Praise for *New York Times* bestselling author Tina Leonard

"Leonard's tough and stubborn characters make a vibrant impression and will stay with the readers long after the last page is turned."

—*RT Book Reviews* on *A Callahan Outlaw's Twins*

"[A] fun, fast-moving story with just enough seriousness to make it a delightfully heartwarming romance."

—*RT Book Reviews* on *Catching Calhoun*

"Leonard's penned the best and funniest so far in the Callahan family saga. Readers are in for a wild ride."

—*RT Book Reviews* on *The Bull Rider's Twins*

Praise for *USA TODAY* bestselling author Marie Ferrarella

"Mixes unmatched humor, poignant situations and whimsical scenes."

—*RT Book Reviews* on *Dating for Two*

"Expert storytelling coupled with an engaging plot makes this an excellent read."

—*RT Book Reviews* on *Cavanaugh Undercover*

"Strong storytelling and sizzling chemistry between Ryan and Susie will keep readers turning the pages."

—*RT Book Reviews* on *Second Chance Colton*

"*Her Mistletoe Cowboy* is filled with moments of joy, caring, awakening and possibilities.... A story that deeply touches the soul."

—*Fresh Fiction*

HOME ON THE RANCH:
TEXAS FOREVER

New York Times **Bestselling Author**
TINA LEONARD

USA TODAY **Bestselling Author**
MARIE FERRARELLA

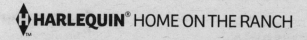

HARLEQUIN® HOME ON THE RANCH
™

ISBN-13: 978-1-335-02039-0

First published as Texas Lullaby
by Harlequin Books in 2008 and
Cowboy for Hire by Harlequin Books in 2014.

Home on the Ranch: Texas Forever
Copyright © 2017 by Harlequin Books S.A.

Recycling programs
for this product may
not exist in your area.

The publisher acknowledges the copyright
holders of the individual works as follows:

Texas Lullaby
Copyright © 2008 by Tina Leonard

Cowboy for Hire
Copyright © 2014 by Marie Rydzynski-Ferrarella

Printed in U.S.A.

www.Harlequin.com

CONTENTS

Tina Leonard is a *New York Times* and *USA TODAY* bestselling and award-winning author of more than fifty projects, including several popular miniseries for the Harlequin American Romance line. Known for bad-boy heroes and smart, adventurous heroines, her books have made the *USA TODAY*, Waldenbooks, Ingram and Nielsen BookScan bestseller lists. Born on a military base, Tina lived in many states before eventually marrying the boy who did her crayon printing for her in the first grade. You can visit her at tinaleonard.com, and follow her on Facebook and Twitter.

Books by Tina Leonard

Harlequin American Romance

Bridesmaids Creek

The Rebel Cowboy's Quadruplets
The SEAL's Holiday Babies
The Twins' Rodeo Rider

Callahan Cowboys

A Callahan Wedding
The Renegade Cowboy Returns
The Cowboy Soldier's Sons
Christmas in Texas
"Christmas Baby Blessings"
A Callahan Outlaw's Twins
His Callahan Bride's Baby
Branded by a Callahan
Callahan Cowboy Triplets
A Callahan Christmas Miracle
Her Callahan Family Man
Sweet Callahan Homecoming

Visit the Author Profile page at
Harlequin.com for more titles.

TEXAS LULLABY

TINA LEONARD

To my sister, Kimmie, who is simply my star, and Lisa and Dean-O, my best friends, and Kathleen Scheibling, who believes in my work, and my gal pals, who are always there for me.

Chapter One

"What doesn't kill a man makes him stronger."
—Josiah Morgan's parting advice to his teenage
sons when they walked out of his life.

The four Morgan brothers shared an unspoken belief,
if nothing else: stubbornness equaled strength. A man
who didn't have *stubborn* etched into his bones hadn't
yet grown into big boots.

Some people used the word *jackasses* to describe the
family of four brothers, but the Morgans preferred to
think of themselves as independent loners. It was common for them to be approached by women who wanted
to relieve their "loneliness." The Morgans had no problem breaking with their routine for beautiful women
bent on their relief.

Fortunately, most people in Union Junction, Texas,

understood that a solitary way of life was a good thing, if it was lived by choice. The Morgan brothers were moving to the area not by choice, but for two different reasons. The first was continued solitude, which had been confirmed by some family acquaintances, the Jeffersons. Men after their own heart, the Jeffersons weren't loners, but they hadn't exactly been hanging out in bars every night sobbing about their sad lives before they'd all found the religion of love. They appreciated the need to be left the hell alone.

Yet the need for peace and quiet was just a cover for the real reason Gabriel Morgan had come home. This was about money. He stared at the two-story sprawling farmhouse set amongst native pecan trees and shouldered by farmland. For this house, this land, the Morgans were called to relocate to the Morgan Ranch near Union Junction. The first thing the brothers had all agreed on in years was that none of them were too happy about finding themselves the keeper of a large ranch. Five thousand acres as well as livestock—what the hell were they supposed to do with it? This was Pop's place. Light-footed Pop and his far-flung dreams, buying houses and land like he was buying up parts of earth to keep him alive and vital.

Pop was the true jackass.

Selling the ranch had been the first thing on Gabriel's mind, and he was pretty certain his brothers had the same idea. But no, Pop was too wily for that. Knowing full well his four sons weren't close, he'd come up with a brilliant plan to stick them all under one roof on acres and acres of loneliness where no one could witness the fireworks.

Pop was in Europe right now, in a new stone castle he'd bought in Pézenas, no doubt laughing his ass off at what he'd wrought. Oh, he couldn't buy just any old French countryside farmhouse—he'd bought an eighteen-hundreds Templar's commandery for a cool four million. It wasn't in the best of shape but just his style, he'd told his sons in the letters they'd each received outlining his wishes. Three floors, ten bedrooms, eight baths, plenty of room should they all ever decide to visit. It even had its own chapel, and he'd be in that chapel praying for them every day.

Gabriel doubted the prayers would help. Pop would be praying for family harmony, and truthfully, some growth in the family tree, some tiny feet to run on the floors of the stone castle, sweet angelic voices to learn how to say Grandpop in French. *Grand-père*.

Like hell. Family expansion wasn't on Gabriel's mind. He was looking for peace and quiet in this rural town, and he was going to get it. He'd live in the house just as his father had decreed, for the year he'd specified, take his part of the bribe money—money was always involved with Pop—and leave no different than he was today. Except he'd be a million dollars richer.

Easy pickings.

Gabriel would take the money. As for the unspoken part of the deal… The pleasure of putting one over on his father, spitting in his eye, so to speak, would be a roundabout kick from one jackass to another. Pop hadn't said his sons had to be close-bonded Templar knights; he'd just stated they had to live in the house for a year. Like a family.

He could do that—if for no other reason than to show the old man he hadn't fazed Gabriel in the least.

"Hi!"

He turned to see a woman waving to him from a car window. She parked, got out and handed him a freshly baked cherry pie.

"Welcome to Union Junction, stranger." Her blue eyes gleamed at him; her blond hair swung in a braid. "My name's Mimi Jefferson. I'm from the Double M ranch, once known as Malfunction Junction. I'm Mason's wife. And also the sheriff."

"Hello, Mimi." He'd met Mason months ago through Pop's business dealings, and Mason's wonderful wife had often been mentioned. "Thanks for the pie."

"No problem." She glanced at the farmhouse. "So what do you think of it? Hasn't changed much since you were last here."

Pop had made some additions to the house, rendering it more sprawling than Gabriel thought necessary. He'd added more acreage, too, but that was his dad's agenda. Always the grand visionary. "I haven't been inside."

She smiled. "It needs work."

That he could see from the outside. "I noticed."

"Should keep you real busy."

He nodded. "Seems that was my dad's plan."

She laughed. "Your father fit in real well here in Union Junction. I'm sure you will, too."

He didn't need to, wouldn't be here long enough to put down deep roots.

"By the way, I believe the ladies will be stopping by with some other goodies. We figured your dad left the fridge pretty empty when he went to France."

"The ladies?"

"You'll see." With a cryptic smile, she got into the truck. "I'll tell Mason you'll be by to see him when you've settled in."

That meant it was time to head into the old hacienda of dread and bar the door. He had no desire to be the target of gray-haired, well-meaning church ladies toting fried chicken. "Thanks again for the pie."

She waved at him and drove off. Gabriel dug into his pocket for the key marked Number Four—he supposed that was because he was the fourth son or maybe because his father had four keys made—and headed toward the wraparound porch. It groaned under his weight, protesting his presence.

Then he heard a sound, like the growing din of a schoolyard at recess. As a code breaker for the Marines, he was tuned to hear the slightest bit of noise, and could even decipher murmured language. But what assaulted his ears wasn't trying to be secretive in any way. He watched as ten vehicles pulled into the graveled drive. His jaw tensed as approximately twenty women and children hopped out of the cars and trucks, each bearing a sack. Not just a covered dish or salad bowl, but a bag, clearly destined for him.

He was going to go crazy—and get fat in the process.

"We're the welcoming committee." A pretty blonde smiled at him as she approached the porch. "Don't be scared."

She'd nailed his emotion.

"I'm Laura Adams," she said. "These ladies—most of us—are from the hair salon, bakery, et cetera, in town. We formed the Union Junction Welcoming Committee some time ago after we received such a warm greeting when we arrived in this town. Many of us weren't raised in Union Junction. Our turn to do a good deed, you might say."

Except he didn't want the deed done to *him*. She

smelled nice, though. Her voice was soft and pleasant and he liked the delicate frosting of freckles across her nose and cheeks. Big blue eyes gazed at him with a warmth he couldn't return at the moment.

The porch shook under his feet with the sound of more approaching women. He hadn't taken his eyes off Laura, for reasons he couldn't quite explain to himself. She opened her pretty pink lips to say more, introduce all her gift-bearing friends, when suddenly something wrapped itself around his thigh.

Glancing down, he saw a tiny towhead comfortably smiling up at him. "Daddy," she said, hugging his leg for all she was worth. "Daddy."

For the first time in his life, including the time he'd temporarily lost part of his hearing from an underwater mine explosion near a sub he'd been monitoring, he felt panic. But the women laughed, and Laura didn't seem embarrassed as she disengaged her daughter from his leg.

"Oh, sweetie, he might be a daddy, or he will be one day. Can you say Mr. Morgan?"

The child smiled at him beatifically, completely convinced that the world was a wonderful, happy place. "Morgan," she said softly.

So he'd be Morgan, just like Pop. He could remember people yelling his father's name, cursing his father's name, cheering his father's name. It was always something along the lines of either "Morgan, you jackass!" or "Morgan, you old dog!"

It didn't feel as bad as he thought it might. Gabriel wondered where the child's father was, and then decided it was none of his business. "I should invite you in," he said reluctantly to the gathering at large, his gaze on

Laura. He could tell by their instant smiles that being invited in was exactly what they wanted. "Too hot in June to keep ladies on the porch. We can all see the new place at the same time and make some introductions."

"You haven't been inside your home yet?" Laura asked. "Mimi said she thought you might have arrived later than you planned."

"Tell me something," he said as he worked at the lock on the front door. The lock obviously hadn't been used in a long time and didn't want to move. "I'd heard Union Junction was great for peace and quiet. Is this one of those places where everybody knows everybody's business?"

That made everyone laugh. Not him—for Gabriel it was a serious question.

"Yes," Laura said. "That's one of the best parts of our town. Everyone cares about everybody."

Great. The lock finally gave in to his impatient twisting of Key Number Four and he swung the door open. The first thing he realized was how hot the house was— like an oven.

The smell was the next thing to register. Musty, unused, closed-up. The ladies peered around his shoulders to the dark interior.

"Girls, we've got our work cut out for us," an older lady pronounced.

"That won't be necessary," Gabriel said as they brushed past him. Laura smiled at him, swinging her grocery sack to the opposite hip and taking her daughter's hand in hers.

"It's necessary," she said. "They can clean this place so fast it'll make your head spin. Besides, we've seen worse. Not much worse, of course. But your father's been gone a long time. Almost six months." She smiled kindly. "Frankly, we expected you a lot sooner."

"I wasn't in a hurry to get here." Neither were any of his brothers. During their curt email transmissions, exchanged since their father's letter had been delivered to them, Dane had said he might swing by in January if he'd finished with his Texas Ranger duties by then, Pete said he might make it by February—depending upon the secret agent assignments he couldn't discuss—and Jack hadn't answered at all. Jack was the least likely of them all to give a damn about Pop, the ranch, or a million dollars.

His chicken brothers were making excuses, putting off the inevitable—except for Jack, who really was the wild card.

"Well, we're glad you're here now." She didn't seem to notice his grimness as she set her grocery sack on the counter. "Hope you like chicken, baby peas and rice."

"You don't have to do that." He heard the sound of a vacuum start up somewhere in the house, and windows opening. The fragrance of lemon oil began to waft from one of the rooms. The little girl clung to her mom, her eyes watching Gabriel's every move. "Really, I'm not hungry, and your little girl probably needs to be at home in bed." It was six o'clock—what time did children go to bed, anyway? He and his brothers had a strict bed-time of nine o'clock when they were kids, which they'd always ignored. Pop never came up the stairs to check on them, and they used a tree branch outside the house to cheat their curfew. Then one year, Pop sawed off the limb, claiming the old live oak was too close to the roof. They devised a rope ladder which they flung out on grappling hooks whenever they had a yen to meet up with girls or camp in the woods.

Or watch Jack practice at the forbidden rodeo in the fields lit only by the moon.

"Oh, Penny's fine. Don't worry about her. You're always happy, aren't you, Penny?"

Penny beamed at Gabriel. "Morgan," she murmured in a small child's breathy recitation. He felt his heart flip over in his chest as he returned the child's gaze. *Heartburn. I'm getting heartburn at the age of twenty-six.*

"I have a smaller version of Penny who is being watched for me right now." Laura smiled proudly as she unloaded the grocery sacks the ladies had loaded onto the kitchen counter. "Perrin is nine months old, and looks just like his father. You love your baby brother, don't you, Penny?" She looked down at her child, who nodded, though she didn't break her stare from Gabriel.

Gabriel felt his heart sink strangely in his chest. This woman was married, apparently happily so.

He was an idiot, and probably horny. The house was swarming with women and he had to get the preliminary hots for a married mom.

Good thing his yen was in the early stages—one pretty face could replace another easily enough. "Listen, I don't want to be rude, but I just got in. I appreciate you and your friends trying to help, but—"

"But you would rather be alone."

He nodded.

"I understand." She flicked the oven on Warm and slid the casserole inside. "I would, too, if I was you."

She knew nothing about him. He decided a reply wasn't needed.

"You know, I really liked your father," she said, hesitating. She stared at him with eyes he felt tugging at his desire. "I hated to see Mr. Morgan go."

"Josiah," he murmured.

"I didn't call him by his first name."

He shrugged. "You didn't know him too well, then."

"Because I didn't call him by his name or because I liked him?"

He looked at her, thinking, *Both, lady.*

"Mr. Morgan was fond of my children."

His radar went on alert. Here came the your-father-wants-you-to-settle-down chorus. He steeled himself.

She ran a gentle hand through Penny's long fine hair. "Of course, he dreamed of having his own grandchildren."

Gabriel frowned. That topic was none of her business. His family was too raw a subject for him to discuss with a stranger.

"You're going to hear this sooner or later." She gazed at him suddenly with clear, determined focus. "I'd rather you hear it from me."

He shrugged. "I'm listening." He reminded himself that whatever she had to say didn't matter to him. What Pop had meant to the town of Union Junction was not his concern.

"Your father put a hundred thousand dollars into a trust for my children."

She'd caught his attention. Not because of the amount, but because Pop had to have lost his mind to have gone that soft. Pop was as miserly as he was stubborn, even complaining over church donations. All he was interested in was himself.

Or at least that had been the Pop of Gabriel's youth. Truthfully, it astonished him that this tiny woman had the nerve to tell him she'd managed to wheedle money out of his father. Maybe Pop had finally begun to crack, all the years of selfishness taking their toll. More importantly, Laura was obviously the kind of woman with whom Gabriel should exercise great distance and caution. "Congratulations," he finally said, trying not to smirk. "A hundred grand is a nice chunk of change."

"Each."

He stared at her. "Each?"

"Each child got their own trust. Penny and Perrin both received a hundred thousand dollars. Your father said it wasn't a lot, but he wanted them to have something later in their lives. He doesn't want them to know about his gift, though, not until they're grown up." She smiled, and it seemed to Gabriel that her expression was sad. "They won't even remember him, then."

He had no idea what the hell to say to this woman. He was suspicious. He was dumbstruck. Perhaps he was even a little envious that she'd gained some type of affection in his father's heart, when he and his brothers had struggled for years and had received none.

She picked up Penny. "I just thought you should know."

He watched as she turned, heading for the front door. Over her mother's shoulder, Penny watched him with wistful eyes. What had been the relationship between Pop and Laura that such an astonishing gift would be given to her kids?

He could remember a cold, wet night in Poland, hunched behind a snowbank, listening to a radio he'd held with frozen fingers to pick up conversation in a bedroom in Gdańsk. He'd retrieved the information he'd needed, turned it in and got cleared to return home.

Chilled, he'd called his father, thinking maybe his soul could use a good thawing and their relationship a delayed shot of warmth. He was young, idealistic, mostly broke, lonely. Damned cold in every area of his life.

He needed a bus ticket from the base, he'd told his father. The military would get him stateside, but he only had a few zloty in his pocket.

Pop had told him not to come crying to him for money. He said the greatest gift he could ever give him was the knowledge of how to stand on his own two feet.

That was ten years ago, and he could still hear the sound of the receiver slamming in his ear. He followed behind Laura, catching up to open the front door for her. "You must have meant a lot to my father."

She turned, slowly, her gaze meeting his, questioning. In a split second, she got the gist of his unspoken assumption. "Your reputation preceded you," she said softly. "You really are a jackass."

The door slammed behind her. Gabriel nodded to himself, silently agreeing with her assessment. Then he went to shoo her well-meaning friends out of the house he didn't want.

Chapter Two

Laura returned to her house, steaming. She put Penny down on the sofa and went to find Mimi, whom she could hear quietly singing to Perrin in the back of the house. "Thank you for watching my little man, Mimi." She looked down into the crib at her baby, and all the tension flowed from her.

Together they walked from the nursery. "So what did you think of Gabriel Morgan?" Mimi asked.

"Not much. He thinks I sucked up to his father to weasel money out of him." Laura shrugged her shoulders. "He's everything Mr. Morgan said he was. Cocky, brash, annoying."

Mimi laughed. "Not a man's best qualities. Wasn't he nice at all? He just seemed sort of shy to me."

Laura went to fix them both an iced tea. "I suppose I compare every man to my husband." Her gaze was reluctantly drawn to the framed, fingerprint-covered photo of Dave. Penny liked to look at the picture of her father, enjoyed hearing stories about him.

Dave had been such a kind man. Warm. Funny. Easy to talk to. Nothing like the man she'd met today. Laura wrinkled her nose and tried not to think so tears wouldn't spring into her eyes. Heaven only knew Dave had his moments; he was no angel. They'd had their spats. But he'd been her first love and that counted for so much. It had been such a shock to lose him.

At least she had his children.

"I suppose it would be hard for me not to compare every man to Mason." Mimi smiled. "No one would measure up."

Laura nodded, appreciating her friend's understanding.

"Some would say there never was a tougher nut to crack than Mason Jefferson."

"Really?" Laura found that hard to believe. Mason loved his wife, loved his kids. Was always looking at Mimi, or holding her hand.

"Suffice it to say he was really difficult to get to the altar. Sometimes I even wondered why I wanted him there." Mimi laughed. "Talk about stubborn and hard to get along with."

"Dave was easy," Laura murmured. "Don't get me wrong, I'm not looking to replace Dave in my life at all. But I was hoping for a connection with Gabriel, something like the one I'd had with his father. I miss the old gentleman." She smiled sadly at Mimi. "I can't understand why his boys don't want to be close with him."

"Mr. Morgan was a different person with us than he was with his sons. They say people show themselves differently to everyone, and we probably saw his best side. He was a good man."

"Obviously his sons believe they understand him better, and they probably do." She and Mimi moved to the kitchen table. Penny came into the kitchen and crawled into her mother's lap. Laura handed her a vanilla wafer from a box left out on the table since yesterday. "I swear I do keep house. We don't always have food left out from the day before." She glanced at the sink where the pots were piled up from making the welcome meal for Gabriel.

"Try living in a house where grown men come and go all the time. They make a bigger mess than the kids." Mimi sipped her tea. "I'll help you clean it up in a bit."

Laura shook her head, appreciating the offer but not wanting the help. She didn't mind washing dishes. It was soothing to have her hands in warm dishwater, and somehow comforting to submerge dirty dishes in suds and then pull them gleaming from the water. "I didn't want him to misunderstand my relationship with his father."

Mimi nodded. "Men don't always temper their thoughts before they speak. Anyway, nobody tells Josiah Morgan what to do. Gabriel knows that."

Gabriel, too, struck Laura as the kind of man willing to fight any battle life threw at him.

"Besides, it's really none of Gabriel's business."

That was also true. She'd only told him about his father's gift to her children because she wanted him to know up front. "Okay, I give up on being mad. It's a waste of time."

Mimi got up from the table. "Let's wash these dishes."

"No, you go on home to your family. You've done enough for me, Mimi. I really appreciate you watching Perrin so he could nap."

"Did the doctor say how long it would take for the medicine to do some good?"

Perrin had colic, long bouts at night that worried Laura. Someone had suggested that the colic was stress-induced, and that Perrin was sensing his mother's sadness. It had been a shock when Dave had died, and she certainly had grieved—was still grieving—but it was an additional guilt that she was causing her son's pain. "The doctor said babies sometimes go through colic. The medicine might help, and putting him on a different formula. Or he could grow out of it."

Mimi patted her hand. "I'll come by to see you later at the school."

Laura nodded. "I'd like that."

She closed the door behind Mimi. Penny handed her a vanilla wafer, and for the first time that day, Laura felt content.

On Friday night, three days later, Gabriel finally drove into the small town of Union Junction. He could see what had drawn his father to this place. For one thing, it looked like a melding of the Old West and a Norman Rockwell card. There was a main street where families were enjoying a warm June stroll, ice-cream cones or sodas in hand. A kissing booth sat in front of a bakery. Other booths lined the street in front of various shops.

He glanced at the kissing booth again, caught by a glimpse of blond hair and the long line outside the booth. All the booths had lines, but none as long as the kissing booth, which Gabriel figured was probably appropriate. If he was offered the choice of getting a kiss or throwing rings over a bottle, he'd definitely take the kiss.

"What's going on?" he asked a young cowboy at the back of the line.

"Town fair." The young man grinned at him. "You're Morgan, aren't you?"

He looked at him. "Aren't you too young to be buying kisses?"

He got a laugh for that. "Get in line and spend a buck, Mr. Morgan."

"Why?" He wasn't inclined to participate in the fun of a town fair. He'd just been looking around, trying to figure out why Pop had settled near here, trying to stave off some boredom.

"We're raising money for the elementary school. Need more desks. The town is certainly growing."

"Shouldn't the town be paying for that from taxes or something?"

"We like to do some recreational fundraising, too."

Gabriel reluctantly fell into line. "So who are we kissing?"

"Laura Adams."

"We can't kiss her!" He had to admit the idea was inviting, but he also wanted to jerk the young man out of line—and every other man, too.

The line kept growing behind him.

"Why not?" His companion appeared puzzled.

Gabriel frowned. "She's married. And she's a mom."

The young man laughed. "Mimi Jefferson was working the booth an hour ago. It's the only time any of us

can get near Mimi without getting our tails kicked by
Mason, so most of us went through twice."

Gabriel's frown deepened.

"It's for a good cause," his new friend said. "Besides
which, Laura's not married anymore."

Gabriel's mood lifted slightly. He felt his boots shuf-
fling closer to the booth behind his talkative friend.
"She's not?"

"Nah. Her husband died shortly after she gave birth
to Perrin." His friend looked at him with surprise. "You
should know all this. Your dad loved Laura's kids. Said
they were probably the only—"

"I know. I know. Jeez." Gabriel rubbed at his chin,
trying to decide if he liked how quickly the line was
moving. And the young man was right. The gentlemen
were leaving the line to catcalls and whistles and hurrying to the back of the line for another kiss. It was
a never-ending kiss line of rascals. "I'm pretty sure I
don't belong here."

"No better way to get to know people," his friend
said cheerfully. "My name's Buck, by the way."

"Hi, Buck." He absently shook his hand. "I guess
kissing's as good a way as any to get to know someone." He supposed he should get to know Laura better
since they sort of had a connection.

Buck stared at him. "Hanging out at the town fair
being sociable is the way to get to know people."

"That's what I meant." Gabriel noticed there were
only five people in front of him now. His heart rate
sped up. Should he kiss a woman his father had such a
close relationship with? Clearly Pop had depended upon
Laura for the sense of family he was lacking. It almost
felt like Laura could be a sister.

He heard cheers as Buck laid a smooch on Laura. To Gabriel's relief, it was mercifully short and definitely respectful. *Just good clean fun.*

He found himself standing in front of her booth, staring down at her like a nervous schoolboy. Her blue eyes lit on him with curiosity and nothing else, no lingering resentment over their initial meeting. He noted a distressing jump in his jeans, a problem he hadn't anticipated. But he'd always been a sucker for full lips and fine cheekbones. He could smell a sweet perfume, something like flowers in summer.

Laura was nothing like a sister to him.

He laid a twenty-dollar bill on the booth ledge and walked away.

Gabriel found a better way to support the local elementary school: drinking keg beer some thoughtful and enterprising young man had set up far away from the kissing booth. Here he was safe. No one bothered him while he sat on a hay bale and people-watched, which was good because he really needed to think. He hadn't expected his father to have a family connection in Union Junction.

He sat up. Surely his father hadn't been trying to build his own family here? With a ready-made mom and grandchildren? All it would take was one out of the four brothers to meet the lady and her children, to whom some of the Morgan money had been put in trust, and maybe, just maybe, Pop might get that family he'd been itching for?

He wouldn't put it past Pop. Throw in a scheme that required all four brothers to be on the premises for a year, and Pop had a one in four chance of seeing that dream come true.

Gabriel resolved not to fall for it. In fact, he congratulated himself for staying one step ahead of the wily old man. He didn't know for sure that was what Pop had been up to, but with Pop there was always an angle.

He'd be very cautious.

"Hi." Someone soft and warm slid onto the hay bale beside him. Laura didn't smile at him, but her lips were full and plump from being kissed. "Guess you changed your mind about kissing me."

He hung between fear and self-loathing for being a coward. "Seems we should keep our relationship professional."

"Awkward."

"That, too."

"Fine by me."

He slid her a glance. She had nice breasts under her blue-flowered dress—very feminine. A breast man by nature, he was shocked he hadn't taken note of her physical charms before. He'd been completely preoccupied by the swarm of women descending upon him. Although he had to admit that after just thirty minutes of being in his house, it looked and smelled more welcoming than it was ever going to be under his watch. But now he was checking out Laura's attributes, a subconscious flick of his gaze that dismayed him. God, they really were gorgeous. And he hadn't noticed her small, graceful hands before, either.

He felt his temperature rise uncomfortably. "Where are the kids?" Not that he was really interested, but it was best to remind himself that this woman was a mother, not someone to be ogled as if she were single and available for some casual fun.

Which was all he was interested in, for now and for always. *Damn Pop for throwing temptation my way.*

"Penny and Perrin are being held by some ladies from the church. They're spoiled rotten by them." She pointed to an outdoor play area that had been set up. Lots of older ladies were inside, holding infants and playing games with toddlers.

He could see Penny's light hair, just like her mother's, as she sat in a woman's lap and colored in a book. It wasn't difficult to see what had drawn Pop to this gentle fatherless trio.

Who would have thought Pop would have had a protective bone in his body?

"You know, we're not swindlers. Nor did we lure your father into feeling like we were his family."

He turned to Laura. "I shouldn't have implied that there was anything unusual about my father leaving someone outside the family money. I apologize for that."

"Thank you." She raised her chin. "I knew you could be a difficult person. I choose to ignore that for your father's sake."

He frowned. "I don't want anything for my father's sake."

She shrugged. "He was a nice old man."

"You didn't know him."

"Maybe not as well as you. But maybe better in some ways."

He couldn't argue that. Didn't even want to. "Why?"

"When my husband got sick with cancer, and then died, your father said the least he could do was make certain my kids had college educations. There was a fundraiser here in town to help us…because Dave had no insurance. He was a self-employed carpenter, a dreamer, really." Her voice got soft remembering. "He loved to build homes. The bigger, the better, the more intricate, the better. He did lots of work on your father's place."

This was all beginning to make sense. "Listen, none of this is my business. What my father wants to do with his time and his life is his concern."

She nodded. "I've got to go back to the booth. I've got one more half-hour shift."

He could see the line queuing from here, could count at least twenty men waiting their turn. It looked as if Union Junction had no lack of horny males. "Do you have to kiss all of them?"

"Most of them just kiss my cheek." She smiled. "Only the younger ones try for something more, and a few of the bachelors."

That's what he was afraid of. He thought about his father, and what a jackass he was. He looked at the line, and the men grinning back toward Laura, obviously impatient for her break to be over.

Out of the corner of his eye, he could see Penny, who'd spotted her mother. Mom and daughter waved at each other, and he could see the longing in Laura's eyes to be with her daughter.

What the hell. He lived to be a jackass. He was just keeping the family name alive.

"All right," he announced loudly, ambling to the front of the line, "I'm buying out Ms. Adams's thirty minutes of time." He placed five one-hundred-dollar bills—all he had on him at the moment besides some stray ones and a couple of twenties—on the booth ledge where everyone could see his money. Grumbling erupted, but also some applause for the donation. He grunted. "Move along, fellows. The booth is closed for this lady."

Chapter Three

Gabriel's buyout of Laura's time in the kissing booth won him lots of winks from the guys and smiles from the ladies as he walked toward his truck. He hadn't said anything to a shocked Laura—just figured he'd introduced himself to the town in the most obvious way he could have for a man who preferred being a loner.

He didn't even know why he'd done it.

Maybe it was Pop, egging him on to be a gentleman, which was a real stinker of a reason. Mason met him at his truck.

"Have a good time?"

Gabriel checked Mason's eyes for laughter but the question seemed sincere. "Seems like everyone is enjoying themselves."

"Good to see you around. We've been wondering

what you're going to do with yourself out there if you stay holed up at the ranch."

"I imagine I'll figure out something."

Mason handed him an envelope. "Mimi said to give you this."

"Mimi?" Gabriel scanned the envelope. It had his name written in his father's handwriting, and no postmark.

"Mimi's the law around here." Mason winked at him.

"What does that have to do with me?"

"Your father left that with her. She asked me to deliver it to you. I've been meaning to get out to your place, but here you are, getting to know the good folks of Union Junction."

Again Gabriel studied him for sarcasm. There appeared to be nothing more to the man's intentions than good old friendliness.

"Why didn't Pop just mail this to me? Or courier it like he did before?"

Mason shrugged. "He said something to Mimi along the lines of when and if any of his sons ever got here, they were to have that. Josiah figured you'd be the first, though. In fact, we wagered on it. I owe your father a twenty." He handed Gabriel a twenty-dollar bill.

Gabriel shook his head. "Put it toward the school fund." He looked at the envelope, wondering why his father would have wagered he'd be the first brother to the ranch. "Who'd you bet on?"

Mason laughed. "Jack. He's the unpredictable one. I always go with the dark horse."

"Cost you this time, buddy."

Mason slapped him on the back. "Sure did. Come

on out to the Double M when you have time. We'll introduce you to the kids."

"Maybe I will," Gabriel said, knowing he probably wouldn't.

"Congratulations, by the way," Mason said as he walked away.

"For what?"

"For spending that much money for a kiss and then not getting it. Nerves of steel." Mason waved goodbye. Gabriel glanced back down at the envelope, aware that Mason was now giving him a gentle ribbing. "Jackass," he muttered under his breath and got into his truck.

But it was kind of funny coming from Mason, and even Gabriel had to wonder why he'd passed up the chance to kiss Laura after he'd so obviously put his mark on her.

Not that he was going to think about it too hard.

"Nothing," Laura told the girls at the Union Junction Beauty Salon. "I'm telling you, there's nothing between us. He didn't kiss me. Gabriel's barely civil to me."

The girls oohed and then giggled. Laura had received a fair bit of teasing and she expected the kissing booth incident had been thoroughly dissected. Privately, Laura wondered what it would have been like to have Gabriel's lips on hers. It had been so long since she'd kissed a man—well, kissed a man as she had Dave. She didn't count those chaste, predictable pecks in the kissing booth. Even the old ladies and the elderly librarian got their turn in the kissing booth, and the men lined up for them just as quickly. The older ladies—particularly teachers—received grandmotherly busses on the cheek from favorite students.

Everyone was anxious to see the elementary school succeed. There was so much goodwill in this town. Laura was never going to regret moving here with Dave those five years ago. He'd said Union Junction was a growing town, he'd have lots of work, they'd make a family and be happy out away from the big city…

It had worked out just that way for just over five years. Five perfect years.

So she shouldn't really be thinking about what it would have felt like to kiss Gabriel. She was twenty-six, too old for dreamy longings; she was a mom and a widow.

"I bet he kisses great," one of the stylists said to another, and Laura blushed.

"Aren't you curious?" someone asked her.

Laura ran her hand through Penny's hair as she often did. The feel of the corn-silk softness comforted her, as did the powdery smell of Perrin. "No," she murmured, easy with the lie. "Gabriel is not my kind of man."

They all fell quiet, silenced by the uncomfortable position they had put her in.

"She doesn't need to tiptoe around Dave forever," someone finally spoke up bravely. "Honey, we know you loved him, but you're alive and he wouldn't want you being sad forever."

Tears jumped into Laura's eyes. Several ladies came over to hug her. She felt Penny press closer to her leg. "I know."

"All right, then." They all patted her, then went back to their places. "So next time you get a chance to kiss a hunk like Gabriel Morgan, you just grin and bear it if you want to, okay?"

"Maybe," Laura said, smiling as she wiped away the unwanted tears.

"Wish he'd buy out *my* booth," someone said, and everyone laughed, even Laura, although she really didn't think it was funny. What they didn't realize is that Gabriel hadn't wanted to kiss her, hadn't even looked tempted. He'd sort of picked up his father's responsibility—and then he'd headed off.

A woman knew when a man was interested in her. All fairy tales included a kiss—a man knew how to get what he wanted, even in books. Dave had been a gentle pursuer, slow and careful as if she were a fine porcelain doll.

Gabriel owned no such gentle genes. If he wanted a woman, she figured the indication of his desire would be swift, like a roiling wave breaking over a boat at sea, claiming it with powerful intent.

Gabriel pretty much turned to stone every time he laid eyes on her.

Dear Gabriel,
By now you are at the house and are beginning a year of time you no doubt resent like hell. But money talks and though it might not talk very loud to you, I know you'll stick out the year just to prove yourself. This need of yours to be a tough guy living on the edge is exactly what I now need to lean on.

Remember when I bought that extra acreage and added on to my own hacienda out here? I bought it from a man who was down on his luck, and partly down on his luck thanks to me, which he has discovered. Now don't go getting all high and mighty like I cheated this man out of his birth-right, because the man is a scoundrel. And any-way, he needed the money.

The problem is, I bought the land suspecting there was an underground oil source. I had it sur-veyed without his knowledge. He has since found out I paid for a geological survey of his property and feels cheated.

Fact is, maybe he was and maybe he wasn't. He could have paid for his own damn survey.

The trouble in this is that the man is Laura Ad-ams's father, with whom she has no contact due to the fact that he didn't approve of her marrying a carpenter. Didn't like her husband, felt he wasn't good enough for his only child, which didn't sit well with Laura. He needed her to marry big to save his sorry ass.

You see my predicament. I could sell the man back his land but the price would include a ter-rific profit which he cannot afford. I gave Laura's children a tiny portion of what is rightfully theirs, since it would have been anyhow, I suppose, though I believe her father would have drunk up the estate. You might say I just hijacked Penny's and Perrin's inheritance, robbing from the poor to give to the poorer.

Unfortunately, the jackanapes took to threat-ening me. He really feels cheated by life, and I suppose he has been, but the big dog runs off the little dog and that's life, isn't it? But for the grace of God go I.

Anyway, you'll be seeing him, as he lives to create trouble. But I have faith that you'll smooth

*everything over in due time, as you were always
the responsible one in the family, even though it
really chaps your ass that I say that. It just happens to be true.*
Pop

"It does chap my ass." Gabriel forced himself not to
shred his father's letter. "It does indeed chap me like
you can't even imagine, Pop."

He did not appreciate being appointed the protector
of the family fortunes, but even less so the knight of
Laura Adams's little brood. He couldn't even make himself kiss her; how the hell was he going to start thinking
of her as part and parcel of the Morgan family?

And yet, according to Pop, they owed her something.

What exactly that was, Gabriel wasn't certain.

The storm that swept Union Junction and the out-
lying countryside that night kept Gabriel inside and
feeling caged. He paced the house, watching lightning
crack through the windows of the two-story house. The
TV had gone out; the phone lines were dead. He could
hear water dripping frenzied and fast into the over-
grown gardens.

There wasn't a lot to do in a house one didn't call
home. So far he'd mainly confined himself to his room
on the second floor, and the den. He passed through
the kitchen occasionally to forage from the goodies the
ladies had left for him. The house, he estimated, was
around six thousand square feet. Eventually, he'd have
to investigate the rest of Pop's place.

Actually, there was no better time than the present,
he decided. The sound of something not quite right

caught his ear; instantly he listened intently, all the old survival skills surging into action. Someone was at the front door; someone with a key that wouldn't fit easily. Gabriel considered flinging the door open and confronting whoever was out there, some idiot so dumb they didn't know it was storming like hell outside, then relented. Let the water drown them. If they made it inside, then he'd deal with them.

He thought about Laura's father's threats against Pop and figured he couldn't kill the man in cold blood. So he selected one of his father's many travel guides he had in the den   the heaviest one, something about the South Seas—and waited behind the door.

It suddenly blew open with a gust of wind and rain and vituperative cursing. Gabriel raised the eight-hundred-page tourist guide high over his head, preparing to crack it over his visitor's skull.

"Damn it, I *hate* Texas with a passion!" he heard, and lowered his arms.

"Dane?"

His brother swung to look at him. "What the hell are you hiding back there for? And with a book on the South Seas?"

"Preparing to coldcock you." Gabriel closed the door.

"I'm *supposed* to be here." Dane glared at him, his coat dripping water all over the floor.

"Your email said you were coming in January."

"And I've since changed my mind. You got a problem with that?" Dane asked as he threw his bags in a corner.

Gabriel sighed. "Calm down, Sam Houston. Food's in the fridge."

"Don't call me that. I detest Texas."

In the kitchen, Gabriel settled into a chair. "Are you starting your year of duty early?"

"Figured I might as well get it over with." Dane stuck his head inside the refrigerator door, ending the conversation for the moment. "Fried chicken! Watermelon!"

Gabriel shook his head and began to read the travel guide to the South Seas, which was starting to sound appealing.

"You get your letter from Pop?" Dane asked while he emptied the contents of the fridge on to the kitchen counter.

"What letter?"

"The one with the sob story about watching over this woman and her twins who have no man in the house."

"Twins?" Gabriel sat up. Laura only had a toddler and a baby—didn't she?

"I despise kids almost as much as I hate Texas," Dane said.

Gabriel couldn't think for the shock of adding more kids to Laura's equation. "You're a Texas Ranger. Get over it."

"I'm done. I retired from active duty."

"Congratulations. So back to the family of four—"

"Yeah. I'm supposed to look out for this little mom because of some mess Pop made."

Gabriel frowned. *He* was supposed to be the reluctant knight in shining armor. Possessive emotions and a sense of *I saw her first* crowded his skull.

Dane shuddered. "Her name is Suzy something."

"Suzy? Not Laura?"

Dane sat down across from him with a beer and a plate of fried chicken. "How do you get Laura from Suzy?"

Gabriel shook his head. "This doesn't sound good."

"Tell me about it. I nearly took off for New York, never to be seen or heard from again. But in the end, I knew I had to do this, or I'd really never be free of Pop. He'll try to rule us from the grave if we don't prove to him that nothing he does can screw up our lives anymore."

"And then there's the million bucks."

"A small price for putting up with Pop," Dane said glumly. "You know it's going to get ugly. *Suzy.*" He shuddered.

At least it wasn't Laura Pop had sent Dane to rescue. It didn't really matter, Gabriel reminded himself. One year and he was gone. *Outta here.*

But now apparently there was a family of four in the mix, and an additional *problem* to be solved. Gabriel stared out the window at the pelting rain.

It was indeed beginning to get ugly.

Chapter Four

"So who's Laura, anyway? Girlfriend?"

Gabriel stared at his elder brother, elder being twenty-eight to his own twenty-six. "Hell, no. I just met her. Pop left her children a trust. It's complicated."

"Isn't everything Pop touches complicated?"

Gabriel nodded. "This as much as anything. So what's the deal with Suzy?"

"Don't really know. The letter just said that he owed her something and he'd like me to see to it."

"Pop's matchmaking by making disasters for us to fix."

Dane quit chewing. "You think?"

"Sure. He wants grandkids. He's been busy finding himself some ready-made families."

"Man," Dane said, "that's not fair. I'm glad you figured that out because I might've stepped right into the snare."

Gabriel nodded. "Pop never does anything without a reason."

"But still…family-making?" Dane shook his head. "That's so underhanded."

Gabriel returned to staring out the window.

"So is Laura at least somewhat easy on the eyes?"

Gabriel shrugged. "She is. But she's not my type."

"That would be pretty hard to identify."

He frowned. "What's that supposed to mean?"

Dane looked at him. "Pop's not a sphinx. He can choose all he wants for us, but he can't figure out who'd be that special girl, which personally, I believe is a fairy tale spun to young boys by parents who want grand-kids. So we're safe."

"Oh." Gabriel relaxed a little now that he under-stood his brother wasn't saying he was tough to please. Then he tensed all over again. Pop *had* selected some-one Gabriel was attracted to, in a breath-stealing, jaw-tightening way he hadn't anticipated. "I'd still be careful," he warned. "Suzy might be just your thing."

"Nah." Dane shuddered. "I could never hear myself saying 'Suzy, make me breakfast, baby.'"

Gabriel stared at his brother. "You wouldn't say that to a woman without getting a frying pan upside the head."

Dane sipped his beer. "I like girls who can cook."

Gabriel considered that. If the chicken and rice and peas were any forewarning, Laura could definitely cook.

"Great cooking, great sex. Very important quali-ties in a woman, if I was looking for one. I'd say Pop's run into a brick wall with me. Now, you might not be as safe."

Gabriel stood. "I'm going to bed. Make yourself at home, such as it is." He wasn't going to think about sex and Laura; he wasn't going to even kiss her. Or imagine what she tasted like.

"You realize if Pop cooked up a mess for me and one for you, the other two probably have assigned families as well," Dane pointed out.

"Yeah, well, good luck with Jack. We haven't seen him in ten years. And Pete, almost as long." He shrugged. "What's a secret agent going to do with a family?"

"I see Jack's scores every once in a while. He posts a few wins, breaks a few bones. Got stomped in Amarillo."

Gabriel looked at his brother. "Stomped?"

"Not bad. Slight concussion."

He sat again in spite of himself. "You've seen Jack."

"I was a Ranger. I have connections. People tell me things, let me know what's happening on the rodeo circuit." Dane finished the chicken and started on some watermelon. "Sure. When he got stomped, I checked in on him at the hospital. Don't think he knew I was there. He was out of it for a while, but I did see him pat the nurse's ass. And he didn't get his hand slapped."

"I didn't know about Jack being in the hospital."

"You weren't stateside much."

That was true. But even if he had been home, he wouldn't have known much anyway. "So since you hear things, fill me in on Pete."

"He slipped into my house in Watauga about a year ago. I thought I was going to have cardiac arrest when he sat down at my breakfast table with me. I hate that spy crap secret agent voodoo thing he's got going on."

Gabriel grunted. "Thought Rangers had sonar hearing and X-ray vision."

Dane laughed. "We're not quite superhuman, jarhead."

He wasn't a jarhead anymore. Since he'd gotten his discharge, his dark hair had grown out some. He'd expected a bit of gray, and saw a few strands mixed in. No bald spot or thinning hair, though, which made him think he might just keep growing the stuff. It felt strange long. Old habits died hard. "So what did Pete have on his mind?"

"Just checking in. He was on his way somewhere. Didn't say. Said he was getting tired."

They were all getting older. Even Gabriel felt the gradual march of time slowing his body down, his need for action yet speeding up. Not military action. Something else he hadn't quite put his finger on.

"I don't know if I can live out here for a year," Dane said. "Watauga seemed like hell to me, but this would be worse."

Gabriel took Dane's plate to the sink. "Do any of us really have a choice?" He walked back to the fridge and tossed Dane a beer. "Look. We have to do this. For the sake of our own futures. Pop's crazy, no doubt, but crazy like a fox. Remember? He was always working a deal."

Dane cracked his beer and focused on the label. "I know you're right but it still stinks. I resent Pop for controlling our lives with a snap of his thin fingers."

"Look," Gabriel said, "what if the old man died?" He looked at Dane with a serious expression. "He'd get the last laugh, man. We'd be holding the whole damn bag of emotional dirt."

Dane shook his head. "That's too 'tortured soul' for me."

"Well, think it over, because it's true." He sighed and leaned back in his chair, not wanting the conversation, not really wanting the beer, not wanting anything but a flight to Tokyo, maybe. Away from here. "So we're going to do this. And what about Suzy?"

"Now, that isn't anything I have to deal with. Whatever mess Pop made, I just have to make certain some money changes hands, some responsibilities are seen to and that's it. I live here for a year, a paltry three hundred and sixty-five days, and then my time is done."

He thought about Laura. "So cut-and-dried."

"So cut-and-dried." Dane nodded. "You got that right."

"Good game plan. I'm turning in."

Gabriel rose, poured the beer into the sink and headed upstairs, mulling over Dane's game plan. It was fairly detached, and Gabriel liked detached and unemotional.

It just might work for him.

Laura frowned at the note that had been stuck to the front door of her small house. *Hey, baby, be by to see you later.*

Chills ran through her. Nobody *baby'd* her—no one except her father. She didn't want to see him. Didn't want him near her children. The fact that he'd found out where she lived made her want to move far away, as fast as she could.

He was her father by blood, but Mr. Morgan had

acted more fatherly toward her. There was something wrong with the man whose genes she bore—Ben had problems with thinking the world owed him something. A chip on his shoulder kept him from being the responsible human he might have been.

Laura wanted no part of him.

She took her children inside and locked the door. Penny went straight to her stuffed animals, so Laura put Perrin in his playpen before she sank into a chair at the kitchen table to think.

There was a reason Ben had chosen this moment to filter back into her life. Months ago, Ben had claimed Mr. Morgan had done him a disservice, which the old man had denied. Ben had told her that Mr. Morgan had cheated him out of money. She didn't think Mr. Morgan was the cheating type but after Dave died, he had put that money into trust for her kids. Was it guilt money? At the time, tired and grief-stricken, she'd assumed it was exactly what he'd said it was, a gift of college education for kids whose company he'd enjoyed. As a teacher, she'd certainly appreciated the gesture. A lot of people had been very generous after the funeral. In fact, the Jeffersons had helped pay down the mortgage on this house so that Laura wouldn't have to struggle so much. It was just the type of caring thing Laura had seen done many times over in this town.

She hadn't thought about guilt money. And Ben had always been the kind of man who whined. It was part of the reason she was determined to shoulder her burdens without complaining, without relying on other people. She wanted independence and that didn't come by whining and blaming.

She thought about Gabriel. He seemed very independent, too. He wouldn't blame other people for any misery he incurred. She'd heard from Mr. Morgan that none of their family was close, a fact that disheartened him. In his twilight years—he'd started to say he was feeling his age—he had hoped to knit his family back together.

He'd never said exactly what the problem had been.

Laura wanted a family for her children, though. If she ever remarried, she would want a man who was close to his kin. Penny and Perrin deserved a father who didn't have skeletons rattling in his closet; they had enough bones with Ben. Although they'd never met him, it was only a matter of time before that family skeleton made a nuisance of itself with some whiny rattling.

She tore up the note and threw it into the trash, pushing it down deep before closing the shutters and checking the locks on the doors.

Two hours later, Laura had the kids in bed. She'd been spending some time making plans for the upcoming school year; it would be her second year teaching seventh-grade science. Laura had plans for setting up some conservation composts and doing a rocket launch. If the students were ready, she planned to jump right into some in-class science projects so that they could record data over the course of the whole year.

She'd completely put Ben out of her mind.

Someone knocked at the door, and the dreaded prickles ran up her back. She closed her eyes, reminding herself that Ben was her father, that he had never been violent. He just hadn't liked Dave and had been disagreeable and opinionated about him.

It was Mr. Morgan he'd really been at odds with. Maybe she'd been influenced by those stories.

Yet there was the money. Funny that Ben would be showing up in her life when he knew that her children had been the recipients of various gifts of goodwill from the town. Ben wasn't a coincidental kind of man; he planned everything almost down to an obsession. Then again, she'd heard through the grapevine that Ben had picked up heavy drinking in the town that bordered Union Junction.

The knock sounded again. Now was as good a time as any to face her father. Then again, it could be Mimi.

Mimi would call first.

"Who is it?"

"Gabriel Morgan."

She put a hand to her chest to still her thundering heart, then realized he made her just as nervous—in an unexpected, different way.

She turned on the porch light and opened the door. "Hello."

There he was, wearing a Western hat and jeans. He wasn't smiling, but he hadn't smiled the other times she'd met him, either. He had bought out her kissing booth—and then disappeared. She'd expected to hear something from him…she hadn't been sure what.

"I would have called, but I didn't have your number. Guess it's unlisted."

She nodded. "It is."

"Would have called Mason for it, but…hope you don't mind me stopping by."

He seemed uncomfortable and Laura didn't blame him. Apparently he was only in the area because of his duty to his father. She held the door open so Gabriel could come inside. "If you'd called Mason, he would have asked why you needed to see me. I can ask you myself." Laura pointed to a sofa so he could sit down. He did, gingerly hovering on the flowered sofa.

"Just seems we got off on the wrong foot."

She nodded. "Maybe. What other foot is there, though?"

He hesitated. "I think I was surprised my father left me instructions about you."

"He did?" That wasn't welcome news. She didn't want Gabriel to feel obligated to her in any way.

"Yeah. Apparently you have some issues with your father, who may or may not have your best interests at heart."

She thought about the note on the door. "It's not something I really want to talk about."

"I fully understand. I don't want to talk about my dad, either."

"So don't." She felt more awkward by the second. "Look, Gabriel, despite whatever your father told you, I can take care of myself. I have lots of friends. I have a great job. I love my kids. I don't need a protector or anything like that."

He glanced down at his hands for a moment before looking back at her. "You're sure you're all right?"

"Of course I am! Your father was ultraprotective of me because of my children. But you don't have to take on a parenting role, Gabriel. I wouldn't want you to. They had a father." She took a deep breath. "He was a wonderful man, and… I'm not looking to fill his role in our lives."

He appeared to consider her words. "You'd let me know if you need something?"

"Honestly, no." She shook her head. "I wouldn't. I'd call Mimi or some of my girlfriends. But I can tell you I would if that's the closure you need. It just won't be true. You're completely off the hook."

A knock at the door startled both of them. A shaky premonition snapped into Laura.

"I'm sorry. I didn't realize you were expecting company." Gabriel got to his feet.

"Laura! Baby! Let me in!"

Gabriel frowned. Laura glanced at the door, making certain it was securely locked after she'd let Gabriel in. To her relief, it was.

"Laura! It's your father. Don't keep me out here!"

"I didn't realize you were still on speaking terms with Ben." Gabriel's eyes searched hers. "Thought I'd heard the opposite."

It was her family's private business. "I don't want to discuss this with you." If she did, he would feel responsible for her.

The glass pane smashed, and Laura screamed in spite of herself. She flung open the door. "Ben, what the hell? You could have hurt one of the children!"

"Hi, baby." Her father tipped unsteadily to one side, listing, before righting himself. "I know I taught you better manners than to leave your old dad standing outside."

She felt Gabriel move behind her. She pushed him back with one hand. This was her problem. "Ben, take your drunk and sorry self off my property and don't come back. We said all we had to say years ago. If you ever come around here again, or if I catch you near my children, I'm going to have you put in jail."

He squinted at her. "Who's that in there with you?"

"Ben, pay attention to what I'm saying to you—" Laura began, but her father shoved the door back so fast she couldn't stop him.

"Morgan," her father said, his tone a curse. "I should have known Morgan's pups wouldn't be far away from the prize."

Gabriel literally moved her from the door, filling the opening with his large frame. "Ben, whatever happened between you and my dad is old news. It has no part with me, and it has no part with Laura. You need to let it go."

"The money your father gets from the oil rights on that property should be mine."

"So take it to court," Gabriel said calmly. "You can't get any money that Laura has because it's all tied up in trust for her children."

"That's why you're hanging around. The children." Ben's face grew surly. "Like little pieces of gold."

"I'd be a fairly useless human if I had to wait around for fifteen years to get some little kid's trust. Move along, Ben. It's all over. Laura said she didn't want you here, and you need to respect that."

"Because you say so?"

Laura tried to edge in front of Gabriel but he held her back.

"Because I say so," Gabriel confirmed. "I'd be going if I was you, or you're not going to be in one piece to do it on your own."

Ben's face wrinkled with hate. "You haven't heard the last of me, Morgan."

"I'm certain of that." Gabriel shut the door, waiting until he heard Ben's boots leave the porch before he turned to Laura. "I'll fix this pane before I go. I can tape it tonight, and then get some glass tomorrow at the hardware shop."

She straightened her five-foot-two frame. "Don't ever fight my battles for me again. Don't assume I can't take care of myself."

"It wasn't about you," Gabriel said, "it was about my father and his schemes." He glanced around the room. "I'll be sleeping here tonight."

Chapter Five

Gabriel's pronouncement clearly didn't suit Laura, but he hadn't expected it would. She gave him a determined stare. "You will not be sleeping here tonight, or any other time."

"Mommy?"

Gabriel turned to face a tiny blue-eyed, blonde version of her mother. Penny stood in the hallway, rubbing sleepy eyes.

"Yes, honey?" Laura said, going to her.

"I heard a loud noise."

Laura shot Gabriel a warning glance. "A pane on the door accidentally broke. Don't worry about a thing."

In the background, Perrin began to cry. Gabriel focused on the sound. If he had to guess—and he had zero experience with infants—it was a *comfort me* cry.

Laura went down the hall to Perrin. Penny looked solemnly at Gabriel. "Who's going to fix the window?"

"I am," he told her. "Tomorrow morning."

"No, you're not," Laura said, entering the family room with Perrin, who was happy now that he was being held. "And you're definitely not—" she glanced at Penny "—you're definitely not staying here," she said in a low voice.

"Either I stay here or your family comes to my ranch. You can't stay here with your father in a hotheaded state." Protective emotions inside him rushed to the surface. Laura looked vulnerable with her two children in her arms. She was trying to be tough but her eyes held confusion. He knew she had to be scared. No woman wanted to sleep in a house with a broken window. If Ben came back—and he probably was watching to see when Gabriel's truck left—he'd simply reach through that pane and unlock the door.

To Gabriel's mind, any battle Ben wanted to put up should be with Gabriel, not Laura. He was after money, pure and simple. The easiest way to get it was to panhandle his own daughter.

"I'm going to put my children back to bed."

Laura turned and went down the hall. Penny followed with a backward glance at Morgan, her face somber. His heart lurched, twisted. Despite his vow to never want children of his own, Penny's big eyes and soft voice saying his name stole his heart. Perrin's plump cheeks and soft hair made him want to see the little boy have his chance at growing up safe and strong. Actually, he would have loved to hold the baby if Laura would let him—but he knew she would not. She had definitely warned him off her deceased husband's territory. He couldn't blame her for that. But she did need some help, whether she wanted to admit it or not.

Maybe Pop hadn't been so crazy after all.

Laura walked into the kitchen with Penny, getting the little girl a drink of water. She held her daughter in her lap, singing softly to her, ignoring Gabriel. That was fine with him. Frankly, he'd never seen anything so beautiful as Laura comforting her daughter.

Then he heard Perrin crying again, an inconsolable sobbing. Gabriel started to mention to Laura that the baby was upset again, then thought better of it. Penny was enjoying her mother's attention. Gabriel quietly went down the hall in the direction of the crying—three bedrooms, bathroom on the hall to the left—and found the nursery.

Perrin had wedged himself under his tiny pillow and flailed a blanket over himself, and was not happy about his predicament.

"Hey, little guy." Gabriel removed the blanket. The baby stared up at him. "Don't be so upset, dude. Your mom's trying to calm your sister down, and they just need a moment together. You've got this soft bed, and everything's going good for you, right? So calm down." He reached into the crib, stroking the baby's cheek. Perrin watched him with big eyes. Gabriel couldn't stand it any longer. Laura would not appreciate this, but the lure was too strong.

He scooped the baby up and cradled him to his chest.

There was nothing, he decided, quite like the smell of a baby. The feel of a baby. And this one...this one was so rotund and squeezable... Gabriel closed his eyes as the baby laid his head against his chest. He felt like he was holding one of those fat cherubim he'd seen in paintings in the Louvre.

The baby had gotten himself agitated with all his wailing. Gabriel swept back Perrin's tiny curls from his forehead. "Little man, you've got to learn to chill. There's nothing quite as annoying as getting yourself wrapped up in your blanket, but you've got to learn to think your way out of your predicament." He leaned his cheek against the baby's head. "When you're older, of course. Right now, you have the luxury of having a good wail on the world. When you're my age, you learn to suck it up." Gently, he placed Perrin back in his crib, and quietly hummed a Texas cowboy lullaby he'd learned long ago. Soothed, the baby curled into his sheet, opened his eyes once more, then shut them peacefully.

Gabriel backed away from the crib, yet kept his eye on the baby, kept humming. That hadn't been so bad.

"What are you doing?"

Gabriel turned. "He was crying."

"I can take care of my own family, Gabriel."

He looked at Laura. "I noticed. Relax. Where's Penny?"

"In bed."

He nodded. "Guess I'll head to the sofa and do the same." Brushing past her, knowing the storm of protest was brewing at his back, he almost smiled. Laura was independent, she was in a bad spot and there was nothing like the combination to make a woman like her mad.

"It's inappropriate for a man to stay in a house with a newly widowed woman and her children. What would my neighbors say?"

"Folks'll understand when they hear about your visitor."

"*I* won't understand!" She had her hands on her hips and was building anger. He gave her credit for stubbornness.

"Suit yourself." He nodded. "I'll be back tomorrow to fix the window."

"I'll call a handyman."

She sure didn't seem to like him. It hurt his feelings a bit since she'd been so fond of his father. Or had she? Had her affection been a ruse for his money?

It didn't matter—all those answers would come in time. "Good night." He headed outside, got in his truck and made himself comfortable.

Ten minutes later, she was at his truck window.

"What are you doing?" she demanded.

He turned down the radio, which was playing soft country tunes. "Watching out for the boogeyman."

"I don't need you to protect me." Laura shook her head. "What's it going to take to get that through your thick skull?"

"Something more than you've got, lady, because I'm not convinced you don't need a little help. And as long as I'm out here, and you're in there, I'd say your virtue is safe."

She gave him a glare that would have curdled milk.

"What's the problem?" he asked reasonably. "I'm not bothering you."

"You're the problem. Go away."

He got out of the truck, considering her. "I'm slowly starting to figure you out."

"You are not."

"Yeah. I am. Here's my offer. I'll stay out here until

I'm satisfied you're safe. In the morning, you call the handyman, or Mason, and I'll go." He put his hands on either side of her, capturing her against the truck. "And in the meantime, I'll be a gentleman. I promise."

Then he kissed her.

Gently, but he kissed her all the same.

At the moment, it felt awesome. For days afterward, he'd wish he hadn't.

Shocked by Gabriel's kiss, Laura pushed his arms away. She stared at him, trying to figure out why he'd done it—hadn't he just said he'd be a gentleman?—then stalked inside her house, locking the door.

She let out her breath and waited for her thundering heart to still. He was everything Josiah Morgan had said his son was: arrogant, opinionated, stubborn.

Nothing like Dave, who'd been gentle, kind, nurturing.

And she'd been lying when she'd told Gabriel she didn't need him standing guard. She was indeed afraid, mostly for Penny and Perrin. Her father wouldn't hurt her children, but it was nerve-racking and wearying when Ben was drunk like that.

Yet no woman wanted to be a responsibility. She knew Mr. Morgan's bequest made Gabriel feel he had to have a part in looking after her and her children.

She touched a finger to her lips, still surprised that she remembered the way his kiss had felt.

She was afraid of feeling anything.

It hadn't been long enough since her husband's passing to feel anything. Hadn't she promised to love and honor Dave until the day she died? Her heart would never forget him.

No other man should have a part in her children's lives. Perhaps that's why she'd felt so comfortable with Mr. Morgan's affection for Penny and Perrin; it was grandfatherly and safe. Their own grandfather was rough around the edges; Dave's family lived up north and sent presents at Christmas. Mr. Morgan had provided the love the children needed through Laura's most devastating hours. She would not feel the same about Gabriel sharing their lives.

Yet he was out in her driveway, standing guard over them. She'd frozen when she'd heard him singing to Perrin; very few men would sing to another man's children. She'd found that quiet act of his astonishingly sexy. Tingles sizzled over her skin, jolting her with a memory she'd shared only with her husband.

Yet those emotions were impossible. Ignoring the tug of desire she would never acknowledge, she went to put on her nightgown and go to bed.

"Then what happened?" Dane stared at his brother. Hot Texas sun rose to nearly overhead, indicating the noon hour. The steaming humidity was suffocating. "Did you kick Ben's ass?"

"No." Gabriel peered at the cracked rocky earth where the old dividing line had been, before Pop had bought Ben's property. "I sent him on his way and then stayed to make certain he didn't return."

Dane knelt, watching Gabriel dig around in the soil. "So now what? What are we looking for?"

"I don't know. Pop and his wild tale of oil under the land he bought from Ben. I don't believe it should be causing this much trouble, because if there was enough oil to fight over, Pop would have had drillers out here by now." He looked at Dane. "So what if it was one of Pop's wild tales? What if he was trying to stir Ben up on purpose?"

"Why would he?"

"I just don't trust Pop." He couldn't tell anything about the earth. The soil didn't look any different to him, from the miles he and Dane had walked together. He didn't really need Dane tagging along, but he couldn't say it had been a bother. Pop had claimed he'd noticed a difference in the soil that led him to speculate that the land was holding a secret, but Gabriel was more inclined to believe a fairy tale had been dreamed up for all of them.

"Well, I will be damned," Dane said, and Gabriel glanced up.

"What?"

"Look what the wind just blew into town."

There wasn't so much as a breeze to stir the humidity. Gabriel turned. "Pete," he murmured, shocked. "I'll be damned right along with you."

Their brother rode up on a horse, a chestnut Gabriel recognized as one of their own. "It isn't February."

"Nope." Pete got down. "But thanks for the trail you left for me."

"Trail?" Gabriel stared at his brother, realizing that the years had left them all a little older, a little leaner, maybe a little meaner. Pete's eyes were a hard dark granite; his cheeks sculpted by whatever demons secret agents battled. He was surprised that he was glad to see his brother. "We didn't leave you a trail."

"Tire marks to the side of the field, hay bent after that. Looked like a bear had crossed the field instead of two men."

"We weren't trying to hide where we were," Dane said. "Good to see you, Pete. Didn't know you were in the country."

"You might have thought about hiding if you knew Ben Smith was at the house, hollering about wanting Gabriel to come out and take his punishment."

"Oh, hell." Gabriel winced. "He's becoming a pain."

"I sent him on his way, but he's convinced we owe him money," Pete said. "He shared that at the top of his lungs, over and over again. Do we?"

Gabriel shrugged. "I doubt it." He glanced at the ground. "Think Pop's got everybody all stirred up for nothing."

"You mean this isn't going to be the next King Ranch?" Pete asked, his hard gaze turning lighter for a moment. "Ben seems to think we're sitting on a Spindletop-sized gusher."

"Don't think so." Gabriel turned toward the truck. "Thanks for the warning, though."

Dane followed, and Pete remounted, riding alongside. "We probably want to keep an eye on him."

Something—maybe a fly—whizzed past Gabriel's ear. He flicked at it, then realized the fly had been accompanied by a sound in the distance.

"What the hell was that?" Dane suddenly flattened Gabriel to the ground.

Gabriel heard hoofbeats rhythmically charging away from them. "Did that sorry sack of crap just take a shot at me?"

"Pete's going after him. Lie low until we know Pete's ridden him down."

Hay crackled in Gabriel's face and itched at his hot skin. He wasn't too keen that his brother felt he had to protect him. "Get the hell off of me. I'm not china, and that goofball couldn't hit the broadside of a barn." Gabriel preferred to take his own hit—he didn't need to rely on his brothers. Dane didn't move, and Gabriel couldn't hold back a snarl. "Get *off,* damn it!"

Dane rolled away. Gabriel jumped to his feet, making a primo target of himself in his red T-shirt and jeans.

"I'd get down if I were you until Pete signals. Who's going to look after Mrs. Adams and the children if you're gone?"

Gabriel glared hotly enough at his brother to scorch the hay around him. "Be very careful, brother."

"Oh, hell. You always were the sensitive one." Dane laughed, untroubled by his brother's foul mood.

Gabriel ignored the desire to jump on Dane and whale him a good one. "I suppose you don't think Pete makes a bigger target on the back of a horse."

"Ben's aiming for you, not Pete."

Gabriel grunted. "I'm walking to the truck. If Ben could have hit me, he would have by now."

"It just takes one lucky shot."

He wasn't going to cower on the ground while his brother fought his battle. If he got his hands on Ben, he was going to wring his skinny neck.

Then again, Ben was Laura's father. Theoretically, he shouldn't strangle the ornery little coward. Laura would probably say he'd bullied Ben, and she sure wouldn't want any help solving her own family issues. Something round in the dry grass caught his eye. Gabriel bent to pick it up. "Not that I'm any happier about a BB, but at least I'm not going to have to kill him."

They got in the truck and he and Dane drove back

to the house in silence. Dane got out and glanced over his shoulder. "Coming in?"

He shook his head. "Got to get some glass for Laura's window in town."

Dane studied him for a long moment, then nodded. "I'll see what Pete found."

Gabriel didn't really care. All he was thinking about was Laura and the kids.

Laura knew Gabriel was out there. She knew when he drove into the driveway. She didn't answer the door when he rang the bell. Holding her breath, she waited for him to leave, knowing she was being unkind, maybe even rude, by not thanking him for his care of her.

She didn't want big, strong Gabriel Morgan pushing his way into her life, storming her heart. It could happen so easily. But she was going to fight the onslaught of his charisma with all her might, for the sake of her own sanity.

Would she even breathe until she heard his truck drive away? She didn't think so; her chest physically pained her. He rang the bell again, calling, "Laura! Your door needs to be repaired!"

He wasn't leaving until he did what he'd come to do. She opened the door silently, unsmiling. He tipped his cowboy hat to her, then puttied in the window efficiently and quietly, never meeting her gaze.

When he finished, he closed the door and went whistling down the porch. Now that he was gone, she could relax. Her house was safe again.

Except it wasn't. There might not be a broken window anymore, but there was a very strong chance of a broken heart that had too few pieces left to risk shattering.

She locked the door.

Laura thought she was free until she heard Gabriel's truck pull back into her drive at eight o'clock that night. She tensed, waiting for a knock on the door, but none came. Burning curiosity tweaked at her. She peeked out the window. He'd simply shut off the engine and pulled out a newspaper.

An hour later she couldn't ignore him any longer. She went outside to confront him. "This is not necessary."

"Caution is a good thing. Besides, your old man took a shot at me this morning."

She gasped, not wanting to believe him. The honest depth of his eyes made her realize he was being completely truthful. She felt sick over her father's spiral into violence. "Did you call the sheriff?"

He shook his head. "Nah. It was only a BB. Pete ran your father down and Ben said he'd just been shooting at a duck. I didn't see any ducks, but whatever." He looked at her with some sympathy. "Maybe there's a way you know of that we can calm him down, get him to stop acting like he's out of his tree."

"I appreciate you trying to be understanding, but I don't know what Ben's problem is. We haven't been close since the day I got married." Instinctively, she lifted her chin. It was still a memory that hurt. "I'm not sure why he'd want to hurt you, though."

"He was just trying to get attention." Gabriel shrugged. "Pete paid him some."

"Pete? How many of you are at the ranch now?"

"Three."

She smiled. "That leaves just one more. Guess your father knew what he was doing."

That rankled. "Go on in before the kids start looking for you. I'm going to read the newspaper."

She sighed, wearing a slightly annoyed expression. "I have a phone. I'll call you if Ben comes back. How's that? You go on home and visit with your brothers, the way your father intended."

He squinted at her. "How do you know what my dad intended?"

She shrugged. "Josiah wasn't exactly quiet about how much he missed his sons being around."

That seemed strange. He'd pretty much run them off when they were old enough to be gone.

"Do you think your father really stole from my father the way Ben claims?"

Gabriel considered that. "I don't know what to believe. And I'm not sure it really matters."

"It matters to Ben."

"Are you taking sides?"

She shook her head. "Merely stating a fact."

"Even if my father did steal from him, that doesn't mean he has the right to knock out your window and take a shot at me."

"I didn't say it did. I simply said that he certainly feels wronged."

"Yeah, well." He wished she'd get on another topic that was friendlier to both of them, and a little easier. Getting a laugh or a smile out of Laura was rare. The shame of it was, he liked looking at her so much. He wished she'd stop cornering him all the time so he could just sit and stare at her full lips and blue eyes. Right now she was wearing a white blouse and a blue skirt that looked cool and feminine. He liked the whole modest thing she had going on. "Well, I'd best turn in," he said, before he started hungering for something he couldn't have.

"Turn in?"

"Get some shut-eye." He settled the newspaper over his face. "I've got some chores to take care of early in the morning."

"Nothing is going to happen. You really don't have to stay."

He slid the newspaper off and met her gaze, not to be polite but because he wanted an excuse to look at her. "I know it won't, not as long as I'm sitting in your driveway."

"You're the most stubborn man I ever met."

"Yes, ma'am."

"Have it your way." She turned away, and without any guilt he watched her fanny sashay to the house and up the steps.

He knew he shouldn't look. A gentleman wouldn't. *Damn.*

Chapter Six

One hour after he'd read the sports section, the business section and the larger community section of Union Junction's newspaper—a one-page epistle—Gabriel was surprised when the passenger-side door of his truck opened and Laura slid into the seat.

"Hello," he said cautiously.

She gave him a determined look. "Why did you kiss me?"

He didn't have an easy answer for that question; he'd pondered it and come up empty. The only reason he could think of was that the old rascal inside him had risen up and acted impulsively. "Paid for it, I guess. Just cashed in a bit late."

She nodded at his reply. "Gabriel, I can't have you sitting in my drive every night. It's only six o'clock now, and here you are already. It's not good for me."

"The neighbors will talk?"

"You and I both know that was just an excuse."

"So what's the real reason you don't want me around?"

She took a deep breath, met his gaze. "I just might fall for you, just like your father probably planned."

His jaw slackened. "Excuse me if I didn't see that one coming."

"Neither did I. But I've been thinking a lot about this, and I realized my heart is just a bit too tender right now. You know, a woman gets lonely. She gets scared at times. And if there's a big, strong man in her driveway, she could just get used to that."

"You're talking in the third person, which means you're not referring to yourself, which means you're likely telling me a story." He frowned at her. "What's the real thing you're trying to tell me?"

She looked at him, silent.

"Correct me if I'm wrong, but you don't strike me as the kind of woman who falls for a man who gives her a light smooch."

Laura sighed. "All right. I am telling you a bit of a story."

"Why?"

"So you'll leave." She shook her head. "I really, really want you to go away."

He was slightly hurt. "All you had to do was ask."

"I have been asking, but you're ignoring me. You'll do whatever you want to, all the time."

"Sorry. Guess I've been on my own all my life."

"Do not try to win pity from me."

He heard her softening and it cheered him. "You didn't have to get my hopes up like that, with all that business about falling for me." Two could play at her game.

She gave him a long stare. "Gabriel, I doubt your hopes were up."

"You never know. I have sensitive feelings."

She looked out the window toward the house, making no comment.

"So you were trying to scare me off with all that business about falling for me. It was just reverse psychology."

She smiled and shook her head. "Obviously it didn't work."

"It did work a little," he said. "I know now that you've been thinking about my kiss. Pretty good for a guy who only got a one-second pass at your lips. Imagine how much more unforgettable I'd be if you'd give me, say, a full hour—"

She got out of the truck and stomped inside. He laughed softly to himself. Maybe she did want him.

If that was the case, he'd probably not say no.

But the children… He was not father material, he knew that. And Laura was not a one-night kind of woman.

Sighing, he turned on his truck, and against his better judgment, acceded to her wishes by leaving her alone. He didn't like it, but she was right: he was too stubborn for his own good.

"Thought you were spending the night out," Dane said, glancing up from the game of chess he and Pete were playing. "It's only six-thirty."

"I was. Sensing that I'm not entirely welcome at the Adams homestead, I decided to come back home and bother you." Gabriel felt restless. He prowled the kitchen looking for something to eat, but he wasn't hungry. Wasn't thirsty. Just had energy to spare.

"She ran you off?" Pete laughed. "To think we used to be such ladies' men, and now we sit here playing checkers."

"Chess," Dane said.

"Whatever. Check."

Dane squinted at the board. "I will be damned. How did you do that?"

Pete leaned back and looked at Gabriel while Dane pondered his next move. "Now what?"

"She thinks we're all square and that we don't owe her anything." Gabriel figured Laura was right. He wouldn't want anybody trying to take care of him, either. He remembered how he'd felt when all the ladies had rushed his house with goodies—he hadn't wanted that at the time. How Laura felt was not that unreasonable.

"Well, while we're all here, we probably ought to discuss what we're going to do about this shack." Pete looked at him. "Don't you think?"

Since Laura didn't need him, it was probably best. She'd really stung him with that drama about how she might fall for him. Part of him had really jumped when she'd started that spiel, and to his surprise, he'd found himself listening eagerly. To find out she'd just been creating a tale to run him off really wounded his pride. "Guess so."

Dane glanced up as the chess clock dinged. He punched the button down. "Your turn. By the way, Gabriel, you realize you're falling into Pop's plot."

"So how's Suzy?" Gabriel asked. "The girl you're supposed to rescue?"

Pete frowned. "Pop didn't send me a letter about anyone. Why'd you guys get one?"

"Be glad." Gabriel sat down. "Or you could have Dane's Suzy."

"Yeah," Dane said. "That'd be awesome."

"So back to this shack of Pop's," Pete said. "We're going to have to hire some people to work it. I'm thinking Ben might be a good first choice."

"Are you out of your mind?" Gabriel demanded.

Pete shrugged. "Best to keep your enemy firmly tucked up against your bosom."

Gabriel blinked, not liking the idea at all. "I don't need Ben around here. He's a lazy drunk."

"Maybe he needs a fair chance." Dane moved a rook on the board and looked satisfied.

"Did you two cook this up while I was at Laura's? I think you're trying to get me killed or something." Gabriel shrugged. "Not that he could get at me. I never knew a man with such bad aim."

Pete nodded. "You'd be safer with him around drawing a paycheck."

"Okay," Gabriel said slowly, "so Ben manages to work one square inch of this ranch. We'll need other hands."

"So are you agreeing?" Dane asked.

"I guess. I can always beat him like a piñata if he acts up."

"No beating the help," Pete said. "That will not win you points with Laura."

"I'll never have points with Laura." As he said it, Gabriel realized it was true, though he hadn't meant to sound so down about it. "We're on different sides of the world, so far apart we'll never run into each other."

His brothers went back to their heated rivalry on the chessboard, the subject closed now that they'd gotten their way about hiring Ben. Gabriel grimaced—what a dumb idea that was. But they were his older brothers, and he'd just get voted down anyway. Life was always hell on the baby.

The notion made him think about Laura and her baby. He wondered if Perrin was suffering from an upset stomach tonight, he wondered if Penny was sleeping soundly tucked in her bed. For that matter, he'd love to know if Laura was sleeping soundly tucked in her bed, then decided that train of thought was fruitless. "Just going to get me in trouble," he murmured, and Pete glanced up.

"What?" his brother asked.

"Nothing," Gabriel said. "See you two troublemakers in the morning."

"Checkmate," Dane said triumphantly, and Gabriel left them arguing over who was the better chess player. They'd both checkmated him, and what he couldn't fathom was why.

Ten years ago, they had been out at a rodeo, all four boys. Pop did not approve of sneaking out, and he despised rodeos with a vengeance. He was determined to keep everyone under his roof, and therefore under his thumb. This came under the heading of good parenting.

The boys chafed, resenting their father's strict rules.

Later, they would think he was pretty reasonable, but then, they deployed every tactic possible to get away from him. Gabriel just wanted to be with his older brothers—he was sixteen, and that seemed reasonable. The boys wouldn't have gone if they hadn't believed they were safe. Jack would never have done anything to harm any of them; he was their hero. Since he was the oldest, Jack took his responsibilities seriously, and yet, Pop considered him a drifter with no purpose in life. Jack hung around rodeos, played his guitar at night, loved the girls a little too eagerly.

Pop had told Jack he belonged in the military when he turned eighteen, and that really began the divide between them. Pop wanted his sons' lives to have a purpose. Jack would not be allowed to live the wild lifestyle of rodeo.

Though Jack was supposed to be helping Pop on the ranch, he'd been riding bulls for years. The brothers never told on him. They decided to sneak out one night and watch him in a town two hours away. Jack had drawn a bull named Ace of Death, a bull in the running for being a registered bounty bull. A rider with big dreams and the determination to stick with it, Jack had looked forward to the challenge.

Six seconds and a fractured spine later, the boys had rushed behind the ambulance, following Jack to the hospital. They got T-boned at an intersection, and though it hadn't been their fault and nobody was hurt, all the brothers had been in for Josiah Morgan's anger. He hadn't spared it. He blamed Jack for luring his brothers out, blamed Pete and Dane for allowing Gabriel to go, blamed Gabriel for not telling his father what the older boys were planning.

Pop's anger had been a terrible thing to witness.

Gabriel shook his head, telling himself that going

back down memory lane wasn't a good idea. Better to live in the present.

He turned and headed back toward his brothers. "When are you going to offer Ben a job?"

"Offer it yourself. He's sitting on the back porch," Dane said.

"Why?" Gabriel wasn't eager to speak to the cantankerous old man.

"He's lonely," Pete said. "He's been quiet as a mouse."

"I don't want any part of this scheme." Gabriel scratched his head. "I don't think you two know what you're doing. He broke Laura's window, you do remember that?"

Dane shrugged. "We can always fire him, Gabriel. It's just best to keep him here—him and his little cap gun."

They listened, hearing the sound of a car pull into the front yard. "Company," Pete said. He peered out. "Looks like Ben has a caller."

Gabriel frowned. "Who would come here to see him?"

"His daughter. And grandchildren, from the looks of things." Dane eyed the black-and-white pieces on the board. "Couldn't hurt to say hello."

Gabriel peered out the window, watching Laura in a pretty sundress step around the back of the house, her two children in tow. "How does she know where he is?"

"We told her," Dane said. "We, of course, wanted her opinion on how she would feel about us offering her father a job."

"And when was I going to be consulted?" Gabriel began to have misgivings about how wise it was for the three of them to be occupying a house together.

"We thought you were at Laura's," Pete said reasonably as Gabriel resumed spying on Laura talking to her father. "We didn't realize when you said you were going to Laura's that you meant no farther than her driveway."

"That's sort of a metaphor, isn't it?" Dane glanced at him, a sly twinkle in his eyes. "The princess won't let the drawbridge down for fair knight."

Pete snickered. "No Holy Grail for him."

"Very funny." Gabriel watched Laura sit down next to her father, gently introducing him to the children. "It seems rude to make them sit outside and visit."

"Nah. They want some time to themselves. Probably like for you to stop staring like a Peeping Tom through the window. I'm getting a beer. You want one?" Pete asked Dane, ignoring Gabriel.

To his credit, Ben seemed thrilled to see the children. He sat up from his slouched position, touching first Penny's hand, then Perrin's. Laura stood back a pace from her father, cautious, yet seemingly hopeful. "Do you think broken families can forget the past?" Gabriel murmured, thinking about the bad feelings between Laura and her father.

"Jeez," Pete said, "no one ever said we had to love each other or anything. We just have to live together. It's one year. No longer than being in a college dorm with a bad roommate."

"Or being married to the wrong woman for a year," Dane said. "Anyway, this house is big enough for three families."

"And we could add on to it if things get really grim." Pete glanced at Gabriel. "As long as we're under this one roof, Pop never said how big the roof had to be."

"We're not adding on to anything. I meant if Laura

and Ben could put their bad blood behind them, we can, too." Gabriel wished he didn't feel so odd man out all of a sudden. Like everybody in the room had been chosen for football and he was designated water boy. "I just don't get the theory behind hiring Ben."

"Every man needs a purpose." Dane looked at him. "Go ask him. You're the human resources director of this ranch."

Gabriel looked at Laura through the slatted wood blinds. "And how did that become my responsibility?"

"You're the baby. Plus, you have a yen for that woman and her children. Pop must have known you better than you know yourself." Dane leaned back in the leather chair, staring up at the rough-beamed ceiling. "I'd almost be scared about Suzy, but I know myself better than that."

"So when do you find out about the mysterious Suzy?" Gabriel put off going out to talk to Laura and Ben. They seemed calm together, maybe even enjoying each other's company for the first time in God only knew how many years.

"Never." Dane grinned, then high-fived his brother. "Dad only said we had to live in the house for a year. The letter asked if I'd take care of Suzy's situation. I did, through a mediator."

Gabriel had to admit it was a smooth move he hadn't considered. "That was smart."

"Watching you moon around after Laura hasn't been pretty. If you got snagged so easily, it could happen to anyone. I had to measure my risk appetite, and I decided it was pretty low."

"I have not been snagged." Gabriel felt his ill humor returning.

"Then back away from the window," Pete said. "I'm sure she can see you from behind those blinds."

Laura probably could. She'd probably be unsurprised that he was keeping watch over her. He sighed, realized she also wouldn't appreciate it and slid away from the window, feeling silly.

"Again, you could just go say hi." Pete stood, stretching. "Anybody for banana fritters?"

Gabriel frowned. "Fritters? Who's going to make those?"

"Laura said she would since she was coming over. It's either that or we grill burgers. I offered burgers because I'm not exactly a banana man. She said the choice was yours since you'd been through a lot lately. We all agreed that was the case."

His life was out of control, hijacked by people he didn't really know that well. He was thinking about the past, and everybody else seemed happy to go along with the cards Pop had dealt them, singularly unsuspicious about the old man's true motives.

"Burgers," he said, "and I guess I'll ring the damn dinner bell." Feeling almost relieved, he jerked open the door. Ben jumped to his feet, startled, and Laura stared at him with shock.

"Morgan," Penny said, a sweet smile on her face.

"Are we bothering you?" Laura asked. "Pete and Dane said we could come inside, but we prefer to sit outside. It's a lovely evening."

"Ben," Gabriel said, "what the hell are you doing on my porch, anyway?"

"Got no place to go at the moment." Ben didn't seem too concerned by that. "Your dad bought my place. This is as close to home as I can get."

"But where were you before that?" Gabriel demanded. "You were somewhere, weren't you?" He looked at Laura, who didn't seem that disturbed by his bad manners. Stepping around him, Dane and Pete went to brush leaves and blown dirt off the picnic table and set up the grill for burgers.

Ben scratched his head. "Well, I've sort of been in this town and that town looking for work. Then you boys came back, and I pretty much figured it wouldn't hurt if I hung around here a bit."

"You tried to shoot me." Gabriel wasn't sure how he was supposed to forget about that. Turning the other cheek in this case would be a trifle hard.

"Didn't try too hard, son. I really didn't give it my best shot. And I was under the influence of some booze and self-pity, I don't mind admitting." The old man scratched his head and rubbed his chin ruefully. "Sorry I scared you, though. Won't happen again. I gave your brothers my word."

"I wasn't scared. It's against the law to take potshots at people." Gabriel felt annoyance rising inside him. This was not a Hallmark card moment, never would be for him. Anger and mistrust were wrung up together inside him. Why did he get the feeling that this new family was being thrust upon him? "I don't trust you, Ben, to be perfectly honest."

"I respect that," Ben said calmly, "but on the bright side, it's not like I'm in the running to be your father-in-law or anything."

Pete and Dane swung around to stare at them. Laura's eyes went huge. The words hung silent and awkward in the twilight air.

Ben glanced around at everyone. "Well, I'm not," Ben reiterated, "so there's the bright side, right?"

It would be hell having Ben for a father-in-law. Whatever foolish daydreams he'd had concerning Laura were blown to dust. He should never have kissed her, should never have toyed with her affections.

Now that she and her father were coming to some type of reunion, he could excuse himself from the picture-perfect moment he didn't want to be painted into. "Think I'll go check on the horses. Good night." He headed off, leaving everyone else to enjoy what had become a family picnic.

Almost.

Laura stared after Gabriel, disappointed by his reaction. She could feel his withdrawal from the gathering, from her. Even from the children, and that hurt the most. He was big and strong and caring, and she had kept him at arm's length. There were reasons for that, but she didn't want him resenting her, or her father.

Although it was easy to resent Ben. He had lost his temper. No one would forgive someone who shot at them.

"I've made a mess of this," Ben said sadly. "I'm never touching another drop of drink."

Dane and Pete went back to scrubbing off the grill. It looked like it hadn't been scrubbed properly or even used in years. "Listen, Ben," she said, sitting down on the porch beside him, "it's great that you're not going to drink anymore. It's great for you, it's great for the kids. You might even consider some counseling or AA. In the meantime, don't worry about Gabriel. There was nothing to mess up."

"I was just so mad thinking Josiah had cheated me. I always hated getting cheated." Ben sniffed, rubbing his nose on his shirt. "Josiah is a tricky one, too. He's a smart man. He didn't get so wealthy by being a sucker." He sighed deeply. "Unlike me."

"This is the time to stop feeling sorry for yourself, don't you think, Ben?" She shifted Perrin in her arms; Penny sat quietly between them. "If you see yourself as a victim, then you'll be one."

He slowly nodded. "I guess I fell into that trap when your mother went away. I thought she was happy with me. Never dreamed she'd go off."

Laura had read the letter from her mother many times over the years. She'd long since made peace with the fact that her mother hadn't been able to handle life with a drifter who moved from town to town. She'd gone back north where she had friends. It wasn't that she didn't love her baby, she'd said in the letter. She just felt Ben would be the better parent.

It had been like being given up for adoption. Painful in the growing years, hard as a teenager and probably contributing to Laura's desire to marry a kind, gentle man who seemed solid as a rock, someone who'd be there for her forever. "Ben, it's all right about Mom. We did fine on our own."

"I've been an ass." He looked down at Penny, who stared up at his whiskered face without judgment. "I'm sorry I was hard on your husband, Laura. When he died, I relapsed. I blamed myself for letting my stubbornness get between us."

The familiar knife of pain went through Laura at all the time wasted between them, when Dave had been alive, when her father could have been part of their family. It was time that could never be replaced.

"And now I've shot at your new boyfriend and ruined things for you," he said. "He's never going to want me around."

"Gabriel's not my boyfriend," Laura said firmly, "and if you're sincere about quitting drinking, I want you around and that's all that matters."

He nodded, glancing at Penny and Perrin wistfully. "I am."

"And no more feeling sorry for yourself."

"No." He shook his head. "I've got a lot to live for now."

"And you forget about that oil business you think Josiah pulled over on you," she said sternly.

A grimace wrinkled his face. "That's a little more difficult. A man hates to have something taken from him."

"I don't think there's anything here. There'd be drillers out here if there was. And do you know what the start-up costs on an operation like that would be?" She looked at her father sincerely. "Unless it was an oil find the size of, I don't know, something in the Gulf, it probably wouldn't be worth the drilling costs."

He blinked. "You're right."

She nodded.

He thought about that for a minute. "But why'd he give you all that money for the kids if it wasn't guilt money?"

"Because Mr. Morgan was a nice old man."

Ben shook his head. "No, Josiah Morgan is not."

"It doesn't matter, does it? He felt like he could

help our family when Dave died. That's a good thing, isn't it?"

Ben glanced over at Dane and Pete. "He couldn't get along with his own family, though. Never did understand how that came to pass."

"It's none of our business. People probably say the same thing about us." She kissed Perrin and Penny on their heads.

"Hamburgers? Or hot dogs?" Pete asked. "What does everyone want?"

Laura stood, feeling awkward. "I'm not sure we should stay for dinner. Gabriel made his feelings about our presence pretty plain."

Pete grinned at her. "Gabriel was always the slow child among us. He'll cool off in a bit."

Dane laughed, overhearing his brother's comment. "Besides Jack, he's definitely the most temperamental."

She sat Penny at the picnic table. Somewhat sheepishly, Ben sat down beside Penny.

"It's awfully nice of you boys to forgive me," Ben said.

"You don't have to sing for your supper, Ben," Dane said kindly. "Let's just enjoy the wonderful summer evening."

"Every one of us here is a sinner," Pete added, plopping a big juicy burger in front of Ben. A hot dog followed for Penny, and then a burger for Laura. Perrin sat in her lap, watching everything with big eyes and his fist in his mouth.

"It's a bit charred because we overfired the grill. We'll get better in time," Dane said.

Dane and Pete served themselves, then sat across from Ben and Laura. "I'll say a blessing," Pete offered, and they all bowed their heads until they heard the back door slam.

They glanced up to see Gabriel standing in the doorway.

"The prodigal brother returns," Pete said. "Grab a burger."

Gabriel looked at the picnic table, divided with Laura's family on one side, the Morgans on the other. He had no appetite, except maybe for Laura, something he'd discovered that was growing in spite of his objection to those emotions. "I don't think I'm going to be able to stay here."

They all stared at him.

"Tonight?" Pete asked.

He couldn't meet Laura's steadfast gaze. "At all."

Chapter Seven

Laura's heart sank at Gabriel's words. He obviously had a problem with her family. He definitely did not want them there. She couldn't blame him, either. She held Perrin tighter to her. Maybe she'd made a bad judgment call, believing that because Mr. Morgan had welcomed them, his sons would, too.

"Ben," Gabriel said, "how are you at doing odd jobs on a ranch?"

Ben looked at him. "Could do a good-sized bit of work in my day."

Gabriel folded his arms across his chest. "Are you wanting a job?"

"Depends." Ben jutted out his chin, letting everyone know his pride was at stake.

Gabriel's gaze briefly flicked to Laura. "We've got one open here. This place needs a lot of work."

Ben's jaw sagged. "Do you mean it?" He glanced around at Pete and Dane, whom Laura noticed were staring at Gabriel with approval.

Gabriel nodded. "My brothers feel you could be helpful. You have good knowledge of a working ranch."

It seemed Ben's eyes shone brighter. "I'll take you up on that offer, then."

Gabriel nodded. "You'll have to ask my brothers the particulars of where you should start." He glanced around at the gathering. "Laura, Ben, thank you for coming by." He fondly tousled Penny's and Perrin's hair, surprising Laura. "I'll be heading out."

They all watched in silence as Gabriel left.

"Uh, anybody want pickles with their burgers?" Dane asked to cover the awkward silence. Penny ate her hot dog, and Perrin strained to get down and crawl on the ground. Laura had the strangest sensation that she was missing something in Gabriel's words. He sure hadn't seemed happy. "Can you watch my kids, Ben?" she asked her dad.

"Sure," Ben said, happy to be asked.

Laura handed Perrin to her father, then hurried around to the front of the house so she could catch Gabriel before he departed. He'd said he wasn't going to stick out the year on the ranch—something was bothering him. Badly.

She had to know it wasn't her—or her family.

"Gabriel, wait." She hurried across to where he was backing his truck down the drive. "What is your problem?"

He gazed at her, his eyes pensive. "If I have one, I'm keeping it to myself."

Wasn't that just stubborn as a mule? She shrugged. "I think something's on your mind."

He resumed backing down the drive. She let him go this time, hating his withdrawal. Hiding your emotions was too easy.

She watched him stop his truck, then pull slowly back up the drive, like a magnet moving toward her.

"Maybe we should talk," he said.

"As long as it's your idea," she said sweetly, and got into his truck.

"It wasn't my idea to offer your father a job," he said, heading away from the ranch.

"I thought not. Why did you?"

"My brothers thought we should. And I'm not exactly objective about the situation, considering I don't completely trust him."

"Nor should you," Laura said, not hurt in the least. "He hasn't always been trustworthy." She took a deep breath. "If it makes your decision any easier, I'm taking some leaps of faith where Ben is concerned these days, as well."

"I don't think I'd be able to be friends as easily with my father if he suddenly came back."

She figured that hadn't been an easy admission to make. "I have children, Gabriel. Ben deserves a chance to be a good grandfather, even if he didn't agree with my choice of life partner. That's always going to hurt, but he regrets it now. And I can't wish those years we spent apart never happened, because they did."

"That's one of the things I like about you. You're steadfast." Gabriel glanced toward her briefly. "I just don't think I'll ever be close to my father, especially now that he's got us all tied here for whatever purpose."

"Parenthood isn't easy at any age."

He stopped the truck outside a roadside ice-cream stand. "Would it bother you if you were part of a setup?"

"No, because I don't see myself that way."

Gabriel looked at her. "Even though Josiah gave your kids money, even though he asked me to look after you, you don't see this as part of a grand scheme?" He sighed. "I do. I resent the hell out of it."

She felt prickles run over her skin. "You're safe from me."

"Oh, I know that. You've got an honest-to-God electric fence up around you." Gabriel stared at her so intently she felt her bones turn to water. "It would almost be easier if you didn't."

"Meaning you could sleep with me and then move on? As easily as you're going to move on from your father's request?" She lifted her chin. "I didn't see you as the type of man who looks for the easy way out. Even Ben's got more spirit than that."

Well, that little minx, Gabriel thought. How dare she decide he was spineless? If she knew how badly he wanted to kiss her, shut those pretty lips up so they'd stop taunting him, she'd jump right out of his truck and run back to her safe little family.

He hated indecision, despised fear and inaction. Strength for a man lay in his stubborn attachment to his ideals, and she was shaking every one he had. He hadn't wanted to hire Ben, but part of him knew he'd win approval from her for it. Now he realized how desperately he craved that approval.

But he didn't want to feel this way, not so deeply. About *any* woman, and no million dollars was worth it. A man worth his salt earned his own damn money, he didn't get paid to go to the altar.

That's what he felt like. That's what he'd really meant when he'd said he might not stick out the year. As ticked as he was at his brothers for making him hire Ben—a problem lodged in his own brain because Pete and Dane seemed to think it was a brilliant plan—he really didn't want to admit his father was controlling his life.

His choice of bride. His will to marry.

Dane, he'd noticed, had to feel the same because he didn't give two flips about who this mysterious Suzy was. "Do you know a Suzy in this town? I believe she may have a few children."

Laura turned big eyes on him. "Suzy? Don't you know, since you're asking about her?"

Gabriel shrugged. "Pop left Dane a letter about someone named Suzy."

"Oh." Laura seemed surprised by that. "She's not exactly his type."

"Really? What type is Dane's?" He watched her, obviously interested in her reply. What made her think she knew his brother at all?

"She has twin baby girls. I'm not certain any of you Morgans would want to take on parenting duties," Laura said slowly, then shook her head. "I see what's bothering you. Your father seemed to have planned to get you brothers women with ready-made families."

"Would be awful devious of him."

She nodded. "What I think you're underestimating is that he wanted grandchildren and doesn't mind adopting them into his family. I don't think he's actually crazy enough to assume he can induce four hardened bachelors to get to the altar."

"Yeah, Pop is that ornery." He nodded. "As least your father only took a shot at me. Mine's trying to shoot holes in our lives."

"You probably learned a lot about being bulletproof in the military," she said smoothly. "But your father wants the same thing mine does—to be close to his family. And if he uses money or connections to make that happen, can you blame him? He's not getting any younger."

"I prefer the direct approach."

She shook her head. "No, you don't. You've been running from me ever since you kissed me."

That was certainly direct coming from a young widow with children. "I've been trying not to do it again. You didn't seem too happy about it, and a gentleman respects a lady's wishes."

"I do appreciate you hiring my father, Gabriel. I saw something come into his eyes I haven't seen in years. I think it was hope. He seems to be changing."

"Wasn't easy. He's made an ass of himself."

She tapped his hand, which was resting on the steering wheel. "All of us probably have. I doubt he'll let you down, though."

"Hope not," he grumbled.

"So you've done what your father asked of you. You've watched out for me, employed my dad. You can go on with your life now and not worry about me."

"It's not that easy," Gabriel said with reluctance. "Your kids have gotten under my skin."

Laura looked at him. "What do you mean?"

"See, this is the part I wasn't expecting," he said, realizing all of a sudden what he hadn't been able to put into words before. "I didn't expect to find myself caring about your children."

She seemed to withdraw from him. He knew he had headed into deep water, and there was no going back to shore. "Guess I see why Pop liked them so much. Penny's adorable and Perrin… I hate it when he cries. He makes me want to comfort him."

Her face was a blank he couldn't read.

"It's okay," he said, steeling his heart. "I just find myself thinking about them…and even if I wanted to leave, I don't think I could leave *them*."

Laura didn't know what to say. Perhaps Gabriel was only offering himself in a brotherly capacity. He didn't act like a man who was interested in her—beyond that initial quick kiss, he hadn't made a move toward her.

He wouldn't. Behind that wolf's coat hid a chivalrous heart. Just like his father, just like his brothers. These men all walked dangerous paths, but they wanted the heart and soul of life: family, friends, community.

They just didn't want to admit it.

"If you're offering to take a man's role in my children's lives, I wouldn't turn that down," Laura said. "Mason spends a lot of time with them, and—"

He took her hand in his. Laura stopped speaking, held herself stiffly. Nothing in her body would relax.

Gently, he pressed her palm to his lips. His eyes were dark and fathomless.

Oh, boy. She was pretty sure he wasn't thinking *uncle* now. Her heart beat too hard; her breath went shallow. She couldn't take her hand away from his warm lips. She couldn't think. She felt herself falling under Gabriel's spell, falling faster than she'd ever fallen in her life. There was nothing safe here; this was not a gentle friendship he was offering.

She knew he was waiting for her to speak. A man like him would probably only offer his protection once…and yet, she could not reach into the flames to feel the desire he was offering to ignite.

She lowered her gaze, her pulse racing. After a moment, he put her hand in her lap and rolled down his window. "Ice cream?" he asked, his tone respectful.

"No, thank you."

"Think I'll get a limeade." He pressed the button, placed an order for two and stared out the front window pensively.

"Gabriel, I—"

"You know," he said, "I'll always be here for you, no matter what."

"For a year."

He nodded.

"Because your father asked you to watch out for me."

He turned to look at her. "It won't hurt me to spend time around your children. I know how to observe the boundaries you've set."

It was over, whatever he'd been offering her a moment ago. "Thank you," she said, her heart jumping too hard.

He nodded, paid for the order when a carhop brought them and handed Laura a drink.

"No problem," he said. "No problem at all."

Chapter Eight

Man, he was a sap.

Gabriel decided his life was a runaway train driven by his father. He'd hired his enemy, fallen for the man's daughter and her kids. He was changing, being changed, and he wasn't sure he liked it. "If we head back now, we can still grab some of those burgers."

"So you're staying in Union Junction?"

"As long as you and I can avoid my father's manipulation, I can probably survive."

She nodded. "I need to put Perrin to bed. It was nice of your brothers to invite us over, though."

Yeah, they'd shanghaied him on that one. "So, back to this Suzy."

He felt her gaze on him as he drove.

"She's a nice lady. Rides a lot."

He grunted. Dane wasn't usually cut out for nice ladies—that had the sound of commitment and wedding bells tied to it. "What did Pop feel he owed her?"

"I don't know." She adjusted her seat belt, then quit fidgeting. "Have you ever considered going over to France to talk to your father?"

"Hell, no. Didn't talk to him in America, sure as hell aren't going to cross the world to do it." Why would he, anyway? They hadn't had anything to say to each other in years.

"So what was it exactly that happened? Do you mind me asking?"

He did mind, but since it was Laura, he could tolerate the question. "There's no easy answer, other than we all got tired of being on the rough side of Pop's tongue." It had been hard facing constant criticism. None of them had ever lived up to Pop's ideals. "Pop was a hard taskmaster."

"I know. It's how he made his money."

"I guess. But his way wasn't my way, nor Dane's, nor Pete's and sure as hell not Jack's." If there was ever a man who'd had all his ambition for steady living driven out of him, it was Jack. Jack was perfectly suited to rodeo because it was a gamble, a walk on the wild side. Just man pitted against beast and a score that determined the outcome.

In other words, it was pretty much a day-to-day test of survival skills. "Beyond the fact we couldn't please Pop and we knew he'd never be proud of us, we did something he just couldn't tolerate. We knew he'd never forgive us, so we left. Unfortunately, when we left, none of us felt good about it, so we sort of drifted apart. Ten years moves a lot faster than you think it might. People say they get busy and they do, but it's just all noise for the relationships they're avoiding."

"Oh, I know how fast time can slip away."

Damn, he'd sounded like he was preaching. "We were pretty much of a handful for Pop to raise. Chafing against authority and all that."

She smiled. "As a teacher, I have to ask if you did well in school."

"None of us did particularly well in regular school. All of us enlisted except Jack, and from there we found our own niches. I'm proud to say that the military put me through four years of college, and then I made top grades."

"Good for you."

"Yeah." He hadn't had Pop chewing on him to do well, so he'd done it for himself. "So then I served out the rest of my time and now I'm answering the call to family duty."

"Very honorable."

"Not really, I guess. Just trying to beat Pop at his own game."

She laughed. "I don't think you realize how much he's mellowed in his old age."

He grunted.

"And I don't really believe the reason you're doing all this is because you're trying to best your father," she said, "because that would mean you still care very much about his opinion, and you don't. Do you?"

Ah, she was being sneaky. He liked that. "Not sure."

"I know families can be messy. I also believe it's best to let the past go, if possible. Even if you felt your father was never proud of you, you're proud of your choices. You're your own man."

"You're a regular mind reader, aren't you?" He wasn't sure he liked her picking at his emotions.

"Teachers do some of that," she said coolly, "but having known your father, I know that he isn't a man who is truly comfortable with his emotions. Most people aren't."

He stopped at the ranch. "I'd better feed you a hamburger before you blow a circuit."

She smiled and got out of the truck. "Do you feel better now that you've cooled off some?"

"Maybe." He stared down at her, thinking he wasn't cool at all. He was on a slow boil around Laura.

"Just don't say you're not going to stick out the year again, at least not because of me." She looked up at him with those endless eyes, and he felt his resistance melting. "You're as easy to get attached to as your father, you know," she told him.

He didn't know what to make of that. Or her. He shook his head and followed her around to the back patio.

Ben was enjoying his grandkids. Pete and Dane were throwing a Frisbee around, and not too well, either. Gabriel scowled at the makeshift family gathering.

Then he looked at Perrin and Penny and broke out in a grin. They were cute, unafraid of Ben. He wasn't sure he could ever forgive Ben—the man could have killed him in a drunken stupor—but Laura was right. It would be better for Penny and Perrin if their grandfather was active in their lives.

If Ben was serious about turning his life around.

"I really do appreciate the job," Ben told him, his eyes shining over the heads of his grandchildren. "Feel like I have a purpose now. Your brothers told me I can start tomorrow."

"Great," Gabriel said, his voice stern. "You have to lock your guns in a gun cabinet or get rid of them altogether now that you've got grandkids. Even BB guns, air rifles, pellet guns. Hell, even water guns." He jutted out his chin.

The Frisbee landed on the grass. Pete and Dane stared at him. Laura nodded.

"He's right, Dad. It's a good idea."

Her gaze met Gabriel's. He knew she understood that he might not ever trust Ben, but she also thought he was trying to be cool about what happened. A man had a right to be ticked about being shot at, didn't he?

"It was a BB gun and he was far away," Pete told him. "Not that it couldn't have harmed you but we're not talking the need for a bulletproof vest, either, bro."

"Yeah, well." He'd been in the military too long to appreciate someone aiming a gun at him. Any kind of accident could happen with toddlers around. "For that matter, we're locking ours away in the attic. I don't think that's too cautious, do you?" He couldn't stand the thought of Penny and Perrin accidentally getting near a hunting rifle or… His chest constricted, his mouth went dry. Clearly his brothers thought he had gone mental, then they shrugged and went on with their game. Laura watched him, her expression concerned, but with a soft smile on her face. His mind raced, still on Penny and Perrin. There was a pond on the property, knives in the kitchen. The fireplace had sharp corners on it where Perrin could fall and hurt himself. There were two staircases that the children could tumble down. Acres of farmland surrounded them. He scanned the perimeter of the property, thinking that if one of the children wandered away, he wasn't sure they could find them easily.

He realized he was panicked. He could count on one hand the times he'd been scared in the military, and that was when he'd been in a war zone.

He couldn't imagine actually being a parent.

"Are you all right, Gabriel?" Laura asked.

He was beginning to wonder.

Dane was wondering, too, mostly what was eating at Gabriel. He jerked his head at Pete and they slipped inside the house. From the kitchen, they watched Laura and Ben play with the grandkids, and Gabriel hover nearby like an uncertain bear.

"Think he likes her?" Dane asked.

"Pop probably hoped he would."

They sprawled in the wooden, rounded-back chairs set at six places around the table. "There were four of us, and Pop. Guess we never needed the sixth chair unless we had company." Dane remembered they all used to toss their coats in the sixth chair, and Pop had gotten so mad.

"If he gets married before his year is up, does that mean he forfeits if he moves away?" Dane was thinking that if Gabriel wasn't open to getting serious, he was probably crazy. Laura was a beautiful woman. She was sweet. Her kids were great. He didn't give Pop much credit for anything, but he'd certainly picked a nice family to associate himself with.

"I don't know." Pete shook his head. "No one knows but Pop. I wouldn't say that to Gabriel, though."

"Oh, hell, no. Although he did consider leaving, briefly."

Pete laughed. "He hates being boxed in. Even when he was a kid, he hated being told what to do."

"So do I." They were all stubborn chips off the block like their dad. "Wonder why Pop never remarried if he was so set on family."

They sat quietly, listening to Gabriel and Laura calling to Penny as they tried to teach her to throw the Frisbee.

"Dunno. Didn't he always say marriage was for suckers?" Pete kicked his boots up onto a chair.

"He did." He'd been pretty bitter when their mom left. Refused to speak of her for years. "So if it's for suckers, he'll understand none of us choosing to settle down."

They heard Perrin's happy squeal, saw Ben go by the window holding his grandchild.

"Maybe one house can only hold so much bitterness," Pete said. "I don't understand why Pop didn't match me to a bride."

"Hey!" Dane sat up. "This Suzy girl is not my match!"

Laura came inside the kitchen, smiling when she saw them relaxing at the table. "Too much activity out there for you boys? You're not used to being around children. They can be overwhelming."

"I can handle it," Dane said.

"That's good." She got out glasses and a tumbler. "Gabriel says you're supposed to meet with Suzy Winterstone at some point? She has darling twins." She filled the pitcher with water and ice.

Dane sat up. "How old?"

"About twelve months old. Why?" She glanced at him curiously.

"Where's the father?" His mouth felt completely dry. Damn Pop! He could almost feel a trap ensnaring him.

"There isn't one. Well, not in residence anyway. Suzy had a boyfriend. She thought they were serious, but apparently, he wasn't. She's not heard from him since he went back to Australia or wherever he was from. Mr. Morgan hired a couple of nannies to help her and now they're doing just fine."

"Nannies?" Dane didn't really know what a nanny did. Didn't they just push around big fluffy strollers with oversized wheels?

"Well, she has the money to have help. Definitely having two children at once is challenging. And being alone would be hard. Plus, she had a C-section that had some complications."

"But if she has money, then she doesn't need…like, a man or anything." Dane knew he sounded like he was desperate to run away from the situation, and he was, but he didn't want to sound completely unchivalrous.

"She has money because of your father's generosity."

She took the tray of drinks outside, leaving Dane to stare at Pete.

"Pretty weird hobby Pop had."

"So was collecting huge acreages. Made him a lot of money, though." Pete sounded untroubled by that.

"You're just not worried because you didn't get a letter of doom." Dane felt annoyed by that. "Maybe Pop only felt that Gabriel and I were suitable choices for—"

"His schemes. I'd buy that. You guys are the youngest. And the most impressionable."

Dane shook his head. "I don't need a woman with two babies. That sounds high maintenance."

Pete laughed. "So is Pop."

* * *

Laura stayed later than she'd planned, watching Ben play with her children, feeling like her life was a completed circle now. Wholeness eased her heart. Penny and Perrin would have a father figure to look up to; Ben appeared to have a new lease on life.

She could forget the past. Not Dave, of course. Her heart still burned with sadness when she thought about him. But healing old pain made her feel brighter about everything. It was the start of summer, a great time for new beginnings.

Gabriel made her feel a snap of excitement, too, as much as she didn't want him to be part of her emotional healing process. With Ben in their lives, the father-figure gap she'd worried about would be alleviated.

She stood. "I have to take the children home and put them to bed. Thank you for a lovely evening."

Penny tiredly rubbed her eyes; Perrin's were drifting shut as he lay against Gabriel's chest. Gabriel and Ben followed her as she picked Penny up and walked her to the car.

"I'll be by tomorrow," Ben said eagerly. "We could take the kids for a ride into town. I'd like to show them off to my buddies."

Laura smiled. "They'd love that."

Ben glanced at Gabriel self-consciously, then said, "Thanks for everything, Morgan."

Gabriel watched as Ben ambled away. "I can't get used to people calling me that in my father's house."

She strapped Penny into her car seat, then took Perrin from Gabriel to do the same. "What did they call you in the service?"

"Morgan. But I hear it here, and I look around for Pop."

"It took me a few weeks to get used to being Mrs. Adams."

It was then that the idea hit Gabriel, blooming big in his brain, like facing the worst fear he'd ever had.

Chapter Nine

"Try getting used to Mrs. Morgan," Gabriel said.

Laura turned around. "What do you mean?"

"It could be your name. For a year, anyway."

Her heart skipped strangely inside her. She wanted to run and hide in the worst way. "I don't want a husband."

"I don't want a wife in the traditional sense. But it wouldn't kill me to have some help making this year more bearable, I'll admit."

She sank into the seat and closed the car door. "I have to get my kids home."

He nodded, his eyes dark, his gaze unfathomable, before his attention switched to the kids in the back-seat. "They look like they've had a full day. I'm glad I got to see them."

She hesitated, Gabriel's words just sinking in. "I'm sorry, but did you just propose to me?"

"I am proposing, yes. You can call it a business proposal, a merger or an idea to make my life easier. Whatever you want to call it."

She shook her head. "You are your father's son."

"Laura, I understand that you're still grieving. Whatever limits you'd want on a partnership between us would be fine by me."

She felt her fingers tremble. He didn't understand that she wasn't that much of a daredevil. Besides the obvious thrill of being married to a man like Gabriel, she wouldn't be able to count on the snuggling, the gentle companionship that Dave had offered.

"Just think about it for now. The option's open. Good night, kids." He reached through the window and touched each child's hand. "See you tomorrow."

She backed up the car and drove away, her mind whirling over Gabriel's proposal. She didn't want to get married. He didn't want to get married.

The only reason he'd asked her was because of his father. It had something to do with the wager his father had set upon his sons.

On the other hand, Gabriel really seemed to enjoy her children. He had even offered Ben a job, which she knew was against his better judgment, and maybe even hers. But the fact that he'd been willing to give her father a chance caught her attention. Sometimes a chance was all someone needed to start over, jump into better luck.

Her eyes widened as she realized he was giving her a chance, much like he had Ben. Gabriel was a giver, hiding behind a gruff exterior. She'd been fooled—or frightened—by his seeming harshness.

Marriage to him would be a business, just like everything else in the Morgan family. Because of their father, they couldn't help but think coolly, strategically.

She missed Dave's uncomplicated style. Day by day, come what may.

However, that lifestyle had led to being alone with two small children and financial hardship. Had it not been for Josiah Morgan—who'd seen fit to give her a chance—she'd still be knocked off her feet.

She was surprised to find herself mulling Gabriel's offer.

The temptation shocked her.

Her gaze found Penny and Perrin in the backseat through the rearview mirror, and she knew she was looking at the one reason she would consider Gabriel's offer. A chance for a wonderful father for her children didn't come along that often. Maybe she was being self-ish, but secretly she longed for that chance for them.

It didn't hurt that Gabriel was sexier than any man had a right to be.

Whatever label anyone wanted to put on marriage—partnership or love at first sight—Gabriel had never considered the option. He was too old to be fooled by sexual attraction, but he was insanely attracted to the little mother. Nor did he care that he was falling into his father's plan willingly.

Fact was, he didn't give a damn what his father or his brothers thought. He liked Penny and Perrin. He liked Laura. The piece of his life they'd begun to occupy felt like home to him, and he was smart enough to realize that all the houses and land Pop had acquired over the years were probably a filler for the feeling of home.

Bottom line, a man shouldn't be so dumb he let his pride rule him.

He knew Laura probably would never love him. Actually, his chances weren't great on that score, since she was still in love with her deceased husband. He understood, but he didn't mind waiting that out. The desire to own that piece of life they'd embedded in his heart, that intangible thing he'd craved all his life, was simply too strong. He was a risk taker; he wasn't afraid of it. In fact, he almost relished the challenge.

A great chunk of the challenge—and he wasn't afraid to admit it—was that he'd never planned to have children of his own. But he could be a father to two kids who needed one—at least he could try. This was the toughest part of proposing marriage: not knowing if he could be an adequate father. It required settling down for real commitment. Living in one town. This town.

And what if they stayed married beyond the year he needed to put in at the ranch? Little League, dance recitals, trying not to beat on teenage boys who would come to date his daughter, learning golf with his son. Golf was probably a good thing to learn, he mused. He'd have to attend church with them, something he had refused to do. God had been a very faraway component of his life in the world's hidden outposts.

He'd have to change a lot about himself. Being a parent required sacrifice. He wasn't afraid of sacrifice.

But the reality that he might let them down sent sweat trickling down the back of his neck. He'd had a stern role model for fatherhood—he hoped Laura didn't factor that into her consideration of his proposal.

He really craved the piece of home she represented.

* * *

"Home, sweet home!"

The bellow from the foyer at 5:00 a.m. shot Gabriel upright in his bed. The voice was a nightmare; he remembered the lashing roughness of it.

It couldn't be. He'd simply had a nightmare.

He heard familiar heavy boots clomping on the hardwood floor downstairs. His pulse rate jacked up. He went to stare over the rail. Dane and Pete met him there.

Suddenly he was an awkward teenager again, wishing he didn't have to face the critical appraisal of his father. "What the hell, Pop?" he demanded.

The white-haired and strong Josiah Morgan looked up at his three sons. "I see money *can* buy a man everything." His weathered face folded into a frown. "Except Jack. Where the hell is Jack?"

"Not being bought," Gabriel replied. "Helluva price to pay for a family reunion, if that's what you wanted."

His father shrugged. "A good businessman checks up on his investments."

"I'm leaving," Dane said under his breath. "I don't need this crap."

Pete nodded. "Damn if he doesn't make me remember all over again how much I despise him. Old goat."

"Shh," Gabriel said. "Don't disrespect the chance to learn from life's mistakes."

"Are you crazy?" Pete asked. "The man isn't a father. He's a human computer."

"Maybe he can be reprogrammed."

"I don't care," Pete said. Their father ignored them, headed into the kitchen. They could hear his boots striding through to the den. "He doesn't own me."

"If Ben can turn over a new leaf, it's possible Pop

can, too." Gabriel wasn't going to run from his father's dark bitterness. "He wouldn't be here if he wasn't up to something. Wasn't it you who said we should keep our enemy tucked close to our chest?"

"Yeah, but that was when it was your ass in hot water," Pete said, and Dane nodded.

"I personally don't believe in that enemy theory," Dane said. "It isn't the way I handled being a Ranger."

"I preferred distance between me and the enemy. The old saw about close enough for hand grenades worked for me," Pete said.

"God hates a coward." Gabriel turned to go downstairs to face his father.

"Nope, God gave me legs to depart." Dane shrugged. "I don't have a big enough shovel for all the crap Pop's gonna give us. And it ticks me off that he lured us here under false pretenses. He just wanted us home."

"I agree with Dane. I'm too old to be trapped into one of Pop's sorry-ass confrontations. His approval hasn't mattered to me in years. Gabriel, you're on your own if you're fool enough to stay." Pete went to his room.

Gabriel figured he was used to that. Hell, they all were. "Well, maybe Pop's carping won't bother me as much as it would you. Otherwise, my backup plan for getting along with Pop is to get married," he said, and grinned when his brothers stuck their heads back into the hall.

"Married?" Pete repeated.

Gabriel nodded. "I asked Laura to marry me."

"Whoa," Dane said, "you're setting a bad precedent here. Do not think that I intend to do the same. In fact, I tore up Pop's letter about that Suzy chick. I'll be telling him that before I leave, too."

"Why are you falling in line with Pop's scheming?" Pete demanded. "This isn't the military, you know. You don't have to jump when sarge commands. Once Pop knows he can buy you, you'll be screwed."

"I'm doing it because Laura needs me," Gabriel said, "although Laura would disagree." Actually that reason was too simplified, but he wasn't going to pour his heart out to his boneheaded brothers. They'd never understand.

"Well, probably no one can save you," Pete said. "Good luck."

"Yeah. Let me know where to send a gift," Dane said.

Gabriel replied, "Here, of course. I'm sticking out my year like I planned."

"With Pop in residence? Does Laura know?" Pete asked. His expression said Gabriel was nuts.

"Doesn't matter to me if Pop's here or not. Doesn't matter to me what Pop thinks about my marriage proposal." Gabriel's heart was singing at the freedom of not caring anymore. "To be honest, I couldn't care less. Everything is in the past and that's where it's going to stay."

"The optimism of a baby," Dane said. "I hope you know what you're doing."

Gabriel shrugged and went downstairs. "So. What ill wind blew you in?"

His father looked up. "How the hell was I to know my place was being looked after?"

"You knew I'd be here. I'd bet you expected all of us to be here." Gabriel slung himself into a leather chair opposite his father. For being apart ten years, he couldn't say there was an outpouring of emotion at the reunion. Nor had the old man changed much. He was craggier, whiter of hair, maybe, but still looked strong as a bull and was obviously marching to his own drummer. "You set this all up knowing we'd all do what you wanted."

"I wish it were that easy." Josiah looked at him. "Are you still in the military?"

"Did my time. Now I'm house-sitting for you."

"Mooching off me, you mean," Josiah said sourly.

"Okay," Gabriel said easily, rising to his feet. "I didn't realize you regretted your own scheme. Ben will be arriving every morning at 5:00 a.m. to water and feed the horses you left for the neighbors to look after."

"Ben? Ben Smith?"

Gabriel nodded. "You said you owed him something. So we gave him a job."

"No one consulted me." Josiah's brows pulled together. "The man is a leech."

"Well," Gabriel said, putting on a hat, "fire him if you want, but you'll let Laura down. Those kids of hers are something, aren't they?" he said, not ashamed to be as sly as his father. "I'll be seeing you."

He went out, not listening to the expletives his father unleashed at him. Getting into his truck, he drove deserted country roads for hours. Then he headed to Laura's. He sat staring at her house, thinking, trying to pull a plan of action together.

He knew she wasn't likely to accept his proposal. But he could use the buffer between him and Pop. Pop liked Laura; she brought out his less antagonistic side.

She opened the door and seemed to hesitate. Then she waved at him to come inside.

He did before she changed her mind.

"I'm glad you came by," Laura said, "because we should probably talk."

That sounded good to him. He slid onto the bar stool she offered and watched as she made lemonade in the small, bright kitchen. "Where are the kids?"

"Napping. They've been tired lately, and I think it's the June heat." She pinched some mint sprigs, and he could smell the sweet green freshness. "The other night, you made me a proposal."

He nodded. He pretty much knew what her answer was going to be. She looked so calm and refreshing in a white top and blue jean shorts, cute sandals. "I probably didn't handle that as well as I should have."

She looked at him. "But you were sincere?"

"Oh, yeah. Definitely."

She took a deep breath. "I'm not going to fall in love with you."

"I know." Still, hearing the words stated so flatly threw a knife into his chest. He knew his odds were slimmer than a crack in a window. He thought about Pop, angry and pissed off at home, and wondered if he'd ever known real love. "I'm not the romantic type who expects notes signed with a heart."

Pain seemed to jump into her eyes. "I'm not looking for romance. In fact, it would bother me if that's what you're looking for. I just don't have that emotion available to me right now."

"I understand."

"I'd like to accept your proposal."

He sat up straight. "You would?"

She nodded, holding his gaze. "With a couple of modifications."

"Name them." Suddenly, his heart was skidding with

joy. He didn't care what the qualifications were; he had never wanted anything so much in his life.

"My children," she said, "come first."

"I wouldn't expect anything else."

"You would in a marriage where you'd been my first love. You would have come first. But I understand that you're offering me a proposition that's pretty much cut-and-dried. As a single mother, I'll admit I see benefits to what you're offering."

She had no idea what benefits he'd be getting. A family. A real wife and kids. Okay, maybe not totally real, but close. Closer than he'd ever expected. "What else?"

For a long moment she looked at him, then took a deep breath. "I know that you're supposed to live in your father's house for a year—"

"He's back," Gabriel interrupted. "As far as I can guess, he's nullified his own game. Pop never did like to give up control."

"I know Mr. Morgan's back." She motioned him to follow her into the garden and turned on a baby monitor. They sat an awkward distance away from each other, but at ten o'clock in the morning, there was no moonlight to confuse romance with negotiations. "Everyone knows he's back. He left a generous donation to the church, the library and the school. And then there's that." She pointed, and Gabriel saw a plastic sandbox shaped like a dinosaur and bags of sand. Shovels and buckets lay in a gaily decorated basket nearby.

"I can't figure him out. Pop came in the house snarling like his old self."

"The whole town is reeling this morning from the gifts." She shook her head. "Maybe you four were problem children?"

"Oh, he'd like you to think that. He'd like everyone to see his good, benevolent side. Thing is, it's so much easier to be nice to people on the surface. Family requires time and effort. It requires being close enough to give a damn."

"Which is why I really shouldn't ask this of you," she said, hesitating, "especially since you should be focusing on your father…"

He was afraid she'd get hung up on Pop and do something generous like decide to crawfish out of his marriage proposal. "Let me worry about Josiah."

"You have to live here with us," she said calmly, her tone serious.

He stared at her, his heart instantly shifting into a slow thudding beat. "Here."

She nodded. "I can't take the children from the only home they've ever known, even if it's only for a year."

"I guess you can't." He wouldn't want them uprooted from their security, especially so soon after losing their father.

"I realize doing so would break the agreement between you and your father—"

"He wasn't going to give any of us a million dollars, anyway," Gabriel said. "It was one of his ruses to trap us. Because he can't come right out and ask for what he wants."

Her eyes went wide at the bitterness in his tone. "I don't want to come between family—"

He got up, pulled her to her feet and kissed her on the mouth, long and hard, definitely not allowing her to retreat. She would never be able to say no to this man about anything, she realized, her heart falling.

Gabriel pulled slowly away from their kiss, brushed

her cheek with his fingers, stroked her neck with his palms. "Don't mention him again. This is the family I want."

"I just think—"

"No, you don't." Gabriel shook his head. "Thinking about the old man invites decay into my life. I choose you and Penny and Perrin."

"Your father has been giving away a lot of money," Laura said. "Maybe he is sincere. Maybe he's using his money to bring you closer to him."

"Then he has no idea what I really want in life." Gabriel kissed her hand. "Your children come first, and I live here with you. Have I got it?"

She nodded.

He felt happier than he had in a long, long time. "I'll move in after we're married."

"All right."

"We can probably get the marriage license and blood work done in a week—"

"Or we could go to Las Vegas," Laura said quickly.

He blinked. Was she hot for him? He didn't think so. If anything, she looked scared to death. "What about the children?"

"Mimi and Mason would be happy to keep them."

He didn't really want an Elvis wedding, or one away from her children. Penny would make a darling flower girl. Perrin would be a cute ring bearer of sorts. "Are you sure?"

"Definitely. As soon as possible. Just the two of us."

"I'll pick you up tomorrow." He walked to his truck, not feeling good about the arrangement.

It didn't matter. He could wait a couple of days to find out what Mrs. Adams had up her sleeve. She was taking advantage of his offer of marriage for a reason—but she was forgetting who'd raised him. He knew all about ulterior motives, and he wasn't afraid of hers.

He was finally getting a real family of his own.

Gabriel figured he'd bunked in enough out-of-the-way places that he could sleep in the foreman's cottage overnight. Hell, he could sleep in a barn if it meant staying away from Pop. Why the hell had the old man really returned? He hadn't accomplished anything he'd supposedly wanted; Pete was gone, Dane had hightailed it and he wasn't providing a sounding board for his father's bitching.

Yep, he'd take the foreman's deserted shack. Unlocking the door with the key hidden in a secret wall crevice, he went inside, glad to be finally alone.

It had been an exciting day. He'd made plane reservations, wedding reservations, had gotten Laura a ring. Of course, he couldn't get married without buying a couple of stuffed animals for his new kids: a soft, fluffy horse for Penny, a paunchy, huggable teddy bear for Perrin. He couldn't wait—he would be a hundred times better father than Pop.

The foreman's shack hadn't changed, and to his relief it wasn't in the terrible condition he'd expected. He and his brothers had spent some happy hours here hiding from their father. They'd used it as a home away from home. Pop had never been able to keep much help around, so the cottage went for long periods of time unoccupied.

He flipped on one of the bedroom lights, and a figure rose from the bed.

"What the hell?" the figure demanded.

Gabriel frowned. "Ben, what the devil are you doing here?"

Ben rubbed his eyes. "Trying to sleep! What are you doing here?"

"This house is on Morgan property," Gabriel reminded him.

"If you want me taking care of your livestock at five a.m., this is my house." Ben stuck out his jaw. "I can't sleep in fields forever."

Gabriel considered that. The man would be his father-in-law tomorrow. He supposed it was churlish of him to begrudge the man a home. "You think you could have asked?"

Ben shrugged. "The door hadn't been opened in probably five years. Didn't figure as it mattered."

It probably didn't. "I'm avoiding Pop."

"You think *you* are?" Ben swung his legs to the side of the bed. "He wouldn't exactly be jumping for joy to find me on his property." He squinted at him. "Did you tell him you hired me?"

"Yeah." Gabriel sank into an old leather chair that had seen better days. "I'd say he wasn't happy, except he wasn't happy about anything. That's sort of the groove he stays stuck in."

"I don't mind sharing the place with you if you'll sleep," Ben said. "Five o'clock comes early, you know, and my bosses are real jackasses." He snickered and slid back in bed. "Nice of them to hire me, though."

Gabriel rubbed his chin. "Yeah, about that, Ben."

"You promised you'd be silent as a mouse," Ben told him. "So far all I hear is yak, yak, yak."

"I'm marrying your daughter tomorrow."
A long pause met his words. Then Ben sat up.
"Nope," he said, "that ain't gonna do."

Chapter Ten

Laura was nervous. Accepting Gabriel's marriage proposal filled her with a strange type of dread. She'd said yes for all the wrong reasons.

Gabriel was a handsome man. He was sexy, the kind of man most women wanted. But there was something she'd kept from him: she was the reason Josiah Morgan had returned.

Mr. Morgan had made her promise that if any of his sons came home to Union Junction, he was to be notified. She didn't know any of the Morgan boys, and innocently, she had thought it was awful the way they never came to visit their father. Maybe she'd even felt a sad yearning for the relationship she lacked with her own father. Because of the gifts Mr. Morgan had given her children, she'd readily agreed to his request.

She hadn't realized how much they despised him—

and she hadn't dreamed he meant to return home to confront them. Mr. Morgan's return had driven Gabriel to a marriage proposal. He claimed he wanted the one thing he'd never had: a real family. Children he could love and hold and call his own. Secretly, she couldn't say that she didn't adore the idea that her children would have a father like Gabriel.

She wasn't going to deny to herself that Gabriel didn't make her blood run hot. A fantasy or two or ten had definitely played in her mind, hotter ones than she'd care to admit.

Yet if he knew that Mr. Morgan had planned to return, had basically lured them, and she had helped—she was pretty certain it was a betrayal that Gabriel would not be able to forgive.

She wasn't going to tell Gabriel. He had offered marriage for one year. She had been honest, told him that she wouldn't fall in love with him. She'd had love before, knew what it felt like, how deep it lodged in her heart. What she felt now was lust and a desire to have safety for her children, nothing more.

And when Gabriel left in a year, she would tell Penny and Perrin that Gabriel would always be part of their lives. He would, she knew, just as Mr. Morgan remained part of their world.

Gabriel just wouldn't stay in hers.

Knowing that kept the guilt she felt at bay. Even if she felt like a traitor, it had been an innocent mistake. She'd thought she was doing the right thing, and she couldn't change that now.

Josiah Morgan had few friends. He had no family who cared for him. It was ironic how much he wanted what he couldn't have, when he could buy everything in sight.

An old journal lay open on his desk. Pictures of him and his wife at their wedding stayed between the pages of the heavy journal; they were slightly grainy with age and wrinkled at the corners. He treasured those two pictures more than anything he owned.

He knew where his wife had gone. With the money he'd accumulated in his life, he'd been able to hire an investigator. Gisella was living in France, in the countryside, with people who remembered her from her childhood. Her own parents were long deceased, but Gisella still fit in to the surroundings of her youth. He would never contact her, but he needed to know where she'd gone.

He'd met Gisella in the military, in London, when he'd been stationed there as a cook. Back then he hadn't had two pounds in his pocket, but Gisella hadn't cared. They'd found plenty of activities to fill their time, and then Jack had been conceived. Head over heels in love, Josiah married Gisella. He smiled, remembering that day. Never had he seen a woman look more beautiful. Nowadays most women wore too much makeup, had their bodies artificially plumped or toned or browned— Gisella had been the salt of the earth.

As soon as he'd gotten out of the military, he'd begun his lifelong habit of acquisition. He was determined to deserve this wonderful woman, give her everything she didn't have. It was rough financially while they were married, but she believed in his dreams. She gave him four beautiful sons.

He was moody, struggling with start-up businesses. He was under the weight of trying to deserve the woman he loved. They fought a lot. Gisella hated being left alone on the ranch; she was afraid of the dark.

Their few cattle started disappearing, and Gisella became nervous with fear. Always edgy, afraid for the boys. Terrified for herself.

He was gone on a business trip to Dallas when he got the worried call from Jack. All of eight years old, Jack tried manfully to tell him his mother was gone—in the end, he dissolved into tears that Josiah would never forget hearing him cry. He hurried home, finding the boys were being kept by Ben Smith, whom Gisella had called for help.

He would never, ever forgive Ben Smith for driving his wife to the airport.

It had been years, and he was still mad as hell. Ben told him that Gisella had planned to call a taxi, but he'd driven her to Dallas to try to talk her out of leaving. Gisella had left a babysitter at the house, with instructions to stay with her sons until their father returned.

He could feel his blood boil all over again. Betrayal, by everyone he knew.

The boys would never understand that from that day forward, he had to teach them to be men. They needed to know that life was hard, and there were disappointments. Nothing was easy, nothing was free. Nobody gave a man a single thing, he earned every bit, and if he was smart, he made that lesson the bedrock of his soul.

Josiah shut the journal and stared at it for a long moment. In the journal, he wrote words daily that he wanted his sons to know about him, about their mother. He was aware they disliked him intensely. But they would know that he had loved them, and whether they considered his love too harsh was something they could decide after he was gone.

His kidneys were failing and he had maybe a year, possibly less. He would not take treatment, would not be chained to a machine. Would not show weakness, nor the fatigue that robbed his strength. Not even the depression that came upon him from time to time. A kidney transplant could save him, but that was not an option he chose. There were many more deserving people in the world who had something to live for. He'd been given his own chances to do something good with his life, and God would judge that.

He'd leave the healing to those who deserved it. He'd struck his deal with life, now he was determined to go out with fireworks. He would be no wimpy candle that blew out unresisting at the slightest puff of wind.

"Nope," Ben said, "you ain't marrying my daughter. And if that's why you gave me a job, then you can sure as hell shove it, Morgan."

Gabriel threw himself on the sofa and closed his eyes. The sofa was scratchy and old, made of a plaid fabric that had seen better days. It felt lumpy and out of shape, but Gabriel was too tired to care. "Go to sleep, Ben. We'll argue in the morning."

"Morning or night, next week or next year, I ain't giving you my blessing. You damn Morgans ruin everything you touch, and you ain't gonna upset Laura."

"Listen, Ben, you're no angel. And Laura's old enough to make her own decisions."

"That's just like a Morgan, thinking they can bend everybody else to their will. I'm telling you, leave Laura and the kids out of your screwed-up life."

Ben had a point. He had several points, in fact, but nothing was going to stop Gabriel from marrying Laura, not even her own father. He wanted her so badly that he could practically taste her. Desire washed through him, tugging at him, binding him to her in a way he could never explain.

"She deserves a man who can love her," Ben said, standing over him, "and you come from stock that loves no one but themselves."

"It's not entirely true." Gabriel grimaced.

"Yes, it is. Your whole clan turns on each other at the snap of a finger. Where are your brothers?"

"Not here."

"And how many words have you spoken to your father?"

"Under fifty, maybe," Gabriel admitted.

"Which is why you're hiding out here, and why you're trying to rope my daughter into marrying you. Fact is, you're doing this to get your father's approval."

Gabriel blinked. "You could have a point."

"Yeah. I do. You know your father provided for my grandchildren. So what do you do? You go and ask their mother to marry you. You haven't even known Laura a week. It's not love at first sight or something romantic like that—it's trophy bagging. Like she's some kind of prized deer you can brag that you shot."

"Hey!" Gabriel jerked up on the sofa. "Ben, shut your mouth before I shut it for you. That's a terrible way to talk about your daughter!" There might have been some family psychology at work—he didn't mind admitting that Laura represented wholeness and a sense of family he craved—but he would never see her as a trophy.

Ben stuck out his chin belligerently. "I'm talking

about you, not my daughter. You're the hunter here. She's just the innocent prey in your quest for game."

Gabriel shook his head. "I don't know what to say, except you sort of worry me. Didn't you act up about Laura's first husband?"

Ben raised a finger, wagging it at Gabriel. "He wasn't good enough for Laura."

"Is anybody?" Gabriel honestly wanted to know.

"Probably not," Ben barked. "She hasn't yet met the man who deserves her. But I don't expect you to understand that, because you're your father's son."

Gabriel sighed. "Ben, you gotta calm down. It's going to be hard to share Christmas dinners if you talk like that all the time."

"I'm being honest."

"And I appreciate that, but I'm not the devil. And Laura's a smart woman. She wouldn't have said yes if she didn't think marrying me had some merit."

Ben snorted. "Laura is a grieving widow. She thinks you'll be a good father. Maybe you can be, but maybe you won't be. But, son, I know more about you and your family than you'll ever know, and I'll be willing to bet you've never had a relationship with a woman that lasted a year."

Gabriel's brows furrowed.

"Have you?" Ben demanded.

"How do my past relationships affect my future ability to be a good husband?"

Ben put a boot on the side of the sofa and leaned close. "Rumor has it you and your brothers make sport of women."

"Not true," Gabriel said defensively. "While I can't

speak for my brothers, I can't exactly say I personally ever met the woman I wanted to spend my life with."

"And did you tell my daughter you planned to stay with her for the long haul?" Ben asked. "I'm just curious, because marriage is a long-term thing. It's a commitment. Something I haven't ever known you Morgans to be good with."

"I was in the military. Can't think of a more demanding commitment than that."

"That's a paycheck. It was also an escape from your father." Ben left the room, heading back to his own exile. "Marriage should not be an escape route, Morgan."

He closed his eyes. "True," he muttered. "I'll take it under advisement."

"I'll be saying the same to Laura."

"Probably a good idea." He'd be worried about having himself for a son-in-law if he was in Ben's boots. Why had he even mentioned it to Ben?

He stared up into the darkness, examining his conscience. It was traditional to ask a father for his daughter's hand in marriage. Perhaps he'd hoped for his future father-in-law's blessing. He really cared about Laura and her family, and that included Ben to some degree. He didn't blame Ben for feeling the way he did. Yet Gabriel knew he was marrying Laura—unless she changed her mind about having him. He briefly considered tying Ben to his bunk, at least until the *I dos* were spoken, but the old man had a right to do his damnedest. It didn't matter what Ben did, anyway. Laura had said yes, and she wasn't the kind of woman to go back on her word.

Chapter Eleven

"I'm getting married," Gabriel told his father the next day before he left to pick up Laura on the way to the airport. "I know news travels fast here, so I wanted you to hear it from me." He figured Ben had probably already run a marathon to tell his old man, but Josiah looked surprised.

"You are?"

Gabriel nodded. "I'm marrying Laura in Las Vegas today. We'll be back by nightfall."

Josiah's brows beetled. "Not much of a honeymoon."

Gabriel shrugged. "She has two young children. She'd rather not leave them long." He wouldn't tell his father they didn't need any real *honeymooning*.

"Penny and Perrin would be fine with me. They like me," Josiah offered.

"Thanks. But Laura's got her heart set on coming home."

Josiah grunted. "Your brothers slunk out of here without saying much to me. Guess you'd be gone, too, if it wasn't for Laura and the kids."

He probably would. Pop's gaze was on him, inspecting him, waiting for an answer. What was the right answer? What did Pop want to hear? He didn't know. "Since you're back, you can take care of the place yourself, right? And you've got Ben."

Josiah scowled. "I don't need Ben."

"Well, get along with him." Gabriel tossed some stuff into his truck. "I probably won't be seeing you for a while."

"You probably won't. I'm planning on going back to France early next week."

Gabriel turned to look at his father. "Why did you really come home?"

Josiah shook his head. "It's my house, isn't it?"

"So what was the deal about the million dollars if we stayed here for a year?"

Josiah fixed dark eyes on him. "None of you seem to be planning to do it, so what does it matter?"

True enough. Gabriel knew his father had simply been moving them around like chess pieces.

"Gabriel, I have to admit I'm glad you and Laura are getting married."

"I guess so. It makes you a grandfather. Wasn't that what this was all about?" Gabriel felt a little bitter about satisfying one of his father's desires, the familiar resentment welling up inside him that Josiah Morgan was always behind every move in his life.

"Actually, I never dreamed she'd have you," Josiah

said. "She was pretty torn up when Dave died. I just wanted you to look after her and the kids while I was gone."

"Did you cheat Ben on purpose?"

Josiah frowned. "I saw value in something that Mr. Smith did not. Including his own family, I might add."

He had a point. But that didn't make it right with Gabriel.

"Pop, have you ever thought that maybe you shouldn't capitalize on people's weaknesses?"

"Hell, no. It's a dog-eat-dog world. Don't kid yourself."

Gabriel shook his head. "Listen, I've got to head out."

He looked at the man who was his father, and yet who felt like he was something else: judge, jury, prosecutor. Time had stretched the bonds between them and deepened the scars. He didn't think either of them would really ever heal the wounds.

"Gabriel, thanks for telling me about the wedding." Josiah turned to go inside his house. For just a moment, Gabriel felt sorry for his father, then decided it was a wasted emotion. Josiah played by his own rules, and they were rules he was comfortable with. Gabriel wasn't going to make the mistake of judging his father.

He drove off to pick up his soon-to-be bride, and it belatedly occurred to him that he had received his father's approval. It felt good.

Marrying Laura would feel good. He'd counted the hours since yesterday.

He was going to be a husband and a father. He couldn't wait.

But when he got to Laura's house, she wasn't there. Instead, he found a note taped to the door.

*Gabriel, Dad was having chest pains. I've taken
him to the hospital. Laura*

Laura was nearly sick with fear. Her father looked so
pale. Nurses scurried to hook him up to various moni-
tors and an IV. She didn't want him to have a heart attack, she wanted him to be well. Life was short, and
she'd wasted time Ben could have had with his grandchildren. She regretted every moment of her stubborn
pride.

She should have tried harder to make her father understand how much she loved Dave—although as much
as she hated to admit it, Dave hadn't helped to ease
Ben's worries. In retrospect, she realized how much
Dave's laconic approach to life had worried Ben.

Ben had mumbled how sorry he was that she had to
take him to the hospital when she was supposed to be
leaving for a wedding in Las Vegas. Laura comforted
her father, telling him that everything would work out
eventually. She didn't want him upset.

Gabriel strode into the hospital, coming straight to
her to close her in his embrace. She allowed herself to
be enveloped in his strong warmth, appreciating his
caring. "He got sick all of a sudden."

He stroked her hair. "He'll be fine."

She wasn't certain. "I hope so." Through the small
window, she could see her father being wheeled down
the hall. "It just came on so quickly."

"They'll get him fixed up."

She looked up at Gabriel. "Sorry about the wedding."

"Las Vegas has weddings every day. We can reschied-
ule."

"Like a business meeting," she murmured.

He stroked her cheek. "Ben was sleeping in the old foreman's shack. He may be getting too old to live the life of a gypsy."

"How do you know where he was sleeping?"

"I found him there. I tried to ask him for your hand in marriage, but it wasn't the most encouraging conversation."

An old, painful memory slid forward. "Oh?"

"Yeah. I can't say he exactly gave me his blessing, but I made it clear how much I wanted to marry you. We left it at that."

Laura doubted anything had been *left*. Ben had refused his blessing when Dave had asked him, as well. And now Ben was in the hospital with sudden chest pains. Was a short-term marriage, a year of life with Gabriel, worth going through this again? She should have seen this coming. Ben was uneasy about the Morgans and he definitely wasn't going to give her away to them without a fight. "Was he upset?"

"No more or less than usual. At least he didn't take another shot at me." He turned her chin up so he could look into her eyes. "Ben's illness is not because we plan to get married."

She hated how worried she'd sounded. "I'd like to wait until he's better before we…before we do anything."

"I agree." Gabriel nodded, gently releasing her. "Where are the children?"

"Mimi's looking after them."

"I'll swing by and grab them, if you want. I can keep them while you're here with your father."

She looked at him, her blue eyes a bit guilty. "Are you sure you're ready for that? They can be a handful."

He grinned. "I think I can handle your crew."

He certainly seemed to look forward to the challenge. "I hope you know what you're signing on for."

He shook his head. "I've enlisted before. This will be a piece of cake. Call me if you need anything."

He went off, not the least bit bothered by her hesitation to marry him, not worried about Ben's non-blessing. Dave had been bothered by it, but she had the sudden impression that Gabriel was not the kind of man who would give a damn. He'd love the blessing, but if not, he sure wouldn't lose any sleep over it.

Maybe Ben had a simple case of heartburn, and then none of this would matter. Perhaps Gabriel had misunderstood her father's reticence about their marriage.

She knew Gabriel had misunderstood nothing.

"Mrs. Adams?"

She turned to face a doctor. "Yes?"

"I'm Dr. Carlson. I understand that you're your father's only relative who can see to his care?"

"I am." Chills suddenly ran through her.

"He's had a mild heart attack. Nothing severe, but we're going to keep him here overnight. We're evaluating his condition and need to run some tests. We'll look for a blockage, or other issue that may have caused this."

"Thank you." She felt ashamed for wondering whether her father had staged a heart attack to keep her from marrying Gabriel. "Can I see him?"

"For a minute. Then I want you to go home and get some rest."

She nodded, following the doctor into her father's hospital room. "How are you doing?"

"I'm fine," Ben said. "These doctors need to let me out of here."

She patted his hand. "Stay calm, Dad. Don't get excited."

He sighed. "I am not a good patient."

She nodded. "Most people aren't. But the doctor says I can only stay a moment."

"Guess I messed up your wedding." He didn't look too unhappy about that. "I told Gabriel I didn't think he deserved you."

"I know. He told me."

Ben twisted his lips. "Guess I worried myself into a little chest pain."

Guilt jumped inside her. "You shouldn't have. I'm a big girl, Dad."

"Fathers worry. That's what we do."

She shook her head. "You need to let go."

He nodded. "I guess it was just a shock. I felt like you and I had just patched things together, and then suddenly I needed to keep you to myself. Felt like I had to fight for you. You know I don't trust those damn Morgans."

"This is my decision, Dad. Gabriel's a good man."

"You say that about Josiah, too, and he's a scoundrel."

She laughed and kissed her father lightly on his forehead. "He's not the only scoundrel in Union Junction."

Ben grunted.

"I'm leaving before your blood pressure skyrockets."

"I think it already did," he said, in a bid to get more attention.

She smiled. "I'll be back tomorrow."

He looked at her, his eyes big and sad. "I wish you could stay my little girl."

She blew him a kiss and backed away, feeling like the worst daughter in the world.

Gabriel smiled when Mimi opened the door. "Hello, Mimi."

"Come in, Gabriel. How's the patient?"

He looked around the big, welcoming entry of the house at the Double M ranch. Gabriel could honestly say he wouldn't mind having a place like this one day, where little feet could run and play, and he and Laura could raise their family.

He seemed to think about Laura and the life he wanted with her all the time. "Nice place, by the way."

"Thank you."

"The patient isn't pleased to be a patient," Gabriel said.

"I wouldn't expect Mr. Smith would be happy to be in the hospital." Mimi ushered Gabriel into the kitchen. Through the window, he could see Penny and Perrin playing with Mimi's brood. Though Mimi's children were a bit older, they included Laura's children in their activities. There was a large swing set and fort, a sandbox and a couple of Hoppity Hops littering the lawn.

He remembered having a Hoppity Hop. Jack had been the best of all of them when it came to racing on them; maybe it had been good early training for the rodeo.

Mimi glanced over her shoulder at the children. "They make me smile, too. Laura's done a great job with her kids."

"Yeah." He couldn't wipe the smile from his face.

"So I hear congratulations are in order?"

He dragged his gaze away from the children. "I

hope so. When Ben gets well, congratulations will be in order."

Mimi smiled. "Laura sounded happy about marrying you."

That shocked him. If anything, she'd seemed reluctant to him. "Glad to hear it."

"She asked me not to tell anyone what you were planning, but she felt like you two are very comfortable despite only knowing each other a short while. I take it you want a low-key wedding?"

He nodded, not certain what Laura would want if the circumstances were romantic rather than advantageous.

"I know you'd planned for an elopement," Mimi said carefully, "but I also know you were having to plan spur of the moment. So Mason and I were wondering if perhaps—when Ben gets well, of course—if you'd like to get married at the Double M."

He blinked, instantly able to see Laura in a pretty dress on the wide green lawns of the Double M. It was the kind of wedding she deserved. "That's very generous of you and Mason."

Mimi smiled. "It would be our wedding gift to you and Laura. Then Penny and Perrin could be at the wedding, and by then Ben will be well enough to give his daughter away."

Gabriel wasn't sure Ben would be up to the task. Laura would have to be pried out of his grasp.

"You know he didn't get to give her away before."

Gabriel shook his head. "I didn't know that."

"Ben was so dead set against Laura marrying Dave that Laura ended up eloping. Coincidentally, they married in Vegas. She said it wasn't what she'd wanted, but she'd had no choice." Mimi put some biscuits on the counter and covered them with a plaid napkin. She set some fresh fruit out in a bowl, and the washed fruit shone in the light. "Laura may feel differently, and my feelings won't be hurt if you don't take Mason and me up on our offer, but it does seem that a woman should have one hometown wedding in her life. Don't you think?"

He certainly agreed. In fact, he wanted no reminders of Laura's first wedding. "Thank you, Mimi. I'll see if I can budge her on the matter." He wasn't sure what Laura would say. Pieces of the future were fitting together in his mind, and the more he thought about a traditional wedding, with vows spoken in front of family, and Penny and Perrin there, the more he knew he wanted this moment to feel like forever.

He could see wanting Laura for the rest of his life.

Now that his father had returned, and the deal was off, he didn't need a one-year marriage. He didn't need to get married at all. He could go back to being as unattached as he was before.

But that wasn't what he wanted, not his freedom nor a one-year marriage. Suddenly, he was grateful that Ben's heart condition had slowed everything down. Somehow he needed to convince Laura that he had changed—she could trust him for something deeper than a fast fix.

Chapter Twelve

Gabriel drove Penny and Perrin to his house, feeling pretty good about how excited they'd acted to see him. Of course, Perrin didn't show his enthusiasm quite like Penny, but the baby definitely seemed pleased. He'd debated whether to take them to Laura's house where they'd be among familiar things, then decided he'd head over to Josiah's. His father would enjoy seeing the kids—it might even soften the old man up a bit.

Penny and Perrin might be the only way to put a smile on Josiah's face. Penny saw Josiah on the front porch and ran to be enveloped in his arms.

"This is a surprise," Josiah told Gabriel. Josiah's eyes glimmered gratefully at Gabriel. In that moment, Gabriel knew he was going to spend extra energy trying to connect with his father. It could be his father lying in that hospital. As cranky as Josiah was, he didn't want to shortchange their relationship.

"Didn't figure you'd mind," Gabriel said.

"Nope. Come out here, kids. I have something to show you."

The four of them walked to a south paddock. A small white pony stood grazing, glancing up at them before returning her attention to the grass.

"Horse!" Penny exclaimed. "Can I ride her?"

Josiah laughed. "As soon as she gets settled in, you may ride her. Perrin, too, when he's old enough. I bought that pony for you kids."

Gabriel raised a brow at his father. "You bought them a pony?"

"Every child should have a pony. At least every child who wants one, and who has a little land."

Gabriel watched as Penny held out a piece of grass to try to lure the pony to her. "You never bought us a pony."

Josiah grinned. "You boys were too busy rappelling out your bedroom window to need a pony. You got plenty of exercise."

"So you cut that limb off on purpose?"

Josiah nodded. "Just hadn't figured on the rope ladder."

It felt good to talk about the past. The moments of ease that peeked into their relationship felt healing.

"So, how's my thin-skinned farmhand doing?"

Gabriel snorted. "Ben's tough."

"I didn't need you hiring half a man to work this place."

Gabriel looked at his dad. "You weren't supposed to be here. So I made an appropriate hire. The man has plenty of experience. Not to mention that you ran off two able-bodied sons."

"I didn't run them off. They deserted."

"You didn't make them feel welcome." He didn't feel welcome, either, but he had Penny and Perrin to think of.

"What was I supposed to do? Buy them a pony?" Josiah asked.

"You're supposed to just be nice," Gabriel said. "It gets you what you want. Especially after you've gone to the trouble to gather everybody around."

Josiah grunted.

"You might as well tell me," he said, helping Perrin to put his feet on the bottom of a wood rail, "why you went to the trouble of scheming to get us all home."

His father picked Penny up, kissed her on the cheek. "So did Ben ruin any chance of you and Laura getting married? You know he's pulling this sickly routine on purpose."

"I don't know that to be true."

"Ah, hell, yeah, Ben was probably one of those kids who threw fits."

"Shh, that's their grandfather," Gabriel cautioned.

Josiah shrugged. "It's true. Anyway, here comes Laura. We'll ask her how the hypochondriac is doing."

"I wouldn't phrase it that way," Gabriel said, making Josiah laugh.

"Hi," Gabriel said, when Laura walked to the fence. "How did you know we were here?"

"Where else would you go?" She looked up at him, her eyes dark with fatigue. "This is your home."

True. He didn't glance at his father. "How's Ben?"

"Fine, for the moment," Laura said. "Still, he needs

a change in diet and an improved lifestyle. The doctor feels he's under too much stress."

Josiah turned away with Penny in his arms. Gabriel thought he'd seen a grin on Josiah's face. "Glad he's going to be all right."

"Gabriel, can I talk to you?"

"I'll take the kids in for a snack," Josiah offered. "Good news about your father, Laura."

"Thank you." She pushed her hair back, though the early-morning breeze pulled it forward again. "Gabriel, maybe we were moving too quickly."

He watched her intently. Damned if Ben didn't appear to be winning the battle. "Maybe. Maybe not."

Laura looked uncertain. "I don't want to cause my father any stress."

"Of course not." Gabriel shook his head in sympathy.

"Since you and your father appear to be getting along better, you probably don't need my help any longer."

"Your help?"

"By marrying you," Laura said quickly.

"Oh." Her face was so drawn that Gabriel realized it was Laura who was stressed, maybe more than Ben. She was afraid. Afraid that her relationship with her father might be forever on hold if he suddenly died. She was afraid that marrying against her father's wishes a second time might be too much for him to take. "I understand your position."

"Thank you," she said on a rush. "I've got to get back to the hospital."

"Leave the kids here," he said quietly. "Dad and I are enjoying them."

"Dad?" she said. "Not Pop?"

He shook his head. "It doesn't matter. You go on. I'll take good care of the children."

"Thank you so much for understanding."

"Yeah. I'm just that kind of a great guy," he said as she got into her small seen-better-days car. He waved as she drove away, though it was hard to pull off the light-heartedness. The pony neared the fence, eying him curiously. "There went my bride," he told the pony. "She has no idea I want to marry her for real. I've fallen in love with her, and I don't think she sees me quite the same way."

It hurt. And he was pretty sure that a gentleman would back off and be an understanding kind of guy. He could do that, in fact, would do that, since she'd asked it of him, but he recognized it was going to take a chunk of his soul to act like he was good with it.

At least he still had Penny and Perrin. He was pretty sure they liked him. He headed inside to find out.

Penny and Perrin were riding on Josiah like he was an energetic *horsey*. For his part, Josiah seemed to enjoy the game as much as the kids. He neighed, pawed the air and generally acted silly. "I can't remember you doing that for us," Gabriel commented.

Josiah let out a gleeful neigh, his white hair shaking as he pretended to be a horse. "Where do you think I got these skills?"

"I thought Penny and Perrin conned you into being a substitute for the pony you bought them. Does Laura know you did that?"

"We need not share that just yet." Josiah carefully rode Perrin across the "creek," a swath of the den where the furniture had been pushed away. "She was in a bit of a hurry to get back to Ben, wasn't she? Think he's really all right?"

"I guess so." Gabriel went into the kitchen to make tea and grab some of the cookies the church ladies had recently left. The realization that Josiah was in town and bearing gifts had brought many containers of delicious treats to their house. It was too bad Pete and Dane had elected to leave—the eats were fantastic. Gabriel munched on a double chocolate chip cookie from a box labeled Thank You For Everything, Mrs. Gaines.

"What'd you do for Mrs. Gaines?" He set the cookie tray on the table and pulled Perrin into his lap. "No cookies for you, sir. You get something more delicious, like one of these meat stick thingies your mom left you. Ugh. Probably better for you, but still."

"She's the town librarian. They had a wish list last Christmas that asked for a new reference set. Times have changed, you know. Nobody hardly wants the big fat books as much. They want the CD versions, or the website subscriptions, and that takes updated technology. I left a little money to cover the technology." He swiped a cookie, set Penny beside him, stuck a napkin in her hand—the picture of a happy grandfather. "It's especially important for the high schoolers who want to study in the library. Not everybody has a computer in their home."

"Yeah, Dad, about that." Gabriel sipped at some iced tea, carefully moving Perrin's hand away from the cookie tray and giving him an animal cracker instead. "I know kids don't always remember everything their parents did for them, but it does seem that you've entered a new, more benevolent stage of your life. One we aren't familiar with."

"You're asking why I didn't coddle you boys since I had so much money. Why I kicked your asses instead of giving out hugs. Why I tried to make men out of you instead of pansy-assed good-for-nothings who were always looking for a handout."

"In so many words," Gabriel said, "I suppose you just gave me the answer."

"Kids who have everything handed to them generally don't fare well. You boys were already a little wild. You had no mother to soften you. I was busy running things and couldn't mother hen you. I figured if you had it in you to be successful, you'd get there on your own. And if you didn't, you'd only have yourself to blame."

Gabriel nodded. "I see your point." He saw it, but that didn't address the affection part of the parenting equation, the pleasure of enjoying your child. "So the reason you're spoiling Penny and Perrin is—"

"I can enjoy being a doting grandfather if I want."

"I can't speak for my brothers, of course, but seeing the softer side of you—"

"I'll tell you something, Gabriel. Since you're being honest, and since you hung around, which frankly shows some of what I was trying to teach you boys sunk in— which is to face the hardest parts of life bravely—I liked watching you kids struggle. I liked seeing you get tough. Raising men is a hard thing. Raising whiners is easy." He kissed Penny on the forehead and handed her another cookie. "But in case you feel left out—and I suspect you do or you wouldn't be trying to improve my parenting skills—I'll tell you a little secret."

"Shoot," Gabriel said dryly. "I'm all ears."

"Now, this is just between you and me—"

"Absolutely," Gabriel said. Who the hell would he tell?

"I put the million dollars that you would have received for staying here one year into a bank draft in your name this morning."

Gabriel looked at his father. "What's the hook?"

Josiah laughed. "There is no hook. You proved yourself. You came here, and you would have stayed. You alone cared enough to try to patch up our differences. I see in you a son I can be proud of."

That meant more to him than the money. "Thank you."

Josiah nodded. "Jack didn't even bother to show up. He doesn't give a damn. He'll still get his chance, but—" Josiah shrugged "—he and the rest of your brothers have to live under the same rules you played by."

"Okay," Gabriel said, "did you come home because you wanted to see us, or was it all just a test?"

Josiah grabbed a red ball, scooted near the fireplace and rolled it to Penny, who rolled it back. He then rolled it to Perrin, who couldn't roll so well, so Gabriel helped him.

"When Laura let me know you had come home, I chose to come home," Josiah said. "It was a test, maybe, but I also wanted very much to see you."

"Laura?" Gabriel frowned.

"Did you think I was psychic?" Josiah grinned. "Laura had instructions to let me know if any of my sons returned."

Gabriel wondered what else she was keeping to herself. "Guess she did her job."

"I'm leaving in the morning." Josiah stood, his

shaggy hair bushing out around his shoulders. "I have to get back to work. It keeps a man alive, you know."

"I hope so." It was all he had right now. "So what are your plans for this place?"

"You're here. You can take care of it. You have the money to do whatever else you like, but I wouldn't tell anyone, if you want to know if they care for you."

Gabriel wondered if that was a veiled reference to Laura, but he didn't think she was fixated on money or she would have said yes to him instead of backing out on him when her father had chest pains.

"There's an account and books for the ranch specifically. I know I can trust you with the running of it."

"Ever thought about selling?"

Josiah shook his head. "Nope. I love my place in France and I'm thinking on buying one in Florida, but this ranch represents what I believe is best about life. Feel free to make it your home as long as you want."

"And if Pete and Dane come back?"

Josiah shrugged and headed up the stairs.

"Jeez," he said to Penny and Perrin. "He's got me stuck right in the middle."

Penny smiled at him. "Morgan," she said, enjoying saying the name.

"That's me," he said, and wondered why he suddenly felt okay with that.

When Laura came to pick up the kids that night, Gabriel had a surprise for her. "Chicken on the grill, canned corn and a salad. Not as good as you made me when I first arrived in Union Junction, but as good as I can do. I know you're probably worn out."

"I'm all right." She glanced at the food. Penny and

Perrin were seated at the table. Somewhere Gabriel had found a small chair he'd sort of roped Perrin into; sailor's knots held her son's roundness into the chair. Mashed peas decorated the table in front of Perrin. "It's hard babysitting when you're not used to it."

"It's good practice for me. And Dad's been helping."

She slid into the chair. "Thank you. It looks delicious."

"So. This is what we'll look like every night if you keep my proposal in mind." He lit two candles in the center of the table with a flourish. "I'm just saying."

"I can't." Laura shook her head. "Ben is just too upset about it. And I can't go through that again. I'm sorry, Gabriel."

"You have no idea what you're passing up." He'd thought a lot about it, and he wasn't about to let this woman go just because Ben was having a coronary. If anything was killing the man, it was his own bitterness.

Steps sounded on the stairs. Josiah came into the room, his laugh booming when he saw the children at the table. "You two don't need to eat. You need to see a pony!"

"Yay!" Penny jumped up from the table.

"Young lady!" Laura shook her head. "Mr. Morgan, they must excuse themselves."

"All right. Excuse us all," Josiah said, rescuing Perrin from his sailor's knots. "We have to go walk a pony, and then I need to do some things in town. I'll only be gone a couple of hours, Laura, so don't get jittery. You and Gabriel enjoy the food. He's been cussing at the grill for an hour."

Gabriel nodded. "It's true. I am not the griller that my brothers are."

"Looks like you did a fine job," Josiah said, looking at the meal, "but the kids and I are having ice cream for dinner. Even Perrin can have ice cream instead of those peas, can't he?" he asked, nuzzling the baby as he carried him out. "And I saw my son feed you that nasty meat stick thingie from a jar earlier. If I was you, Perrin, I'd complain. Come on, Penny, honey, you and I will have a swirl with candies on top."

The door closed behind them. Gabriel shook his head. "I didn't even know he knew that there was a roadside ice-cream store that offered swirls with candies on top."

"He's always been this way with my children." Laura seemed resigned to it. "The gifts are getting bigger, however."

He'd just had a huge one tossed into his life. He wasn't sure how to take the fact that he now had a million dollars to his name, free and clear. He didn't even have to live here, didn't have to put up with Josiah, didn't have to take care of Laura.

He was free.

"So, Laura," he said, "I understand you're the little birdie who let Josiah know I was here."

She hesitated as she served them corn. "Yes, I did."

"You weren't going to tell me."

"No. Do you have a problem with that?"

He grinned. "I probably should, but I like that mysterious edge you've got going on." Reaching over, he captured her hand in his. She dropped the spoon into the corn as he pulled her into his lap. "Suddenly, this dinner doesn't seem as inviting as what I've got in my lap right now."

He kissed her, and Laura had no desire to pull away. She knew her father would be so angry—Ben really thought he was looking out for her best interests—but just like before, she was falling for the man and not the approval. Gabriel kissed differently than her husband had and she relished that. She wanted everything about this to be different.

It was important that she never look back. She didn't ever want to feel the same. She wanted this, and more and everything Gabriel wanted to give her—except marriage. She couldn't do that. She knew that now. Ben falling ill had convinced her that she had agreed to marriage for all the wrong reasons. She was agreeing to marry for stability, when all she really wanted was to feel alive again.

Gabriel moved his hand to her waist, and then along her sides to her breasts. Her breath caught. She sensed him waiting, asking permission. Gabriel was a gentleman; he would never override her wishes. But she wanted him, wanted what he was offering her and so she kissed him back, letting her hands move down his chest—and then lower.

His breath hitched, and she knew he wanted her the way she wanted him.

"You're making me crazy," he told her.

"I want to."

"I'm going to drive you crazy, too," he said, "and then make you the happiest woman on earth."

He already was. Her blood steamed in her body, her skin craved his touch. But she feared Josiah and the children would walk in and see them.

Gabriel carried her upstairs, laid her in his bed. Kissed her inch by inch, her entire body, chasing away her fears. Made her know that everything about this moment would be different from anything she'd ever known—and when he finally claimed her, Laura knew she'd never be the same again.

Hunger had been born inside her, and only Gabriel could satisfy it.

"Get out of bed, old man."

Josiah looked down at his nemesis, allowing his lips to curl. Ben's eyes flew open—then he grinned at Josiah.

"I'm quite comfortable, thank you. Appreciate the visit, though." Ben glanced around. "What brings you? An apology?"

"Hell, no. What would I apologize for?"

"For trying to kill me when you learned I took Gisella to the airport. I was trying to do a neighborly deed, caught between a rock and a hard place was I—"

"Let's not live in the past," Josiah snapped. "Forgiveness isn't one of my more saintly qualities."

"I'll say." Ben shuddered. "They'll not be putting your name forth for beatification no matter how much money you give away."

Josiah sighed. "The kids want to see their sad sack of a grandfather. Right now, they're eating fruit cups in the cafeteria with a nurse friend of mine. You and I have something to discuss."

Ben glared at him. "I'm on my deathbed."

"You're throwing a pity party, and I want it to cease. Or I'll consider myself invited."

Ben wrinkled his face. "You've never been much fun at a party."

Josiah laughed heartily. "Now, listen, old man, you think you're playing me and everyone else like a well-strung fiddle. But you leave Gabriel and Laura alone."

Ben's gaze narrowed. "Why should I? He's trying to marry my daughter, and that just ain't gonna happen."

"Thanks to you, it probably won't."

"I see no reason to mingle my blood with yours, Morgan. It would dilute the purity of my good name."

"Ben, you sorry ass—if you weren't connected to an IV, I'd kick your selfish butt."

Ben shrugged. "And everybody would say look at poor Ben being picked on by that awful Josiah Morgan."

"No, they wouldn't. They'd say poor Josiah Morgan, having to put up with that conniving Ben Smith."

"Damn you!" Ben looked like he wanted to hop out of bed and take a swing at Josiah. "I'm not a conniver! No more so than you, Josiah Morgan!"

"You are if you're lying in this bed making your daughter feel guilty about wanting to be with my son."

"How the hell do you expect me to feel? After you cheated me?"

Josiah grimaced. "I didn't cheat you. You think you put one over on me, and I'm letting you gloat on that, but if you don't give my son your blessing, I'm going to put an end to your game."

Ben looked at him suspiciously. "What are you talking about?"

Josiah tapped him on the arm. "Old friend, I'm talking about that false rumor you put about that there was oil on your property."

Ben blinked. "Don't know what you're talking about."

"Sure you do. You told everyone you thought there might be oil. Then you asked me to buy your land at an inflated price. Then you ran around screaming about how I'd taken advantage of you. I knew there was no oil, I knew there was little value to your land and that you were hard up for cash. What happened to that cash, by the way?" Josiah asked, a gleam in his eyes.

"It's…in a safe." Ben waved a hand. "Anyway, it's none of your business."

"Funny how you're shacking up in my foreman's house if you have the money somewhere. Over a half million dollars, and you don't even buy your grandchildren a trip to the county fair. Yet I hear you going all over town about how I cheated you."

"Probably you did, Josiah. You always get the best of a person."

Josiah's white brows raised. "Did you gamble away that money?"

"No!"

"Did you drink it up?"

"No!"

Josiah leaned close. "Then tell me what happened to it."

Ben sighed. "I put it in a vault in the bank so it couldn't be traced to me for taxes."

Josiah frowned. "You would have had to report the sale of your land."

"That's why I tell everyone you cheated me. So I won't have to pay capital gains."

Josiah wondered if the man truly didn't understand the law. "Do you understand that few people cheat Uncle Sam and get away with it?"

"Do you understand that that is the only time I'll see that much money? Do you know how hard it is to make it as a farmer?" Ben crossed his arms. "I'm not giving one cent of it to the government. I've paid taxes for years. When did the government ever help me?"

Josiah scratched his head. "At the very minimum,

when you get caught, you'll have to pay interest on what you owe."

"I'll be dead by then."

Josiah shrugged. "And your estate will still have to pay. I'm not sure what you've done helps Penny and Perrin."

Ben sighed. "It was just hard to give up any of that dough. I wanted money all my life, just a little something in the bank that gave me security. Something I could pass to my daughter without everybody thinking I'd been a failure all my life."

"Don't you think she'd have been just as happy with you being honorable?"

Ben shook his head. "I can take care of her, and my grandkids, without asking anybody for a dime if we ever fall on hard times."

"Laura seems independent to me. Besides, Ben, sleeping in my foreman's shack isn't exactly living the high life."

"It's free. Seems like a bargain to me, and I'm satisfied with that."

Josiah had to admire the man's desire to keep what was his. "But you've just about done in your ticker."

"That's because your son is trying to take my daughter away from me."

"You're just trying to keep her away from me." Josiah sat down near his nemesis. "Be honest and don't juggle facts for a change."

Ben snorted. "I don't completely cotton to Morgans, I'll admit. Some are better than others."

"But is that fair to your grandchildren?" He leaned close to stare Ben down. "Gabriel would do fine by them."

Ben's gaze slid away. "Not sure about that. But if it'll make you quit harping on me, I promise to pay the taxes on the money you paid me for the land."

Josiah sighed. "Don't get me back on that. This entire matter is between you and me, and you need to butt out of Laura's life. You nearly got yourself sidelined for good, you know. Interfering is not healthy."

"Says the greatest interferer I ever met." Ben's eyes closed. "Anyway, you don't even like your own sons. Why should I?"

Josiah shook his head. Ben had it all wrong. He clearly didn't understand the Bible's instruction: *What son is there whom a father does not chasten?* The way he'd raised his sons was the only way to raise good men. But Ben was so stubborn it was hard to move him. Laura probably had some of those stubborn genes in her, which didn't bode well for Gabriel, who was pretty mulish himself.

Josiah wished he could make it all better, but he couldn't. The die had already been cast. He went to get Penny and Perrin to sneak them in to see their grandfather—no kids allowed in this area, especially past visiting hours—but he figured what the hell. He'd given enough money to the hospital to buy beds for a new wing. One day, it might be him lying in one of these beds, and he sure hoped Ben would care enough to sneak the kids in to see him.

Maybe he would, and maybe he wouldn't. Josiah couldn't divine whether forgiveness lay in store for him, from anyone. But life was all about family, and Josiah was doing his damnedest to try to build one.

Chapter Thirteen

The moment he made love to Laura, Gabriel was even more determined to romance her until she couldn't say no to his marriage proposal. But he was aware this wouldn't be easy. He moved her arms above her head, trapping them against the pillows, then languidly licked each nipple. He loved the gasp he pulled from her.

"Gabriel," she murmured, a slight protest, and since he knew she was going to use going to visit her father as an excuse, he slid inside her, keeping her with him for a few more minutes.

"Yes?" he asked.

She moved up against him, welcoming him. "Don't stop."

He laughed. "Are you sure?" He teased her with another slow thrust.

She clutched at him, pulled his head down so that

he could kiss her. This closeness with one person was what he'd been missing all his life. He kissed her fast, hard, possessively, and let himself enjoy the feel of her unresisting in his arms.

An hour later, Laura gasped and jumped from the bed, grabbing at her clothes. "I hear your father's truck!"

"It's all right. It'll take him a minute to get the kids out of their seat belts."

Laura gasped again, jumping into her clothes. "The children can't see me like this! Hurry, Gabriel!"

The joys of parenthood. Gabriel grinned. "That's what you said not an hour ago."

"Don't tease me now," she said. "No mother wants her children to find her naked in bed with a man she's not married to."

"Yes, we should fix that."

She tossed him his shirt. "Some things can't be fixed, you know."

He handed her the tiny black panties that had gotten hung on his belt buckle. "Female undergarments amaze me. Are they utilitarian or just for turning a man on? These certainly seem more sexy than functional. Can't say that's a bad thing."

"Gabriel!" She moved his boots over to him and slipped on her panties and then her sandals. Her fingers flew through her hair as she glanced out the window. "Oh, they're looking at the pony. Why did your father buy a pony when he won't be here long?"

"He bought it for your kids," Gabriel said absently, thinking through the logic of what Laura had just said. He followed her down the stairs. Josiah had said he was leaving in the morning. Why would he have bought a pony that couldn't be ridden yet?

"My kids! Penny and Perrin aren't really old enough to ride. Besides, we're never over here."

"I know." They sat down at the dinner table they'd abandoned two hours ago. The candles were burned down to the sticks and had put themselves out. The food was cold, but Gabriel would have eaten it anyway except for the look on Laura's face. "What?"

"He bought a pony for my children," she repeated. "Obviously he plans on them being around here. With you."

"You'd have to ask Pop about that. I don't really understand him myself. I'm just now learning the whole father-son thing in a new way. It's a whole new language I'm decoding."

"Gabriel!"

"Yes?" He looked at Laura. "Do you know you're beautiful when you're not wearing makeup and your hair is out of place?"

She opened her mouth to say something when Josiah walked in with the kids. He had Penny by the hand and Perrin soundly sleeping tucked up against his chest. "You two still eating?" Josiah asked. "Must be some hungry folk."

He glanced at the plates and saw that they hadn't been touched. "Ah, you know in France and Italy people tend to take longer meals. It's good for the digestion," he said to cover Laura's embarrassment. She could barely look at Josiah.

He handed her Perrin gently. "This one's a snoozer. He was awake for visiting your father, though."

"My father?" Laura looked at Josiah. "You went to see Ben in the hospital?"

"Sure." He put Penny in a chair at the table, glancing at Gabriel like he had something he wanted to say but wouldn't share it in front of Laura. "He's my employee."

Could Ben and Josiah spend five minutes in the same room without a battle breaking out? Gabriel wasn't sure. "So how did that go?"

"He was his usual irascible self, which I attribute to his general well-being." Josiah tucked in to cold corn and chicken. "This is delicious, Gabriel. For a man who lived off of military grub, you seasoned this chicken just right."

"Mr. Morgan," Laura said sternly, "you did not go to pay a social call to Ben."

"I took the grandkids by." Josiah shrugged, his face innocent. "I had some things to say to him. Never know when I might see him again."

Gabriel stared at his father, the pieces falling into place. "Dad," he said, "you gave us a referendum and a game plan, but then you came home in the middle of the playing rules. You gave me money I wasn't expecting. You're gifting the whole town. You bought these kids a pony they're not really old enough to ride and which you will not be here to put them on. You've gone to see your archenemy or rival or whatever you want to call the relationship you've had over the years with Mr. Smith."

Josiah looked at him, his brows furrowed. "So?"

Gabriel glanced at Laura, then at the kids and saw the family setting his father wanted so badly. "A man would have to be knocking on heaven's door to change as much as you are," he said quietly.

Josiah blinked. He didn't reply, confirm, deny.

"Are you sick, Dad?" Gabriel asked.

Josiah shrugged. "Depends upon a man's perception of himself. I happen to think I'm just fine."

"But the doctors don't agree?" Laura asked.

"Now, missy, you just worry about your own father," Josiah said.

Laura shot back, "You're family, too!" which brought an amazing change to Josiah that Gabriel had never seen in all his life.

Tears in Josiah Morgan's eyes.

Laura was shocked by the look on Gabriel's face. He looked heartbroken by his father's slight admission of illness. Briefly she wondered how ill Mr. Morgan could truly be—certainly he looked fit. But he wouldn't lean on frailty to get his way, something Ben might do, she conceded unwillingly.

Here at this table sat many of the people she knew as family, and yet one of them had been holding up all the rest of them. "I'm worried about you," she told Mr. Morgan.

"Don't," he said shortly. "Damn doctors don't know what's in God's plan."

"True, but is there something I can do for you?" She glanced at Gabriel, saw that he appreciated her asking the question he apparently could not. Gabriel looked like he'd had his horse shot out from underneath him. He'd made a lucky guess on his father's latest machinations, trying to second-guess him when the truth was much more simple. The man was trying to cobble his family back together.

"No, thank you," Mr. Morgan said, "it's not in my hands."

"Excuse me." Gabriel left the room.

"Now, see, I don't want anybody worrying," Gabriel's father said. "There's too much of life to live without everyone being down."

"He is your son," Laura said gently. "Wouldn't you expect him to be concerned?"

"I'd rather him focus on getting married and having a family. He's traveled around for years," Mr. Morgan said, warming to his subject. "The honest truth is that family is a great thing. I made a lot of mistakes, I know, but family gave me more pleasure in my life than anything else, including making money. Some people would find that shocking."

Laura felt it was best to skip the marriage comments. "I don't think Gabriel getting married will help your health issue."

"Sure it will. That old geezer you call Ben is lying up in a bed because he doesn't want you to marry my son."

Laura sighed. "Mr. Morgan, it's not that easy. And anyway, you can't really say that Ben doesn't know what's best for me when you're busy impressing your will upon your sons, claiming you know what's best for them."

"True," he answered, "but I have to consider my own longevity. And, Laura, won't you please start calling me Josiah?"

Laura refused to allow him off the topic. "You and my father both think that parenting is managing. I'm going to try not to do that with my children." Penny got down from Josiah's lap and went to find her ball. Perrin snoozed comfortably on her shoulder. She loved her children; she could see how she might want to make decisions for them.

"Well, enough of that kind of talk," Josiah said. "I heard there were chocolate chip cookies in the kitchen, so if you'll excuse me, I think I'll brew up some coffee and have a few."

He got up from the table. She watched him walk into the kitchen, big and broad-shouldered. He appeared more robust than Ben, but he wouldn't fake an illness. He wanted to see his sons married more than anything.

She understood that—but it was not something she could help with. Making love with Gabriel had clearly been a mistake. There was no future for them; she knew in her heart she could not go into a second marriage—not now. When they'd planned a temporary marriage, when she'd thought she was helping Gabriel, that had been different. She'd been able to see the beginning and the end of their marriage. Open and shut, like a book. No emotions.

Now it was too complicated. She couldn't see the end, or where the heartache was. She'd barely pulled herself through the abyss this time; she didn't know if she could rescue herself again. The Morgans were unpredictable men. No matter how much she'd fallen for Gabriel, she had to keep herself from the edge, especially for her children's sakes.

Slowly, she stood. "Will you tell Gabriel I said goodbye, Josiah?"

He came out of the kitchen. "Must you leave so soon?"

She knew Gabriel was upset by his father's news. He needed time to think. "I need to get to the hospital early in the morning in case they release Ben."

He nodded. "Let me know if I can help."

She shook her head. "I appreciate everything you've done, Josiah. Everything except the pony."

He grinned. "Every child should ride."

"I'd tell you to quit scheming," she said, "but maybe it's medicinal for you. It's probably keeping you alive."

He roared with laughter, pleased by her outspokenness. But she had a feeling she was right.

Gabriel watched from his window as his father said goodbye to Laura and the kids. He saw Josiah kiss each child, saw him laugh at something Laura said before hugging her. Gabriel saw softness and kindness that he'd never experienced from his father, and realized Josiah had reprioritized his life. It wasn't so much Perrin and Penny that had changed his father, though that had something to do with it. Gabriel saw that Josiah had accepted the changes life was pressing upon him. His father was a different man.

He felt sad for all the time that had passed between them, when he had allowed silence to set solid and inflexible between them. After a moment, he pulled out his cell phone.

He hunted around for Dane's number, then made the call. "Dane," he said. "It's Gabriel. Got a minute? I need to talk."

"Great," Dane said, "I was just about to call you. Have you heard from Pete yet?"

"No." Gabriel watched Laura drive away, saw his father look after the car until it was long gone and then still he stood, eyeing the distance. "What's up?"

"You might want to think about a road trip and be quick about it," Dane said. "Jack took a real ass-stomping in Kearney and this time he's hurt pretty bad."

Chapter Fourteen

As he stared at Jack in intensive care, wired into every machine known to man, Gabriel knew he had to change his whole life. His brother lay very still, his head bandaged, his eyes closed. Pete and Dane had visited first, then Gabriel went in with Josiah. Josiah hadn't had to be dragged to see his son, which surprised Gabriel. In fact, his father had seemed eager to get to Kearney, his fingers drumming anxiously on his knees as Gabriel drove.

Josiah's drawn face hovered over the face of the son he hadn't seen in ten years. Gabriel wanted to push back time. Jack was battered, bruised—almost unrecognizable. "Jack," he whispered, but his brother didn't move. Josiah's shoulders slumped. Slowly, he reached to touch his eldest son's hand, his fingers trembling.

"Has he spoken?" Gabriel asked the nurse, who was changing a bag of IV fluids.

"No. But we know from the cowboys who rode in the ambulance with him that he had a helluva ride before the bull caught him against the rail and dragged him off. His foot caught in a stirrup and he couldn't free it. The clowns did what they could, probably saved his life, according to your brother's friends."

It was the risk that came with rodeo. Gabriel shook his head. They all worked dangerous jobs, and each of them loved their chosen professions. They had the fever to live on the edge. Many times he'd sat shivering in Gdańsk, or baking in San Salvador, wondering why he did what he did.

The answer was easy: the Morgan brothers all did what they did to prove themselves to the old man. And the old man was keeping his own secret of fallibility. *So we're just bashing ourselves on the rocks, trying to get to someplace that doesn't exist.*

"Jack," he murmured again, hoping to see his brother's eyes move. Josiah looked truly distraught. Gabriel wanted to comfort him but he didn't know how. He did know, however, that their father had raised them as he'd thought best as a parent.

Gabriel sighed. The nurse glanced at him. "I'm sorry, we have to keep his visits very short."

"I understand." Gabriel stood, but Josiah lingered at the bedside of his firstborn.

"Come on," Josiah said. "Jack?"

But Jack didn't move. Josiah turned and silently left the room.

"We'll be back tomorrow," Gabriel told the nurse. "Will you call us if there's any change?"

But the only change the next day was that they were told Jack didn't want visitors. Nor the next day. At the end of the week, the family was told that he'd checked himself out. The hospital could give them no further information.

The three remaining brothers and Josiah stood awkwardly in the waiting room digesting the news. Josiah looked as if he'd aged fifteen years. Gabriel watched as Pete and Dane tried to absorb what they'd learned. Finally, they left after giving Josiah an awkward handshake.

Josiah looked at Gabriel. "Was I that bad a parent?"

Gabriel sighed, shaking his head. "We all make mistakes. I've made more than my share." He pulled his stunned father to the sliding doors leading outside. "Come on, Dad. Let's go home."

Laura had just put the kids to bed when she heard a knock on the door, an impatient rapping she recognized. She hurried to open the door. "How is your brother?" she asked Gabriel.

"Tough as cowhide." Gabriel reached to grab her, not allowing her to keep an inch between them.

"And your father?" Laura asked breathlessly.

"Equally tough."

His lips searched hers hungrily. "Wait." She pulled away, feeling a new intensity in him. "What happened?"

"Jack disappeared. Crawled off like a wounded animal, I guess. He just went away before any of us ever got to see him conscious."

She gave him a gentle push toward the sofa, which he sank into. "Where are the kids?"

"In bed. Do you want a drink? Food?"

He shook his head. "I'd like to see the kids. I was hoping to catch them before they went to sleep."

As if she'd been listening at the door—and probably she had—Penny came into the room. She crawled up in Gabriel's lap. A warning flashed in Laura's mind. Her daughter was becoming attached to Gabriel, as was she. There was no denying it. Panic spread through her as she recognized a blossoming hope in her chest. She got up to get Perrin out of his crib so they could all be together.

The three of them looked at her with winsome eyes. She knew Gabriel wanted to be with the children; she knew he had to be upset from visiting his brother. "It is a special occasion," she said.

They snuggled up to Gabriel, each child resting against one side of his body. Perrin put his thumb in his mouth, then thought better of it. Penny's eyelids slowly lowered.

"Life is short. Let's make this more than a special occasion," Gabriel said.

Laura looked at him, her senses on alert.

"I want this to be an every night thing," he told her. "You deserve a guy like me, Laura."

She couldn't say no. In spite of her misgivings—and she was scared to death—she couldn't look in those dark eyes and honestly say she didn't want to be his, didn't want him to be a father to her children. "All right," she said, knowing there was no turning back now and not really wanting to anyway.

Mimi was delighted to help plan a wedding for Laura. She had a friend in a neighboring town who made bridal gowns, so she dragged Laura over to Tulips, Texas, to have her fit in something that "would make Gabriel's mouth water," Mimi said with a flourish. In town, Valentine Jefferson would make her a lovely wedding cake. Mimi assured her no one did them better.

They had Perrin outfitted in a little tuxedo and Penny in a darling flower girl gown. Mimi agreed to serve as the matron of honor. The ladies of the Union Junction salon agreed to do the hair for the wedding, and even trim Gabriel's just a bit. Not enough to take away from the rascal look he had going on, they assured her. They liked his hair growing out of its military cut.

Ben had recovered enough to give Laura away, though he was balking. "Don't know if I should willingly give you to a Morgan," he said, before asking Josiah if he planned on hanging around or hotfooting around the globe. This seemed to annoy Josiah for a minute, before he recovered his good humor at being invited to the wedding.

Pete and Dane sent congratulations. Jack, they never heard from at all. Gabriel was worried, but he knew that his brother was still recovering. He tried not to think about the fact that none of his brothers would be at his wedding, and asked his father to be his best man, an invitation which Josiah readily accepted. His return to France was postponed.

It would have been perfect except that before the rehearsal dinner, Gabriel discovered just how cold his bride's feet actually were. He went by to give Laura the ring he'd bought weeks before and knew by the pink of her nose that she'd been crying.

"You're not having second thoughts?" he asked, remembering how anxious she'd been to marry him before and then how quickly she'd backed away when her father became ill. It was all understandable—but he had to admit to a spur of worry.

She shook her head. "I'm just nervous, I think. You?"

"No way. I'm going to be a husband and a father. Life is good."

She took a deep breath. "Thank you."

"For what?"

"For not being afraid of…stepparenting."

He laid a finger over her lips. "Parenting. No *step*. When we slow down and you catch your breath, I'd like to adopt Penny and Perrin, if you'll let me."

"I—I have to think about that," she said, wondering why she held back. But the very act of allowing the children to be adopted seemed to push her deceased husband very far into the children's background. Was that the right thing to do?

"There's plenty of time. Right now I'm going to drink a beer with Josiah as my bachelor celebration. I'll see you at the rehearsal tonight." He kissed her goodbye. More than anything, Laura was afraid that she was going to awaken and find this had all been a fairy tale dream just beyond her grasp.

And then she realized why: Gabriel had never told her he loved her. That he was *in* love with her. He loved her children. He really wanted to be a father.

As for love—that word had never crossed Gabriel's lips.

The rehearsal would be an easy step toward marrying Gabriel. Laura tried to keep calm, telling herself that just because the wedding had grown a little bigger and more elaborate than she'd expected, this was no cause for nerves. Nor was marrying one of the finest men she'd ever met. If she was a little disappointed

Gabriel hadn't ever actually said he loved her, she was sure that was something that would come with time.

She reminded herself she was the one who'd insisted on boundaries when he'd first asked her. He was probably trying not to scare her. This time, there was no reason for them to be marrying, except good old-fashioned romance.

The dress she was wearing tonight was a straight column of light silk she'd worn to church many times. Gabriel would never know this gown was old. But her wedding gown was brand-new. Designed by Mimi's friend in Tulip, it was a shell-pink wrapping of silk and lace, falling straight to her ankles without any fuss. She loved the simplicity of it. Nothing about it reminded her of her first wedding, and she felt beautiful when she put it on.

Gabriel would be very handsome in a charcoal-gray tuxedo. She got the kids ready, and headed over to the Morgan ranch. Picnic tables and chairs had been set up on the lawn for the rehearsal dinner. White tents protected the guests from any shower which might fall, but the skies were clear.

She pushed down her rising panic, resenting it. Where were these feelings of worry coming from? Normal bridal nerves, she assured herself. Every bride probably got them.

She hadn't when she'd married Dave.

But she'd been young and idealistic then. Now there were many more people counting on her to make the right decision. The diamond Gabriel had given her sparkled on her finger. It was a bigger diamond than she expected; she'd never dreamed of owning anything so beautiful. Despite the sun, goose pimples ran over her arms.

The minister had asked them to be early, so that he could have a private discussion with Gabriel and Laura. She saw his car parked in the drive so she hurried to knock on the door. It swung open, and Josiah engulfed her in a hug. "You're family now! You don't have to knock on the door like a guest, Laura!"

"Thank you," she said, letting herself enjoy Josiah's bear hug. Across the room, Gabriel smiled at her. The minister smiled at her. It was a happy occasion— nothing to be afraid of.

"I want to go over the solemnity of the vows with you and Gabriel," Pastor Riley said. "This is just some quiet time for us to reflect on the meaning of the ceremony before you say your vows in front of your guests."

"All right." She slid into the chair he held out for her, unable to meet Gabriel's gaze.

"Did either of you want to write any of your own vows?" Pastor Riley asked.

"I don't think so," Laura murmured. They hadn't talked about it—maybe traditional vows were best. Gabriel shook his head.

Nodding, Pastor Riley put on his glasses. "Marriage is a holy occasion, as you know. From the beginning of the vows, which ends with the final instruction 'till death do you part—'"

Laura stood. Gabriel followed suit, surprised. "I'm sorry. I can't do this. Gabriel, forgive me. I truly thought I was having simple bridal nerves. But it's more than that." She took a deep breath, struggled for the right words. "This feels like a test I know I'm not going to pass."

"Laura," Gabriel said, his tone sympathetic, "would a few moments alone with Pastor Riley help?"

She shook her head, alarmed by the panic spreading inside her. They couldn't possibly understand. She'd done the death-do-you-part thing once. Death did part her from her beloved, cruelly early, and she'd never be able to say those words again knowing how sinister they were. They weren't romantic at all.

"I'm sorry," she repeated. She handed Gabriel the ring and backed away from the table. "I— Maybe it's just too soon," she said.

Gabriel followed her. "Laura. Are you all right?"

She gathered up Penny and Perrin, walking them to the car. She strapped the children into their seats. "I can't do it. I suppose in retrospect I wanted a Vegas drive-through type of wedding so it wouldn't seem so momentous. I realize that now. I'm just too scared to get married again, Gabriel. Which sounds silly, I know, but it's not like falling off a bicycle. As Pastor Riley said, the vows are solemn and meaningful—but they don't always last."

"All right. Don't worry. Somehow we'll get this to work out."

"I don't want you to think I'm crazy," she said, trying not to cry.

"No crazier than anybody else around here. Frankly, if we got to the altar without a couple of misfires, we probably wouldn't be doing ourselves any good. Practice makes perfect."

"Do you mean it?" Laura wasn't sure she deserved this much forgiveness.

"Oh, hell, yeah." He shrugged. "Go home. Change

your clothes. Forget about this whole thing. Call me when…when you can."

She nodded. "Thank you."

He shrugged. "Bye, Penny. Bye, Perrin."

They looked at him through the window and Laura turned on the car and drove away, feeling like she'd just given up the best thing that could have ever happened to her.

"I am so, so sorry," she murmured to the children. "You have no idea what your mother just took from your life."

She had taken the coward's way out, and now she knew she was in love with Gabriel Morgan. And the thought of losing him, the way she had Dave, was a fear she could not face.

"What the hell just happened?" Josiah demanded. Pastor Riley looked at Gabriel sympathetically.

Gabriel shrugged. He appreciated the concern, but he really wasn't surprised. "My bride got the jitters."

"Huh." Josiah shook his head. "Laura's always been a cool, practical kind of girl. Usually knows what she wants."

"Oh, she knows what she wants. She just can't figure out how to get there." Gabriel ushered the minister into the kitchen and poured them all some tea. "I bet wedding cake freezes just fine. Tuxes can be reordered. Pastor, you can use the flowers for this weekend's services, can't you?"

"Or I can have them delivered to some older folks' homes. They'd really appreciate that, Gabriel." Pastor Riley shook his head. "I've known Laura Adams a long time. She's a wonderful woman. She'll come around."

"I know. She's just not a marrying kind of girl. At least not right now," Gabriel replied.

"You know, I think you have a point," Josiah said. "The best things in life don't come easy."

"See? All those good lessons you gave us growing up are coming in handy now," Gabriel said wryly. "A lesser man might give up on a good thing if he hadn't learned that patience is a virtue."

Josiah grunted. "You didn't learn patience in my house."

"That was the military. You taught me life wasn't always easy. I can wait on Laura."

Pastor Riley nodded. "I'll notify Mimi, and she can help me let the guests know. I'm always available when Laura is ready."

"Thanks." He walked Pastor Riley to the door, then headed upstairs. Grabbing a duffel bag, he tossed in shirts, jeans, all his clothing. His father stood in the doorway, watching.

"What are you doing now?"

Gabriel wasn't sure how to explain his plan. "For now, leaving Ben with the upkeep of the ranch."

"I thought you said you were okay with Laura having second thoughts."

Gabriel looked at his father. "She says it's the ceremony she can't go through again. I think she was fine up until the 'I do forever' part." He shrugged. "Luckily for her, I learned life could be very short in the military. If she doesn't want to put the words on it right now, I understand. But I'm still going to be with her, as a husband, and as a father to her children."

Josiah handed him his boots. "And what if she says—"

"She won't," Gabriel said. He'd held that woman, made love to her. He knew how she felt about him. "It's up to me to give her space."

"By moving in with her?"

"By going slow." Gabriel picked up his duffel and shook his father's hand. "When are you leaving for France?"

Josiah grunted. "I was leaving after we threw the paper hearts at the happy couple."

Gabriel grinned. "Plan on making a return trip in the near future."

He walked away, confident that Laura and he could pass whatever test she was worried about—together. She just needed a teacher to help her study, and he had lots of lessons left to give her.

And a wedding ring.

Chapter Fifteen

"I'm so sorry, Mimi, about all your hard work." Knowing that guests needed to be notified, Laura had driven from Gabriel's ranch straight to the Double M. "I just couldn't make myself do it. It was like there was a giant sign that said Go The Other Way flashing at me."

"Well, you're not exactly a runaway bride," Mimi said, hugging her. "You told Gabriel what was happening, and he understood. Believe me, there are a lot of couples in this town who didn't make it to the altar smoothly, and I'm one of them."

Laura couldn't imagine Mason and Mimi not having an easy courtship, but she did remember rumors that Mason had jumped through a few complicated hoops to win Mimi. "Thank you."

"I bet Josiah just about cried." Mimi smiled. "He's been itching to get his boys to the altar."

Laura didn't feel good about that. Josiah had been so good to her and she felt she'd let him down. "I left so quickly I barely saw Josiah. But he'd been so nice, even telling me not to knock on the door anymore now that I was family."

Mimi patted her hand. "You're still family. Josiah made that clear a long time ago."

She felt better. Slowly but surely, her panic ebbed away.

"You did the right thing," Mimi said. "It's never good to feel pushed toward a decision."

"I really do like Gabriel."

Mimi smiled. "I know."

Laura hoped she hadn't lost any chance she'd had with him. He was gorgeous, sexy, kind. Loving. She was in love with him. "I think I was a little nervous that he hasn't told me he loved me."

Mimi paused in the wrapping up of some hors d'oeuvres that had been meant for the rehearsal dinner. "He hasn't?"

Laura shook her head.

"Men don't always talk about their emotions. Sometimes they expect us to divine their feelings."

"I'm not good with divining," Laura said, and Mimi laughed.

"I can't remember how long it took for Mason to tell me he loved me, but it does seem like forever. It was like pulling a mule out of a barn in winter." She put some food into the refrigerator. "Gabriel seems a lot like Mason. You can read a lot about their feelings from their actions."

Gabriel was a man of action. She could count on him to never be boring. "Can I help you with anything?"

Mimi shook her head. "Right now, I want you to go home and put your feet up. Play with your children. Do something relaxing. You've been through a lot lately. Take some time to smell the roses, as they say."

Laura gathered up her children and embraced her friend. Mimi held her for a good long hug, and Laura thought for the hundredth time how lucky she was to have such wonderful people around her.

She drove home, realizing she'd expected Gabriel to be parked in her driveway. He walked over to help her take the kids out of the car. "I hope you know how glad I am to see you," she told him.

He nodded, grinned at her. Desire melted through her, right down to her bones. "I know you want me."

She shook her head and helped Penny to the house; Gabriel carried Perrin. "I wonder why you still want *me*."

"Because I do. That's all I know," Gabriel said, putting Perrin on the floor with his toys. "I'm moving in, unless you object."

"I was hoping you would," Laura said, surprising herself.

"And what about gossip?" he asked.

"I'll try to save your reputation eventually," she said.

He slid her ring across the kitchen table. "Put that in your jewelry box until you're ready for it."

She picked up the beautiful sparkling ring, then handed it back to him with a shake of her head. "Thank you for trying to be a hero. It hasn't gone unnoticed."

He shrugged and got down on the floor with Perrin. Penny came to sit beside him. "I'm going to like this parenting stuff."

* * *

Gabriel told himself he was doing the right thing. Even if Laura looked nervous, she hadn't kicked him out.

He decided the best path was to start off as friends.

It was going to be hard, but he vowed to go slow. Let her make all the moves. The prize would be worth it in the end.

A persistent ringing of the doorbell sounded. He glanced around for Laura, but she'd gone to the back of the house. Shrugging, he decided that since this was now his home, he could open the door just as well.

Dane and Pete grinned at him. "Hey. You're not supposed to see the bride before the wedding," Pete said. He came inside the house, looking around with approval. "Small. Clean. Bright. I like it."

"The wedding is canceled. Sorry you made the trip." Gabriel looked his brothers over. "You look like just fell out of a laundry bag."

"We've been doing something I never thought I'd do," Dane said. "We volunteered as clowns at a rodeo. Then made a side trip. Can we sit down or not?"

"It's not really my house," Gabriel said, then remembered he was practicing fathering and marriage. "Sure, have a seat. Play with my kids."

Pete eyed him as he sat. "How are they yours if the wedding is canceled? Sorry about that, by the way."

"Don't be. Some things turn out for the best."

"Always the optimist. Did you get cold feet?" Dane shook his head. "Marriage and Morgans don't mix well."

"Laura had second thoughts. So I decided to move in and show her what she's missing out on."

"Brave. Egotistical, but brave." Dane grinned. "I decided that while I was in town for your nuptials, I'd best take a look at this Miss Suzy Winterstone."

"And?" Gabriel pulled Perrin in to his lap.

"I'm so glad I didn't allow Pop to guilt me into anything. She isn't my type."

"How do you know? Did you talk to her?"

"I watched her playing at the playground with her twins." He glanced at Penny and Perrin. "I'm not cut out for the playground lifestyle. I'm not even cut out for living in Texas."

"You live in Watauga, you're a Texas Ranger," Gabriel reminded him for the hundredth time. "I've never understood you being something you didn't want to be."

"What, like a housemate instead of a husband?" Dane asked, taking a small dig at Gabriel's circumstances. "Jeez, Gabriel, take it easy on a guy. Part of my issue is that I let Pop kick me into the military. I got out as fast as I could, but what else was I suited for besides protecting, keeping order and handling guns?"

"Sounds like an excellent résumé to me," Gabriel said dryly. "So back to the playful Miss Winterstone."

"Okay. She's cute, I have to admit, but a little fuller-figured than I like."

"Because she has year-old twins."

"Perhaps. But I sense she's just one of those big-boned girls."

"Not a bad thing, in my book." Laura was nice and petite, but nobody would call her thin. She had lots of curves he'd love to discover all over again.

"I think she might be German or French or something." Dane shook his head. "If I'd had your skills, I could have probably understood what she was saying to her children."

"Yeah." Gabriel grinned. It sounded as if his brother had happened upon the babysitter at work, but he wasn't going to share that. Let Dane figure it all out on his own—it was more fun that way. "So where are you headed now?"

"Well, since there'll be no wedding, I guess I'm free for the weekend. What's Pop doing?"

"Last I heard, he was heading out."

"And you're staying here?"

"Nothing's moving me," Gabriel said. "This is my family now."

"Wow." Pete shook his head, walked to the door. "You actually already seem like an old married man. Congratulations."

"Thanks." He hated to ask but made himself do it. "Ever hear from Jack?"

"Nah. He went off to lick his wounds. We'll probably never know what happened, you know?" Pete said.

Pete and Dane seemed resigned to this, but it bothered Gabriel. Their family was so sporadic, unsettled. "Keep in touch, all right?"

"I will." Dane waved at him. "Give my regards to the family."

"Why? Aren't you stopping by to see Josiah?"

Dane shook his head. "I've been thinking about that million dollars Pop promised us if we lived in the house for one year."

"Oh, yeah?" Gabriel kept his face blank. "What about it?"

"Do you think he ever meant to give us any money? Or was he just playing a game? Not that it matters, as far as the money goes. I just resent being jerked around by Pop. Don't think I can forgive that."

Gabriel thought about the money that was already in his bank account. His father had sworn him to secrecy, and he figured Josiah knew something about what he was doing. "Can't say, myself."

"You're not going to live there, though."

"Laura wants her children to stay here where they can keep some stability in their life."

"Doesn't bother you to live where her husband lived?" Pete asked.

Gabriel paused. "Can't say it's going to bother me." Pop was right; some things were better left unsaid.

"Sorry. Shouldn't have opened my big fat mouth."

"Don't worry about it. I'm not." He waved goodbye to his brothers and closed the door. Home was where the heart was; he knew that from spending too much time in dangerous places hungering for the promise of home. Penny and Perrin and Laura belonged here. Hopefully he did, too.

"Who was that?" Laura asked, coming into the room. She was freshly showered, her face glowing. He loved seeing her completely natural; he loved being with her in her home.

"Nobody but trouble," he said.

When the doorbell rang an hour later, Gabriel half expected to see another wedding guest who hadn't yet received the news about the postponement—he refused to say *cancellation*. He and Laura were simply delaying the inevitable.

It was Ben standing on the porch, looking like he'd

rather be anywhere but his own daughter's house. "Hi," he said, walking inside. "Can I talk to you, Gabriel?"

"Sure." Why the hell not? Apparently it was his day for surprise visitors, misery loves company for the jilted groom. He motioned Laura's father over to where he'd been sitting with the children.

"Hi, Dad," she said. She walked into the room with her kids. "We're going outside to play in the new sandbox now that it's all put together."

"You do that," Ben said. "I need to talk to Gabriel for a moment."

"Oh? About what?" Laura asked.

"Now don't you worry about that." He kissed his daughter on the forehead. "Sorry about the wedding, but I do understand. Perhaps it's a wee bit soon."

Her glance slid to Gabriel. "I think so."

"Have fun," he told her.

She managed a tentative smile for Gabriel and closed the door behind them.

Ben wasted no time getting to his topic. "Gabriel, I'm sorry as hell the wedding didn't go off like you wanted."

Gabriel looked at Ben, not completely certain he was being truthful.

"But I hear from your father that you're planning on moving in here with my daughter. I have to be honest with you, I don't think that's a good idea."

"Because?"

"Son, you're rushing things. The girl is still grieving for her husband. Not that he was any great favorite of mine, as you know, but I know Laura, and she's a one-man woman."

That didn't make him feel better. "She didn't seem unhappy to have me here."

"See, that's the problem. Laura doesn't know what she wants. Ever since Laura was a baby, she's known exactly what she wanted and had no trouble speaking up about it. This is why I think you're making a terrible mistake."

Gabriel looked at the man he'd known could be both slippery and untrustworthy. "Why would you try to help me?"

"Because of Perrin and Penny," he said simply. "I knew Laura wasn't ready to get married. I believe I tried to steer you away from that."

That's not exactly what he would have called it, but whatever. "I think it's just marriage she was saying no to, not me."

"Well, it's all wrapped up together." Ben raised his hand and waved it airily. "It's all pressure."

Gabriel considered that. "I can see your point."

"I know you want to be here, understand that you want to make a family with my daughter. Truth is, you haven't even taken care of your own house, son. And now you're staking a claim on Laura, when maybe you should be giving her some breathing room."

"I'll take it under advisement." Gabriel didn't like anything he was hearing. He wasn't certain he could trust Ben.

What worried him was wondering if Laura would ever trust him, and want him despite her fears. A cramp hit his gut. He wanted to be here with Penny and Perrin; in fact, he wanted an even bigger family with Laura.

But her father knew her best, and he believed Laura wasn't ready for marriage.

He saw Ben out, then considered his options. Tonight he was going to spend time with the family he wanted.

Later, he'd figure out whether his father-in-law-to-be dispensed helpful advice or not.

From the kitchen window he could see Laura and her kids building a small sand castle. It wasn't as grand as the knight's castle Josiah had purchased in France, but big or small, everyone wanted their own castle. He wanted sand castles and Little League and high school proms in his kids' lives. It did his heart good to see Laura enjoying her family. If he was very lucky, maybe one day they would have a child together.

A child seemed like a faraway dream right now. He went into the kitchen and grabbed some hamburger to make patties, veggies for a salad, a little fruit for a child-friendly dessert. He set the table for four and brewed up fresh tea.

Laura smiled when she came inside. She was tousled from playing with Penny and Perrin, and he liked seeing the happiness in her eyes. "You're making dinner?"

"I'm at your service. What time does the family normally eat?"

"This crowd likes to be at the table by six. We eat, then play, maybe watch a video for thirty minutes, have our bath and they go right to bed." Laura seemed uncertain about how much he could stand of kid play. "Feel free to skip the *Little Bear* video if you want."

He shrugged. "It all sounds great."

She smiled. "I'm going to wash the children up. We hosed off outside but we're still a wee bit sandy."

He wanted to help with that but Ben's words held him back. He hated that he felt he had to retrench his emotions; he felt more like a visitor than a part of the family.

Whether he liked it or not, that was exactly what he

was, until Laura said *yes*. Said *I do* with enthusiasm and true joy.

When Laura came back to the table, she sensed a subtle change in Gabriel. He'd gone from being upbeat to quiet. This was supposed to be their rehearsal dinner night, and here he sat eating burgers and watching *Little Bear*.

She didn't want to lose him. He could have had his choice of women, but he'd picked her and her brood. "I'm sorry about tonight, Gabriel. And the wedding."

"Don't be. Everything works out for the best usually."

But she sensed a lack of conviction in his words, as if he was repeating them simply to reassure himself.

Chapter Sixteen

Gabriel had finally figured out his father. Money wasn't everything to Josiah, though he'd kept a penny-pincher's handle on every cent until lately. Josiah had given Gabriel his portion of the one-year money because he had made an honest effort to rebuild the relationship with his father. Family was more important to Josiah than money.

Gabriel wanted family, too. This family he was watching play on the floor after dinner. He wanted Laura to want him as much as he wanted her. Ben's words rang true to him now. Maybe he'd never be certain of Ben's motivation, but staying here wasn't the way to find out if Laura would ever want him the way he hoped she would.

He stood. Penny and Perrin looked up. Laura looked at him, too. This was going to break his heart, but in the end, it had to be Laura who felt sure of what she could handle in life. "I'm going to head to the ranch."

She hesitated. "I thought you were staying here."

He nodded. "I had planned on it, but I accomplished what I came here for. We shared our evening together. I don't need a rehearsal to know how much I want to marry you, but I did want to be with you and the children tonight." Gently, he ran a palm over her cheek. "I'll show myself out."

She followed him to the door. "I don't know what to say right now. I think I understand how you feel, but part of me isn't sure."

He smiled. "It'll all get straightened out in time."

He leaned down and kissed her lightly on the lips. "Be seeing you," he said, and went to his truck.

Leaving didn't feel good, but it did feel like the only right thing to do. His heart heavy, knowing now the agony his father had felt wondering if his boys would ever come home, Gabriel drove toward the Morgan ranch.

"Well," Laura said to her children, "let's pick up these toys. Maybe we should crawl in my bed together and watch a movie."

The children were silent, helping their mother tidy up. Perrin didn't really help but he picked up a block and handed it to his mother. Penny industriously put the toys in the toy box before turning to look at her mother. "Where is Morgan?"

"He's gone to his house, sweetie," Laura said, before realizing what her daughter called Gabriel. She had always called him Morgan—but Laura knew he wanted to be called *Dad*. He'd gone from calling his father *Pop* to *Dad,* a subtle but noticeable shift in their relationship. She liked that Gabriel was stubborn; he hung on to a situation, no matter how unpleasant or awkward, until he had the right answer. He had commitment bred into his soul.

She knew he would always be there for her and her children.

The only thing holding her back was the fear of the unknown.

"Perfectly normal," Valentine Jefferson said the next day when Laura went to thank her for the lovely wedding cake, which had ended up in the freezer. "My path to the altar with Crockett was definitely not easy."

"It's a lovely cake." Laura smiled. "Thank you for everything."

Valentine smiled. "Believe it or not, you'll probably appreciate Gabriel more now that you've been through this."

Laura left the shop and went to visit the girls at the Union Junction salon to apologize for taking a day out of their appointments for a wedding that didn't happen.

"Love is a wonderful thing," Delilah said. The head hairstylist had married her truck-driver beau, Jerry, and all had been right in her world ever since. "It just takes time and understanding. You'll know."

Laura shook her head. "I hope so. I thought I was ready—I just didn't realize I wasn't."

"You have a lot to fit into your life." Delilah sat her down, pulled her hair into a ponytail, pressed it into some pretty curls. "Where's my little Penny and Perrin? Perrin should be just about ready for his first haircut."

Laura shook her head. "Gabriel came by and got

them this morning. He said he wanted to get to know them, and that it was a day without Mom. He wanted me to have some time to myself. I have a suspicion that he wanted to get them on the new pony Josiah bought and didn't want me around worrying."

Delilah smiled. "He sure does like those kids of yours."

"They like him, too." The knowledge gave her a sense of comfort.

"And your father?"

"Ben hasn't said much lately," Laura said. "It's odd for him, because he had plenty to say about Dave, and about Gabriel, too, at first. Once Dad turned over a new leaf, he seems to be determined to stay in everyone's good graces."

"I've seen people change for the better that I never thought would," Delilah said. "My sister and I battled for years, but once Marvella decided to make positive decisions in her life, she's been a completely different person. She's a joy to be around."

Laura thought about Delilah's words for a long time after she left the salon. Then she realized that everybody around her was making changes in their lives—everyone except her. It was as if she were stuck, rooted to one spot, wanting everything in her world to stay completely still and unmoving. She would always love Dave; he was the father of her children. But what she felt for Gabriel was more mature, more balanced. She didn't need to be ashamed of her feelings or feel obligated to Dave's memory. He'd always hold a special place in her heart.

As Gabriel did now. The place he had in her heart felt warmed, and loved.

She went home to her house. Hesitating only a moment, she went and pulled out the family photo album, wistfully opening it.

The first pages showed photos of her and Dave on various dates: at the movies, snuggling on the sofa, hanging out with friends. A few wedding pictures followed, both of them smiling with happiness. There were many photos from when the children were born; she'd forgotten how snap-happy Dave had been. He'd spent hours compiling photos in an orderly fashion that chronicled pregnancies, first steps, first teeth. Tears of happiness and sadness jumped bittersweet to her eyes. The last photo was of Dave, taken by Laura, of him holding both the children. When he learned he had a life-threatening disease, he said he wanted a photo of him and the children so they would always remember what he looked like when he'd been strong and fit. He wanted them to know he'd loved them.

She closed the album and cried one last time for the innocence of her marriage and the good friend she'd lost.

But Dave would know she had loved him, grieved for him, and he'd also want her to move on with a good life for their children. He would not want her making a silent shrine to his memory. The husband, the father in the album he had put together, was the man he'd wanted remembered.

She drove to the Morgan ranch, smiling when she saw Penny on top of the white pony. Perrin was held securely in Gabriel's arm as he walked the pony by halter. Each child wore a cowboy hat. Nearby, Ben took pictures, grinning as he recorded his grandchildren's first ride for posterity.

Ben was a changed man, no doubt about that.

She got out of her car and walked to the fence. "Hey, cowboy," she called.

"Hey," Gabriel said, "you made it in time for the big event."

"What's the pony's name?"

"Sugar." Gabriel grinned proudly. "Penny says she's white as sugar. I figured snow was the obvious choice, but she surprised me."

Laura smiled. "Hi, Dad."

Ben held up the camera. "Step inside the paddock and let me snap a photo." He seemed to consider his words. "A family photo."

Laura ducked under the fence and went to stand beside Penny. Gabriel held Perrin and stood stiffly next to Laura.

"Closer," Ben said with a wave of his hand. "I can't fit everything into the picture."

Gabriel and Laura moved slightly together.

"Closer," Ben instructed. "It's hard to get everybody in the shot 'cause Penny's on the pony."

They moved together again. Laura was pretty sure they were close enough for the smallest camera in the world.

"Closer!" Ben examined the picture he'd just taken. "Gabriel, you have to—"

Laura tugged Gabriel's face toward hers and gave him a meaningful kiss. "Close enough?" she asked her father.

"That one's a keeper," Ben replied.

Gabriel looked down at her, his gaze questioning. "Am I getting a message here?"

"I don't know. How are your code-breaking skills?"

"They were always pretty good." Gabriel grinned. "Try me again to make certain I got the right information."

She kissed him, and he held her tightly against him, despite Perrin's attempt to squiggle free and Penny's giggling behind them.

Gabriel's eyes warmed. "That code was easy to decipher."

She took a deep breath. "After everything I've put you through, do you still want to marry me, Gabriel?"

"You're worth the wait," Gabriel said huskily. "You're talking to a man who waited ten years to be a son. I would have waited forever for you. Fortunately, you come around more easily than I do."

"Dad, hand me that camera, please," Laura said. "And if you don't mind, go stand next to the kids and your future son-in-law."

Ben hopped over the fence and stood next to Gabriel, smiling proudly. Laura clicked the camera, then checked the photo. Everyone was smiling and happy. Tears of happiness jumped into her eyes. She would treasure this picture of her new family for always.

Gabriel helped Penny down from the pony. "There'll be steaks and potatoes tonight for dinner," Gabriel said as they walked toward the house. "Stay and eat with us, Ben."

"I'm going to put Sugar up and bed down for the night." Ben grinned at his daughter. "Think I'm going to try to talk my boss into a new bed and maybe some sheets and blankets for the foreman's house. That plaid stuff is old as the hills, and I'm developing a taste for the finer things in life."

Gabriel snorted. "Get what you need, Ben. The cottage needs an update and you might as well make it yours for as long as you want it."

Smiling, Laura took the children upstairs to wash up. Gabriel looked at Ben. "Are you good with me marrying your daughter now?"

Ben gave him a toothy grin. "She came here on her own, didn't she?"

Laura had, indeed, surprising him. She didn't seem so spooked anymore; instead, she radiated calm and happiness. "Yeah. She did."

"I told you you'd be happier if you waited. Good thing you listened to me. Does no good to rush a woman."

"So, Ben," Gabriel said, "there's one thing I have to know. Did you pull a fast one on my father about oil on your property?"

Ben gave him a coy look. "No one pulls a fast one on Josiah Morgan."

He left, and as he walked to his truck, Gabriel saw the old man jump up into the air and kick his heels. He was celebrating, and Gabriel felt like doing the same.

"Hey," Laura said, as she put her children on the floor, "what can I help with?"

He took her into his arms. "Teaching me how to be a good father and husband."

She smiled up into his eyes. "I think you're already on your way. In fact, I was thinking that maybe it's time for me to give you something you say you want. Weddings are a good time for new beginnings of all kinds, right?"

"Definitely. What am I getting?" he asked, playfully picking her up.

"I was thinking adopting Penny and Perry might make you the—"

"Luckiest man in the world?" He kissed her with gratitude and joy. "I've waited a long time for this moment, and it feels even better than I imagined it would."

Happiness shone in his eyes, and Laura was glad she could bring him joy.

"Home really is where the heart is," Gabriel said, his voice catching. He kissed her again, taking his time to show her how much he cared for her. "I'm in love with you, little mama. I liked you the minute you stood on my porch with chicken and peas."

Hearing Gabriel say he loved her was a pleasure Laura hadn't expected again in her life. "I fell in love with you when I realized you loved my kids like your very own." There was a time she might not have wanted that, but now she knew how blessed her family was to have Gabriel's love.

"I used to think I didn't want kids," he said. "Good thing I'm not stubborn or anything."

She smiled. "Penny and Perrin will try your patience. Be forewarned."

He laughed. "I waited out their mom. I'm a very patient man."

He kissed her, long and sweet, and Laura knew she would always be safe with Gabriel. But even more important, she knew they would always be a family.

Epilogue

This time Gabriel and Laura's wedding went off without a hitch. They married two weeks later on a beautiful cloudless day, and invited everyone in Union Junction who wanted to come celebrate with them. Laura said they'd just needed time to work the kinks out of things, and Gabriel said he was going to keep her busy working kinks out of him for the next fifty years so waiting two weeks hadn't killed him. But happily he'd slid her engagement ring back on her finger, a sweet reclaiming of the woman he loved.

Gabriel thought Laura was the most beautiful bride he'd ever seen. She made him hungry for her just walking around in her shell-pink wedding gown, holding Perrin and keeping a sweetly-dressed Penny at her side. His mind took rapid-fire pictures of his new family, putting them in a mental photo album he would always treasure. Perrin never had colic anymore, and Penny was becoming quite the little pony rider, all positive changes for which Gabriel felt some proud dad ownership.

Ben gave his daughter away willingly. Josiah grinned, a proud best man, his face alight with joy. His approval meant everything to Gabriel, and just seeing his father's happiness healed the old emotional scars for good.

Pete and Dane made it to the wedding this time to serve as groomsmen, and though they never heard from Jack, Gabriel figured his brother's well wishes were with him. Peace was coming over the family, and it felt good to Gabriel. They had a long way to go in the Morgan clan before all the old wounds were healed. Dane and Pete were having a harder time with forgiveness than Gabriel, but the Morgans were getting closer to harmony than they'd been in a decade.

"You've made me a happy man," he told Laura, pulling her to him for a kiss. "Have I told you yet that I love you? Because if I haven't, I'm happy to tell you that I love you, Mrs. Morgan."

Laura laughed. "Not that I'll ever get tired of hearing it, but you have said it a few times in the last hour."

Gabriel grinned at his bride. "When Pastor Riley said I could kiss the bride, I wanted to grab you and never let you go."

Laura smiled at her handsome husband. "*Did* you let go of me willingly? I thought your father tapped you on the shoulder to remind you our wedding guests were waiting for some wedding cake and dancing."

"Remember the kissing booth?" He ran a hand down her back, giving her a gentle hug. "I wanted to beat all those guys away from you. I figured today they can just sit and suffer watching me romance my bride. They'll never get another kiss from you."

She gave him a teasing smile. "Mason lets Mimi volunteer at the kissing booth."

"That's Mason," he said. His eyes held a possessive gleam that made Laura shiver with delight. "I'm a Morgan, and we have never been ones to play well with others."

"We play well together," Laura said. "I love you just the way you are." Their children snuggled close, and Gabriel wrapped them all into his embrace. For Gabriel, this was heaven, his very own Texas lullaby come true.

* * * * *

Marie Ferrarella is a *USA TODAY* bestselling and RITA® Award–winning author who has written more than two hundred and fifty books for Harlequin, some under the name Marie Nicole. Her romances are beloved by fans worldwide. Visit her website, marieferrarella.com.

Books by Marie Ferrarella

Harlequin Western Romance

Forever, Texas

Visit the Author Profile page at Harlequin.com for more titles.

COWBOY FOR HIRE

MARIE FERRARELLA

To
Dianne Moggy,
for being nice enough
to call and reassure me.
Thank You.

Prologue

There had to be more.

There just had to be more to life than this.

The haunting thought echoed over and over again in Constance Carmichael's brain as she sat in her father's dining room, moving bits and pieces of chicken marsala around on her plate.

Her father was talking. But not to her—or even *at* her, as was his custom. This time his words were directed to someone on the other end of his state-of-the-art smartphone. From what she had pieced together, someone from one of his endless construction projects. Carmichael Construction Corporation, domiciled in Houston, Texas, had projects in different stages of completion throughout the country, and Calvin Carmichael thrived on the challenge of riding roughshod on *all* of his foremen.

The table in the dining room easily sat twenty. More if necessary. Tonight it only sat two, her father and her. She was here by mandate. Not that she didn't love her father, she did, but she had never been able to find a way to bond with him—not that she hadn't spent her whole life trying. But she had never been able to approach him and have him see her as something other than the ongoing disappointment he always made her feel that she was.

Calvin Carmichael didn't believe in pulling any punches.

Rather than sharing a warm family dinner, Connie had rarely felt more alone. She felt utterly isolated— and distance was only part of the reason. Before the call came in, her father had insisted that she sit at one end of the table while he sat at the other.

"Like civilized people," he'd told her.

He was at the head of the table and consequently, she was at the foot—with what felt like miles of distance between them.

If merely sharing a meal had been her father's main objective, it could have been more easily attained than this elaborate command performance. Connie was aware of restaurants that were smaller than her father's dining room. She'd grown up in this enormous house, but it had never felt like home to her.

She watched Fleming, her father's butler, retreat out of the corner of her eye. It was no secret that Calvin Carmichael enjoyed with relish all the perks that his acquired wealth could buy, including not just a cook and a housekeeper but a genuine English butler, as well. The latter's duties included serving dinner, even if the only one at the table was her father.

Connie sighed inwardly, wondering when she could safely take her leave. She knew that if her sigh was audible, her father would make note of it. Moreover, he'd grill her about it once his phone call was over, finding a way to make her feel guilty even if he was the one at fault.

Sitting here, toying with her food and watching her father, Connie felt a numbing malaise, a deadness spreading like insidious mold inside her. Surrounded by wealth, able to purchase and own any object her heart desired, no matter how extravagant, she found she desired nothing.

Because nothing made her happy.

She knew what she needed.

She needed to feel alive, to feel productive. She needed to accomplish something so that she could feel as if she finally, finally had a little of her father's respect instead of always being on the receiving end of his thinly veiled contempt.

"You're not eating. I invited you for dinner, you're not eating. Something wrong with your dinner?"

Connie looked up, startled. Her father had been on the phone for the past twenty minutes, but the slight shift in his tone made her realize that he had ended his conversation and had decided to find some reason to criticize her.

Connie lifted her shoulders in a careless, vague shrug. "I'm just not hungry, I guess," she replied, not wanting to get into an argument with the man.

But it seemed unavoidable.

"That's because you've never *been* hungry. Had you grown up hungry," Calvin stressed, "you would never waste even a *morsel* of food." Crystal-blue eyes narrowed beneath imposing, startlingly black eyebrows. "What's wrong with you, little girl?" If the question was motivated by concern, there was no indication in either his inflection or his tone.

Little girl.

She was twenty-seven years old, and she *hated* when her father called her that, but she knew it was futile to say as much. Calvin Carmichael did what he pleased *when* he pleased to whomever he pleased and took no advice, no criticism from anyone. To render any would just get her further embroiled in a heated exchange. Silence usually won out by default.

"Haven't I given you everything?" Calvin pressed, still scowling at his only daughter. His only child according to him. He had long since disowned the older brother she had adored because Conrad had deigned to turn his back on the family business and had struck out on his own years ago.

Connie looked at her father for a long moment. This feeling wasn't about to go away, and if she didn't say anything, she knew it would only get worse, not to mention that her father wouldn't stop questioning her, wouldn't stop verbally poking at her until she told him what he claimed he wanted to know.

As if he cared.

"I don't want to be *given* anything," she told her father. "I want to *earn* it myself."

His laugh was belittling. "Earn it, right. Where's this going, little girl?"

She pressed her lips together for a moment to keep from saying something one of them—possibly both of them—would regret. Her father didn't respond well to displays of emotion.

"I want to helm a project." It wasn't really what was bothering her, but maybe, just maybe, it might help squash these all but paralyzing doldrums that had infiltrated her very soul.

"You? Helm a project?" Piercing blue eyes stared at her in disbelief. "You mean by yourself?"

She tried not to react to the sarcasm in her father's voice. "Yes. My own project."

He waved a dismissive hand at her. "You don't know the first thing about being in charge of a project."

Anger rose within her, and she clutched to it. At least she was finally *feeling* something. "Dad, I've worked for you in one capacity or another for the last ten years. I think I know the first thing about being in charge of a project—and the second thing, too," she added, struggling to rein in her temper. An outburst would only tilt the scales further against her.

Her father was a formidable man, a man who could stare down his opponents and have them backing off, but she was determined not to allow him to intimidate her. She was fighting for her life—figuratively and, just possibly, literally.

Calvin laughed shortly. But just before he began to say something scathing in reply, his ever-present cell phone rang again.

To Connie's utter annoyance, her father answered it. It was time to leave, she decided. This "discussion," like all the others she'd had with him over the years, wasn't going anywhere.

But as she pushed her chair back and rose to her feet, Connie saw her father raise a finger, the gesture meant to keep her where she stood.

"Just a minute."

She wasn't sure if he was speaking to her or the person on the other end of the call. His next words, however, were definitely directed at her.

"Forever." For a moment, the word just hung there, like a single leaf drifting down from a tree. "Let's see what you can do about getting a project up, going and completed in Forever."

Something in her gut warned her she was walking into a trap—but she had no other choice. She had to do it—whatever "it" turned out to be.

"What kind of a project?" she asked warily.

Her father's attention already appeared to be elsewhere. "I'll have Emerson give you the particulars," he said in an offhanded manner, referring to his business manager. "Just remember, little girl, I started with nothing—I don't intend to wind up that way," he warned her, as if he was already predicting the cost of her failure.

Adrenaline was beginning to surface, whether in anticipation of this mysterious project or as a reaction to her father's condescending manner, it was hard for her to tell—but at least it was there, and she was grateful for that.

"Thank you," she said.

But her father was back talking to the person on the other end of the cell phone, giving that man his undivided attention.

She had a project, Connie thought, savoring the idea as it began to sink in. The world suddenly got a whole lot brighter.

Chapter One

"I can't believe what you've done to the place," Brett Murphy said to Finn, the older of his two younger brothers, as he looked around at what had been, until recently, a crumbling, weather-beaten and termite-riddled ranch house.

This morning, before opening up Murphy's, Forever's one and only saloon, he'd decided to look in on Finn's progress renovating the ranch house he had inherited from one of the town's diehard bachelors. And though he hadn't been prepared to, he was impressed by what he saw.

"More than that," Brett added as he turned to face his brother, "I can't believe that you're the one who's doing it."

Finn never missed a beat. He still had a lot to do before he packed it in for the day. "And what's that supposed to mean?" he asked. He'd been at this from first light, wrestling with a particularly uncooperative floorboard trim, which was just warped enough to give him trouble. That did *not* put the normally mild-tempered middle brother in the best frame of mind. "I built you a bathroom out of practically nothing, didn't I?" he reminded Brett. The bathroom had been added to make the single room above the saloon more livable. Until then, anyone staying in the room had had to go downstairs to answer nature's call or take a shower.

Brett's memory needed no prodding. It had always been a notch above excellent, which was fortunate for his brothers. It was Brett who took over running Murphy's and being financially responsible for them at the age of eighteen.

"Yes, you did," Brett replied. "But don't forget, you were the kid who always wound up smashing his thumb with a hammer practically every time you so much as held one in your hand."

His back to Brett as he continued working, Finn shrugged. "You're exaggerating, and anyway, I was six."

"I'm not—and you were twelve," Brett countered. He inclined his head ever so slightly as if that would underscore his point. "I'm the one with a head for details and numbers."

Finn snorted. It wasn't that he took offense, just that their relationship was such that they took jabs at one another—and Liam—as a matter of course. It was just the way things were. But at bottom, he was fiercely loyal to his brothers—as they were to him.

"Just because you can add two and two doesn't make you the last authority on things, Brett," Liam informed his brother.

"No, running Murphy's into the black pretty much did that."

When, at eighteen, he had suddenly found himself in charge of the establishment, after their Uncle Patrick had died, he'd discovered that the saloon was actually *losing* money rather than earning it. He swiftly got to work making things right and within eight months, he'd managed to turn things around. It wasn't just his pride that was at stake, he had brothers to support and send to school.

"Look, I didn't swing by to squabble with you," Brett went on. "I just wanted to see how the place was coming along—and it looks like you're finally in the home stretch. Liam been helping you?" he asked, curious.

This time Finn did stop what he was doing. He looked at Brett incredulously and then laughed. "Liam? In case you haven't noticed, that's a box of tools by your foot, not a box of guitar picks."

Finn's meaning was clear. Of late, their younger brother only cared for all things musical. Brett still managed to get Liam to work the bar certain nights, but it was clear that Liam preferred performing at Murphy's rather than tending to the customers and their thirst.

"I thought Liam said he was coming by the other day," Brett recalled.

"He did." Finn's mouth curved. "Said watching me work inspired his songwriting."

"Did it?" Brett asked, amused.

Finn shrugged again. "All I know was that he scribbled some things down, said 'thanks' and took off again. I figure that *he* figures he's got a good thing going. Tells you he's coming out here to help me then when he comes here, he writes his songs—and calls it working." There was no resentment in Finn's voice as he summarized his younger brother's revised work ethic. For the most part, Finn preferred working alone. It gave him the freedom to try different things without someone else second-guessing him or giving so-called advice. "Hey, Brett?"

Brett had wandered over to the fireplace. Finn had almost completely rebuilt it, replacing the old red bricks with white ones. It made the room look larger. "What?"

"You think our baby brother has any talent?" he asked in between hammering a section of the floorboard into place.

"For avoiding work?" Brett guessed. "Absolutely."

Finn knew that Brett knew what he was referring to, but he clarified his question, anyway. "No, I mean for those songs he writes."

Brett could see the merit in Liam's efforts, especially since he wouldn't have been able to come up with the songs himself, but he was curious to hear what Finn's opinion was. Since he was asking, Brett figured his brother had to have formed his own take on the subject.

"You've heard him just like I have," Brett pointed out, waiting.

Finn glanced at him over his shoulder. "Yeah, but I want to know what you think."

Brett played the line out a little further. "Suddenly I'm an authority?" he questioned.

Down on his knees, Finn rocked back on his heels, the frustrating length of floorboard temporarily forgotten. Despite the fancy verbal footwork, he really did value Brett's take on things. Brett had been the one he'd looked up to when he was growing up.

"No, not an authority," Finn replied, "but you know what you like."

"I think he's good. But I think he's better at singing songs than he is at writing them," he said honestly, then in the next moment, he added, "But what I *do* know is that you've got a real talent for taking sow's ears and making silk purses out of them."

Never one to reach for fancy words when plain ones would do, Finn eyed him with more than a trace of confusion.

"How's that again?" he asked.

Brett rephrased his comment. Easygoing though he was, it wasn't often that he complimented either of his brothers. He'd wanted them to grow up struggling to always reach higher rather than expecting things to be handed to them—automatic approval readily fell into that category.

"You're damn good at this remodeling thing that you do."

Finn smiled to himself. Only a hint of it was evident on his lips. "Glad you like it."

"But you don't have to work on it 24/7," Brett pointed out. Finn had immersed himself in this huge project he'd taken on almost single-handedly. There was no reason to push himself this hard. "Nobody's waving a deadline at you."

"There's a deadline," Finn contradicted. He saw Brett raise an eyebrow in a silent query, so he stated the obvious. "You and Lady Doc are still getting married, aren't you?"

Just the mere mention of his pending nuptials brought a wide smile to Brett's lips. Just the way that thoughts of Alisha always did.

Until the young general surgeon had come to town, answering Dr. Daniel Davenport's letter requesting help, Brett had been relatively certain that while he loved all the ladies, regardless of "type," there was no so-called soul mate out there for him.

Now he knew better, because he had met her. Not only was she out there, but he would be marrying her before the year was out, as well.

"Yes," Brett replied. "But what...?"

Finn anticipated Brett's question and cut him short. "This is my wedding present to you and Lady Doc—to say thanks for all the times you were there for Liam and me when we needed you—and even the times when we thought we didn't," he added with a touch of whimsy. "And this is, in a small way, to pay you back for staying instead of taking off with Laura right after high school graduation, the way she wanted you to.

"In other words, this is to say thanks for staying, for giving up your dream and taking care of your two bratty younger brothers instead."

While Finn and Liam were aware of Laura, he had never told them about the ultimatum she'd given him. Had never mentioned how tempted he'd been, just for a moment, to follow her to Los Angeles. All his brothers knew was one day, Laura stopped coming around.

He looked at Finn in surprise. "You know about that?"

Finn smiled. "I'm not quite the oblivious person you thought I was."

"I didn't think you were *oblivious*," Brett corrected him. "It was just that you saw and paid attention to things the rest of us just glossed over." His smile widened as he looked around the living room. Finn had outdone himself. "But seriously, this is all more than terrific, but this is *our* ranch house," he emphasized, "not just mine."

Finn looked at him and shook his head in wonder before getting back to work. "You bring that pretty Lady Doc here after you've married her and she finds out that she's sharing the place with not just you but also your two brothers, I guarantee that she'll walk out of here so fast, your head'll spin clean off."

He might not be as experienced as Brett was when it came to the fairer sex, Finn thought, but some things were just a given.

"Now, I don't know nearly as much as you do when it comes to the ladies, but I do know that newlyweds like their own space—that doesn't mean sharing that space with two other people. Liam and I'll go on living at the house. This'll be your place," he concluded, waving his hand around the room they were currently in as well as indicating the rest of the house.

"But the ranch itself is still *ours,* not just mine," Brett insisted.

"Earl Robertson left it to you," Finn stated simply. The man, he knew, had done it to show his gratitude because Brett had gone out of his way to look in on him when he had taken sick. That was Brett, Finn thought, putting himself out with no thought of any sort of compensation coming his way for his actions.

"And I've always shared whatever I had with you and Liam," Brett stated flatly.

Finn allowed a sly smile to feather over his lips, even though being sly was out of keeping with his normally genial nature.

"I see. Does that go for Lady Doc, too?"

Brett knew that his brother was kidding and that he didn't have to say it, but he played along, anyway. "Alisha is off-limits."

Finn pretended to sigh. "It figures. First nice *thing* you have in aeons, and you're keeping it all to yourself."

"Damn right I am."

Finn changed the subject, directing the conversation toward something serious. "Hey, made a decision about who your best man is going to be?"

Brett was silent for a moment. He'd made Finn think he was debating his choices, but the truth of it was, he'd made up his mind from the beginning. It had been Finn all along.

"Well, Liam made it clear that he and that band of his are providing the music, so I guess you get to be best man."

His back to Brett, Finn smiled to himself. "I won't let it go to my head."

"Might get lonely up there if it did," Brett commented with affection. He glanced at his watch. "Guess I'd better be getting back or Nathan McHale is going to think I've abandoned him," he said, referring to one of Murphy's' two most steadfast patrons.

Finn laughed. "Wonder how long he'd stand in front of the closed door, waiting for you to open up before he'd finally give up."

Brett began to answer without hesitation. "Two, maybe three—"

"Hours?" Finn asked, amused.

"Days," Brett corrected with a laugh. The older man had been coming to Murphy's for as many years as anyone could remember, motivated partially by his fondness for beer and most assuredly by his desire to get away from his eternally nagging wife, Henrietta. "I'll see you later tonight."

Finn nodded. "I'll be by when I get done for the day," he said. He was back to communing with another ornery section of floorboard before his brother walked out the front door.

Connie had decided to just drive around both through Forever and its surrounding area to get a general feel for the little town. For the most part, it appeared she'd stumbled across a town that time had more or less left alone. Nothing looked ancient, exactly, and there were parking places in front of the handful of businesses rather than hitching posts, but all in all, the entire town had a very rural air about it, right down to the single restaurant—if a diner could actually lay claim to that title.

She'd been amused to see that the town's one bar—how did these cowboys survive with only one bar?—had a sign in the window that said Hungry? Go visit Miss Joan's diner. Thirsty? You've come to the right place. That had told her that there was obviously a division of labor here with territories being defined in the simplest of terms.

Given its size and what she took to be the residents' mind-set, Connie doubted very much if a place like this actually *needed* a hotel—which, she had a feeling, had probably been her father's whole point when he had given her this *project,* saying if she wanted to prove herself to him, he wanted to see her complete the hotel, bringing it in on time and under budget. The budget left very little wiggle room.

"Newsflash, Dad. I don't give up that easily," she

murmured to the man who was currently five hundred miles away.

Challenges, especially seemingly impossible ones, were what made her come alive. At first glance, the sleepy little town of Forever needed a hotel about as much as it needed an expert on wombats.

It took closer examination to see that the idea of building a hotel had merit.

Connie could see the potential of the place forming itself in her mind's eye. She just needed the right approach, the right thing to play up and the hotel-to-be would not only become a reality, it would also be a success and eventually get its patrons.

But it wouldn't get anything if it wasn't first built, and she had already decided that while she could have materials shipped in from anywhere in the country that could give her the best deal, to get the structure actually built, she was going to use local *talent,* so to speak.

She naturally assumed that living out here in what she viewed as *the sticks* made people handy out of necessity. Unlike in the larger cities, there wasn't a range of construction companies, all in competition with one another, all vying for the customer's money. Driving down here from Houston, she had already ascertained that the nearest town, Pine Ridge, was a minimum of fifty miles away. That alone limited the amount of choices available. If anything, out here it was the unhandy customer who wound up searching to find someone to do the work for them.

Just like faith, the right amount of money, she had learned, could move mountains.

She had no mountains to move. But she did have a building to erect, and in order not to be the outsider, the person who was viewed as invading their territory, she would need allies. In this particular case, she needed to have some of the men from Forever taking part in making the hotel a reality.

Granted that, once completed, the hotel would belong to the Carmichael Construction Corporation until such time as they sold it, but she had to make the locals feel that building the hotel would benefit the whole town as well as provide them with good-paying jobs during construction.

Connie knew the importance of friends; she just didn't exactly know how to go about making them.

But she had done her homework before ever getting behind the wheel of her vehicle and driving down here.

As she drove around now, Connie thought about the fact that on the other side of the town, located about ten miles due northwest, was a Native American reservation. She couldn't remember which of the tribes lived there, but perhaps they would welcome the work, along with Forever townspeople. Given the local state of affairs, who wouldn't want a job?

So, armed with her GPS, Connie was on her way there. She was driving slower than she was accustomed to for two reasons: one, she didn't have a natural sense of direction, and she didn't know the lay of the land and two, she wanted and *needed* to get to know this land she was temporarily camping out on.

The reservation was her destination, but something—instincts perhaps—made her closely scan the immediate area she was traversing.

Which was when she saw him.

At first she thought she was having a hallucination, a better-than-average morning fantasy that could easily trigger her latent libido if she let it. The trick to being a driven woman with not just goals, but also the taste of success tucked firmly under her belt, was the way she responded to things that needed life-long commitments. It required—demanded, really—tunnel vision. Eye on the prize and all that sort of thing.

Even so, Connie slowed her pristine, gleaming white BMW sports car down to an arthritic crawl as she stared at the lone figure in the distance.

No harm in just looking, she told herself.

Even at this distance, she could easily make out that the man was around her own age. She was keenly aware that he was bare-chested, that his muscles were rippling with every move he made and that, pound for pound, he had to be the best-looking specimen of manhood she had seen in a very long time.

Moving closer, she could see that perspiration covered his body, causing practically a sheen over his chest and arms.

At first she wasn't aware of it, but then she realized that her mouth had gone bone-dry. She went on watching.

He didn't seem to be aware of the fact that he was under scrutiny. The worker turned his back to her and went on doing whatever it was that he was doing. She couldn't quite make it out, but it had something to do with construction because there were tools on the ground, surrounding an empty tool chest.

As she continued observing him, Connie saw that the man appeared as if he not only knew his way around tools, but he also definitely seemed comfortable working with his hands.

It came to her then.

He was just the man she was looking for to be her foreman, to act as her go-between with whatever men she wound up hiring to do the actual work. Watching him, she couldn't help wondering how well someone who looked like that would take instructions from a woman.

Or was he the type who didn't care who issued the orders as long as there was a guaranteed paycheck at the end of the week?

Enough thinking, start doing, she silently ordered herself.

The next moment, she turned her vehicle toward the cowboy and drove straight toward him.

Chapter Two

He'd been aware of the slow-moving, blindingly white sports car for some time now. It was a beauty—much like the woman who was driving it.

But unlike the woman behind the wheel, the vehicle, *because* of its make and model, stuck out like a sore thumb. Regardless of the season, Forever and its outlining area didn't see much through traffic. Every so often, there was the occasional lost traveler, but on the whole, that was a rare occurrence. Forever was *not* on the beaten path to anywhere of interest, except perhaps for the reservation and a couple of other tiny towns that had sprung up in the area. On its way to being a ghost town more than once, the town stubbornly survived despite all odds. Like a prickly pear cactus, Forever, a few of the much older residents maintained, was just too ornery to die.

The owner of the sports car, Finn decided, had to be lost. Nobody driving that sort of a vehicle could possibly have any business being in or around Forever. Even Dan, the doctor who had initially come to town out of a sense of obligation mixed with a heavy dose of guilt, hadn't been driving a car nearly that flashy and unsuitable for this terrain when he'd arrived.

As the vehicle came closer, Finn tossed down his hammer and approached the car. The woman, he couldn't help noticing, was even better-looking close up than she was at a distance.

"You lost?" he asked her, fully expecting her to sigh with relief and answer "Yes."

She didn't.

Instead, she shook her head and said, "No, I don't think so."

Finn regarded her thoughtfully. "In my experience, a person's either lost or they're not. There is no gray area."

The woman smiled at him. "Didn't think I'd find a philosopher all the way out here."

"It's not philosophy, it's just plain common sense," Finn told her.

To him, so-called *philosophers* referred to the gaggle of retired old men who got together every morning and sat on the sun-bleached bench in front of the general store, watching the rest of the town go through its paces and commenting on life when the spirit moved them. He was far too busy to indulge in that sort of thing.

"Well, if you don't need directions, then I'll get back to my work," he told her. The woman was clearly out of her element, but if she didn't want to talk about what she was doing out here, he wasn't about to prod her. Lost or not, it was strictly her business.

"I don't need directions, but I do have a question." She raised her voice as if to get his attention before he began hammering again.

Finn turned back to face her. She looked rather fair. He could see a sunburn in her near future if she didn't at least put the top up on her car. Skin that fair was ripe for burning.

"Which is?" he asked casually.

"Did you build this yourself?" The woman got out of her car and crossed to the freshly rebuilt front steps of the house.

Thanks to Brett, honesty had always been at the core of his behavior. His older brother expected and accepted nothing less than that. Anyone can lie, Brett maintained, but it took a real man to tell the truth each and every time, even when it wasn't easy.

"No," Finn replied. "The ranch house was already here. I just changed things around a little, replaced what needed replacing, added a little here, a little there—that kind of thing," he told her simply.

He made it sound as if he'd hammered down a few loose boards, but one look at the exterior told her that the man with the impossibly appealing physique had done a great deal more than just that. The structure looked brand-new. She knew for a fact that this part of the state was hard on its buildings and its terrain. Summers could be brutal, and they left their mark on practically everything, especially structures. The ranch house she was looking at had been resurfaced, replaced and renovated—and recently.

Connie couldn't help wondering if that craftsmanship extended to the inside of the building, as well.

There was only one way to find out.

"Could you take me on a tour of the inside of the house?" she asked brightly.

"I could," the cowboy answered but made no effort to follow through on her request.

"But?" she asked.

She made him think of a stick of dynamite about to go off. He was about ten inches taller than she was, but a stick of dynamite didn't have to be very big to make a sizable impression.

Just who was this woman, and what was she doing here? "But I don't even know who you are."

"I'm not dangerous, if that's what you're thinking," she told him.

Like he believed that.

Finn's mouth curved ever so slightly, the left side more than the right. He wondered just how many men this woman had brought to their knees with that killer smile of hers.

"There's dangerous, and then there's *dangerous,*" he replied, his eyes never leaving hers.

She raised her chin just a little, doing her best to generate an air of innocence as she assured him, "I'm neither."

The cowboy continued looking at her. The image of a human lie detector flashed through her mind for an instant. She discovered that breathing took a bit of concentration on her part.

"I don't know about that," he said. But the next moment, he seemed to shrug away his assessment of her and said, "Okay, why not? Don't lean against anything," he warned before going up the porch steps. "The paint's still fresh in places."

She had no intentions of taking away any part of

this house on her person. "I'll keep that in mind," she told him.

Connie waited for her tour guide to open the front door. If the inside looked nearly as good as the outside, she was ready to be blown away.

"After you," the cowboy told her once he'd opened the front door.

Connie crossed the threshold, taking it all in at once.

She hadn't missed her guess. The inside of the house was simplistic and all the more captivating for that. It was a house that emphasized all things Western, with just the right touch of modern thrown in to keep the decor from being completely entrenched in the past.

There were only a few pieces of furniture. For the most part, the house was empty, but then, she hadn't asked to come in just to see the furniture. She was looking to take stock of the workmanship firsthand.

She hadn't been wrong.

This cowboy did have a gift for bringing things together—and apparently, a knack for knowing just when to back off.

"How long have you been working on this?" she asked, wanting as much input from the man and *about* the man as she could get.

"Awhile," Finn replied vaguely, as if wondering just what her end game was.

While this woman had apparently been taking stock of the house as he went about showing her around the two floors, Finn did the same with her. So far, he hadn't come to any useful conclusion. She hadn't really volunteered anything except a few flattering comments about his work. He still had no idea what had brought her to Forever, or even if she *meant* to come to Forever, or was just passing by on her way to somewhere else.

"Awhile," the woman repeated, going back to what he'd said about his timetable. "Does that mean six months or six years or what?"

"Awhile means awhile," he replied in a calm voice, then added, "I'm not exactly keeping a diary on this."

"Then you're just doing this for fun?"

"Not exactly." Because he could see that she intended to stand there, waiting, until he gave her some sort of a more satisfying answer, he told her. He saw no reason not to. "It's a wedding present."

"For your bride?" she guessed.

Finn nearly choked. He didn't intend to get married for a very long time. Possibly never.

"No," he denied with feeling. "For my brother. It's *his* wedding."

"And this is his house?" she asked, turning slowly around, this time taking in a three-hundred-sixty-degree view. No doubt about it, she thought. The work done on the ranch house was magnificent.

"He says it belongs to all three of us, but Earl Robertson's will left it to him." And as far as he and Liam were concerned, this was Brett's house.

"Honor among brothers. That's refreshing."

He thought that was an odd way to phrase it. "Don't know one way or the other about *refreshing.* Do know what's right, though, and this house is right for Brett and Lady Doc."

"Lady Doc?" she repeated, slightly confused.

"That was the nickname my brother gave Alisha when she first came to Forever. Alisha's a doctor," he told her by way of a footnote. "Look, lady, I'd love to

stand around and talk some more—it's not every day
that we see a new face around here—but I really do
have to get back to work."

The woman raised her hands in mock surrender,
showing the cowboy that she was backing off and giving him back his space. "Sorry. I didn't mean to take
you away from your work."

Having said that, she turned on her heel and headed
back to her vehicle.

As he watched her walk away, Finn found himself
captivated by the way the woman's hips swayed with
every step she took. It also occurred to him at the same
time that he didn't even know her name.

"Hey," he called out.

Ordinarily, that was *not* a term Connie would answer
to. But this one time, she made an exception. People
acted differently out here. So rather than get into her
car, Connie turned around and looked at him, waiting
for the cowboy to say something further.

Raising his voice, Finn remained where he was. "You
got a name?" he asked.

"Yes, I do," Connie replied.

With that she slid in behind the steering wheel of her
car, shut her door and started up her engine.

Always leave them wanting more was an old adage
she had picked up along the way, thanks to her grandfather. Her grandfather had taught her a great many
things. He had told her, just before he passed away, that
he had great faith in her. The only thing her father had
ever conveyed to her was that she was a huge and ongoing source of disappointment to him.

Her grandfather, she knew, would have walked away
from her father a long time ago. At the very least, he

would have given up trying to please her father, given up trying to get him to take some sort of positive notice of her.

But she was too stubborn to give up.

Knocked down a number of times for one reason or another, she still got up, still dusted herself off and was still damn determined to someday make her father actually pay her a compliment—or die trying to get it out of him.

Connie spent the rest of the afternoon driving around, getting marginally acquainted with the lay of the surrounding land. She took in the reservation, as well—if driving around its perimeter could be considered taking it in. She never got out of her vehicle, never drove through the actual terrain because even circumnavigating it managed to create an almost overwhelming sadness within her.

Her father had been right about one thing. She was a child of affluence. The sight of poverty always upset her. But rather than fleeing and putting it out of her mind, what she had seen seemed to seep into her very soul. She could not imagine how people managed to go on day after day in such oppressive surroundings.

It also made her wonder why the reservation residents didn't just band together, tear some of the worst buildings down and start fresh, putting up something new in their place.

Not your problem, Con. Your father issued you a challenge. One he seemed pretty confident would make you fall flat on your face. It's up to you to show him once and for all that he's wrong about you. That he's underestimated you all along.

* * *

That thought was still replaying itself in her head when she finally drove back into Forever late that afternoon. She was hungry, and the idea of dinner—even one prepared at what she viewed to be a greasy-spoon establishment—was beginning to tempt her.

But as much as she wanted to eat, she wanted to finish up her homework even more.

In this case, her homework entailed checking out the local—and lone—bar to see the kind of people who hung out there. She wanted to meet them, mingle with them and get to know them, at least in some cursory fashion. She was going to need bodies if she hoped to get her project underway, and Murphy's was where she hoped to find at least some of them.

Right now all she knew was that her father had purchased a tract of land within Forever at a bargain price because no one else was interested in doing anything with it. A little research on her part had shown that the town was deficient in several key departments, not the least of which was that it had nowhere to put up the occasional out-of-town visitor—which she just assumed Forever had to have at least once in a while. That particular discovery was confirmed when she went to book a hotel room and found that the nearest hotel was some fifty miles away from the center of Forever.

The hick town, her father had informed her through Emerson, his right-hand man, needed to have a hotel built in its midst. Giving her the assignment, her father washed his hands of it, leaving all the details up to her.

And just like that, it became her responsibility to get the hotel built for what, on paper, amounted to a song.

Her father had hinted that if she could bring the project in on time and on budget—or better yet, *under* budget, he might just take her potential within the company more seriously.

But she needed to prove herself worthy of his regard, of his trust. And until that actually happened, he had no real use for her. He made no effort to hide the fact that he was on the verge of telling her that he no longer needed her services.

Connie had every intention of showing her father just what a vital asset she could be to his construction conglomerate. She also promised herself that she was going to make him eat his words; it was just a matter of time.

Stopping her vehicle behind Murphy's, Connie parked the car as close to the building as she could. The gleaming white sports car wasn't a rental she was driving, it was her own car. She wasn't superstitious by nature, but every good thing that had ever happened to her had happened when she was somewhere within the vicinity of the white sports car. It was, in effect, her good-luck talisman. And, as the embodiment of her good fortune, she wanted to keep it within her line of vision, ensuring that nothing could happen to it.

She intended on keeping an eye on it from inside the bar.

However, Connie quickly discovered that was an impossibility. For one thing, the bar's windows didn't face the rear lot.

Uneasy, she thought about reparking her car or coming back to Murphy's later, after dinner.

But then she reminded herself that her car had a tracking chip embedded within the steering wheel. If her car was stolen, the police could easily lay hands on it within the hour.

Provided they knew about tracking chips and how to use them, she qualified silently. She took measure of the occupants within the bar as she walked in. The first thought that crossed her mind was that the people around her could never be mistaken for the participants in a think tank.

Still looking around, she made her way to the bar, intending on ordering a single-malt beer.

A deep male voice asked her, "What'll it be?" when she reached the bar and slid onto a stool.

The voice sounded vaguely familiar, but she shrugged the thought away. She didn't know anyone here. "What kind of beer do you have on tap?" she asked, continuing to take inventory of the room.

"Good beer."

The answer had her looking at the bartender instead of the bar's patrons. When she did, her mouth dropped open.

"You," she said in stunned surprise.

"You," Finn echoed, careful to hide his initial surprise at seeing her.

Unlike the woman seated at that bar, he'd had a couple of minutes to work through his surprise. It had spiked when he first saw her walk across the threshold. Disbelief had turned into mild surprise as he watched her make her way across the floor, weaving in and out between his regular patrons.

When she'd left the ranch this morning, he'd had a vague premonition that he would be seeing her again— but he hadn't thought that it would be this soon. He should have known better. The woman had asked too many questions for someone who was just passing through on her way to somewhere else.

"So what are you?" The woman posed the question to him. "A rancher or a bartender?"

"Both," he said without the slightest bit of hesitation. Around here, a man had to wear a lot of hats if he planned on surviving. "At least, that's what my brother says."

"The one who's getting married," she recalled.

So, she had been listening. That made her a rare woman, Finn concluded. The women in his sphere of acquaintance talked, but rarely listened. "That's the one."

"You have any more brothers?"

"Yeah, he's a spare in case I wear the other one out."

The woman looked around, taking in the people on either side of her. The bar had its share of patrons, but it was far from standing-room only. Still, there were enough customers currently present—mostly male—for her to make a judgment.

"Something tells me that the men around here don't wear out easily."

"You up for testing that theory of yours out, little lady?" Kyle Masterson proposed, giving her a very thorough once-over as he sidled up to her, deliberately blocking her access to the front door.

Chapter Three

Although he remained behind the bar, Finn's presence seemed to separate the talkative cowboy from the young woman who had wandered onto Brett's ranch earlier. Finn was 85 percent certain that Kyle, a rugged, rather worn ranch hand, was harmless. But he was taking no chances in case Kyle was inspired by this woman and was tossing caution to the wind.

"Back to your corner, Masterson," Finn told him without cracking a smile. "The lady's not going to be testing out anything with you tonight."

Kyle, apparently, had other ideas. "Why don't you let her speak for herself, Murphy?" the other man proposed. "How about it, little lady?" he asked, completely ignoring Finn and moving in closer to the woman who had caught his fancy. "We could take us a stroll around the lake, maybe look up at the stars. See what happens."

His leer told her exactly what the hulking man thought was going to happen. Amused, Connie played out the line a little further. "And if nothing happens?" she posed.

"Then I will be one deeply disappointed man," Kyle told her, dramatically placing a paw of a hand over his chest. "C'mon, little lady. You don't want to be breaking my heart now, do you?" He eyed her hopefully, rather confident in the outcome of this scenario he was playing out.

"Better that than me breaking your arm, Masterson," Finn informed him, pushing his arm and hand between them as he deliberately wiped down the bar directly in the middle.

Kyle glanced from Finn to the very appealing woman with hair the color of a setting sun. It was obvious he was weighing his options. Women came and went, but there was only one saloon in the area. Being barred from Murphy's was too high a price to pay for a fleeting flirtation.

"Oh, is it like that, now?" the cowboy guessed.

"Like what?" Connie looked at the man, not sure she understood his meaning.

Amazingly deep-set eyes darted from her to the bartender and then back again, like black marbles in a bowl.

Kyle grinned at the bartender. "Don't think I really have to explain that," he concluded. Raising his glass, he toasted Finn. "Nice work, laddie." And with that, the bear of a man retreated into the crowd.

Brett approached from the far side of the bar. "Problem?" he asked, looking from his brother to the very attractive young woman at the bar. He'd taken note of the way some of his patrons were watching her, as if she were a tasty morsel and they were coming off a seven-day fast in the desert. That spelled trouble—unless it was averted quickly.

"No, no problem," Finn replied tersely. As grateful as he was to Brett and as much as he loved and respected him, he hated feeling that his older brother was looking over his shoulder. He wasn't twelve anymore, and hadn't been for quite some time. "Everything's fine."

"That all depends," Connie said, contradicting Finn's response. She had a different take on things, one that had nothing to do with the hulking cowboy and his unsuccessful advances.

Brett looked at her with interest. "On?"

"On how many men I can get to sign on with me," Connie replied.

The sudden, almost syncopated shift of bodies, all in her direction, plainly testified that the exchange between the young woman and two of the saloon's owners was far from private. Leers instantly materialized, and interweaving voices were volunteering to sign on with her no matter what the cause.

In Finn's estimation, it was obvious what the men's leers indicated that they *believed* they were signing up for—and tool belts had nothing to do with it.

To keep the crowd from getting rowdy and out of control, Finn quickly asked the question, "Sign on to what end?" before Brett could.

Crystal-blue eyes swept over the sea of faces, taking preliminary measure of the men in the saloon. "I need a crew of able-bodied men to help me build a hotel," she answered.

"Build a hotel?" an older man in the back echoed

incredulously. By the way he repeated the proposed endeavor, it was obvious that a hotel was the last structure he would have thought the town needed. He wasn't alone. "Where you putting a hotel?"

Connie answered as if she was fielding legitimate questions at a business meeting. "The deed says it's to be constructed on the east end of town, just beyond the general store."

"Deed? What deed?" someone else within the swelling throng crowing around her asked.

Connie addressed that question, too, as if it had everything riding on it. She had learned how *not* to treat men by observing her father. He treated the men around him as if they were morons—until they proved otherwise. She did the exact opposite.

Employees—and potential employees—had her respect until they did something to lose it.

"The deed that my company purchased a little less than three weeks ago," she replied, then waited for the next question.

"Deeds are for ranches," Nathan McHale, Murphy's' most steadfast and longest-attending patron said into his beer, "not hunks of this town."

Connie shifted her stool to get a better look at the man. "I'm afraid you're wrong there, Mr—?" She left the name open, waiting for the man to fill it in for her.

Nathan paused to take a long sip from his glass, as if that would enable him to remember the answer to the newcomer's question. Swallowing, he looked up, a somewhat silly smile on his wide, round face.

"McHale."

"Don't worry about him, missy. Ol' Nathan's used to being wrong. The second he steps into his house, his wife starts telling him he's wrong," Alan Dunn, one of the older men at the far end of the bar chuckled.

Nathan seemed to take no offense. Instead, what he did take was another longer, more fortifying drink from his glass, this time managing to drain it. Putting the glass down on the bar, he pushed it over toward the bartender—the younger of the two behind the bar.

Connie noticed that the latter eyed his customer for a moment, as if deciding whether or not to cut the man off yet. She knew that she definitely would—and was rather surprised when the bartender decided not to.

For all his girth and folds, McHale looked like a child at Christmas, his eyes lighting up and a wreath of smiles taking over his rounded face. He gave the bartender who had refilled his glass a little salute as well as widening his appreciative smile.

Using both hands, he drew the glass to him, careful not to spill a single drop. Then, just before he took his first sip of his new drink, McHale raised it ever so slightly in a symbolic toast to the newcomer. "You were saying?"

"I was saying—" Connie picked up the thread of her conversation where it had temporarily stopped "—that my construction company has purchased the deed for a section of the town's land."

"You here to see if the town wants to buy it back?" Brett asked, curious.

There'd been complaints from time to time that there was nowhere to stay if anyone was stranded in Forever overnight. But things always got sorted out for the best. The sheriff enjoyed telling people that was how he and his wife, Olivia, had first gotten together. On her way to track down her runaway sister, Olivia'd had no intentions of staying in Forever. Her car had had other ideas. She'd wound up relying on the hospitality of the town's resident wise woman and diner owner, Miss Joan.

"No," Connie replied patiently, "I'm here to build a hotel."

"A hotel?" It was someone else's turn to question the wisdom of that. Obviously, more than one person found this to be an odd undertaking. "What for?" the person asked.

"For people to stay in, you nitwit," the man sitting on the next stool informed him, coupling the sentence with a jab in the ribs.

"What people?" a third man asked. "Everyone around here's got a home."

Connie was ready for that, as well. She'd read up on Forever before ever setting out to see it. She knew her father wouldn't have given her an easy project. That had never been his way.

"Well, if there's a hotel here," she said, addressing her answer to the entire bar, "it might encourage people to come to Forever."

"Why would we want people to come here?" the man who'd asked her the question queried again. "We got all the people we know what to do with now."

Several other voices melded together, agreeing with him.

Connie was far from put off, but before she could say anything, the good-looking man she'd seen this afternoon beat her to it.

"She's talking about the town growing, Clyde," Finn pointed out. "You know, *progress*."

Connie fairly beamed at the bartender, relieved that

at least *someone* understood what she was trying to convey. "Exactly," she cried.

"Hell, progress is highly overrated," Clyde declared sourly. He downed his shot of whiskey, waited for it to settle in, then said, "I like this town just fine the way it is. Peaceful," he pronounced with a nod of his bald head.

This was not the time or the place to become embroiled in a hard sell. The land officially now belonged to her father's company, thanks to some negotiations she had not been privy to. That meant that the decision as to what to do or not do with it was not up to the people lining the bar.

Be that as it may, she was still going to need them, or at least some of them, to help with the hotel's construction. That meant she couldn't afford to alienate *any* of them. Besides the fact that local labor was always less expensive than bringing construction workers in, hiring locals always built goodwill. There wasn't a town or city in the country that hadn't felt the bite of cutbacks and didn't welcome an opportunity to obtain gainful employment, even on a temporary basis.

This was not the first project she was associated with, although it was the first that she was allowed to helm on her own. She already knew she was going to need a few skilled workers, like someone who could handle the backhoe, and those people would be flown in. But as for the rest of it, the brawn and grunt part, those positions she hoped she would be able to fill with people from in and around the town. The one thing she knew she could count on was that extra money was always welcomed.

Connie raised her voice, addressing Clyde. "I promise not to disturb the peace." For good measure, she elaborately crossed her heart. "I came here to offer you jobs. I need manpower to help me make this hotel a reality."

This time it was Kyle Masterson who spoke up. He hired out to some of the local ranchers, but he had never been afraid of hard work. "What kind of money we talking about?"

She made eye contact with the big man. "Good money," she responded in all seriousness.

"How much?" Brett asked, trying to pin her down not for himself, but for the men who frequented Murphy's, men he knew were struggling with hard times and bills that were stamped *past due*.

"Depends on the level of skills you bring to the job," she replied honestly. "That'll be decided on an individual basis."

"Who's gonna do the deciding?" another man at the bar asked.

The question came from behind her. Connie turned to face whoever had spoken up. They were going to find out sooner or later, might as well be sooner, she thought. "I am."

"Big decisions," the man responded with a laugh. He eyed her in clear amusement. She obviously looked like a slip of a thing in comparison to the men she was addressing. "You sure you're up to it, honey?"

Connie had never had any slack cut for her. Her father had made sure that she was treated like a crew member no matter what job she was doing. The fact that she was willing to—and did—work hard had not failed to impress the men, even if it seemed to have no effect whatsoever on her father.

Connie looked the man asking the question directly in the eye and said with no hesitation, "I am. Are you?"

Her answer generated laughter from the other men around the bar.

"She's got you there, Roy. Looks like you better make nice if you want to earn a little extra for your pocket," the man next to him advised.

"It'll be more than just a *little extra*," Connie was quick to correct. "And if you work hard and get this project in on time and on budget, everyone on the project will get a bonus."

The promise of a bonus, even an unspecified one, never failed to stir up positive goodwill, and this time was no exception. Snippets of responses and more questions furiously flew through the air.

"Sounds good!"

"Count me in."

"Hey, is the bonus gonna be as big as the salary?"

"You calculating that by the hour or by the day?"

Finn had stood by, holding his tongue for the most part. The woman doing the talking had intrigued him right from the start when she'd first approached him this morning. Since his bent was toward building, anyway, he figured that he might have to do a little negotiation with Brett to get some free time in order to get involved on this construction project.

But he didn't see that as being a problem. Brett was fairly reasonable when it came to things like this. He'd given Liam a lot of slack so he could practice and rehearse with his band. As far as older brothers went, a man would have to go to great lengths to find someone who was anywhere near as good as Brett.

"Looks like you've got them all fired up and excited,"

Finn commented to the young woman as he checked her glass to see if she needed a refill yet.

"How about you? Do I have you all fired up and excited?" she asked, going with his wording. Connie shifted the stool to face him. The man was still her first choice to head up the work crew. The other men might be good—or even more capable—but so far this so-called bartender's handiwork had been the only one she'd seen firsthand.

But the moment she phrased the question, she saw her mistake.

Finn had every intention of giving her a flippant answer, but there was something in her eyes, something that had him skidding to a grinding halt and reassessing not just his answer, but a hell of a lot of other things, as well. Things that had nothing to do with tools and construction.

The woman on the stool before him probably had no idea that she had the kind of eyes that seemed to peer into a man's soul while making him reevaluate everything that had happened in his life up to this singular moment in time.

A beat went by before he realized that she was still waiting for him to respond.

"Yes," he answered quietly, his eyes on hers. He found he couldn't look away even if he wanted to—which he didn't. "You do," he added in the same quiet tone.

Despite the surrounding din, his voice managed to undulate along her skin and lodge itself directly beneath it.

It took Connie more than a full second to come to, then another full second to find her voice and another one after that to realize that her mouth and throat had gone bone-dry. If she said more than a couple of words, they could come out in a comical croak, thereby negating whatever serious, or semiserious thing she was about to say.

Taking the drink that was on the bar before her, she emptied the glass in an effort to restore her voice to its initial working order. Tears suddenly gathered in her eyes as flames coasted through her veins. She'd forgotten her glass contained whiskey, not something less potent.

"Good," she managed to say without the word sticking to the roof of her mouth. Taking a breath, she willed herself to be steady and then completed her sentence. Nothing could interfere with work. She wouldn't allow it to. "Because I have just the position for you."

Most likely not the same position I have in mind for you.

The thought, materializing out of nowhere, took Finn completely by surprise. He was extremely grateful that the words hadn't come out of his mouth. It wasn't his intention to embarrass either himself or the young woman.

But he found that he was having trouble banishing the thought out of his head. The image seemed to be all but burned into his brain. An image that was suddenly making him feel exceedingly warm.

Finn focused on the hotel she had been talking about. This represented the first move toward progress that had been made in Forever in quite some time.

"What kind of a position?" he asked her out loud, rubbing perhaps a bit too hard at a spot on the bar's counter.

"Is there someplace we can talk?" she asked him.

Finn thought of the room that was just above the saloon. Initially, their uncle Patrick had lived there when he'd owned and operated Murphy's. On his passing, it had been just an extra room that all three of them had sporadically availed themselves of if the occasion warranted it. Currently, however, Brett's fiancée was staying there, but only when she wasn't working—or staying with Brett at the ranch. The clinic was still open, which meant that the room would be empty.

But Finn didn't feel comfortable just commandeering it—besides, Brett would undoubtedly have his head if he found out.

The next moment, Finn felt he had come up with a viable alternative. "Have you had dinner yet?" he asked the woman.

"No." She had been so worked up about this project, so eager to get it going, that she had completely forgotten about eating.

"Then I know just the place we can talk. Brett," Finn called, turning toward his brother. "I'm taking my break now."

Motivated by his interest in anything that had an effect on the town, Brett had discreetly listened in on the conversation between Finn and this woman. He appeared mildly amused at his brother's choice of words. "You planning on being back in fifteen minutes?"

"A couple of breaks, then—plus my dinner break," Finn added for good measure.

"You already took that, don't you remember?" Brett deadpanned.

"Then my breakfast break," Finn shot back, exasperated.

Brett inclined his head. "That should work," he told

Finn. "Just don't forget to come back," he called after his brother as Finn made his way around the bar.

Escorting the woman through the throng of patrons, most of whom were now keenly interested in what this newcomer to their town had to offer, Finn waved a hand over his head. This signified to Brett that he had heard him and was going to comply—eventually.

"Where are we going?" Connie asked once they made it through the front door.

"To dinner," Finn repeated.

"And that would be—?"

Finn grinned. "At Miss Joan's," he answered.

"Miss Joan's?" she repeated. The name meant nothing to her.

"The diner," Finn prompted. "It's the only restaurant in town."

For now, Connie corrected silently. Plans for the hotel included a restaurant on the premises.

But for the time being, she thought it best to keep that to herself.

Chapter Four

Since she had already ascertained that it was the only so-called restaurant in town, Connie had initially intended on checking the diner out after she left Murphy's. But seeing the cowboy who had, she admitted—although strictly to herself—taken her breath away—both because of his craftsmanship *and* his physique—she'd temporarily lost sight of the plan she'd laid out for herself to round out her first day in Forever.

The bartending cowboy opened the door for her and she stepped into the diner. Connie scanned the area, only to discover that everyone in the diner was looking right back at her.

Before taking another step, she unconsciously squared her shoulders.

Inside the brash, confident young woman who faced

down all sorts of obstacles, beat the heart of a shy, young girl, the one whose father had always made her feel, through his words and through his actions, that she wasn't good enough. That she couldn't seem to measure up to the standards he had set down before her.

Even though he had told her, time and again, that she was a source of constant disappointment to him, Calvin Carmichael had insisted that, from the relatively young age of fourteen, his only daughter replace her late mother and act as a hostess at the parties that he threw for his business associates.

It was while acting as hostess at those very same parties that she developed her polish and her poise—at least on the surface. Only her father knew how to chip away at that veneer to get to the frightened little girl who existed just beneath that carefully crafted surface.

To be fair, her father had been just as demanding of her brother, Conrad. But Conrad had been far more rebellious than she ever was. He absolutely refused to be bullied and left home for parts unknown the moment that he turned eighteen.

She would have given *anything* to go with him, but she was only fourteen at the time, and Conrad had enough to do, looking after himself. He couldn't take on the burden of being responsible for a child, as well.

At least that was what she had told herself when he'd left without her.

So Connie resigned herself to remaining in her father's world, desperately treading water, determined to survive as best she could. Not only surviving, but vowing to one day make her father realize how wrong he'd been about her all along. It was the one thing that had kept her going all this time.

The *only* thing.

Was it her imagination, or were the occupants of the diner looking at her as if she were some sort of an unknown entity?

She inclined her head in her companion's direction, lowering her voice to a whisper. "You weren't kidding about not many tourists passing through this town. These people really aren't used to seeing strangers walking their streets, are they?"

Finn's mouth curved ever so slightly. "Forever's not exactly on the beaten path to anywhere," he pointed out. Although, even if Forever was a regular bustling hotbed of activity, he could see this woman still turning heads wherever she went.

"That's becoming pretty clear," Connie whispered to him.

"Been wondering when you'd finally step in here," the thin, older woman with the somewhat overly vibrant red hair said as she sidled up to the couple to greet them. "What'll it be for you and your friend here, Finn?" she asked, nodding her head toward the other woman. "Table or counter?"

Connie was about to answer "Counter," but the man the hostess had referred to as "Finn" answered the question first.

"Table."

The woman nodded. "Table it is. You're in luck. We've got one table left right over here." So saying, the redhead led them over to a table near the kitchen. There was only one problem, as Connie saw it. There was a man still sitting at it.

Connie regarded the other woman. "But it's occupied," she protested. Did the woman think they were going to join the man?

The woman appeared unfazed. "Hal here finished his dinner," she explained, indicating the table's lone occupant. "He's just a might slow in getting to his feet, aren't you, Hal?" she said, giving her customer exactly ten seconds of her attention. Then she looked around for the closest waitress and summoned her. "Dora." She beckoned the young blonde over. "Clear the table for Finn and his friend, please." She offered the couple just a hint of a smile. "I'll be back to get your orders in a few minutes. Sit, take a load off," she encouraged, patting Connie on the shoulder. And then she added, "Relax," and turned the single word into a strict command.

Dora was quick to pick up and clear away the empty dinner plate from the table. Within two minutes, Dora retreated, and Connie realized that she and the cowboy were left alone with their menus.

Connie was only mildly interested in glancing over the menu and that was purely out of a curiosity about the locals' eating preferences. As always, eating, for Connie, took a backseat to orientation.

She decided to begin with the very basics. Names. Specially, his name. "That woman, the one with the red hair, she called you Finn."

"That's because she knows my name," he replied simply. Finn had a question of his own to ask her. "But I don't know yours."

"I didn't tell you?" The omission on her part surprised her. She'd gotten so caught up in getting her operation set up and hopefully rolling soon in this tiny postage-stamp-size town that common, everyday details had slipped her mind.

"You didn't tell me," Finn confirmed, then added with yet another, even more appealing hint of a smile, "I'm not old enough to be forgetful yet."

Not by a long shot, Connie caught herself thinking. Just for a moment, she got lost in the man's warm, incredibly inviting smile.

Get back on track, Con. Drooling over the employees isn't going to get this project done—and it just might mess everything all up.

One way or another, she'd been lobbying her father for a chance to show her stuff for a while. Now that she finally had it, she was *not* about to allow something as unpredictable as hormones betray her.

"My name is Constance Carmichael," she told him, putting out her hand.

"Nice to meet you, Ms. Carmichael." Her hand felt soft, almost delicate in his, he couldn't help thinking. His hand all but swallowed hers up. "I'm Finn Murphy."

"Like the bar?" she asked, trying to fit two more pieces together.

"Like the bar," he confirmed.

"My father's Calvin Carmichael," Connie added.

She was accustomed to seeing instant recognition whenever she mentioned her father's name. The second she did, a light would come into people's eyes.

There was no such light in the bartending cowboy's eyes. It prompted her to say, "He founded Carmichael Construction Corporation."

Still nothing.

Finn lifted his broad shoulders in a self-deprecating shrug and apologized. "Sorry, 'fraid it doesn't ring a bell for me."

That was when it hit her. "I guess it wouldn't," Connie said. "The corporation only erects buildings in the larger cities." The moment she said it, she knew she had made a tactical mistake. The man sitting across the table from her might take her words to be insulting. "I mean—"

Finn raised his hand to stop whatever she might be about to say. "Forever *is* small," he assured her. "And that leads me to my question for you."

Her eyes never left his. "Go ahead."

Having given him the green light, Connie braced herself for whatever was going to be coming her way. Something told her that Finn was one of the key players she would need to solidly win over and keep on her side if she hoped to not only get this project underway, but completed, as well.

"If your dad's company just builds things in big cities, then what are you doing scouting around someplace like Forever?" It didn't make any sense to him. He loved the place, but there wasn't anything exceptional about Forever to make outsiders suddenly sit up and take notice.

It's personal, Connie thought, silently answering him.

Granted, the man was pretty close to what one of her friends would have termed *drop-dead gorgeous,* but she didn't know a single thing about him other than he was good with his hands and could tend bar, so trusting him with any part of her actual life story would have been beyond foolish, beyond reckless and definitely stupid.

Connie searched around for something neutral to say that would satisfy Finn's curiosity. And then she came up with the perfect response.

"He's branching out," she told him, then fell back on

what had always been a surefire tactic: flattery. "Besides, there's a lot of potential in little towns like yours."

Though he wasn't quite sold, Finn quietly listened to what this stunningly attractive woman had to say. For now, he'd allow her to think he'd accepted her flimsy explanation. Since she was obviously sticking around, he figured that eventually, he'd find out just what part of what she had said was the truth.

Miss Joan picked that moment to all but materialize out of nowhere, a well-worn pad held poised in her hand. "So, you two ready to order yet?" she asked them.

Finn had barely glanced at the menu, but then, he didn't really have to. His favorite meal was a permanent fixture on the second page.

"I am," he told Miss Joan, "but I don't think that Ms. Carmichael's had a chance to look at the menu just yet."

Rather than go with the excuse that Finn had just provided her with, Connie placed her menu on top of his and told the woman, "I'll just have whatever he's having."

"How do you know it's any good?" Finn challenged, mildly surprised by her choice. "Or that you'll like it?"

"I'm a quick judge of character, and you wouldn't order anything that was too filling, or bad for you. You told your brother that you were coming back to work the rest of your shift. That means that you can't be too full or you'll get drowsy," she concluded. "Besides, I'm not very fussy."

Miss Joan smiled in approval, then nodded toward her as she said to Finn, "This one's smart. Might want to keep her hanging around for a bit. Okay, boy," Miss Joan said, shifting gears when she saw the slight change of color in Finn's complexion, "what'll it be?"

Finn placed his order, asking for a no-frills burger and a small order of home fries, along with some iced coffee. Miss Joan duly noted his order, then murmured, "Times two," before she glanced over toward Finn's companion. She waited for the young woman to change her mind.

She didn't.

About to leave, Miss Joan turned abruptly and looked at Finn's tablemate. "Ms. Carmichael," she repeated thoughtfully.

"Yes?" Connie considered the older woman, not quite knowing what to expect.

The light of recognition came into Miss Joan's sharp, amber eyes. "Your daddy wouldn't be Calvin C. Carmichael now, would he?"

"You know my father?"

She would have expected the bartender and the people around his age to know who her father was. Since he apparently didn't, she felt it was a given that someone around this woman's age—someone she assumed had been born here and most likely would die here—would have never even *heard* of her father.

"Mostly by reputation," Miss Joan admitted. She thought back for a moment. "Although I did meet the man once a long time ago. He was just starting out then," she recalled. And then her smile broadened. "He was a pistol, all right. Confident as all get-out, wasn't about to let anything or anyone stop him." Miss Joan nodded to herself as more facts came back to her. "He was bound and determined to build himself an empire. From what I hear now and again, he did pretty much that."

Rather than wait for any sort of a comment or a confirmation from Finn's companion, Miss Joan asked another question, a fond smile curving her mouth. "How's your mother doing?"

"She died a little over twelve years ago," Connie answered without missing a single beat, without indicating that the unexpected reference to her mother felt as if she had just been shot point-blank in her chest. Twelve years, and the wound was still fresh.

Usually, she had some sort of an inkling, a forewarning that the conversation was going to turn toward a question about or a reference to her mother. In that case, Connie was able to properly brace herself for the sharp slash of pain that always accompanied any mention of her mother. But this had been like a shot in the dark, catching her completely off guard and totally unprepared and unprotected.

Sympathy flowed through Miss Joan and instantly transformed and softened the woman's features.

"Oh, I'm so sorry to hear that, dear." She placed a comforting hand on the younger woman's shoulder. "As I recall, she was a lovely, lovely woman. A real lady," she added with genuine feeling. Dropping her hand, Miss Joan began to withdraw. "I'll get that order for you now," she promised as she took her leave.

The woman sitting opposite him appeared to be trying very hard to shut down, Finn thought. He was more than familiar with that sort of reflexive action, building up high walls so that any pain attached to the loss was minimized—or as diminished as it could be, given the circumstances.

"I'm sorry about that," Finn said to her the moment they were alone again. "Miss Joan doesn't mean to come on as if she's prying. Most of the time, she just has a knack for getting to the heart of things," he told her gently.

"Nothing to apologize for," Connie answered, shaking off both his words and the feeling the older woman's question had generated. "The woman—Miss Joan, is it?" she asked. When Finn nodded, Connie went on. "Miss Joan was just making idle conversation."

Her mouth curved just a little as she allowed herself a bittersweet moment to remember. But remembering details, at times, was becoming harder and harder to do.

"She actually said something very sweet about my mother. At this point, it's been so long since she's been gone that there are times I feel as if I just imagined her, that I never had a mother at all." She shrugged somewhat self-consciously. She'd said too much. "It's rather nice to hear someone talk about her, remember her in the same light that I do."

Because his heart was going out to her, Finn had this sudden desire to make her realize that she wasn't the only one who had suffered this sort of numbing loss so early in her life.

"I lost my mother when I was a kid, too. Both my parents, actually," Finn amended.

Despite his laid-back attitude about life and his easygoing manner, to this day it still hurt to talk about his parents' deaths. One moment they had been in his life, the next, they weren't. It was enough to shake a person clear down to their very core.

"Car accident," he said, annotating the story. "My uncle Patrick took my brothers and me in." A look Connie couldn't fathom crossed his face. The next moment, she understood why. "A few years later, Uncle Patrick died, too."

Completely captivated by his narrative, she waited for Finn to continue. When he didn't, she asked, "Who took care of you and your brothers after that? Or were you old enough to be on your own?"

"I was fourteen," he said, answering her question in his own way. "Brett had just graduated from high school. He was turning eighteen the following week, so he petitioned to be officially declared our guardian."

What he had only recently discovered was that his brother had done that at great personal sacrifice—the girl Brett loved was setting out for the west coast. She'd asked Brett to come with her. Given a choice between following his heart and living up to his responsibility, his older brother had chosen responsibility—and never said a word about it.

"I guess you might say that Brett actually raised Liam and me—it just became official that year," Finn concluded fondly.

He and Brett had their occasional differences, but there was no way he could ever repay his brother for what Brett had done for him as well as Liam.

Connie laughed shortly. "When I was fourteen, my brother took off." She said the words dismissively, giving no indication how hurt she'd been when Conrad left her behind.

"College?" Finn guessed.

She actually had no idea where her brother went or what he did once he left her life. She hadn't heard from him in all these years.

"Maybe." She thought that over for a second. It didn't feel right to her. Conrad had been neither studious nor patient. "Although I doubt it. My father wanted my brother to go to college, and Conrad wanted to do whatever my father didn't want him to do."

"Is that why you're working for Carmichael Construction?" he asked. "Because your father wants you to?"

Remembering the look on her father's face when they had struck this deal, Connie laughed at the suggestion. Having her as anything but a lowly underling in the company was *not* on her father's agenda. The man was not pushing her in an attempt to groom her for bigger, better things. He was pushing her because he wanted to get her to finally give up and settle into the role of family hostess permanently.

"Actually," she replied crisply, "my father doesn't think I have anything to offer the company. I'm working at the corporation because *I* want to," Connie emphasized.

Reevaluating the situation, Finn read between the lines. And then smiled. "Out to prove that he's wrong, is that it?"

It startled her that he'd hit the nail right on the head so quickly, but she was not about to admit anything of the kind to someone who was, after all, still a stranger.

She tossed her hair over her shoulder. "Out to build the very best damn hotel that I can," she corrected.

Her voice sounded a little too formal and removed to her own ear. After all, the man had just been nice to her. She shouldn't be treating him as if she thought he had leprosy.

So after a beat, she added, "And if that, along the way, happens to prove to my father that he'd been wrong about me all these years, well, then, that's just icing on the cake."

Icing. That was what she made him think of, Finn realized. Light, frothy icing—with a definite, tangy kick to it.

Finn leaned back in his chair, scrutinizing the woman he'd brought to the diner. The next few months were shaping up to be very interesting, he decided.

Chapter Five

"How would you like to come and work for me?"

The question caught Finn completely off guard, but he was able to keep any indication of his surprise from registering on his face.

Rather than laughing or turning the sexy-looking woman down outright, he decided to play along for a little while and see where this was going.

"Doing what?" he asked her, sounding neither interested nor disinterested, just mildly curious as to what was behind her offer.

He'd lowered his voice and just for a split second, Connie felt as if they were having a far more intimate conversation than one involving the construction of the town's first hotel.

His question caused scenarios to flash through her brain, scenarios that had absolutely *nothing* to do with the direction of the conversation or what she was attempting to accomplish.

Scenarios that included just the two of them—and no hotel in sight.

She'd never had anything that could be labeled as an actual *relationship,* but it had been a while between even casual liaisons. The truth of it was, she'd gotten so involved in trying to play a larger part in the construction company, not to mention in getting her father to come around, she'd wound up sacrificing everything else to that one narrow goal.

And that included having anything that even remotely resembled a social life.

Just now, she had felt the acute lack.

The next second, she'd banished the entire episode from her mind.

Without realizing it, she wet her lips before answering his question. "I want you to head up my construction crew for the new hotel."

She might not have been aware of the small, reflexive action, but Finn definitely was. It drew his attention to the shape of her lips—and the fleeting impulse to discover what those lips would have felt like against his own.

Reining in his thoughts, Finn focused on what she had just said. The only conclusion he could reach was that she had to be putting him on.

"The fact that I've never headed up a construction crew before doesn't bother you?" he asked, doing nothing to hide his skepticism.

Connie shrugged carelessly.

"There always has to be a first time," she told him.

That wasn't his point. "Granted, but—"

She wanted him for the job, but there had to be others in this blot of a town who were qualified for the position. What she'd seen at Murphy's convinced her of his leadership qualities. She was not about to beg.

"Look, if you don't want the job, just say so. I'll understand."

He raised his hand to stop her before she could go off on a tangent—or for that matter, leave. When he came right down to it, he'd be more than happy to accept her offer. But there were extenuating circumstances—even if he was to believe that she was really serious.

"Trust me," he told her, "it's not that I don't want to."

If this had been a legitimate offer, he would have snapped it up in an instant. He'd had a chance to compare how he felt when he was working on making something become a tangible reality—first the bathroom for the room above the saloon, and then restoring and renovating Brett's ranch house. He had to admit that was when he felt as if he'd come into his own, when he felt as if he'd finally found something he enjoyed doing that he was really good at.

Those were all reasons for him to pursue this line of business—God knew there was more than enough work for a builder in the area.

But that notwithstanding, Constance Carmichael had no way of knowing any of that. The woman had only been in Forever a few hours, not nearly enough time to orient herself about anyone or anything. Besides, there wasn't anyone to talk to about the quality of work he did because Brett—and Alisha—were the only ones who would have that sort of input for this woman. As far as he knew, Connie hadn't talked to either one of them about him—or about anything else for that matter.

Since she'd seen for herself that strangers really *were* rare in Forever, her fishing around for workers would have instantly become the topic of conversation.

He had no doubt that now that they had left Murphy's, the rest of the patrons were busy talking about the hotel that she had come to build. The skeptics would maintain that the project would never get off the ground because Forever didn't need a hotel, while the hopefuls would declare that it was high time progress finally paid Forever a visit.

Every one of those patrons would secretly be hoping that the promise of extra employment would actually find its way to Forever, at least for the duration of this project.

And he was definitely in that group.

"It's just that," he continued honestly, "I don't quite understand why you would want me in that sort of capacity."

The simple truth was that Connie had good gut instincts, and she'd come to rely on them.

"When I drove by the ranch house this morning, I liked what I saw."

The second the words were out of her mouth, Connie realized what they had to have sounded like to Finn. It was a struggle to keep the heat from rising up her cheeks and discoloring them. She did her best to retrace her steps.

"I mean, you looked like someone who knew what he was doing." That still didn't say what she wanted to say, Connie thought in frustration.

She tried again, deliberately refraining from apologizing or commenting on her seemingly inability to say what she meant. She did *not* want this cowboy bartender getting the wrong idea.

Trying it one more time, Connie cleared her throat and made one last attempt at saving face as well as stating her case.

"What I'm trying to say is that I was impressed with what you had apparently done with the ranch house you said that your brother inherited."

"How do you know what I did and what was already there?" Finn asked.

"When you've been in the construction business for as long as I have, you develop an eye for it," she told him.

Finn didn't bother challenging that outright, instinctively knowing that she would take it as a personal attack on her abilities. But what he did challenge was her timeline, her claim to having years of experience.

"And just how long have you been *in the business?*" he asked. "Ten weeks?" he hazarded a guess, given her fresh appearance and her less than orthodox approach to the work.

Connie's eyes narrowed. Maybe she was wrong about this cowboy. "Try more like ten years."

Finn stared at her. The woman before him was far too young to have had that many years invested in almost *anything* except for just plain growing up. "You're kidding."

"Why would I joke about something like that?" she asked, not understanding why he would ever *think* something like that. "I got a job in the company right out of high school, working part-time. What that amounted to was any time I wasn't in college, working toward my degree, I was on one site or another, learning the trade firsthand."

Since she'd brought the subject up, he was curious. "What was your major in college?"

"It was a split one, actually," she answered. "Architecture and engineering. And I minored in business," she added.

New admiration rose in his eyes as he regarded her. "A triple threat, eh?"

She didn't see herself as a triple threat, just as prepared—and said so. "I wanted to be prepared for any possibility."

Finn nodded. His opinion of her was taking on a different form. The woman sitting opposite him, seemingly enjoying a rather cheap dinner, was multidimensional. To begin with, she had the face of an angel and the body, from what he could tell, of a model.

If she wasn't exaggerating about her background, the woman wasn't just a triple threat, she was a barely harnessed dynamo.

"Well, I think you've covered that," he told her with no small appreciation.

Because of her father, Connie was accustomed to being on the receiving end of a great deal of empty flattery uttered by men who wanted to use her as a way to get ahead with her father. She would have been inclined to say that was what was going on now, but something told her that Finn Murphy wasn't given to offering up empty flattery—or making empty gestures, either. That put his words under the heading of a genuine compliment.

"Thank you," she said quietly.

Finn leaned across the table. "Let's say, for the sake

of argument, that I'm interested in working for you,"
he began. "Exactly what is it that you see me doing?"

"What I already said," she told him. "Heading up
the work crew."

"You mean like telling people what to do?"

She nodded. "And seeing that they do it," she added
with a hint of a smile. "That's a very important point,"
she underscored.

This didn't seem quite real to him. Who did business
this way, just come waltzing into town, making snap
decisions just by *looking* at people?

"And you really think I'm the one for the job by
spending fifteen minutes looking at my handiwork on
the ranch house?" he asked her incredulously.

"That and the way you handled yourself at the bar,"
she told him.

"You intend to have me serve drinks on the job?"
he asked wryly. In actuality, he had no idea what his
job at Murphy's would have to do with the job she was
supposedly hiring him for.

"The way you handled *the men* at the bar," Connie
corrected herself, emphasizing what she viewed was the
crucial part. "You have an air of authority about you—
it's evident in everything you do. And just so you know,
that air of authority doesn't have to be loud," she told
him, second-guessing that he would point out that he
had hardly said a word and when he had, none of the
words had been voiced particularly loudly.

"The upshot of all this is that men listen to you,"
she concluded.

She was thinking specifically of the man who had
tried to hit on her at the bar. Finn had made the man back
off without causing a scene of any sort, and she appreci-

ated that—and saw the merit in that sort of behavior—on many levels.

"When's this job supposed to start?" he asked. "Brett's getting married in a couple of months. I can't just leave him high and dry. He needs someone to run Murphy's while he and Alisha are on their honeymoon."

She assumed that *Alisha* and the woman he had referred to earlier as *Lady Doc* were one and the same, although she wasn't really interested in names.

"We can make arrangements regarding that when the time comes," she promised. "Besides, I gather that most of Murphy's' business is conducted after six." She raised a quizzical eyebrow, waiting for his confirmation.

"Most of it," Finn agreed. "But not all of it. Brett opens the doors officially at noon, just in case someone really needs to start drowning their sorrows earlier than six."

"There's a third brother, right?"

"Liam's more into providing the music for Murphy's than he is into actually serving the drinks."

"But he can, right?"

Finn inclined his head. "Right."

That meant the solution to Finn's problem was a very simple one.

"Then you or Brett tell Liam that his services as a bartender are more important than his playing whatever it is that he plays."

"Guitar," Finn prompted. And family pride had him adding, "And he's pretty damn good. A better musician than a bartender," he told her.

That might be so, but in her estimation, this third brother's talent was not the source of the problem. Apparently, Finn needed a little more convincing.

"I guess it all boils down to what do *you* want more? To continue working at the bar, or to stretch your wings and try doing something new, try challenging yourself," she urged. "Maybe," she concluded, "it's time to put yourself first for a change."

What she had just suggested he saw as being selfish and self-centered. "That's not how family works," he told her.

"That's *exactly* how family works," she corrected with feeling. "*If* the members of that family want to get ahead in the world," she qualified, her eyes meeting his, challenging him to say otherwise.

For a moment, Finn actually thought about terminating the informal meeting then and there. He debated getting up and walking out, but then he decided that the young woman with the blue-diamond eyes apparently was here on her little mission and that if someone didn't come to her aid and pitch in, this whirling dervish in a dress would spin herself right into a huge pratfall—and a very painful one at that.

But first, she needed to be straightened out.

"I think there's something you have to realize," he told her in a slow, easy drawl that belied what he felt was the seriousness of his message.

"And that is...?" she asked.

"The people in Forever aren't really all that interested in 'getting ahead in the world' as you put it," he told her. "If they were, they would have left the area when they graduated high school, if not sooner. We're well aware that there's a big world out there, with bigger opportunities than Forever could *ever* possibly offer.

"But that's not what's important to us," he stressed, looking at her to see if he was getting through to her at all. It wasn't about the money or getting ahead; it was the pride in getting something done and done well. "You might find that bit of information useful when you're working with us."

This is a whole different world, Connie couldn't help thinking. It was totally foreign from anything she was accustomed to. But there was a bit of charm to this philosophy, to this way of viewing things—she just didn't want that *charm* getting in the way of her end goal: completing the hotel and ultimately getting it on its feet.

"I appreciate you sharing that with me," she told Finn.

He grinned. He could still read between the lines. "No, you don't. You think what I'm saying is hopelessly lazy at its worst. Horribly unproductive at its very best."

"Fortunately, I don't have to think about it at all," she told him, then smiled broadly. "Because I have you for that—" And then she realized that he still hadn't accepted the job in so many words. "Unless you've decided to turn down my offer."

"It's not an offer yet," he pointed out to her. "It's only a proposition. To be an offer," he explained when she looked at him in confusion, "you would have had to have mentioned a salary—and you haven't."

"You're right," Connie realized, then nodded her head. That, at least, could be fixed immediately. "My mistake." She rectified it in the next breath by quoting Finn a rather handsome salary.

"A month?" Finn asked, trying to put the amount in perspective. She had just quoted a sum that was a more than decent amount.

Connie shook her head. "No, that's payable each week," she corrected.

Finn stared at her. It was all he could do to keep his jaw from dropping open. The amount she'd quoted was enough to cause him to stop breathing for a moment, sincerely trying to figure out if he was dreaming or not.

"A week," he repeated, stunned at the amount of money that was being bandied about. "For someone with no work experience in the field?" he asked incredulously.

She had to be testing him, he concluded. To what end he had no idea, but nobody really earned that sort of money in a week, not unless they were crooked.

"You have life experience," she countered. "That trumps just work experience seven ways from Sunday."

Hearing the phrase made him grin.

"What?" she asked.

"Nothing." He began to wave the matter away, then stopped. What was the harm of sharing this? "It's just that I haven't heard that phrase since my mom died. She liked to say it," he confessed.

That in turn brought a smile to *her* lips.

Small world, Connie couldn't help thinking. The phrase had been a common one for her own mother.

"Wise lady," she said now.

"I like to think so." Finn gave it less than a minute before he nodded his head. "She would have liked you," he told Connie. And as far as he was concerned, that cinched it for him. Besides, it wasn't like he was signing away the next twenty years of his life.

Putting out his hand, Finn said to her, "Well, Ms. Carmichael, looks like you've got yourself a crew foreman."

Connie was fairly beaming when she said to him with relish, "Welcome to Carmichael Construction," and then shook his hand.

Chapter Six

"Well, you two seemed to have come to some sort of an amicable agreement," Miss Joan noted.

Having covertly observed the two occupants of the table from a discreet distance for the duration of their conversation, Miss Joan decided that now was the proper time to approach them.

Not that she was all that interested in restraint, but this was someone new to her, and she wanted to start out slowly with the young woman. Picking up a coffeepot as she rounded the counter, she used that as her excuse to make her way over to their table.

It was time to see if either of their coffee cups was in need of refilling. High time.

Pouring a little more coffee into both their cups, Miss Joan looked from the young woman to Finn. They had dropped their hands when she had come to their table and had now fallen into silence.

Silence had never been a deterrent for Miss Joan. On the contrary, it merely allowed her to speak without having to raise her voice.

"Anything I might be interested in knowing about?" the older woman asked them cheerfully.

Connie could only stare at the other woman, momentarily struck speechless. Granted, she was accustomed to her father's extremely blunt approach when he wanted to know something. The man never beat around the bush. His demand for information was nothing if not direct.

However, everyone else she'd ever dealt with was far more subtle about their desire to extract any useful information from her.

Miss Joan, apparently, was in a class by herself. Polite, but definitely not subtle.

Since she was in Forever for the singular purpose of getting this hotel not just off the ground but also completed, and to that end she was looking to hire local people, Connie told herself that she shouldn't feel as if her privacy had been invaded—even though she had a feeling that Miss Joan would have been just as straightforward and just as blunt with her query.

You're not here to make lasting friendships—just to get the hotel erected, Connie told herself sternly. *Act accordingly.*

So Connie smiled at Miss Joan, a woman her gut instincts told her made a far better ally than an enemy, and said to her, "Mr. Murphy here has just become my first hire."

Miss Joan's shrewd eyes darted from Finn back to

the young woman. "You're looking to hire men?" she asked with a completely unreadable expression.

Finn could see that Connie's simple statement could easily get misinterpreted and even once it was cleared up, there would undoubtedly be lingering rumors and repercussions. He came to Connie's rescue before she could say anything further.

"Ms. Carmichael is going to be building a hotel in town, and she's looking to hire construction workers," Finn told Miss Joan succinctly.

Miss Joan leaned her hip against the side of the table, turning his words over in her head.

"A hotel, eh? Something tells me you'll get the show on the road a hell of a lot quicker if you two stop referring to each other as *Ms.* and *Mr.* and just use each other's given names." And then she considered the project Finn had mentioned a moment longer. Her approval wasn't long in coming. "Might not be a bad idea at that, putting up a hotel around here. Give people a place to stay if they find themselves temporarily in Forever for one reason or another."

She straightened up then and looked directly at the young woman. "Speaking of which, where is it that you're going to be staying for the duration of this mighty undertaking, honey?" she asked.

Connie wasn't used to being accountable to anyone but her father, so it took a second to talk herself into answering. The woman was just being nosy.

"I've got a room reserved at the hotel in Pine Ridge," Connie replied, thinking how ironic that had to sound to anyone who was listening.

"Pine Ridge?" Miss Joan repeated incredulously. The expression on her face went from disbelief to dismissive. "That's at least fifty miles away from here. You can't be driving fifty miles at the end of the day," Miss Joan informed her authoritatively. "You'll be too damn tired, might hit something you didn't intend to."

As opposed to something she *had* intended to hit? Connie wondered. She shrugged in response. "I'm afraid it can't be helped."

"Sure it can," Miss Joan insisted. "You can come and stay with me and my husband. I've got an extra bedroom you can have. No trouble at all," she added as if the discussion was over and the course of action already decided.

But it wasn't decided at all. Again, Connie could only stare at the other woman, completely stunned. How could this Miss Joan just come out and offer her a bed under her roof? Things like that just weren't done where she came from.

Wasn't the woman afraid she might be taking in a thief—or worse? Apparently, people around here were far less cautious.

"But you don't know me," Connie pointed out.

Miss Joan snorted as if that made no difference at all.

"Finn here seems to trust you, and that's good enough for me," the older woman told her. "Besides, you just said you were building a hotel here. That'll put some of our boys to work, earning more money than they have in a long while, and that's *really* good enough for me. Especially if you include some of those boys on the reservation. They're a proud bunch, but they need work just like the others." Miss Joan leveled a gaze at the younger woman. "Whatever you need," she told Connie, "you come check with me first. I'll see that you get it."

With that, Miss Joan took her leave and sauntered away.

Finn could almost see what his table companion was thinking by the stunned expression on her face. Survivors of a hurricane had the exact same expression.

"Well, that's Miss Joan all right," he commented. "She's pretty much a force of nature. But she means well. She comes through, too. And just so you know, you wouldn't be the first person who's stayed with her when they first came to town."

Connie didn't care if the woman had a guest registry a mile long, she wasn't about to accept anyone's charity. "Thanks, but I do have that hotel room reserved, and I don't mind the drive."

The latter statement wasn't really true. Connie very much *did* mind the drive, especially since she was going to be doing it at night. She was, perforce, independent, but that didn't mean that she wouldn't have preferred not having to drive a long, lonely, relatively unknown stretch of road in the dark. But she had no choice—unless she got a pup tent and camped out.

What she *did* plan on getting sent down, once the work got underway, was an on-site trailer. She'd definitely be able to sleep in it. That way, all she'd have to do was step outside her door, and she would be at work. And once her day was over, her bed wouldn't be far away.

"Suit yourself," Finn was saying. "But if I know Miss Joan, her offer stands and will continue to stand until either the hotel is finished or you actually move into someone's place here in Forever."

Connie paused for a moment, captivated by what he was saying despite the fact that her mind was racing around a mile a minute, pulling together myriad details and things she had to take care of before this work got fully underway.

She was having a hard time accepting what he was telling her. "Are you people really this open and generous?"

The corner of Finn's mouth rose in an amused semismile, just like the one, he was told, that on occasion graced his older brother's face.

"I wouldn't know about open and generous," he confessed. "We see it as business as usual," Finn told her matter-of-factly. "Everyone just looks out for everyone else here in Forever."

Any moment now, the people here were going to join hands and sing, Connie thought sarcastically.

"Yes, but I'm not an insider," she pointed out— needlessly, in her opinion. "I'm an outsider."

He laughed at her statement. "An outsider is just an insider who hasn't come in yet," Finn informed her very simply.

He was kidding, right? "That's very quaint," she told him.

He took no offense at the dismissive note in her voice. Finn had learned that some people needed a little more time to come around. He had no doubts that once her hotel was framed, she would see things differently. He could wait.

"And also true," he added.

"If you say so." Connie looked down at her plate. Dinner had somehow gotten eaten without her taking much note of it or of the process of consuming it.

Okay, it was time to call it a day for now, Connie

decided. She discreetly pushed back her plate, away from her.

"Thank you for dinner," she told him, rising to her feet. "I'm going to start heading back to Pine Ridge now, but I'll be back here in the morning. We can start signing up workers then."

Finn was on his feet, as well. Knowing the prices on the menu by heart, he took out several bills and left them on the table.

"Sounds good." Getting up from the table, he walked her to the front door, acutely aware that Miss Joan was watching their every move, no matter where she was in the diner. "Where do you plan to set up?"

She stepped across the threshold. "Set up?"

He nodded. "I figure I can spread the word, round up a bunch of people for you to interview, but you're going to need to set up somewhere so you can conduct these interviews."

He was right; she needed a central place, somewhere everyone was familiar with and felt comfortable in. It took Connie less than a minute to think of the perfect place.

"How about at Murphy's? Could you open early for me?" she asked, turning directly toward him. "I could conduct interviews there, although if you vouch for the people you bring to me, I don't foresee the interview process taking very long."

She supposed that her father would have accused her of being crazy. She'd had just met this man, and she was behaving as if he was a lifelong trusted friend. But there was just something about Finn Murphy that told her he was the kind of man who always came through, who wouldn't let a person down, not even for his own personal gain. If he told her that someone was worth hiring, she saw no reason to doubt his assessment.

"Murphy's is doable," he told her.

Brett might take some convincing, Finn thought, but he had no reason to think that his brother wouldn't come around. After all, this was ultimately for the good of the town, something that always interested Brett.

"How soon are you looking to get started?" he asked.

"Yesterday," Connie answered.

He believed her.

"Then *we* have some catching up to do," he told her, walking her to her car.

It was a long drive, Connie thought as she *finally* saw the lights of Pine Ridge come into view in the distance.

It wasn't a drive she relished. Maybe she'd see about having that trailer brought in as soon as possible. Granted, the road between Forever and Pine Ridge was pretty empty, but that didn't mean she couldn't find herself accidentally driving into some sort of a ditch, especially if she fell asleep. The road was exceedingly deserted and boring. Monotony put her to sleep, hence her problem.

Mornings wouldn't be a problem. She'd be fresh in the morning, far less likely to have an accident. But even so, it was still time wasted, time she was taking away from getting the actual hotel completed.

For the good of the job, Connie began to seriously entertain taking Miss Joan up on her offer. God knew she valued her privacy, and she liked keeping to herself, separating the public Connie from the private one, but this was business and, as such, she was willing to sacrifice a lot of her own personal beliefs.

Anything to show her father she could live up to her word and be the asset to the company he was always saying he wanted.

The first thing she did when she got into her room at the hotel—besides immediately kick off her shoes and allow her toes to sink into the rug—was place a call to her father's business manager on her cell phone.

Stewart Emerson answered on the second ring. "Hello?"

The familiar, deep voice vibrated against her ear, magically creating a comfort zone for her. "Stewart, it's Connie."

Instant warmth flooded his voice. "By the tone of your voice, I take it that all systems are a go."

She laughed. Good old Stewart. The man seemed to be able to read her thoughts before she ever said anything. She'd discovered long ago that a simple hello could tell the man volumes.

Ever since she could remember, Emerson was like the father that Calvin Carmichael wasn't, the man who made her feel that she had a safety net beneath her if she ever really needed one.

She knew without being told that he had her back in every project she had ever gotten involved in. He'd always made sure that her father only received the positive reports.

Granted, the senior Carmichael paid his salary, but Calvin Carmichael's lifelong associate reasoned that his boss's daughter had a great deal to contend with as it was; he just wanted to make it a little easier for her. He knew the sort of demands that Carmichael placed on his daughter—and he also knew that each time she came close to meeting those demands, Carmichael would raise the bar that much higher.

He had watched her grow from a little girl to the woman she had become. Watched, too, as she heart-breakingly attempted to cull and gain her father's favor, only to fail, time and again. Carmichael was the type to drive himself—and everyone in his world—hard. It made for a very successful businessman—and at the same time, a rather unsuccessful human being.

Emerson strived to somehow prevent the same sort of fate from ultimately finding Carmichael's daughter.

"So tell me how everything's going," Emerson encouraged.

"I found someone in town who's willing to help hire the right people for the crew," she told him.

"Does he have any kind of experience with construction?" Emerson asked her.

"I came across him rebuilding a ranch house. I was really impressed with what I saw," she told him.

"Are you talking about the man, or the job he did?" He put the question to her good-naturedly.

"The job he did. I don't have time for that other stuff," she told him.

"Maybe you should make time," Emerson tactfully suggested.

"Someday, Stewart," she promised strictly to placate the man. "But not today. Anyway, from the looks of it, the man seems pretty skilled."

"And you can work with him?" Emerson questioned.

"I think so," she answered honestly. There was only one problem in the foreseeable future. "But I'm still worried that it might be hard meeting the deadline Dad set down."

"You'll do it," Emerson told her with no hesitation whatsoever.

"Thanks, Stewart." And then, radiant even though there was no one to see her, or to appreciate the sight, she added, "Hearing you say that means a lot to me."

"I'm not just saying it, Connie. I know you. You're just as determined and stubborn to succeed as your old man. The only difference is that you're still human," he qualified. And then he warned her, "Don't drive yourself too hard."

She smiled to herself. "I won't."

There was a slight pause, and then he asked her, "Are you remembering to eat?"

Connie caught herself laughing at that. "Now you're beginning to sound like my mother."

"There are worse people to sound like," Emerson responded. There was a fond note in his voice, the way there always was when the conversation turned toward her mother.

Connie had long suspected that there had been a connection between Emerson and her mother. He'd never actually said as much, and she hadn't asked him. But one day, Connie promised herself, she intended to ask him. Not to pry, but to feel closer to not just her mother, but to the man she was speaking with, as well.

Her father had been no kinder to her mother than he had been to her brother, or to her. It would make her feel better to know that while she was alive, her mother'd had an ally in Stewart, someone she could turn to for emotional support, even if not a single word had been exchanged between them at the time.

That was Stewart Emerson's power, she thought now. He could make a person feel safe and protected without saying a single word to that effect. He conveyed it by his very presence.

"How about the supplies?" she asked, suddenly stifling a yawn. "Are they still coming?"

"They're already on their way," Emerson confirmed. "Now if you've had dinner, I suggest you get to bed and get some rest. If I know you, you're going to drive yourself relentlessly tomorrow—and all the tomorrows after that," he added.

Because no one ever fussed over her, she allowed herself a moment just to enjoy Stewart behaving like an overprotective mother hen.

"Been looking into your crystal ball again, Stewart?"

"Don't need one where you're concerned, Connie," he told her. "I know you like a book."

She didn't bother stifling her yawn this time. Instead, still holding her cell phone to her ear, Connie stretched out on her bed for just a moment. With little encouragement, she could allow her eyes to drift shut.

"You need new reading material, Stewart," she told him with affection.

"No, I don't. You are by far my very favorite book. You don't get rid of a favorite book, Connie, you treasure it and make sure nothing happens to it. Now say good night and close your phone," he instructed.

"Good night," Connie murmured obediently.

She was asleep ten seconds after she hit End on her cell phone.

Chapter Seven

Connie was not unaccustomed to sleeping in hotels. In the past few years, she'd had to stay in more than her share of hotel rooms, most of which were indistinguishable from the hotel room she now had in Pine Ridge. Despite all this, it was not a restful night for her.

Exhausted though she was, Connie found she couldn't sleep straight through the night. Instead, she kept waking up almost every hour on the hour. The cause behind her inability to sleep in something more than fitful snatches was not a mystery to her. She was both excited and worried about what the next day held.

There was a great deal riding on this for her and although, despite her father's mind games Connie *did* have faith in herself, she was not narcissistic enough to feel that everything would turn out all right in the end—*just because.* That was her father's way of operating, not hers.

As a rule, Connie tried to proceed confidently, but keeping what to do in a worst-case scenario somewhere in the back of her mind. She knew better than to believe that the occasion would never come up. She was also well aware that while she seemed to have the beginnings of a decent relationship going with the man in charge of the crew, she wasn't exactly home free in that department yet.

Added to that, she wanted the people who would be working for her to like her. It just stood to reason that employees worked a lot better for people they liked and admired than for people whom they feared and who rode roughshod over them. This would not be an ongoing job for the people she hired but rather a one-time thing. She had to get the very best out of them in the time that she had.

And, if that wasn't enough to prey on her unguarded mind, there was that added *thing* that kept buzzing around in her brain. She had no succinct description for this feeling, other than to call it unsettling. She could, however, easily trace it back to its source: one Finn Murphy. There was something about him, something above and beyond his capability, his craftsmanship and his obvious connection to the men of the town.

Though she would have rather not put a label on it, Connie had always been honest and straightforward with people—and that included herself.

With that in mind, she forced herself to admit that there was no other way to describe it. The man was sexy—not overtly, not in a showy, brash manner, but more in an inherent way. It was part of the fabric of his makeup. Sexiness seemed to be just ingrained in him. There seemed to be no way to separate the trait from the man. They were, apparently, one and the same. But no matter how she described it, how she qualified it, the bottom line was that she was attracted to him.

This was going to be a problem, she thought uncomfortably.

Only if you let it be, her inner voice, the one that always kept her on an even keel, told her firmly.

The internal argument continued back and forth for the duration of her morning drive from Pine Ridge to Forever, blocking out whatever songs were being played on the radio station.

The argument was so intense, she wasn't even aware of the time as it went by. One moment she was half asleep, slipping behind the steering wheel of her car, aware that she wanted to arrive in town early, the next, miraculously, she found herself there, parking in front of Murphy's, wondering if Finn had remembered their conversation about conducting the interviews in his establishment.

She shouldn't have worried, Connie realized as she got out of the vehicle. There was a line of men that went out the saloon's front doors and wound its way down the street.

Some of the men were standing in clusters, talking, others were on the ground, sitting cross-legged and giving the impression that they had been sitting there for a while. A handful looked as if they had just stepped out of a movie about cattle ranchers from the last century, complete with cowboy hats, worn jeans and dusty boots, and still others appeared downright hungry for work.

The last group was the one she paid attention to most

of all. Born into the lap of luxury, she nonetheless had an endless capacity for empathy and could just imagine how it had to feel, facing financial uncertainty each and every morning.

The moment the men saw her approaching, everyone got to their feet, their posture straightening as if they were elementary school students, lining up for the teacher and hoping to pass inspection.

Connie glanced at her wristwatch, half expecting to discover that she had somehow managed to lose an hour getting here.

But she hadn't.

She was early, just as she'd initially intended. The men were even earlier.

Butterflies suddenly swooped in, clustering around her stomach, pinching her. Connie did her best to ignore them.

Approaching the entrance to Murphy's, she greeted the hopeful applicants. "Hi, I'm Constance Carmichael. I'll be conducting the interviews today." She quickly scanned the line, amazed at how many people had turned up. Finn was to be commended—either him, or Miss Joan, she amended. She had no doubt that the older woman had been quick to pass the word along that there would be jobs available. Still, she thought it judicious to ask, "Are you all here about the construction crew jobs?"

To a man they all answered in the affirmative, the chorus of *yeses* all but deafening.

Connie nodded, letting the moment sink in. She felt a little overwhelmed but she did her best not to show it.

"Okay, then I guess we'd better get started. Give

me five minutes to get things together and then we can begin."

Hurrying past the long single line, Connie made her way into the saloon.

In contrast to the way it had looked when she'd first seen it, the place was lit up as brightly as any establishment that didn't require an ambiance for its clientele.

Finn was there along with his older brother, Brett, and another, younger man with blond hair. She took a closer look at the latter and realized that this had to be Liam, the youngest of the Murphy brothers. The family resemblance was hard to miss.

But Finn wasn't talking to either one of his brothers when she walked in. Instead, he seemed to be deep in conversation with a tall athletic man with straight, thick, blue-black hair, and skin that looked as if it would be right at home beneath the hot rays of the Texas sun.

The other man's bone structure intrigued her for a moment. It was all angles and planes, and there was almost a regal appearance to it. The man's most outstanding feature, at least for the moment, was that he was wearing what she took to be a deputy sheriff's uniform.

Did they expect things to get a little rowdy? she wondered uneasily.

Only one way to find out, Connie decided, braced for anything.

Walking up to Finn and the man he was talking to, she greeted one and introduced herself to the other. "Hi, Finn, I didn't think you'd be ready so early. I would have been here sooner if I knew," she told him honestly. Her eyes darted over to the other man. "I'm Constance Carmichael. Is there something wrong, Officer?"

"Deputy," the man corrected her. "I'm Deputy Sheriff Lone Wolf, but you can call me Joe, and no, there's nothing wrong."

Finn joined in. "Joe brought some of his friends from the rez with him when he heard you were hiring."

"The rez?" she questioned uncertainly.

"That's short for reservation," Finn explained. "Everything gets shortened these days."

Joe had been around long enough to be aware that there were those who still viewed Native Americans differently from others. He'd come to unofficially make sure that there would be no trouble erupting due to any misunderstandings that might flair up.

"You *are* hiring, right?" Joe asked the young woman.

"Absolutely," Connie answered with enthusiasm.

She knew what it was like to have a strike against her for no apparent reason other than a preconceived— and false—notion. Contrary to some opinions, her name did *not* open doors. In some cases, it actually slammed them in her face. Her father was a powerful man, but he was definitely *not* liked.

"I'm looking for able-bodied men with strong backs who don't mind working in the hot sun for an honest day's wage," she told the deputy, summarizing exactly what her criteria was. Once that was met, everything else could be taught.

"How many men are you going to need?" Finn asked her.

"How many men have you got?" she countered, indicating that the number of positions she was looking to fill was far from small.

Finn grinned. This really was going to be good for the town. "Let's get started," he told her.

He gestured to a table he'd set up for her. He and his

brothers had temporarily cleared away the others, putting them off to the side for the time being, until the interviews were over for the day.

"Let's," she echoed.

Sitting down, Connie beckoned to the first man in line.

She kept at it, nonstop, until she had seen and talked to every single man in line. She reasoned that if they could stand in line all this time, waiting to talk to her, the least she could do was interview them.

Except for a few who had shown up out of idle curiosity, or had decided after the interview that the work would be too physically taxing, she wound up hiring all the men she interviewed.

Since that number turned out to be higher than she'd initially intended, rather than work a given number of employees full-time, she'd decided to spread the work out, employing all of the men she'd hired on a part-time, as-needed basis. Some, she discovered during the course of the interviews, already had jobs and had approached this position as a way to pick up some extra money, while others were looking to this construction job as a way of feeding their families.

In making her preliminary decisions about the schedule, Connie gave the latter group the most hours while the people in the former group, since they already had some sort of gainful employment, she used accordingly.

In the end, the general schedule Connie ultimately wound up putting together looked a bit complicated, but she was satisfied that she had done the very best job she could and more important to her, had done right by some of the town's residents.

She also found that her initial instincts involved in selecting Finn were right. Finn had remained with her through the entire ordeal. He'd stood off to the side to give her space, but he always remained close enough to be there if she decided she needed backup for some reason, or to resolve some issue.

While acting as her more or less silent second in command, he'd also gotten to observe her more than holding her own. Finn found himself impressed by the way she did business as well as her underlying sincerity. Any doubts he might have still been entertaining about her were laid to rest by the end of the long session. The woman wasn't here just to take advantage of the labor or the town.

Right from the first interview, she made no secret of the fact that this hotel was important to her, but so were the people she was hiring. She made a point of telling them that she wanted them to speak up if at any time they were dissatisfied with the work conditions or the treatment they received from a superior.

All in all, he thought that this newcomer in their midst conducted herself better than some far more experienced people that both he and Brett had dealt with at one time or another.

When the last man had finally filled out a form and given it to Connie, then left the saloon, Finn came up behind her, leaned over and said, "You look like you could use a drink right about now."

Turning her head, her eyes met his, and she allowed herself a weary smile. That had been grueling, she couldn't help thinking. Even so, she felt wired—and very pleased with herself.

"Quite possibly more than one." The one thing that hosting those parties for her father and hanging around with his associates had taught her, other than how to listen and absorb information, was how to hold her liquor.

"That can be arranged," Finn told her. "I happen to know the bartender in this joint. It's a pretty well-established fact that he's a pushover for a pretty woman's smile."

God, but she felt stiff, Connie suddenly realized. She'd been sitting so long in one spot, she felt as if she could have very well melded into the chair.

"Do you know where we can find one?" she murmured, rotating her head from side to side. She could almost hear it making strange, creaking noises.

"I'm looking at one," Finn told her very simply, his eyes on hers.

Connie caught herself raising her chin. It was a purely defensive move on her part. She was waiting for some sort of a disparaging remark to follow because right about now, she felt about as pretty as a dried-up autumn leaf.

"This bartender doesn't set the bar very high, does he?" she quipped dismissively.

"On the contrary, it's pretty much an absolute," he told her.

He realized that she wasn't being cute or angling for some sort of a bigger compliment. She actually meant what she'd said. She didn't think of herself as attractive. How was that even possible? he couldn't help wondering. One glance at her more than established that fact.

"You do have mirrors in your house, don't you?" he asked. How could she possibly not see just how really gorgeous she was? He would have been willing to bet that a number of the men who had lined up today would have been willing to work for her without any monetary compensation, as long as she was on the job with them every day.

"I don't need mirrors," she answered. "I've got my father. He does more than an adequate job of keeping me aware of myself."

He was about to say that, obviously, it was her father who was suffering from some sort of blindness, but Finn never got the chance. Their conversation was abruptly curtailed when one of Miss Joan's waitresses—Dora—walked into the saloon, clutching a large insulated carrier in both hands.

She went directly to the table where Connie had set up her *office*. Seeing that it was covered with stacks of papers, she turned toward the bar instead.

"Miss Joan said you need to keep your strength up," Dora announced, setting the rectangular carrier she'd brought in on the bar.

Unzipping the insulated carrier on three of its sides, Dora extracted what turned out to be a complete three-course meal, along with a container of coffee and a huge slice of coconut cream pie.

The pie was her favorite, Connie thought. Was its inclusion in the meal just a coincidence? Or was this a further example of Miss Joan's talked-about, unusual abilities? At this point, she really didn't know what to believe—or what she ultimately felt comfortable believing.

So instead, she pretended as if all this was just commonplace. "This is for me?" she asked, feigning surprise.

"Miss Joan told me not to let anyone else pick at it but you," Dora told her.

Dora looked at Finn. A rather sharp *no trespassing* look passed between them because the latter looked rather interested in the pie.

Flashing a smile at the waitress, Finn, along with his brother, brought over one of the tables that had been pushed to the side and set it up beside the other one.

Dora brought all the items from the carrier over to that table.

Connie moved her chair over to the new table and regarded the unusual spread. She wasn't accustomed to having anyone concern themselves with her welfare. "I don't know what to say."

"Don't have to say anything," Dora told her, zipping up the carrier and then slinging the straps over her shoulder as if it was nothing more than an oddly shaped shoulder bag. "Miss Joan said for you to consider it her investment in the hotel—and the future."

Connie was unclear as to the message that was being conveyed. She glanced at Finn. "What's that supposed to mean?"

Finn laughed. "You got me. Half the time we're not sure exactly *what* Miss Joan's saying, only that, somehow, in the long run, that very sharp lady always turns out to be right."

"I don't have any great insight in the way people think," Joe began, joining the circle of people, "but offhand, I'd say that Miss Joan just wants to make sure you don't waste away. She doesn't like anyone being as skinny as she is," the deputy added with a dry laugh. He turned toward Brett. "I'll be heading back now." His attention shifted for a moment back to the young woman he had initially come to see this morning. "Thanks for hiring some of my friends."

"No reason to thank me." She thought for a moment, then added just before he walked toward the door, "If there's any thanks to be given, I should be the one to be thanking you for bringing them here today."

"Then you can thank Finn," Joe told her. The man he'd just mentioned had temporarily stepped aside to talk to Brett. "He's the one who told me about this hotel your company's building." He nodded, as if agreeing with something he was thinking before he said out loud, "Finn's a good man."

Connie had no intentions of disputing that. Her gut instincts had already told her the same the morning she had seen him standing before the ranch house, tool belt dipped provocatively at his hips, causing his jeans to dip with them. It had brought a whole new meaning of *fine craftsmanship* flashing through her mind.

Out loud, she murmured to Joe, "I'm beginning to see that."

The problem, however, was that she was also beginning to see a lot more, and that could only have a negative effect on her ultimately getting the job done the way she wanted to.

Chapter Eight

"I'll take that drink now," Connie said, slipping onto the bar stool.

Finn seemed somewhat surprised to see her sitting there. The woman had somehow managed to make it from her table to the bar without a single telltale sound to alert him that she was moving in his direction. Glancing around her, he saw Joe just as the latter went out the front door. He couldn't see the deputy's face from where he was—not that it would have done any good even if he had. As a rule, Joe's face was completely unreadable, giving nothing away that he didn't want to.

"Joe giving you a hard time?" Finn asked her, curious.

It took Connie a second to connect the face with the name. She'd spoken to several "Joes" during the marathon interviewing session today.

"Oh, you mean the deputy?" she finally concluded. "No, he was nice as pie."

Pouring her a shot of Kentucky bourbon, Finn moved the partially filled glass in front of her. "Not that I didn't offer you one just a few minutes ago, but why do you suddenly look as if you actually need this drink?" he asked.

She raised the glass, but rather than throw back the drink or sip it, she just studied the amber liquid in it, moving it slowly from side to side.

"So I can talk myself out of the idea that I'm in over my head," she replied.

He hadn't expected her to say that. From what he had seen, Connie Carmichael struck him as being equal to anything she tackled. But he'd learned long ago that self-image had a lot to do in making decisions that affected more than just yourself.

"Is that how you feel?" he asked.

She laughed shortly, shaking her head. "You're not much of a bartender, are you?"

Although, she silently had to admit, Finn Murphy with his lean, sculpted torso, sexy smile and magnetic green eyes, was every woman's fantasy come to life. She would have to watch her step with him. Really watch her step.

"Come again?" Finn asked.

"Well, isn't this the part where you tell me that, 'no, you're not in over your head. Everything's going to work out just fine and we'll stand to gain from this experience when it's all behind us.'" Her tone of voice was only partially sarcastic.

"Don't see why I should. You seem to have taken care of that part pretty much on your own."

Connie frowned, still regarding the drink in her hand. "Yeah, except that I don't believe myself." And with that, she took a long, savoring sip from her glass. Closing her eyes, she allowed herself to focus on the fiery path the alcohol took through her body. He noted that she didn't toss her drink down, the way people would when they were trying to erase a reaction or memory of a sore point.

"Maybe you should," he told her. "From where I'm standing, you seem like a very capable person. Notice I said *capable,* not *superhuman,*" he pointed out. "If you were shooting for superhuman, I'd say that you had unrealistic expectations. But since you're not, I'd say that everything was A-okay. Now why don't you take that drink—" he nodded at it "—go back to your table and have that dinner Miss Joan sent over before it gets cold?" he suggested. "If I don't miss my guess, Angel made that dinner special, just for you."

"Angel?" Connie tried to recall if she'd met anyone answering to that name in the last two days. She came up empty.

"Gabe Rodriguez's wife," Finn told her. "Miss Joan's got her working at the diner, and that lady's got a way with food that's nothing short of heavenly." He paused to inhale deeply even though it was literally impossible to catch a whiff of the aroma of the meal. The distance was fairly substantial. "I'd recognize Angel's fried chicken *anywhere.*"

He sounded as if he'd enjoy the meal a lot more than she would, Connie thought. Her stomach was badly knotted. As far as she knew, he hadn't had a chance to eat anything, either, so she beckoned him over before she even sat down at the table again.

"Why don't you join me, then? There's more than enough here for both of us," she told him, indicating the food that was on the table.

Finn glanced at the heaping basket of fried chicken that had been placed beside her plate. He knew Miss Joan and the way the woman thought. She had people and their appetites down to a science, and she wouldn't have sent over that much food if she thought that Connie would be eating it by herself. What he was looking at was a deliberate double portion, generous, yes, but definitely a double portion.

Why Miss Joan had sent a double portion, he could only speculate, but he had a feeling that if Connie suspected this was what the older woman had in mind—that they share a meal together for the second time—it just might be the added pressure that would cause Connie's undoing. The woman currently had more than enough on her mind without trying to fathom what was going on in Miss Joan's head.

"Well, if you insist," Finn allowed, crossing over to her table.

"I do."

"Then how can I say no? You're the boss lady," he told her agreeably as he took a seat opposite her at the table.

Boss lady.

That sounded good, Connie couldn't help thinking. She just hoped that this wouldn't turn out to be an isolated incident.

She gazed at the food again and shook her head in amused disbelief. "Miss Joan must think that I have an absolutely *huge* appetite."

"Miss Joan likes to think that when it comes to the

food she serves at the diner, *everyone* has a big appetite," Finn told her. "I think that woman feels it's her
mission in life to fatten everyone up."

As he spoke, he reached into the basket for another
piece of chicken—at the exact same time that Connie
went to take one herself. They wound up both reaching
for the *same* piece of fried chicken, which was why, just
for a second, their fingers brushed against one another.
Contact generated a spark that had no business being
there, and no tangible explanation for being there, either.

They both pulled their hands back almost simulta-
neously.

"Sorry," Connie murmured. She was *really* going
to have to be careful, she warned herself. Everything,
including her entire future, was riding on her success
with this project.

"No, my mistake. Go ahead," he urged, gesturing
toward the basket. "After all, you're the one Miss Joan
sent this to. It's her way of looking out for you," he
added.

"Why would she even concern herself with me?"
Connie asked. "I mean, not that it's not a nice feeling
to know that someone cares whether I eat or not, but
she really doesn't know me from Adam."

"Oh, I think she's got that part pretty much figured
out," he told her with a grin. "There's definitely no mis-
taking you for any guy named Adam. As for the rest of
it, Miss Joan likes to think of herself as a great judge
of character. To give the woman her due, I don't think
there was a single time that anyone can recall Miss Joan
being wrong about anything."

"Bet that must make her hard to live with," Connie
commented.

She knew firsthand what her father would be like under those circumstances. The man already felt he couldn't be opposed, and he had been wrong at least several instances that she knew of. Most likely more that she *didn't* know about, she was willing to bet.

"You'd think so, wouldn't you?" Finn agreed, then went on to say, "But I don't think there's a nicer person in Forever than Miss Joan. Oh, she comes off all prickly and distant at times, you know, crusty on the outside. But she's kind of like French bread in that way. Soft on the inside," he told her with a wink. "Miss Joan's got that famous heart of gold that so many people have benefited from. She thinks you're going to be good for the town, so that's why she's behind you the way she is," Finn told her.

Because her father had made her leery of being on the receiving end of praise, she'd never been one to take a compliment lightly or at face value.

"I don't know about *me* being good for the town," Connie said, "but the hotel's bound to be. If there's a hotel in town, people'll be more inclined to stop here rather than somewhere else. That means they'll eat their meals here, maybe spend a little money here—" And that was when an idea hit her. She looked at Finn hopefully when she asked, "Anything like an annual rodeo take place here?"

Now *that* had come out of left field, he thought. "Nope."

The woman amused him, she really did, Finn thought. It was obvious from the way she conducted herself that she was a city girl—even if she hadn't told him that her father's company was domiciled in Houston, she had the word *city* written all over her. Yet here she was, acting like some kind of an activities director, coming up with ideas about what she thought would be best for a town she'd only set foot in yesterday.

It took a great deal of self-confidence to come across like that—yet when he looked into Connie's eyes, he could see the slight element of fear lurking there. Fear of failure, he assumed. That kind of a thing might ultimately cause her to second-guess herself, which, in his experience, never amounted to anything positive in the long run.

"Maybe you should consider holding a rodeo here," she encouraged. God knew she could picture Finn on a bucking bronco, every muscle tense as he focused on the longest eight seconds of his life.

A warm shiver went up and down her spine. It was an effort to get herself under control and act as if images of Finn hadn't just taken over her brain.

"I'll do that," he told her with a wink, unable to put a lid on his amusement any longer. "I'll consider holding an annual rodeo."

"I'm serious," she told him, leaning in closer over the table. "That would really bring in more people to Forever."

"People who would have to stay at the hotel," he said with a straight face.

"Yes." And then she took a closer look at him. It wasn't that he thought she was kidding; he thought she had a screw loose, she realized. "You're laughing at me."

He did his best to turn down the wattage of his grin—but she was so damn cute when she tried to be so serious. "Not at you, with you."

Connie frowned. "You might not have noticed this, but I'm not laughing."

"But you will be. Sooner or later, you will be," he assured her. "One thing you should know about the people in Forever is that they kind of move at a slower pace than what you're probably used to."

Connie immediately interpreted the words to mean something that affected her. Instantly on the alert, she asked, "What are you telling me, that we're not going to make the deadline?"

"Oh, no, you'll make the deadline," he told her quickly, wanting to make sure she didn't misunderstand him. "That's a real hardworking bunch of men you just hired today."

Her eyebrows seemed to knit themselves over her narrowed eyes. Finn had lost her. "Then I don't understand…"

"People in Forever are slow when it comes to making changes. They take their time embracing progress, if you will."

"Everything has to embrace progress," Connie doggedly insisted. "If something isn't growing, then it's dying." It was one of the first lessons she'd ever learned—and it had come from Emerson, not her father.

"Or maybe it's just being," he suggested.

"Being?" she asked, not understanding what he was trying to tell her.

"Existing," Finn said, putting it another way. "In general, people work hard to make a living, and they feel that they're entitled to just sit back and enjoy that accomplishment. You know, sit back, take a look around and just be happy that they've managed to come this far and survived. It's not always about reaching the next major goal, or getting the next big-screen TV. In other words, it's not always about getting something bigger, or better, or faster. Sometimes, it's just about enjoying the prize that you have, the thing—however small—you succeeded in doing."

He realized that Connie hadn't said anything in a couple of minutes, hadn't attempted to interrupt him. Not just that, but she was looking at him in a very odd way, like he was speaking another language.

He'd overstepped his bounds, Finn thought, upbraiding himself. The woman wasn't ready to hear this countrified philosophy when all she was interested in was getting a good day's work out of them.

He tried to backtrack as gracefully as he could. "Hey, but that's just me," he concluded, easing himself out of the conversation.

But Connie continued to watch him in what he could only describe as a thoughtful, strange way. It was obvious that if they were to move on, he had no recourse but to ask her, "What?"

As Finn had talked, she'd stopped embracing the credo that had governed most of her life, and instead listened to what the cowboy was telling her. It didn't take a scholar to realize—rather quickly—that she was hearing the antithesis of her father's number one philosophy.

Her father would probably have this man for lunch—or try to—saying that if everyone was like him, the country would have withered and died a long time ago.

But maybe it wouldn't have, Connie now thought. Maybe the country would continue thriving because people were satisfied and that in turn made them happy. Was that so bad, just being happy?

She couldn't recall the last time her father, with his

countless mind-boggling triumphs and successes, had been happy for more than a fleeting moment or two.

For Calvin Carmichael, it was always about the next project, the next conquest. Bigger, better, more streamline, all that was her father's primary focus. That was what had always kept him going even more so since her mother had died.

And, until just now, that was what kept her going, as well. But maybe not, Connie amended. "You sound like the exact opposite of my father," she told him.

"I meant no disrespect," he told her. "I just think that maybe there's room for both those points of view. Think about it," he urged. "Why should someone work so hard for something and not stop to at least enjoy it for a bit?" he asked.

Connie realized that he probably thought she was trying to find a nice way of saying that he was wrong. But the truth of it was, upon reflection, she didn't believe that he was. What Finn had done was succeed in making her think a little—not to mention that he'd managed to generate a feeling of—for lack of a better word—relief within her.

There *was* room for more than just her father's work ethic out there. That was a fact that was good to keep on the back burner, she decided.

"I didn't say I thought you were wrong. I just said you and my father would be on opposite sides of the fence when it came to your idea of what life was all about." She smiled, more to herself than at the man with whom she was sharing this impromptu dinner. "You might have guessed that my father is not the kind of man you could get to stop and smell the roses. He's more inclined to stomp on the roses as he made his way to the next rosebush—just to reach it, not to try to savor it or appreciate it," she confessed.

At this point, Connie decided that a change of subject might do them both some good. This was just the beginning of their working relationship. It wasn't the time to get into philosophical discussions regarding—ultimately—the meaning of life. Or any other serious, possibly life-altering topic. Not if it didn't directly relate to the job at hand.

So instead, Connie turned her attention to the meal they were sharing. "You were right."

"About?" Finn asked.

"This has to be the best fried chicken I've ever had. Does Angel do something different when she makes this?"

"I'd say that would be a safe guess," Finn answered her. "But if you wanted to know exactly what she does, that's a discussion you're going to have to have with Angel."

She understood that chefs had their secret recipes, and she wasn't trying to pry. Her eye was on a much larger prize at the moment.

"You know, Miss Joan might do well if she thought about looking into maybe having a chain of restaurants, or selling a franchise—including this recipe and a few others in the package—" She looked at Finn, her momentum growing. "I'm assuming fried chicken isn't the only thing Angel does well."

She said this as she finished yet another piece of the chicken. Rather than become full, Connie only seemed better able to savor each bite the more chicken she consumed.

"Everything Angel makes is pretty tasty," Finn answered. "She has a whole bunch of regular customers who faithfully turn up at the diner since she came to work there."

"I knew it," she said with feeling. Plans and possibilities began to multiply in her head. "Angel and Miss Joan are missing a golden opportunity," Connie told him.

"I'll let them know you said so," he told her. "But for right now, I think you're missing a golden opportunity yourself."

"What do you mean?" she asked.

Finn smiled at her. It wasn't a patronizing smile. Instead, it was indulgently patient. The kind of smile a parent had while waiting for their child to catch on to something all by themselves after all the clues had been carefully and discreetly laid out.

But, Finn quickly realized, they came from different worlds, he and this woman, and thus had been raised completely differently, with a different set of rules to guide them. She would need more than just a hint to catch on.

"You're forgetting just to enjoy the moment. Just for a little while, why don't you forget about the project, your father and everything else and just enjoy the meal and what's around you without trying to see if you can maximize it or improve it or market it? Maybe I'm talking out of turn, but you're going to wind up wearing yourself out before you get a chance to make that mark on the world you're so keen on making."

She pressed her lips together. She hated to admit it, but Finn was right.

At least about the last part.

Chapter Nine

The next moment, Connie pulled herself back mentally and rallied. Maybe if she'd lived here, in this tiny speck of a town all of her life, her view of life might match the handsome cowboy's, but she wasn't from Forever. She was from Houston, and things were a lot different there, not to mention that it moved a great deal faster in the city. Oh, she was certain there were people in Houston with the exact same approach to life as Finn had just emphasized, but they were the people who were content never to get anywhere. To be satisfied with their small lot in life and just leave it at that.

But she wasn't. Her father had drummed it into her head over and over again: you were only as good as your next accomplishment.

Finn might not have a father he needed to prove himself to—once and for all—but she did, and until she accomplished that mission, those roses that needed smelling would just have to wait.

Finished with her dinner, Connie pushed herself away from the table and rose to her feet. "As tempting as just kicking back and savoring the moment sounds, I've got a full day tomorrow. We both do," she reminded him pointedly. "And I've still got a fifty-mile trip ahead of me."

It was that fifty-mile trip that was going to wear her out faster than the rest of it, he couldn't help thinking.

"Why don't you reconsider and just stay in town?" Finn suggested. "That way, you could give yourself a little while to take a well-deserved deep breath, relax and enjoy the rest of today before you go full steam ahead tomorrow."

He made it sound so very simple—but she'd learned the hard way that *nothing* was ever simple.

"And just where do you suggest I spend the night?" Connie asked him. "My car's a little cramped for sleepovers," she added in case Finn was going to suggest that she sack out in her sports car.

"I wouldn't have even thought about you sleeping in your car," he told her. "That's a surefire way to guarantee waking up with a stiff neck. Not exactly the way you'd want to start out," he predicted. "Besides, plenty of people in town would be willing to put you up for the night," he assured her.

And just how did he propose that she go about making that a reality? Connie wondered with a touch of cynicism. "I'm not about to go begging door to door—" she began.

Finn cut in. "No begging. A lot of people here have an extra bedroom." Hell, until Brett and Alisha got married and moved into the ranch house he'd inherited, for all intents and purposes, he and his brothers didn't just have an extra room, they had an extra *house*. "All you'd have to do was say that you needed a place to stay and—"

He didn't get a chance to say that people would line up with offers to accommodate her because Connie cut him off. "Which is just another way of begging," she pointed out, stopping him in his tracks.

But Finn, she quickly learned, was not the type to give up easily. "Miss Joan offered you a room at her place," he reminded her. "That was without you saying anything about even *needing* a place."

She was not about to impose on anyone, or approach them, hat in hand, like a supplicant. "I already told Miss Joan I had a room in the Pine Ridge Hotel. To arbitrarily just ask her if I could stay at her place after that wouldn't seem right." She wanted the workers to trust her, not think of her as some sort of a giant sponge.

"What it would seem," Finn argued amicably, "is practical, and there's nothing Miss Joan admires more than someone being practical."

Judging by the look on Connie's face, he hadn't won that argument, Finn thought. He gave getting her to agree to remain in town overnight another try by offering her another option to consider.

"Or if you really can't bring yourself to do that, my brothers and I have a house right here in town not far from this saloon," he told her. "It's plenty big."

She looked at him incredulously. Was he actually saying what she thought he was saying? "And what, I should stay with you?"

"And my brothers," Finn tacked on for good measure.

"Even better," she murmured to herself, rolling her eyes. If she gave him the benefit of the doubt, best-case scenario, the man thought he was being helpful. She told herself to keep that in mind. "I realize that appearances don't count for very much in this day and age," she began, "but it wouldn't look right, my staying with my crew foreman in his house. Look, I'm not an unreasonable boss to work for, but there are certain lines that just shouldn't be crossed. You've got to know that," she said, searching his face to see if she'd made an impression on the cowboy.

Finn ran the edge of his thumb ever so lightly along the area just beneath each of her eyes. Initially, she began to pull back—then didn't.

There it was again, she realized, that lightning, coursing through her veins. Immobilizing her.

"Only lines I'm worried about seeing are the ones that are going to be forming right here, under your eyes, because you didn't get enough sleep," Finn told her in a low voice that made her scrambled pulse go up several more notches. "And that'll be in large part because of your fifty-mile, round-way trip from Pine Ridge to Forever. Seems like a lot to sacrifice just for appearances' sake."

Finn dropped his hand to his side. "C'mon, Ms. Carmichael, we're both adults," he coaxed gently. "Adults handle situations. Nothing's going to happen if we don't want it to."

If. He'd said if. *Not* because *but* if. *Was that a prophesy?*

Only if she let it become one, Connie silently insisted.

She supposed, in the interest of being here very

early—Emerson had promised that the machinery she required to begin the excavation would be here first thing in the morning—finding a place in town to crash for the night was the far more practical way to go. And while staying with Miss Joan seemed to be an acceptable concept, the older woman seemed the type to subject to her a battery of questions. And Connie would feel obligated to answer in repayment for the woman's hospitality.

That was an ordeal she would definitely rather not face.

She slanted a glance toward the man standing beside her.

"What would your brothers say about your impulsive burst of hospitality?" she asked, covering up the fact that she found herself suddenly nervous with rhetoric.

Finn shrugged, as if she'd just asked a question that was hardly worth consideration. "Brett wouldn't say anything because when he knocks off for the night, which is pretty damn late, he usually goes home to the ranch house you saw me working on. Lady Doc stays there, as well, whenever she gets a chance. So Brett's not even in this picture if you're worried about what he thinks," Finn guaranteed. "As for Liam, well, Liam doesn't exactly think," he said with a dismissive laugh.

"What do you mean?" she asked, doing her best to be tactful in her inquiry.

The last thing she wanted to do was insult someone in Finn's family.

"Liam's just plain challenged—challenged by anything that's not a musical note in a song he had a hand in writing. In other words, what I'm trying to say is that if you're not shaped like a guitar, there's little chance that he'd even notice you, even if you stripped down buck naked and pretended you were the dining room tablecloth. On second thought," he amended, taking another look at the woman beside him, "maybe he's not really that far gone yet."

"As intriguing as that sounds," Connie began, but got no further.

Seeing his advantage, Finn pushed to the goal line. "Take me up on the offer. You'll be driving yourself plenty once this thing is in full swing. I can tell just by looking at you," he said, surprising her. "This might very well be your last chance to take in a deep breath and relax. If you don't want to listen to me telling you this as a friend, then maybe you'll listen to the man you're paying to head up your crew and tell you the way he sees things."

Connie stared at him for a moment, confused. "But that's you."

The smile he flashed at her cut right through the cloud of confusion that threatened to swallow her up. "Exactly," Finn agreed. "And the way I see it, your getting a good night's sleep is more important than you worrying about what a couple of people may—or may not—say about you staying at my house," he underscored.

Having laid out his argument, he took a step back. He had a feeling that crowding this woman was *not* the way to go.

"Final decision," he told her, "like with the project, is ultimately yours. But I'd like to think you'd respect my opinion and give it its due consideration. Otherwise, there's really no point in you hiring me. Think of it this way," he added, suddenly coming up with another argument in his favor. "You wouldn't have any objections to staying in the same hotel as I was in, right?"

"Right," she agreed warily, waiting to see where this was going.

"Well, then think of my house as a hotel," he told her, adding with a grin, "a very small, rather limited hotel."

The man really knew how to use his words. To look at him, she wouldn't have thought that he could actually be so persuasive.

"Bed-and-breakfast inns are larger than your house," she told him.

"So, after your hotel is completed, I'll see about adding on some extra rooms to the house," he told her. "You can think of it as a bed-and-breakfast inn in the making," he added with a wink.

She felt something flutter inside her chest and told herself it was just that she was tired. Her reaction had nothing to do with the wink.

"My clothes are all at the hotel," she suddenly remembered, which, in her book, should have brought an end to this debate.

She should have known better.

Finn took a step back and regarded her thoughtfully for a moment. "Lady Doc's about your size, as is Dr. Dan's wife. One of them can lend you something to sleep in. The other can give you a change of clothes for tomorrow. And once we get the assignments straightened out for the day, I can send someone over to Pine Ridge to get the rest of your clothes." He grinned at her. "See? Problem solved."

And just possibly, a brand-new one started, she couldn't help thinking.

"So you've taken care of everything, just like that?" she asked out loud.

There was a note in her voice Finn didn't recognize, but he had a hunch that weather watchers would point out that it might have to do with a coming storm. He quickly got ahead of it—just in case.

"What I've done—just like that—was make suggestions," he told her. "You're the one who makes the final decisions and ultimately takes care of everything," he concluded, looking like the soul of innocence.

It was Connie's turn to look at him for a long moment. And then she nodded, suppressing what sounded like a laugh. She gave him his due. "Nice save."

Finn did not take the bait. "Just telling it the way it is," he countered.

Connie merely nodded, more to herself than to him. She definitely didn't want to spend the rest of the evening arguing—especially unproductively. Instead, she silently congratulated herself on going with her gut instincts. She'd made the right choice putting Finn in charge of all the others. If the man could pull off this side-step shuffle effectively with her, he could do it with anyone. After all, she had seen something in him from the very first moment she laid eyes on him, and it wasn't that he had looks to die for. It was a vibe she got, a silent telegraphing of potential that felt so strong, it had taken her a few minutes to process.

But just for a moment, she had to deal with his suggestion not as his boss, but as a woman. Looking at him intently, silently assuring herself that if he was selling her a bill of goods, she'd be able to tell, she had one more question for him.

"And you're *sure* neither one of your brothers—

wherever they might roam—won't mind my crashing at their place—and don't tell me again that they won't be there. It's their place. That counts for something."

"They won't mind," he assured her with feeling.

"Okay, I'll stay in town," she agreed in pretty much the same tone that someone agreed to have a root canal done. She only hoped she wouldn't wind up regretting a decision of so-called convenience.

"In the interest of full disclosure," Finn went on, "I just want to warn you that neither one of my brothers— or I—are exactly good at housekeeping. I mean, it's livable and all that," he was quick to add, "if you don't mind dirt, grime and dust like you wouldn't believe." He looked a little embarrassed as he added, "Lost civilizations have less dust piled on top of them than some of the rooms in this house.

"The place is in sturdy condition," he went on to assure her. "Either that, or the dust is acting like the glue that's holding all this together," Finn told her with a hearty laugh.

Connie couldn't help wondering just how much of what the cowboy was telling her had more than an ounce of truth in it. Instead of repulsed, she found herself intrigued. Now she *wanted* to take a tour of this place where he had lived his entire life, just to see if it was in the less-than-savory condition he was describing.

"Remind me not to put you in charge of the new hotel's travel brochure," Connie told him with a shake of her head.

"I don't think you're going to need someone to remind you of that." And then it hit him. They were about to walk out of Murphy's, and Finn caught hold of his boss by the arm. He didn't want to lose sight of her until he had gotten at least this part straight. "Wait, are you saying that I managed to convince you?" he asked her, genuinely surprised. "You've decided that you're staying in Forever tonight?"

"That's what I'm saying," Connie answered—and then she paused. "Unless you've changed your mind about the offer."

"No way," he told her with enthusiasm. "You won't regret this," he promised.

She didn't know about that. Part of her already *was* regretting her decision. As a rule, while she remained friendly and outwardly approachable, she didn't really get too close to the people who essentially worked for her. The reason for that was that she never knew if they were being friendly because they liked her—or because they were using her to get to her father.

Not that that approach ever really worked, since her father could never even come close to being accused of being a *doting* father.

She looked at Finn, hardly believing that she'd actually agreed to allow him to put her up for the night. "So, is this the part where you go asking your friends to donate their clothes to me?"

"No, that comes a little later," he told her. "This is the part where you look up at the sky, say something about being awestruck over how there looks as if there's twice as much sky here as in places like Houston or Los Angeles, and I agree with you—even though I know it's not true. Then I tell you that if you see a falling star, you have to pause and make a wish. Sound too taxing?" he asked her, a hint of a smile on his face.

They had stopped walking again and were standing, in her opinion, much too close, at least for her comfort.

This was a mistake. A big one.

But if she suddenly announced that she had changed her mind about staying the night in his guest room, she'd seem flighty—worse than that, she'd seem as if she was afraid, and she'd lose any chance she had at commanding respect—from him and most likely, from the rest of the men working for her.

Her only recourse was to brazen it out.

Heaven knew it wouldn't be the first time.

"No, I think I can handle making a wish if I see a falling star," she told him.

"Well, then I'd say you've got everything under control."

Finn watched her for a long moment, thinking things that he knew he shouldn't be thinking. Things that would probably get him fired before he ever began to work on the project. But there was something about the woman, a vulnerability despite the barriers she was trying to rigidly retain in place, that reached out and spoke to him. It brought out the protector in him.

He wondered what she would say if she knew. Probably, *You're fired.*

"It's going to be fine," Finn told her.

Startled, she looked at him. "What?"

Connie wished she had as much confidence in her succeeding as Finn apparently had—if she was to believe what he'd just said.

But you don't have everything under control, do you?

She felt another knot tightening in her stomach.

This had to be what opening-night jitters felt like for actors, she theorized. It felt as if everything was riding on this.

"I said it's going to be fine," Finn repeated. "For

a second you looked as if you were a million miles away—and you were frowning, so I thought maybe you were worrying about the site. I have to ask—you always this nervous before a project?"

It was on the tip of her tongue to tell him that her emotions were none of his business, that she hadn't hired him to subject her to countless questions, but that would really be starting out on the wrong foot, and he did seem genuinely concerned.

"No, I have to admit that this is a first."

He nodded, giving her the benefit of the doubt. "You've hired on a good bunch of people, and they'll work hard to deliver whatever it is you need done," he assured her, then asked, "Anything I can do to help squelch your uneasiness?"

She smiled at him. "You just did it."

"Good to know," he told her.

They were outside the saloon now. Finn had gently coaxed her over to the side, out of the way of any foot traffic. He directed her attention toward the sky, pointing to a cluster of stars.

"Look." He indicated a constellation. "Isn't that just the most magnificent sight you've ever seen?" he asked.

To oblige him, she looked up when he told her to. Ordinarily, before tonight, the thought of a heaven full of stars did nothing for her. But looking up now, at Finn's request, she found herself at first interested, then deeply moved. The vastness spoke to her—and she could relate. Relate to feeling isolated, desolate and alone.

Shake it off, Con, she ordered herself. *Sentimental and sloppy isn't going to build the future. It's not you, anyway.*

"Beautiful, isn't it?" he asked again.

She couldn't very well pretend to be indifferent. Because she no longer was.

"Yes," she agreed, "it is. It kind of takes my breath away."

She heard him laugh. When she looked at him quizzically, he merely said, "I know the feeling."

Except that when he said it, he wasn't looking at the sky. He was looking at her.

She told herself to ignore it, that she was misreading him. But even so, Connie could feel herself growing suddenly very warm despite the evening breeze.

Growing very warm and yearning for him to kiss her.

That's the alcohol talking, a voice in her head insisted. But she had only had the one drink, a short one at that, and she could hold far more than that and still remain lucid and steady.

It wasn't the drink. It was the man. But that was an admission she intended to take with her to the grave.

"I think we'd better get going," he told her. "The whole idea of you staying in town was for you to get extra rest—and if we stay out here like this any longer, I might wind up doing something that's going to cost me my job before I ever set foot on the construction site."

Her cheeks heated up and for just a second, she felt light-headed and giddy, like a schoolgirl. She hadn't experienced this sensation even when she had been a schoolgirl.

But the next moment, she regained control over herself and willed the moment to pass. "You're right. Let's get going."

Chapter Ten

"If you need anything," Finn told her almost an hour later as they stood on the second floor of his house, "I'm just down the hall." He pointed to the room that was located on the other side of the small bathroom he had already shown her.

Suddenly bone-tired, Connie nodded, murmuring, "Thanks."

They had stopped on the way to his home to borrow the things that she needed in the way of clothing for tonight and tomorrow. Finn couldn't think of a single other thing she needed to know at this point, so he began to withdraw from the room.

"Okay. Then I guess you're all set. See you in the morning," he told Connie.

Again she nodded, softly repeating the last word he'd just said, as if in agreement. "Morning." With that, Con-

nie retreated into the room that he had just brought
her to.

Closing the door, Connie took another, longer, closer
look around what he'd referred to as the guest room.
It looked even smaller now than it had at first glance,
barely the size of her closet back home. Perhaps even
smaller. There was enough space for a double bed, one
nightstand with a lamp and a very small dresser.

The closet itself, which curiosity prompted her to
check out, was large enough to accommodate less than
half the clothing she'd left at the hotel in Pine Ridge.

Yet from the way Finn had talked about the house
as they drove over to it, she got the impression that this
small, cramped house had seen a great deal more happiness and love than her father's seven-thousand-square-
foot-plus mansion ever had.

There was a kind of worn-down-to-the-nub warmth
emanating from the sixty-three-year-old, two-story
house that was sorely missing from the place where
she had grown up and still vaguely thought of as home.

She found herself envying Finn and his brothers a
great deal.

*Get it together, Con. You've got a full day ahead of
you. Save the pity party for later.*

Taking care to lock her door, Connie pushed the
room's mismatched chair against it by way of an extra
precaution. It wasn't that she didn't trust Finn, because
oddly enough, she did, despite knowing the man for less
than forty-eight hours. She'd been taught that taking an
extra ounce of prevention was always a wise thing to
do—just in case.

That hadn't come from her father, but was something
that Emerson had taught her. The man at one point had

worked as her father's head of security before becoming his general business manager. Emerson had always seemed to be aware of *everything*. She doubted there was a situation in the world that Stewart Emerson was not prepared to handle.

It never occurred to her to dismiss what he said as being useless or inapplicable. She looked to him for guidance the way one should a father. Emerson was the one who always had time for her.

Her father did not.

Connie remembered changing for bed—donning the nightshirt that Brett's fiancée gladly lent her. The verbal exchange between them, with Finn in the middle, had been fleeting. To her chagrin, she could barely recall what the woman had looked like.

But then, she was running perilously close to empty. Connie could vaguely remember lying down.

She didn't remember falling asleep, but she obviously had to have because the next thing she knew, she was looking at the watch she always wore and realizing that it was six in the morning.

Six?

Connie bolted upright. She'd wanted to be up and ready by five. Not because she thought anything actually needed attending to at that time, but because she wanted to be ready—just in case. It was always good to be prepared.

Happily, as far as she knew, everything was proceeding as planned. The necessary machinery was on its way and being delivered by a contractor Emerson had been dealing with for the past fifteen years, Milo Sawyer. Both Emerson and Sawyer knew that failure was not an option for her. Failure would have been worse than death. Emerson had told her that Sawyer took an oath on a stack of figurative bibles that everything would be there when she needed it—if not sooner.

Scrambling, silently lamenting the fact that she needed to sleep as much as she did, Connie was up, dressed and ready in less than twenty minutes.

Her heart kept pace by slamming against her rib cage, reminding her that she was, beneath it all, nervous as hell.

She looked down at what she was wearing. She wasn't keen on starting her first day on a brand-new site in someone else's clothes, but apparently she and Forever's first resident doctor's wife were the exact same size—just as Finn had predicted—and the woman seemed to think nothing of lending her a pair of jeans and a jersey.

Or so Finn had told her when he'd darted into the doctor's house and gotten the items for her. It seemed people just *gave* each other whatever was needed without questioning it. For the umpteenth time it struck her how very different her world was from the world she found herself operating in at the moment.

Moreover, it occurred to Connie, as she glanced in the small oval mirror perched on top of the bureau, that she was wearing something borrowed—the entire outfit—and something blue—the jersey. Not to mention, she also had on something old. Unlike her car, which she laughingly described as her lucky charm, the boots she was wearing were her one *real* concession to superstition: they were her *lucky* boots and they hadn't been considered *new* in the past fourteen years.

Longer, really, because the boots had once belonged to her mother. Unbeknownst to her father, she'd kept her mother's boots in the back of her closet and as luck would have it, when she reached her present adult height and weight, she discovered that the boots fit her perfectly. She had worn them on every occasion that something good had happened to her.

Connie sincerely hoped that they would continue exerting their *magical* influence and make the hotel's construction come off without a single hitch.

Ready and anxious to begin her day, Connie moved the chair away from the door and pushed it back against the wall where it had been. Unlocking the bedroom door, she ventured down the stairs silently.

Her intention was to slip out of the house and drive over to the site—her car was conveniently parked in front of Finn's house. But when she came to the bottom of the stairs, the deep, rich smell of freshly brewed coffee surrounded her before she knew what had hit her—followed by the aroma of bacon and eggs, a classic one-two punch if ever there was one.

Unable to resist, Connie glanced toward the only source of light on the first floor at this hour. It was coming from the kitchen.

The debate between following her nose or leaving while there was no one watching her was a short one that abruptly ended when her stomach rumbled rather loudly, casting the deciding vote.

She went toward the light.

Finn was standing by the old-fashioned stove. He glanced over his shoulder in her direction the moment she stepped over the threshold. It was almost eerie, as if he instinctively knew she would come. He supposed that some people would have said they had some sort of a "connection." He could think of worse things than being connected to a woman who could scramble his insides just with a toss of her flowing, shoulder-length auburn hair.

"You're up," Finn declared by way of a greeting.

"So, apparently, are you," she countered, nodding toward the stovetop. He had three frying pans going at once.

"Everyone gets up early around here. If you don't, you're either sick—or dead," Finn told her matter-of-factly.

"That doesn't exactly leave a wide range of choice available," she commented.

He laughed and shrugged before gesturing toward the kitchen table.

"Sit down," he told her. "Coffee's hot. I'll pour you a cup."

"I can serve myself," she told him as she crossed to the counter.

She looked around for a coffeemaker, but didn't see one. But she did notice a coffeepot on the last burner on the stovetop.

Talk about old-fashioned, she thought. Connie dutifully poured the extra-black substance into her cup and retreated back to the table, getting out of Finn's way.

"Where is everyone?" she asked. She glanced out the kitchen window to see if perhaps one of his brothers was outside, but they weren't. The small area was desolate.

"Liam's holed up in his room, working on another song for his band—he decided he didn't like his last couple of efforts—and I'm guessing that Brett's over at the other ranch house like I said he'd be." Finn was smiling as he turned away from the stove. "He likes the job I did renovating the ranch house so much, he decided he wanted to stay there, getting it set up for Lady Doc and him once they're married."

Holding the steaming mug of coffee with two hands, Connie made herself comfortable at the table. "Have you thought of taking up that line of work permanently?" she asked.

He frowned ever so slightly, not at her suggestion but over the fact that he had lost the thread of the conversation. "What line of work?"

"Construction, renovations," she elaborated. "That sort of thing. There has to be better money in it than there is in bartending," she insisted. Why was the man wasting his time bartending when he could be earning *real* money?

Finn shrugged indifferently. "I wouldn't know. So far, I've never been paid anything for doing that kind of work."

Connie stared at him. Had she gotten her information mixed up? "I thought you said you installed a bathroom over the bar."

"I did," he confirmed. "But that was for the apartment above the bar—all that belongs to my brothers and me. Seems pretty silly to charge myself," Finn commented.

"And the ranch house?" she asked, referring to the first time she had seen him. He'd certainly been working hard that day. Free of charge?

"The same," he replied. "Besides, I told you, that's my wedding present to Brett and Lady Doc. I couldn't charge them," he said, shooting the mere notion down as beyond ludicrous.

She had no idea that they *made* men like this anymore. Connie looked at him with renewed admiration. "That's exceptionally generous of you."

He shrugged away her comment. "So, how do you like your eggs?" he asked.

"In the chicken," she quipped.

Finn stared at her. "Wanna run that by me again?" he requested.

She appreciated what he was trying to do, but there was really no need. "I don't eat eggs," she told him. "Never have, never will. I just plain don't like them no matter what you do to them," she added.

He nodded and said, "Fair enough. Got an opinion about bacon?" he asked, testing the waters cautiously.

There was bacon sizzling in the large skillet on the left back burner. "It smells good," she was forced to admit.

Finn's grin hinted of triumph. "Tastes even better," he assured her. Without waiting for her to respond, he proceeded to place four strips of what looked like perfectly fried bacon on her plate. But that obviously wasn't enough as far as he was concerned, so since she had vetoed eggs, he gave her other options: "Pancakes, waffles, French toast or…?"

She regarded him with what could be described as innocent confusion. "What about them?"

"Which do you want for breakfast?" he asked patiently.

He'd already gone out of his way more than was required. He might work for her, but there was nothing in the fine print about serving her hand and foot, and she didn't want him feeling as if this was part of his job description.

"The bacon is more than enough," Connie assured

the man. "I usually have just coffee in the morning, nothing else."

Finn frowned, obviously displeased with the answer. "You can't tackle a new day on just coffee," he told her. And then he seemed to study her for a long minute, as if he was making some sort of a major decision.

It took everything she had to wait him out, but she had a feeling that she could lose him if she began to ask him too many questions. So she did her best to appear patient—even if it was the last thing in the world that she was right now.

He was probably trying to browbeat her into eating. Simple enough fix, she decided. "Okay, I'll have toast," Connie finally conceded.

"Just toast?" he asked her.

She stuck to her guns. If she began giving in now, that would carry over to the work site, and she would quickly lose any ground she might have had to begin with. "Just toast," she confirmed. And quite honestly, she didn't even really want that.

Finn frowned for a moment longer then suddenly brightened—as if an idea had literally hit him—and went to work. A few minutes later, he deposited two large so-called *slices* onto her plate.

Stunned, Connie could only point out the obvious. "I agreed to toast. What is that?" she asked. Whatever it was, it was thick, and it was huge.

"Toast," Finn responded innocently, then a smile slipped through. "Texas style."

Each piece was the size of three regular slices of bread and together with what she had before her comprised more than a full breakfast in her opinion.

She sighed and shook her head, knowing that if she

protested, she would wind up with something even bigger. And she had to admit that the aroma was definitely working its magic on her, arousing her taste buds. For the first time in years, she was hungry enough to eat something for breakfast.

"You know, it works better if you pick up a fork and put the food into your mouth instead of staring at it," he advised, sitting down opposite her.

He'd put a plate down for himself. Finn's plate was all but overflowing with bacon, eggs, toast and a sprinkling of hash browns.

Connie could only stare at the heaping plate in complete wonder. "You're really going to eat all that?" she asked him.

"I *need* to," he emphasized. "If I don't, I'll run out of steam in a couple of hours—like clockwork," he assured her.

However, listening to him, Connie sincerely doubted what he'd just said. She'd come to quickly realize that Finn might appear laid-back, but the man was all go all the time.

"Who taught you how to cook?" she asked as she resigned herself to the meal before her.

She half expected Finn to say that he had picked things up while watching his mother fix meals in the kitchen.

He summed it up in one word: "Brett."

Connie blinked and stared at him. "Your brother?" she asked incredulously.

To her best recollection, her own brother couldn't boil water. She fervently hoped he'd learned how by now, wherever he was.

Finn nodded, seeing nothing out of the ordinary with

what he was telling her. "Everything I know how to do, Brett taught me."

"Even construction?" she asked, thinking that perhaps she should have approached the older Murphy brother with a job offer, as well—because what she had seen with the ranch house had impressed her no end, and if Brett had had a hand in that, as well…

"Even construction," Finn echoed. "He taught me the basics. I kind of took off with it on my own after that," Finn admitted without a drop of conceit. "Brett's abilities—and vision—kind of went in a different direction from mine," Finn went on to tell her. "Let me put it this way. Brett can fix a leaky faucet—I can install a new one along with a new sink," he explained in an effort to illustrate his point. "Besides, Brett was always busy. He didn't have time to get caught up in anything fancy. He was keeping our family together, especially after Uncle Patrick died. Brett's the really practical one in the family," he added, as if that explained everything.

She tried to glean what he was actually telling her. "And that makes you what, the dreamer?"

"No, that's Liam. He's the dreamer in the family. Me, I'm just the guy in the middle." He grinned as he illustrated his point for her. "The guy not *too*."

If anything, that made things only more obscure in her opinion. "I'm sorry," she told him. "I don't understand. Not too…?" she repeated, at a loss as to what that meant or was supposed to illustrate for her.

Finn nodded then went on to give her examples. "Not too practical, not too dreamy. You know, not too hot, not too cold, that kind of thing. Always staying on an even keel, never too much of anything, just enough to satisfy requirements."

She held up her hand to get him to stop. Was that how he saw himself? That was awful. "You make it sound so bland," she told him.

Finn laughed softly. "Probably because it is."

Connie looked at the man sitting across from her for a very long, quiet moment, thinking of the way this man she still hardly knew seemed to stir her in ways that she'd never experienced before.

"Not by a long shot," she finally told him, though a little voice in her head warned her that she was giving too much away far too quickly.

"You want seconds?" he asked out of the blue. When she eyed him questioningly, trying to comprehend what he'd just asked, he nodded at her plate—which was somehow miraculously empty. When had she eaten everything? "Do you want seconds?" he repeated.

"No. No, thank you. It was all very good, but in the interest of not waddling onto the construction site, I think I'll just stop here," she told him, pushing back her plate.

That was when he took her plate from her, put it on top of his own and then carried both to the sink. Connie bit her lower lip, curtailing the impulse to offer to wash them for him.

The next moment, as she watched, he quickly rinsed off both plates and stacked them in the dishwasher.

An efficient male, she thought to herself.

She took a deep breath.

It was time.

Chapter Eleven

Looking back at the end of the day, as far as first days went, this had to be the very best one she had ever experienced. The machinery showed up early, as did the men who were to operate it. That meant that excavation and ground preparations could begin right on schedule and even a little bit ahead of it.

Because of the work schedules she had laboriously written up ahead of time, everyone she had hired knew almost from the very beginning exactly what to do and what was expected. Detailed schedules were conspicuously posted in a number of places.

The biggest surprise of the day for her occurred shortly before two o'clock.

Stewart Emerson walked onto the construction site, managing to catch her completely off guard.

Connie had been in the middle of a conversation with

Finn, outlining what she hoped would be the project's progress for that week, when she heard a gravelly voice behind her call out her name.

Stopping in midsentence, she turned away from Finn to see exactly who sounded so much like the man she thought of as her rock.

Her mouth fell open the second she saw him.

"Stewart?" Connie cried in disbelief as the big bear of a man strode in her direction.

As Finn looked on, he watched the rather petite young woman being enfolded and all but swallowed up in the embrace of a man who could have easily doubled as Santa Claus—if the legendary figure had been a towering man given to wearing three-piece suits.

"In the flesh," Emerson confirmed. "I guess I'd better put you down. The men might not react well to seeing their boss whirled around the construction site like a weightless little doll." Emerson's deep laugh filled the immediate area.

With her feet firmly back on the ground, Connie made no effort to put space between herself and the older man. "I wasn't expecting you. What are you doing here?" she asked.

Finn stood by, wondering who this man was to her. He would have had to have been blind not to notice how radiant she suddenly looked. She was all but glowing and her smile resembled rays of sunshine reaching out to infinity. He'd thought she was a beautiful woman before, but what he'd been privy to before didn't hold a candle to what he was seeing now. Whoever this man was, he clearly lit up her world.

The one thing he did know was that this couldn't be the father who was always criticizing her.

"I thought you might need a little moral support," Emerson confessed, then laughed at his own words as he took a long look around the area. The entire grounds were humming with activity. "But you're obviously doing just fine—not that I ever thought you wouldn't. You don't lack for bodies, that's for sure," he ascertained.

"Did he send you to check up on me?" Connie asked out of curiosity.

There was no accusation in her voice. She knew that despite the fact that Emerson had been her mentor and all around best friend all these years, the man did work for her father, which meant that he had to abide by whatever wishes Calvin Carmichael voiced whenever possible. The last thing she wanted was to have Emerson terminated because of her. She knew she wouldn't be able to live with this.

"Oddly enough, no, he didn't," Emerson told her. "I meant what I said. I came down because I thought you might need a little moral support, this being your first real solo project and all. I mistakenly thought you might be in need of a pep talk, but here you are, all grown up and following in your dad's footsteps," he chuckled. "The old man would be proud of you if he saw this." Emerson gestured around the busy construction site.

"No, he wouldn't," Connie contradicted him knowingly. "You know that. If he were here, he'd be pointing out all the things he felt that I neglected to do, or had begun to do wrong…" Her voice trailed off as she eyed the heavyset man.

"All right, he wouldn't," Emerson conceded. "But just because he's always looking to find ways in which you can improve doesn't mean you're not doing a fine job to begin with."

She knew what Emerson was trying to do, and she loved him for it, but she was beginning to resign herself to what she was up against when it came to her father—a bar that was forever being raised no matter how great her achievements.

"It's okay, Stewart, really," she told the man, laying a hand on his arm. "My reward will be in a job well-done, not in any praise I'm hoping to get that'll just never come."

Out of the corner of her eye, she saw that Finn was still standing just on the outskirts of her conversation. "Oh, sorry, I guess your visit threw me. I'd like to introduce you to someone, Stewart. This is my foreman, Finn Murphy," she told the older man, hooking her arm through Finn's and drawing him into the small circle that she and Emerson formed.

"Finn, this is Stewart Emerson, the man who really runs Carmichael Construction Corporation." And by that she meant the man who provided the corporation with a heart.

Emerson pretended to wince. "Ouch, don't let your dad hear you say that or I'll have my walking papers before you can say, 'here's your hat.'" Leaning past the young woman he considered to be the daughter he never had, Emerson grasped the hand that her foreman offered and shook it heartily. "Foreman, eh?" he repeated. He released Finn's hand, but his eyes continued to hold the other man's. "You've done this kind of thing before?" Emerson asked.

Connie immediately placed herself between the two men again. "Don't browbeat my people, Stewart.

I wouldn't have hired Finn for the position if I didn't think he could do the job."

Emerson looked at her knowingly. "You'd hire a puppy to do the work if it looked at you with eyes that were sad enough. No offense, Murphy," he quickly told Finn.

"None taken," Finn replied, then added, "as long as you don't think that's why I have this job."

The look in the older man's gray eyes was unreadable. "So this isn't your first time as a foreman? You've been one before?" Emerson asked him.

For the second time, Connie came to the cowboy's defense.

"You're doing it again. You're browbeating. And as to your question, Finn knows how to get men to follow orders." Which, she added silently, he did, just that he did it in his role as a bartender.

"Does he issue those orders himself, or does he let you do all the talking for him?" Emerson asked, a healthy dose of amusement curving his rather small, full mouth.

"Well, I do know enough not to get in her way if she decides she wants to say something," Finn told the other man politely.

Emerson regarded Connie's foreman thoughtfully. For a second, Finn thought that the older man might have felt that he'd overstepped the line. But the next moment, what he said gave no such indication.

"I just want to make sure that Connie's not being taken advantage of—by anyone," Emerson emphasized pointedly.

"Understood," Finn replied with sincerity. "But Ms. Carmichael isn't someone who *can* be easily taken advantage of. In case you haven't noticed, sir," he pretended to confide, "she's very strong-willed and very much her own person."

"Excuse me, I'm right here," Connie reminded the men, raising her hand as if she were a student in a classroom, wanting to be called on. Dropping her hand, she got in between the two men again, looking from one to the other. "I appreciate what's going on here, but I *can* fight my own battles, you know," she informed them, the statement intended for both of the men on either side of her. "Now, then, Stewart, let me take you into that trailer you remembered to send out for me and show you the plans I drew up. Maybe I can renew your faith in me once you review them."

"My faith in you never faded," Emerson informed her as he followed her to the long trailer that was to serve as both her on-site office and her home away from home, as well.

Finn hung back. He'd already seen the plans, both the ones that she herself had drawn up—strictly from an architectural standpoint—and the ones that the structural engineer she'd consulted with had put together.

In addition, he thought that if he tagged along, his presence might be construed as an intrusion under the circumstances.

Sexy and stirring though he found her, she was, after all, the one in charge of all this and ultimately, no matter what sort of feelings he might have for her, she was his boss. He had absolutely no business viewing her as anything else.

However, he silently promised himself, walking back to the backhoe, once this project was completed—and before she left Forever for Houston or her next assignment—he intended to carve out a little time alone for the two of them. There was no two ways about it. The lady most definitely intrigued him.

But he could bide his time and wait.

Patience, his older brother had drilled into him more than once, was the name of the game, and anything worth getting was worth the effort and the patience it took to wait it out.

Stewart Emerson had been around the world of construction, in one capacity or another, for a very long time. Ever since fate had stepped in one night, putting him in the right place at the right time to save Calvin Carmichael from being on the receiving end of what could have been a fatal beating.

He had not only pulled the drunken, would-be muggers off Carmichael, but by the time he was done, he had also sent the duo to the hospital—which seemed only fair inasmuch as their plan apparently had been to send Carmichael straight to the morgue.

Shaken for possibly the first—and last—time of his life as well as uncharacteristically grateful, Connie's father had immediately offered the much larger—and unemployed—former navy SEAL a job as his bodyguard.

As the business grew, so had Carmichael's dependence on Emerson, causing the latter's responsibilities to increase, as well.

Taking nothing for granted, Emerson made it a point to become familiar with everything that his employer concerned himself with and thus, while he couldn't draw up his own plans from scratch, he developed an eye for what was constructually sound, as well as what made good business sense.

Emerson made it a point to become indispensable to the corporation—and the man—in many ways.

But to Connie, the tall, heavyset, bearded man who could have easily been mistaken for Santa Claus these days would always be her one true confidant, her one true friend.

While for years, she had wanted nothing as much as to finally win her father's approval, nothing meant more to her than Emerson's opinion.

It still did.

"Well, what do you think?" she asked, gesturing toward the two large drawings that were tacked up side by side on the bulletin board that hung opposite the trailer's entrance. Between the two plans, they encompassed both the esthetics and the practical side of the building that was destined to be Forever's very first hotel.

Emerson spent a good five minutes studying first one set of plans, then the other. Finally, he stepped back and nodded his shaggy, gray head.

"I must say that I'm impressed. But then, I'd expect nothing less than the best from you," he told her, hooking his bear-like arm around her waist and pulling her toward him affectionately.

She laughed softly to herself, happily returning his hug. "That makes one of you."

Emerson released his hold from around her shoulders and did what he could to hide his sigh. There were times when he despaired if the man he worked for would ever realize exactly what he had and what he was in danger of losing.

"Your father's a hard man to please, Connie. We both know that. Did I ever tell you about the time that, after standing at the edge of the Grand Canyon, looking down for a good ten minutes, he turned to me and said, 'I could have done it better in probably half the time.' If your dad thinks he can criticize God's handiwork like that, the rest of us can't expect to be treated any better."

Though she gave Emerson no indication, it wasn't the first time she'd heard him tell her the story. Emerson had told it to her at least a couple of times, the first being a long time ago in an effort to make her feel better after her father had mercilessly taken apart a venture she'd been very proud of undertaking.

That was when she'd finally realized that *nothing* was ever going to be good enough to meet her father's standards, no matter how hard she tried.

But she wouldn't be who she was if she didn't keep on doing just that.

Trying.

Over and over again.

"I suppose I shouldn't care about pleasing him," she told Emerson, "but he put so much on this project turning out right, I feel that if I don't meet his expectations, that's it, I'm out of the game. Permanently," she added flatly.

"You'll never be permanently out of the game," Emerson told her, even though he knew that was what he'd heard Carmichael tell her. "Doesn't matter what he says at the time. He needs you, needs your energy, needs you to keep going, to be his eyes and ears in places he can no longer get to. He'll come around," Emerson promised in a tone that made an individual feel that he could make book on the man's words and never risk a thing.

"Meanwhile," Emerson continued, his eyes on hers, "you seem to have put together a pretty good crew. They're moving back and forth like well-trained workers. And that foreman of yours—" He paused for a moment, looking at her significantly. "I'd keep my eye on him if I were you."

"Why?" Connie asked. "Don't you trust him, Stewart?"

Emerson heard the slight defensive tone in her voice and wondered if she was aware of it herself. He had a better-than-vague idea just what it meant in this instance. "Hasn't got anything to do with trust," he told her.

She was trying to follow Emerson's drift, but he did have a habit of going off on a tangent at times. This seemed to be one of those times.

"Then what...?"

For once, Emerson didn't hide his meaning behind incomprehensible rhetoric that left the listener baffled for days—because he wanted to be certain that she was aware of what was going on. It was one thing for him to catch her off guard, and another to have some stranger do it.

"Your foreman looks at you as if you were a tall, cool drink of water, and he had just come crawling in on his chafed hands and knees across the length of the desert."

Connie stared at him in bewildered disbelief. "What does that even mean?" she asked. Finn had been nothing if not polite. If anything, she had been the one who'd stared at him that first day.

Emerson grinned. "That means, don't work any long hours alone with the man or you might find something besides this building being created."

What would Stewart say if he knew that she'd spent the night in Finn's house? Connie couldn't help wondering. She was fairly confident that Stewart would ultimately believe anything she would tell him. However, she was also certain that he'd worry twice as much as before—for no reason.

She shouldn't worry. She trusted Finn implicitly— and more important, even though she was admittedly more than just mildly attracted to Finn, she trusted herself not to jeopardize the project.

That was what was important here. Not the blush of a possibly fleeting romance, but the project.

The hotel.

Winning this invisible wager with her father and being assured that her career with the company was a done deal. Anything else came in a distant second— if that.

"I never knew you had such a rich imagination, Stewart," she said, grateful that her cheeks hadn't suddenly rebelled and given her away. "Finn only thinks of me as his boss. There are plenty of women around for him to choose from if he has other inclinations," she added innocently.

"I think he's already made his choice," he told her pointedly.

"And I think you're being way too protective of me— not that I don't appreciate it," she added, lovingly patting the man's cheek. "So, how long do I have you for?" she asked, effectively changing the subject.

In response, Emerson looked at his watch. "Just another couple of hours, I'm afraid. I'm flying back to Houston at four-thirty," he told her. "Your father's looking into acquiring another company to extend his domain, and I told him I'd be there to sit in on the meeting."

"Extension? Again?" she asked with a shake of her

head. Wasn't it ever going to be enough for him? she wondered.

Emerson raised his wide, wide shoulders and then let them fall in a vague shrug. "Your father does have the resources."

Connie sighed and shook her head. "That's not the point. Is it really a smart move to spread himself so thin? What if he suddenly experiences a cash-flow problem? What then?"

Emerson laughed at the objections she raised because those were the exact same ones he'd raised with his employer. "And that's one of the reasons he has his suspicions that you're more mine than his." And then he went on to say what they both knew to be true. "Your father doesn't think that way, and ultimately, he's the boss."

"Still doesn't make him right."

"No," Emerson agreed. "It doesn't. But it also doesn't give us anything to fight with, either. He does what he wants to when he wants to."

Truer words were never spoken, Connie thought. She picked up a clipboard from the table. The next week's schedule was attached to that, as well.

"Well, I've got to get back to work." She paused and then quickly kissed the older man's cheek. "Thanks for coming to check up on me."

"Wouldn't have missed it for the world," he told her in all honesty. "And Connie?"

At the door, about to step out, she paused to look back. "Yes?"

"For what it's worth, I like him. Your foreman," he specified. "I like him."

She hadn't expected that warm feeling to go sweeping through her. It threw her for a second.

"Good. I'll let him know. Maybe the two of you can make an evening of it sometime," she said with a straight face.

The sound of Emerson's booming laugh followed her out of the trailer.

It was, for her, the most heartwarming sound she knew.

Chapter Twelve

Connie looked up from the wide drawing board in her trailer, startled to see Finn walking in. She knew the broad-shouldered man was only six-one but somehow, he just seemed to fill up the entire trailer with hi presence. Given the size of her trailer, that was saying a lot.

"I knocked," he told her. "Twice."

She had no doubt that he had. She'd been lost in thought, oblivious to her surroundings, for the last half hour or so.

Connie merely nodded at his statement. "Is there a problem?" she asked, ready to send him on his way if there wasn't. She was having trouble concentrating, and the schedules were overlapping in areas where they really shouldn't.

He and Connie had been working closely now for the past four weeks, and he'd gotten somewhat accustomed to her being braced for something to go wrong. Thus far, nothing had. If anything, it had been the complete opposite since they'd started work on the hotel.

But that still didn't change her attitude.

"No, no problem," he assured her. "As a matter of fact, it's going pretty damn well, don't you think?"

It did look that way, she had to silently concede. Working in what amounted to two complete shifts, utilizing whatever daylight was available and relying on strobe lighting that she'd had brought in less than six days into the job, Connie had to admit that Finn and the crew had made tremendous headway. The two backhoes were kept humming sixteen hours a day until the excavation was completed.

In addition, the weather had been incredibly cooperative. They had no rain days to interfere with the schedules she'd so carefully drawn up. All that had put them ahead of schedule, something she was not about to take for granted.

"We still have a long way to go before we're done," she pointed out.

Despite everything he had said to her at the outset, he noted that the woman just did not know how to relax or even coast along for a minute. He was just going to have to keep at her, Finn decided.

"But not as long as when we first got started," Finn countered.

"No, of course not. The double shifts have gotten us ahead of schedule—but all it'll take is a few rain days and we'll backslide."

It had to be really taxing, he thought, anticipating the worst all the time. She needed to break that habit—or he had to do it for her.

"Weatherman says no rain for the next week," he told her mildly.

Connie stated what she felt was the obvious. "Weathermen have been wrong."

"Look on the positive side," he coaxed.

Easy for him to say, she thought. He didn't have everything riding on this the way she had. Connie glared at him, debating just murmuring some noncommittal thing, then decided that after the way he'd gotten the crew to operate like a well-oiled machine, maybe she owed him the truth.

So, in a rare unguarded moment, she admitted, "I'm afraid to."

"Nothing to be afraid of," he told Connie. "As a matter of fact, I was going to suggest that maybe, for once, we could keep it down to a single shift and even have everyone knock off early."

"Early?" she echoed. "Why?" Her voice instantly filled with concern as she assumed the worst. "*Is* something wrong?" she asked again.

"No, nothing's wrong," he assured her again in a soothing voice.

"Then why would they want to stop early?" she asked. The crew was being paid, and paid well, to work. She didn't understand the problem.

He crossed to her, gaining a little ground. He glanced at the papers she had spread out over the large drawing board. It was a wonder she didn't have a constant headache, he marveled. He got one just glancing at it.

The scent that he was beginning to identify with her—lilacs and vanilla—began to slowly seep into his consciousness. He assumed that it was a cologne, but maybe it was her shampoo. Whatever it was, he found it both pleasing and arousing—a little like the woman herself, he couldn't help thinking.

He'd come here with an ultimate goal in mind, and he forced himself to get back to it.

"Maybe because all work and no play…you know the old saying."

Connie laughed softly to herself. "In my house, we weren't allowed to mention that old saying," she told Finn. "My father did *not* believe in 'playing.' Or smelling the roses, or anything that didn't have goals and work attached to it."

He'd thought he and his brothers had had it rough as orphans. Despite certain financial hardships, their life seemed like a positive picnic in comparison to the one she must have had.

"Your father's not here," he tactfully reminded her, then quickly added, "and Brett and Alisha are having their engagement party at Murphy's tonight, so, if it's okay with you, everything's temporarily on hold until tomorrow morning."

She looked at him for a long moment. He wasn't challenging her, she realized. If he was, then her reaction would have been completely different. Still, she wanted to push the imaginary envelope just a little to see what would happen.

"And if I say that the work has to go on?"

He didn't look away but continued to meet her gaze head-on. "You'll generate a lot of ill will, and you don't want to do that," he said quietly.

Connie suppressed a sigh. No, she didn't. While she wanted to continue meeting and even surpassing her deadlines, the way her father's crews all did on their construction sites, she really did not want to maintain the kind of tense atmosphere that always existed on one of those work sites.

So, after another moment's debate, Connie nodded and gave her approval. "Fine, tell the men they have the rest of the evening off—but I'll expect them in on time tomorrow," she added, wanting to make sure that Finn didn't lose sight of the fact that she and not he was the one in charge.

"They will be. By the way, you're invited, you know."

She'd already turned her attention back to the schedules, which, in light of the lost shift, now had to be revised.

"To what?" she asked absently.

"To the engagement party."

That had her looking up at him again. "Oh. Well, thank you." She reached for a fresh piece of paper. Instead of using a laptop, she always liked to write her first draft of anything in pencil. "But I think I'll pass." She expected that to be the end of it.

It wasn't.

"Mind if I ask why?"

She indicated the drawing board before her. "If I'm losing an entire eight to ten hours of work, I've got to find somewhere to make it up."

To her surprise, rather than just go along with what she was saying, the way he had been since they had begun working together on the site, Finn took her hands in his and drew her away from the drawing board, saying, "No, you don't."

Stunned at the apparent mutiny, she blinked and stared at him. "Excuse me?"

"You heard me," he told her amicably. "No, you don't," he repeated, then added, "you don't have to do it tonight. Connie." He went on patiently. "It can't always be all about work."

Somewhere in the past few weeks, they had gone from his calling her Ms. Carmichael to using her first name. She wasn't sure exactly when, only that it had evolved rather naturally. She supposed that should have concerned her, but it hadn't.

However, she didn't appreciate being lectured to—especially when she knew in her heart that he was right. "Is this the *look up at the stars* speech again?"

"Think of it as the *let me take you to a party because life is more than just one big work schedule* speech," Finn told her, an amused smile playing along his lips.

She didn't want to be rude, but she couldn't go—for more than one reason. "Finn, I appreciate what you're trying to do—" she began.

"Good, that makes two of us," he replied. "Now, you're coming with me to this thing, and I'm not taking no for an answer."

Connie stared at her foreman in utter wonder. "You're actually going to give me a hard time about this?" she questioned.

"I'm going to *hog-tie* you if I have to," he corrected, "but you are definitely coming to the party."

She didn't understand what difference it made. "Why is it so important to you?"

He never hesitated. "Because you're important to me."

Her mouth dropped open. Did he just say what she thought he said? "What?"

Finn had no doubt that she had heard him the first time. Nonetheless, he went through it again.

"You heard me—and I *am* prepared to hog-tie you

if I have to," he said with finality. "Now, are you going to sacrifice your dignity, or will you come along with me quietly?"

She looked into his eyes and had her answer. He wasn't kidding. She definitely didn't want to put him in a position where he had to carry out his threat.

"I guess I don't have a choice in the matter," she said.

"No," he agreed. "You don't. Besides, seeing you join the party will make the men respect you even more."

She was certain that if her work ethic didn't do it, it would take more than just joining in a toast to make her become one of the crew.

"I really doubt that," Connie told him.

She meant that, he realized. Finn shook his head, feeling genuinely sorry for her. "Then you have a few things to learn about the men who you have working for you."

But as he drew her over to the trailer's door, Connie suddenly looked down at what she was wearing. Jeans and a work shirt. She definitely wasn't dressed for any kind of a party.

"I can't go like this," she protested, digging in her heels.

He gave her a quick once-over. She looked fine to him. Better than fine, actually, though he didn't say so out loud.

"Why?"

"Because I'm not dressed for a party."

"You might not be dressed for one of those fancy parties your father throws in Houston," he told her, "but trust me, you'll fit right in here."

Connie looked at him, surprised at his assurance.

"How do you know about my father's parties?" she asked.

Rather than take offense, Finn merely grinned at the woman's question. "Oh, it's amazing what you can find on the internet when you know where to look. We're not nearly as backward here as you seem to think."

Color flashed across her cheeks. She hadn't meant to insult him. It was just that Forever seemed so self-contained and removed from the world she was familiar with.

"I never thought you were backward," Connie protested.

"Sure you did. But that's okay. You can make it up to me by coming to my brother's engagement party," Finn told her. "C'mon, let's go, boss lady. We're wasting time here."

To emphasize his point, he pulled the trailer door closed firmly behind him then immediately turned around and took her arm. Smiling, Finn guided her over to his truck. As he did so, he waved to the men, who appeared as if they were all looking in his direction, and called out, "She says it's okay!"

Instantly, a cheer went up.

Finn grinned in satisfaction. "See? You're responsible for instant happiness. Feels good, doesn't it?"

She had to admit that it did.

The enticing sound of laughter coming from Murphy's reached them even before they ever pulled up before the saloon.

There were only a few vehicles, trucks like Finn's for the most part, that were actually parked near the saloon. It appeared that most of the people attending the engagement party that Finn and Liam were throwing for their older brother and his fiancée had walked to the saloon. That way, driving home would not be a problem or hazardous to anyone in the vicinity. The town jail was not built large enough to accommodate more than four offenders at a time.

Connie wasn't sure exactly what she expected to find once she walked into the saloon—maybe seeing the patrons line dancing—but what she did see wasn't all that different from other parties she'd attended. The clothes were definitely not as fancy, but there was live music, thanks to Liam and his band, and appetizing food arranged on side tables, buffet style, courtesy of Angel, Gabe Rodriguez's wife and Miss Joan's resident chef.

It was, all in all, a combined effort with everyone, first and foremost, wanting the future bride and groom to have a good time.

The warmth within the saloon was unmistakable.

Connie fully expected to feel awkward and more than a little out of place at such a gathering. She was afraid she'd be regarded in much the same light as a parent who was looking over their child's shoulder on the playground during recess.

But to her surprise, she wasn't. She was not only greeted by everyone she walked past, but she was also swiftly made to feel welcomed, as if she *belonged* here with the others, celebrating the fact that two very special people had managed to find one another against all odds.

Connie would have been content to sit on the sidelines, quietly nibbling on the fried chicken that Angel had painstakingly prepared and listening to people talk.

But she quickly realized that Finn apparently had

other ideas for her. He waited until she'd had a beer to toast the happy couple—who she confided looked absolutely radiant—and had finished the piece of chicken he'd gotten for her.

Once she had put the denuded bone down on her plate, Finn took the plate from her and put it down on the closest flat surface. She looked at him in confusion. Had she done something wrong without realizing it?

"What are you doing?" she asked him.

"You can't dance with a plate in your hands," he told her simply.

Dance? He couldn't be serious. "I can't dance without one, either," she informed him.

Finn was already drawing her to her feet, away from the table where she'd left her near empty bottle of beer. "Sure you can."

Connie shook her head. "I'm serious, Finn. I don't dance." She had two left feet, and she knew it.

But Finn obviously wasn't accepting excuses. "Don't? Or won't?"

"I won't because I don't," she insisted. With every word, he was drawing her further away from any small comfort zone she'd hoped to stake out and closer to the dance floor.

He laughed at the sentence she'd just uttered. "Practice saying that three times fast," he told her, all the while drawing her closer and closer to the area in the saloon that had been cleared for dancing.

She did *not* want to make a fool of herself in front of him.

"Finn, no, really. I'm going to wind up stepping all over your feet," she warned him.

Her excuse made no impression on him whatsoever.

"They can take it. Besides, you're light, how much damage can you do? Don't worry, I'll teach you a few steps. You'll look like a natural," he promised.

Famous last words, she couldn't help thinking. Finn had no idea what he was getting into—but she did, and it was up to her to stop him before it was too late.

"Others have tried and failed miserably," she warned him.

"'Others' weren't me," he told her with a confidence that was neither cocky nor self-indulgent; it merely *was*. He took one of her hands in his and pressed his other hand against the small of her back.

"It's a slow song," he said, bringing her attention to it. "All you have to do is sway with the music and follow my lead."

All. Ha! The man had no idea what he was asking of her.

"I have no rhythm," Connie protested. She wasn't proud of it, but there it was. Connie Carmichael had less rhythm in her body than the average rock.

But Finn was obviously not accepting excuses tonight. "Everyone has rhythm, Connie," he countered easily. "You just have to not be afraid to let it come out. Now, c'mon," he coaxed, "let yourself feel the music. Close your eyes," he urged, "and just *feel* it," he stressed, gently guiding her movements.

This was an experiment that was doomed to fail from the very start, didn't he realize that? "You're going to be sorry," Connie warned him, even as she allowed herself to rest her head against his shoulder.

"I really doubt that," he assured her, his voice low, a whisper only she could hear despite the general din in the room.

A moment later, her eyes flew open.

She could actually feel it. Not just the rhythm, the way Finn had promised her that she would, but she slowly felt the effects of the music as it seemed to seep into her.

Or was that her reaction to the way his body was pressed ever so gently—and incredibly seductively— against hers?

Connie wasn't quite sure, but she could definitely feel herself reacting to the music—as well as to the man.

Her heart got into the act, revving up its pace.

When the music stopped, Connie was almost sorry to hear the notes fade away.

Raising her head from his shoulder, she realized that Finn was still swaying, still moving his feet to a beat that was no longer there.

"Song's over," she told him, whispering the words into his ear.

"Shh," he responded, a mischievous smile playing on his lips. "There'll be another one to take its place in a second."

And then Liam, looking his way, struck up another slow song with his band. Couples around them began dancing again.

"See?" Finn said. "What did I tell you?"

"I should have never doubted you," she told him with a laugh.

"No," Finn agreed, looking far more serious than she would have thought the moment warranted, "you shouldn't have."

She wasn't sure just how long she and Finn danced like that. Three, four songs came and went, all surprisingly slow in tempo. For her, it felt like just one long, timeless melody that went on.

"I haven't stepped on your foot yet," she marveled when she finally realized that she was *really* dancing and not just keeping time with her hips.

His laughter, soft and warm, ruffled her hair ever so slightly. Ruffled her soul a great deal more.

"The evening's still young," Finn told her. "You'll have more opportunities to live up to that threat if you really want to."

She liked what was happening now. It couldn't continue and she knew it, but just for now, she was content to pretend that it would.

"Actually, I kind of like the fact that I haven't yet," she told him. "How do you do it?" she marveled quietly.

"Do what?" he asked as he whirled her around ever so gently. The movement was so subtle, he had a feeling she didn't even know she executed it.

"How do you get me to move this way?" she asked, mimicking him step for step. "I'm usually completely uncoordinated."

"Magic," he said, whispering the word into her ear. "I do it with magic."

A warm, tantalizing shiver shimmied up and down her spine, instantly spreading out to all parts of her. Claiming her.

Just the same way that the man did.

She knew that Finn was just putting her on with that answer. The funny thing was, though, just for a moment or two there, she could have sworn that it actually *felt* like magic.

Or, at the very least, she was more than willing to pretend that it *was* magic.

Chapter Thirteen

Living under her father's roof, Connie had hosted more than her share of parties and so-called casual get-togethers, all to the very best of her ability.

Initially, she'd imagined that she fell woefully below the standard that her late mother had set. Victoria Carmichael had a charming, outgoing personality and the ability to make each person she spoke with feel as if they were the only person in the room. In addition, Victoria had a way of lighting up any room she entered. While Connie knew that her father had never said as much to her mother, after Victoria's death he was always quick to point out how incredibly short of the mark she fell each time he ordered her to take over her mother's role as hostess.

Eventually, through sheer perseverance, Connie grew into the role and became more at ease with the part she had to play. However, she'd never enjoyed herself during any of those gatherings the way she was enjoying herself tonight, here in the small, jam-packed bar, talking with people her father would have been quick to judge, cut off and summarily dismiss as being beneath him.

She began the evening as an outsider and was certain she would remain that way throughout the entire night, but she hadn't counted on Finn taking her in hand, hadn't taken into account the character of the people attending this engagement party.

She'd just assumed that they would regard her as an intruder and laugh about how she didn't fit in behind her back. Instead, to a person, they all went out of their way to make her feel welcome.

She thought perhaps this was because of Finn, that this was somehow his idea, and he had found a way to convey his wishes to the others attending the party. But she never saw him signal anyone, never saw him indicate to the people around them that he wanted them to treat her with kid gloves.

In a way, the opposite of the latter happened because as the evening wore on, she was being teased and kidded, all in such a way that she took no offense and found herself responding lightheartedly.

By evening's end, she came away with the feeling that the people she worked with, the people who essentially worked *for* her, actually *liked* her. Liked the fact that she had come out of her trailer after hours to meet them on their own ground and celebrate that two of their own were getting married.

Each time someone proposed a toast, she was right there with them, lifting her own glass and adding her voice to the well-wishers. And each and every time she did, she was aware of Finn beside her, smiling at her and approving the way she conducted herself.

For the most part, she had lived without approval for a very long time.

As she finished her glass of champagne in what felt like an umpteenth toast, laughter bubbled up within her as she leaned into Finn and whispered, "You were right."

Turning to look at Connie, he nodded. "Of course I was— About what, specifically?" Finn tagged on after a beat.

Her smile was wide and totally uninhibited. She must have looked like that as a child, Finn couldn't help thinking. "I am having fun."

"Yes, you are," he agreed with a laugh.

He noted that she was all but completely effervescent at this point. Connie leaned back a little too far, and he quickly put his arm around her waist to keep her from sliding off her stool. Finn gently took the empty glass from her hand and placed it on the first flat surface he saw on the bar, thinking that was safer than having her accidentally drop it. He knew that once this evening was behind her, she wouldn't appreciate being allowed to look foolish—or tipsy.

"Possibly just a tad too much fun," he speculated.

"There's no such thing as too much fun," Connie murmured. Standing up, she nearly went straight down, feeling as if her legs had mysteriously turned into tapioca pudding right beneath her. "Whoops." She grabbed hold of Finn by his shirt to keep from sinking to the floor. "I swear I only had one drink. Was there something special in it?" she asked, punctuating her question with a laugh that was mingled with a giggle.

"Nothing that wasn't in all the others," he assured her. And then he took a closer look at her. All her features had definitely mellowed. There was only one thing that could accomplish that to such a degree at this point. "How many have you had?" he asked her.

Finn hadn't bothered keeping track of the alcohol she consumed, but then, he hadn't thought he had to. Since she was so straitlaced, he assumed she'd keep track of herself.

Apparently, he was wrong, he realized.

"Just one," Connie said. "That's usually enough…"

She appeared so serious, it was hard for him not to laugh. "You're a cheap date." *Not that this is a date,* Finn added silently.

But he knew she'd be self-conscious later when she realized she'd been slightly tipsy, or even cutting loose. He took better hold of her arm to escort her out of the saloon.

Brett saw them leaving just as the couple reached the massive front door. Excusing himself from the people he was talking to, he quickly made his way over to them.

"Everything okay?" Brett asked, coming up behind the pair.

"Everything's wonderful," Connie answered in a gush before Finn could. "You throw a very mean party," she told the oldest Murphy brother.

"Actually, Finn here and Liam threw it," he gently corrected, "but on their behalf, thank you," Brett responded with a smile as he looked at her. Raising his eyes to Finn, he asked, "Are you taking her out for some air?"

"And then home," Finn added.

Connie whirled around to look at him. "You're taking me to your home?" she asked, visibly beaming. "Good, I've missed it."

Her comment took both men by surprise, especially since her stay at the ranch house had been limited to a single day.

"She's not going to remember saying that in the morning," Finn told his brother.

The latter nodded. Finn had cut her off just in time. "You need any help?" he asked Finn.

Finn smiled as he slanted a glance at the petite woman. "She's a live wire, but I can always tuck her under my arm if I have to."

"Good luck," Brett said before he turned back to the party.

"Why do you need luck?" Connie asked as Finn took her outside. And then she suddenly grinned from ear to ear. "Oh, I get it. You're looking to get lucky. Why didn't you say so?" she asked with a laugh.

"Because I'm not looking to get lucky," he told her patiently, although the idea of getting lucky with her had more than a little to recommend it. He forced himself not to think about it. He'd only be torturing himself. "I'm just looking to get you home."

"Where you'll have your way with me," she concluded with a nod of her head, as if it were already a foregone conclusion.

Finn watched as she got into the passenger side of his vehicle. "I'm not looking for that, either," he told her matter-of-factly, doing his best to bury the fact that this new uninhibited version of her was beginning to stir him.

"Why not?" she asked, confusion highlighting her expression. "Why don't you want to have your way with me? Don't you think I'm pretty?"

They were driving now, and Finn stepped down harder on the gas pedal, going faster than the posted speed limit, but just this once. He figured he could be forgiven for that. There was no one else out on the streets and the entire sheriff's department was back at Murphy's, anyway. He needed to get Connie back to her trailer before his restraint dissolved just like soap bubbles in the spring air.

Because she was staring at him, waiting for an answer, Finn finally said, "Yes, I think you're pretty. Beautiful, actually," he amended.

"But you don't want me," she concluded sadly.

She was making it very, very difficult for him. "You're my boss," he told her, hoping that would be the end of it.

"I know that, but you can still want me," she insisted.

He could almost *feel* his defenses crumbling. "Okay, I want you. But that still doesn't mean I'm going to do anything. It wouldn't be right," he informed her firmly.

He put his truck into Park. They'd arrived at her trailer none too soon, he thought, because he was quickly losing this battle of good intentions allied with restraint. She kept leaning into him, despite the seat belt that should have kept her on her side of the cab. Her hair was seductively brushing against his neck and cheek, making him yearn for her.

Unbuckling his seat belt, Finn quickly got out of the driver's seat and rounded the hood of his truck to get to Connie's side.

She was fumbling with her belt when he opened her door.

She raised her head and he'd never seen her look so vulnerable. "It won't open," she complained.

Finn reached over and uncoupled the seat belt, freeing her. The second he did, she all but slid into him as she got off the seat and out of the truck.

Looking up into his face, she declared, "I give you permission."

"Permission?" he echoed. Very carefully, he made sure she could stand, then removed his hands from her waist. "Permission for what?"

She stepped in closer again, as if there was a magnetic charge between her body and his. "Permission to do something about wanting me."

Oh, God, if only... He caught himself thinking before he shut down his thoughts.

"Connie, you're a little tipsy. Maybe this isn't the right time," he began, desperately trying to do the right thing. But the ground beneath his feet was swiftly eroding.

"I know exactly what I'm saying," she corrected. "What I don't have the courage to say during regular hours."

Finn told himself not to listen, and he tried to get her to go into the trailer. Instead, she whirled around, made a funny little noise about how dizzy that made her feel. Then, before he knew what was happening, she had anchored her arms around his neck, pushed herself up as high as she could and before he could stop her, she'd managed to press her lips against his.

At first, it was just the excitement of making contact that zipped through him like static electricity. But as she pulled herself up a little higher and pressed her lips against his a little more forcefully, all sorts of tantalizing things began happening all through his body.

And not just his body, he realized a second later because the woman on the other side of her all-but-death grip was definitely responding to him. He could feel her body, soft and pliant, against his. Could feel her lips against his, no longer just a target, a passive receiver, but most definitely in the game.

All the way in the game.

Before he knew what was happening, he found himself responding to Connie. *Wanting* Connie with a level of desire that took him completely by surprise and totally threw him off his game.

He enfolded her in his arms, deepening the kiss she had begun even as it took him prisoner.

And then, as a sliver of common sense returned, pricking at his conscience, Finn forced himself to stop kissing her. Forced himself to put some distance, however minuscule, between them.

Taking hold of both her arms—to keep himself at bay as well as her—he gently pushed Connie back and said, "You don't want to do this."

There was a very strange light in her eyes, mixing in with the definite glimmer of mischief.

"Guess again," she said in a low, husky voice just before she retargeted his mouth again, sealing hers to it.

Finn knew damn well that he was supposed to be the sane one here, the one who was supposed to push her away again for her own good and keep pushing until she finally stopped coming at him. But he had used up his small supply of nobility quickly and she had refused to listen, refused to back away the way he'd told her to.

And damn, he'd been wanting this since the first time he'd turned around and saw her out there on the ranch, standing next to her less-than-useful sports car, looking at him as if she'd never seen a bare-chested man sweating in the hot sun before. She had generated a strong wave of desire within him then, and that wave had never really subsided, never receded so much as an iota.

Instead, it had remained suspended, waiting to be released.

Waiting for an opportunity like this.

Before he knew what he was doing and could discover a way to talk himself out of it, he swept Connie up into his arms. Then, pushing his shoulder against the trailer door to open it, Finn carried her inside.

The second the door was closed—and even before—Connie was all over him—marking his total undoing.

He could hardly keep up with her.

Her hands were everywhere, tugging at his clothing, skimming along his body, coaxing him to let go of his last thread of sanity and come to her.

And then he did.

He remembered the whole scenario taking place in what amounted to a hot haze, a frenzy of activity. A strange wildness had seized him as he found himself wanting her so very badly that it actually physically *hurt*. Wanting her and waiting for even an instant hurt in such a way that it felt as if it almost turned the air in his lungs to a solid substance.

She was going to regret this, a little voice in her head told her over and over, taunting her. Pointing out obvious things.

The actual deed couldn't possibly live up to the expectations she had built up in her head. She was just setting herself up for a fall.

And worst of all, he was going to brag about this to his friends, tell them that she was an easy mark and not really worth the effort in the end.

He'd disappoint her and she him.

All these things raced through her mind at top speed, repeating themselves over and over again. They should have stopped her.

On some level, she knew that.

But even so, her body was begging her not to listen to anything but its own rhythms, its own demands. All along, if she was being honest with herself, she had known that this man was going to be her downfall and yet she'd still hired him, still kept him around. Still allowed his presence to fuel her dreams at night, when her guard was so woefully down.

She couldn't put a stop to it, couldn't rescue herself at the last moment because she discovered that every moment was just too delicious for her to voluntarily end.

She reveled in the way his lips felt against her skin, creating an excruciatingly wondrous moist trail of kisses that covered her breasts, went down to her belly and even farther than that, creating a dizzying warmth at the very core of her.

A warmth that coupled with a fire, which reduced her to a mass of rejoicing whimpers as climaxes blossomed within her over and over again.

Encased in dusky desire, Connie uttered not a single murmur of protest as she heard rather than saw Finn sweep away the schedules she'd labored so hard over, sending them all tumbling to the floor as he cleared the drawing board for her.

For them.

Squeals of ecstasy escaped her as he pushed her down onto the cleared flat surface and proceeded to make love to every inch of her, using his hands, his lips, his very breath to claim each part of her as his very own.

And when restraint tore at the weakened ties that were meant to keep her in place, when she arched and bucked against his body, silently begging for the union it'd promised, he gave in and took her, capturing her mouth at the last second so that they were joined together at all possible points.

The eternal dance began, and it was one that, to her stunned delight, Connie quickly mastered, getting in sync with each of his movements so that only a moment into the dance, they began to move as one, increasing the tempo as one.

And reaching the highest peak of pleasure as one, as well.

She felt the rainbow reach out and claim her, filling her with such exquisite euphoria that she didn't want to ever let it go.

This was where true happiness had been hiding from her all along.

And he had brought it to her.

Chapter Fourteen

Sanity returned far too swiftly.

It wore spurs on its boots and tracked a layer of mud all over Finn's conscience. The weight of his conscience was almost too oppressive to bear.

Pivoting on his elbows, Finn did his best to create space between their bodies, then moved over to one side, separating from her completely. He didn't know whether to apologize to her for what had happened, or just allow the silence to grow until it filled the room and overtook them, leaving no opening for conversation.

Rather than turn from him the way he expected her to, Connie just watched him. If she'd been giddy and tipsy before, she appeared to be totally clear-eyed now.

Was she angry? Did she think he took advantage of the situation and of her?

Did she hate him for it?

The silence continued to grow, becoming unwieldy to the point that he felt he just couldn't tolerate it any longer. Silence had never bothered him before, but it did now.

"Say something," Finn finally urged. But even as he was on the verge of begging her to speak, he braced himself for what he felt was inevitably coming: a barrage of words that would most likely compare him to the very lowest life form on the face of the earth.

What he found he wasn't prepared for was the actual word that did leave her lips.

"Wow."

Finn blinked, utterly positive that he had misheard her. Almost hesitantly, he whispered in confusion, "Say again?"

"Wow," she repeated, this time accompanying the word with a breathy sigh. "You know, I think the earth actually moved." She turned into him to see his face more clearly. "You don't have earthquakes down in this part of Texas, do you?"

"No," he replied uncertainly, studying her. Was she pulling his leg? Getting him to lower his guard before she hit him with a lethal punch?

"Didn't think so," she said, the smile taking on a dreamy quality. "Then I guess *wow* stands."

Her reaction just wasn't sinking in. He was still waiting for an explosion. "You're not angry?" Finn asked, still more than a little uncertain as he studied her demeanor.

"No, why would you think that I was angry?" She sat up for the first time. "Do I look angry?" Connie asked, glancing around to see if there was some sort of a reflecting surface available to her. She wanted to see herself so she could ascertain whether or not *she* thought she looked angry.

"No, you don't," he told her, treading very lightly. "But I thought…well… I thought that you'd feel I took advantage of you, and also you're my boss."

So that was it, Connie thought. At that moment, Finn went up another notch in her estimation. He really *was* a good guy.

"I had one drink," Connie admitted. "Not so much that I can't remember that I was the one who made the first moves—" she pointed out. "I kissed you first, not the other way around."

"So you're not angry," he concluded, wanting to be absolutely sure.

"Right now I'm still too tingly to be angry," Connie freely admitted—another first for her, she thought. She'd made love before, but each time all her feelings, all her reactions, were neatly compartmentalized. This deliriously happy feeling was definitely something new—and it thrilled her. Probably more than it should, she realized. But she just couldn't get herself to put a lid on it. So, just for tonight, she allowed herself to enjoy it.

Connie glanced down on the floor at the flurry of papers scattered there. "I will, however, be upset in the morning when I try to put all those schedules into some kind of order again."

That *had* been his fault. He'd swept her schedules to the floor. "I can help with that," Finn quickly volunteered.

"How?" Connie asked with a laugh. "By sweeping them out of the trailer?" she asked, amusement playing on her lips.

"By organizing them for you on my own time," he

told her, sitting up beside her and looking at the mess below their feet. He was acutely aware of her sitting like that beside him. "But right now, if you're sure you're not angry…"

She turned her face to his and softly whispered, "Yes?"

He'd just had her and here he was wanting her again. Wanting her so badly, he felt himself literally *aching* for her. "I'd like to make love to you properly."

She pretended to look at him with wide-eyed confusion. "Oh, then what we just did, that was improper?"

He was fairly certain there were several states where what they'd just done would have been banned. "Highly."

"I see," she murmured thoughtfully. "And now you'd like to show me how it should have actually been done, is that it?"

His smile reached out to all parts of him, shining in his eyes as well as on his lips and in his demeanor. "Yes, I would."

Connie slid off the drawing board, her bare feet touching the scattered papers on the floor. She nodded her head slowly, as if she was thinking it over. "Never let it be said that I refused to leave myself open to a learning experience."

Finn followed suit, standing up beside her. It was all she needed. Connie wound her arms around his neck, vividly aware of the fact that they were both still very nude.

She smiled up into his eyes. "You do realize that I'm still just a little dazed."

His arms went around her, bringing her even closer to him than a sigh. "I'm counting on it." When he saw her raise an eyebrow at his statement, Finn was quick to explain, "You're a lot less inhibited—and a great deal more trusting."

She saw no reason to argue that. He was right. "I'll have to work on that. Tomorrow," she decided. "I'll work on it tomorrow."

Because tonight, she knew she would be otherwise occupied.

And thrilled because of it.

Finn approached her carefully a little after eight the next morning, not quite sure what to expect or how to behave. He'd slipped out quietly from her trailer an hour before dawn. He'd wanted to give Connie her privacy, and he wasn't sure just how she would deal with the sight of him in her bed now that they had to go back to work.

If there was shame and discomfort on her part, since he was the cause of it, he wanted to spare her the sight of him for as long as possible.

At the same time, he knew he didn't have the luxury of simply going into hiding. He was her foreman, her second in command and as such, he had to be there, available for her *to* command.

Approaching her trailer, he knocked lightly, gave himself to the count of three, braced his shoulders and then walked in, every part of him prepared for some form of rejection, denouncement or whatever it was that would make Connie feel vindicated.

Finn was far too much of a realist to believe that fairy tales went on forever. He was just hoping that she didn't ultimately hate him for last night because for him, last night would live on in the annals of his mind for a very, very long time.

When she heard the door opening, Connie glanced over her shoulder. "Morning. I was beginning to think you were going to sleep in today."

Connie waved her hand, indicating the tall, covered white container on the side of her drawing board. An opened, partially empty container was standing right next to it.

"Got you some black coffee at Miss Joan's," she went on, turning back to her work. "The woman is selling India ink as coffee, but she swears that it gets your motor running, so drink up. We've got a really full day ahead of us if we've got a prayer of keeping this puppy on schedule."

Though he'd always thought of himself as being able to roll with punches, Finn was having trouble processing what was going on. Not because he was hungover, but because Connie seemed so different, so much—*looser* for lack of a better word—than she had been before. And definitely more upbeat and cheerful. She still looked like the same woman, the same beautiful blue eyes, the same killer figure, but it was as if she was a newer, more improved version of heresf. If she'd been a software program, he would have thought of her as Connie 2.0. He stared at the covered, oversize paper container she'd pointed to on the drawing board. "You got me coffee?" That alone was enough to throw him for a loop.

She nodded again. "Just in case you were having trouble getting in gear this morning."

"You have any of this?" he asked.

"I don't drink India ink," she informed him matter-of-factly. "I did get myself a cup of regular coffee, though. Just enough coffee to give the creamer something to work with and lighten," she told Finn. Now that he looked into her container, he could see that the contents appeared to be exceedingly light, close to the color of milk itself. "Now drink up, Finn," she was saying, "we're wasting daylight."

That was an exaggeration. "It isn't even eight yet," he pointed out.

But Connie absently nodded, as if he'd just agreed with her. "Like I said, we're wasting daylight."

Shaking his head even as humor crept in and curved the corners of his mouth, Finn took the lid off his container and took a very long, savory drag of his very black coffee.

As hoped for, the caffeine hit him with the kick of a disgruntled mule.

From that day forward, work continued at an almost effortless pace. There were a few hitches, and one on-site near accident with a girder, but overall, they kept on track, and the hotel took on its desired shape.

As it transformed from a hole in the ground to an edifice of impressive lines and structure, the citizens of Forever began to redesign their paths so that it took them by the excavation site. They came to note the progress or simply to watch some of their own operate the sophisticated machinery with precision.

They came to watch girders, posts, bolts and nails become something greater than the sum of their initial parts.

And a number of them, mostly the younger females, came to observe bare-chested men sweat and strain as they diligently created something they would all be proud of.

As Connie oversaw each and everyone's progress as they approached the end goal, occasionally issuing orders, or changing directives, her project, the bet she had with her father, turned into something far more meaningful to her. It no longer represented just winning an impulsive bet.

She was no longer the girl who was trying everything she could to get just a drop of her father's praise. There was far more going on here now.

The hotel became not only *her* project, but the crew working on its completion also became *her* men. And, she was delighted to discover, she was proud of them—proud of each and every one of them because of what they contributed to the whole.

And she fervently hoped that they returned the feeling, at least to some degree.

Somewhere along the line, shortly after Brett's engagement party—and her awakening as a woman—Connie began to document the crew's progress with the hotel. She would aim her smartphone at anything she felt should be preserved. This was her very first solo project and as such, like a first-born, each tiny milestone deserved to be forever frozen in time.

What she felt were the best shots she passed on, not to her father, but to Emerson, trusting him to choose which photo her father should see and which he might have found some minor, underlying fault with. It was a given fact that Calvin Carmichael was not known for his tact or restraint, especially where the company logo was involved. Emerson knew her father the way no other living soul did, and she trusted him to make the proper judgment calls on her behalf.

She could also trust him to be on her side. True to his nature, Emerson would send back an encouraging text that praised not just her efforts, but also her progress and the way the hotel was obviously shaping up. He was her own personal cheering section, and Connie loved him for it the way she knew she could never hope to love her father. On the home front, her life was also progressing equally well.

What could have become a very awkward situation between her and Finn—with neither of them knowing how to behave or react to one another—became, in fact, a very comfortable existence that they found themselves falling into without any actual discussion on their parts. Certainly no attempts to lay down any groundwork for themselves.

Connie was a woman who had, from a very young age, lived by her schedules. She always had to have her days mapped out from moment one to way beyond the final time frame. It made her feel as if she had control. And yet this sort of spontaneous forward movement worked for her. Not knowing worked for her. As did the delicious warmth of anticipation. And holding her breath when Finn walked up behind her, waiting for the first moment that his hand would brush against her shoulder, or touch her face.

Or the first moment that he would make her insane with desire.

They made love every night, the perfect ending to a perfect day. She had never been happier—as long as she didn't allow herself to dwell even fleetingly on the specter looming in the background: the completion of her project.

For now, she just took heart in the fact that the project was progressing well ahead of schedule and she, well, she was progressing in directions she had never dreamed she would.

As the days and weeks went by, Connie began to think of Forever as her special magical place, except that she knew Forever was real, too.

Still, because it had become so very special, she fervently hoped that Forever—and Finn—wouldn't disappear.

"What's that you're humming?" Finn asked her as they stood off to the side one day, observing the day's progress.

"I didn't realize I was humming," she confessed. "Just some nameless tune to keep my spirits up."

She didn't want to admit that what was actually keeping her spirits up was the fact that he was at her side from morning to night—and thereafter.

Work-wise, there had been a problem with the design when it came to the plumbing on the ground floor, but she had managed to resolve it with a few key strokes of her pen on the blueprints, then conveyed what needed to be done by way of integral changes to the men installing the pipes.

All of which had left Finn in complete awe of her—and also drove home the stark realization—again—that she didn't belong here. It was further proof to him that once this hotel, which was so very important to her, was finally finished, Connie would go back to her upscale world and be permanently gone from his life.

Which, had this been any one of a number of other

times in his life—involving other women—would have been fine with him.

But it wasn't fine this time.

Because this wasn't like any of those other times. This time, he admitted to himself, was different because *she* was different.

And he was different because of that.

Different because he was in love with her.

It had hit him one night as they were making love in her bed. Hit him with all the subtlety of a rampaging mustang trying to divest itself of a newly cinched saddle. He felt a tenderness toward her, a sensation he hadn't experienced before, a desire to protect her not just for a little while, but for all the years to come.

That part had become clear to him when he discovered his desire to shield Connie from her father's harsh behavior. Something had been bothering her for the past few hours. He was aware of it even as they were making love.

"What's wrong?" he asked her as they lay there together, the sounds of heavy breathing mingling and fading.

"Nothing."

"I know you. That's not *nothing*. Now out with it— or do I have to torture you to get it out of you?" As if to make good on his threat, he wiggled his fingers before her as if he was about to tickle her. The second he brushed his fingers against her, Connie quickly surrendered.

"It's nothing, really. I sent my father a text update, complete with photos and the fact that we were way ahead of schedule."

"Did he respond?"

"Oh, he responded all right. He texted back 'Stop bragging. It's not finished yet. You could still fail.'" Connie shrugged. "I suppose it's just the way he is, and I shouldn't have expected any other response from him. It's just that every once in a while, I keep hoping he'd change. That this one time, he'd tell me he was satisfied."

"And that he was proud of you?" Finn guessed.

"Yeah, there's that, too," Connie admitted with a shrug.

Finn could feel anger building up. Anger aimed at a man who had no idea how lucky he was to have a daughter like Connie. "Leopards don't change their spots," he told her gently.

A smile played on her lips. She knew he was trying his best to cheer her up, to make her focus on what she had and not feel inadequate because of what she'd failed to achieve.

"Very profound."

"Also very true," he pointed out.

She sighed and nodded. Finn was doing his best, and she was grateful to him for it. "My father doesn't matter."

"Damn straight he doesn't matter," he'd told her, surprising her with the fierceness in his voice because up until now, Finn hadn't really commented on her father at all. "He's never going to be satisfied and even if he thinks you've done better than fantastic, he's not about to tell you because somehow, he feels that would be cutting down *his* image." His eyes held hers as he tried to make her understand what seemed so obvious to him. "Connie, you could do the best damn job in the whole world, and that man isn't going to tell you. He's just going to look for something, *anything,* to point to and find it lacking." He raised her chin with the crook of his finger when she tried to look away. "But you and I know the truth."

"And what's the truth?" she asked with a glimmer of a smile forming on her lips.

"That no one holds a candle to you. That you've got a crew that'll follow any order you give them not because it's an order but because you were the one who gave it. They're not just a crew, Connie, they're *your* crew. I know these guys. Trust me when I tell you that really has to count for something," he told her.

The smile that rose to her lips told him that, at least for tonight, he'd gotten his point across.

Chapter Fifteen

When her cell phone rang the following morning, Connie was busy finalizing the next week's schedule, which was, happily, far ahead of her original schedule. Things were moving right along, and she was exceedingly pleased with herself and with life in general.

She couldn't remember a time when she was happier—or even just as happy—than she was right now.

Pulling the phone out of her pocket, she pressed Accept without looking at the caller ID. Emerson called her almost daily to find out how things were going, and it was his voice she expected to hear on the other end when she said, "Hello."

But it wasn't Emerson.

It was her father.

Carmichael began without exchanging any pleasantries or even offering a perfunctory greeting. As always, he was all business. "I went over your latest report last night."

When he paused, she knew better than to press him for his opinion. It would come soon enough.

She was right. "I must say, you didn't mess up as badly as I expected you to."

Could she have expected anything more? Connie asked herself wearily. "Heady praise, Dad."

"I'm not in the business of heady praise," he told her curtly. "In case you've forgotten, I'm in the construction business. Which leads me to my next point. I've got a new project for you to supervise—it's a museum. Right up your alley. It's on the east coast so I'm pulling you off the hotel."

She felt as if she'd just walked across a land mine and it had gone off. "But the hotel's not finished," she protested.

"I'm not blind. I can see that," he snapped. "I'll be sending Tyler Anderson to oversee its completion. It's not your concern anymore, Constance. Pack. I want you here by morning."

"But—" She heard a strange noise on the other end of the line and found herself talking to dead air. Her father had terminated the call.

Frustration flared through her. "Damn," Connie muttered to herself as she continued to stare at the now silent phone in her hand.

There was a quick knock on her trailer door and the next moment, Finn stuck his head in. "Hey, we're sending out lunch orders to Miss Joan's, and I just wanted to ask what you wanted to eat today."

That was when he saw the shell-shocked expression

on Connie's face. Lunch was forgotten. Finn came all the way into the trailer and crossed to her.

"What's wrong?" he asked.

And then he noticed the cell phone in her hand. His mind scrambled to put the pieces together. Had she just gotten bad news? Was that what was responsible for that completely devastated look on her face?

"What happened?" he prodded again. "Did your father just call?" She raised her eyes to his but still wasn't saying anything. "Talk to me, Connie. I can't help if you don't talk to me."

"You can't help even if I do," she answered quietly, staring unseeingly straight ahead of her. She felt as if everything was crumbling within her.

Taking hold of Connie's shoulders, he gently guided her to a chair and forced her to sit down.

"It was your father, wasn't it?" It was no longer a guess. Only her father could make her look like that. After a moment, Connie nodded. "What did he say? Because no matter what that man said, you know you're doing a damn good job here and—"

Her quiet voice cut through his loud one. "He wants me to come home."

Finn tried to make sense out of what she had just said. "When you finish?"

Connie slowly moved her head from side to side. "No, now."

That didn't make *any* sense. From what she'd told him, her father was obsessive about projects being completed on time, under budget and to reflect everyone's best work to date.

"But the hotel's not finished. You still—"

Connie turned to look at him, focusing on his face for the first time. She was struggling very hard not to cry.

"He's sending someone else to finish overseeing the job. He says he has another project for me. Seems there's a museum going up on the east coast he wants me to be involved in."

"The east coast?" Finn echoed. That was half a continent away. *She'd* be half a continent away, he thought, something twisting in his gut.

"The east coast," she repeated numbly.

"Are you going?" he asked, doing his best to suppress his anger at this unexpected, sudden blow.

Connie released a huge sigh that felt to her as if it went on forever. "He's my boss. I have to."

Finn wanted to argue that, but he knew he had no right. All he could do was ask questions. "Did he say why he wanted you off this project?"

Connie shook her head. "He's the boss. He doesn't have to explain anything. He never has before."

Finn told himself that his feelings about this unexpected turn of events, his feelings about her, didn't matter. That he'd known all along that this day was coming. It had just arrived a little sooner than he'd anticipated.

The important thing here was Connie. This was what she'd wanted all along, to have her father recognize her ability to helm projects. The man clearly wouldn't be sending her to begin another one if he didn't feel that she was good when it came to setting things up and getting them rolling.

"How soon?" he asked her, the words tasting bitter in his mouth.

Her eyes shifted to his. "Soon" was all she said in

reply. She couldn't bring herself to say "immediately" just yet. She knew that she would break down if she did.

"Well," Finn began, doing his best to sound philosophical and supportive instead of angry and exasperated, "this is what you've been hoping for all along, right?"

"Right," she answered without even attempting to sound enthusiastic.

She slanted a glance at Finn. Why wasn't he as upset about this as she was? Did he actually *want* her to go? Didn't he care that she wasn't staying?

Finn was doing his best to find his way through this emotional maze he suddenly found himself in. "In his own way, I guess your father's telling you that he thinks you're capable of representing him, of helming an important project. He's not asking you to accompany him but to go to the location without him. This means that he's admitting that you *can* fly solo," he said with as much enthusiasm as he could summon—all for her sake. But then he looked at her closely. "You're not smiling."

"Sure I am," she responded evasively. "On the inside."

"Oh. Sorry, I left my X-ray-vision glasses in my other jeans," he told her sarcastically. The next moment, he told himself that wasn't going to get him anywhere. He ditched the attitude. "So how much time *do* you have?" he asked, acutely aware of the minutes that were slipping away, out of his grasp. Quite possibly his last minutes with her.

"He wants me to be in Houston in the morning. That means I have to leave by tonight at the latest."

She was saying the words, but they still hadn't sunk in yet. She was leaving. Leaving Forever. Leaving crews who weren't just crews anymore; they had become her friends. Leaving a man who had her heart in his pocket.

"Tonight?" Finn questioned, his voice echoing in his own head. "He really does want you back immediately, doesn't he?"

Don't cry. Don't cry, she kept telling herself over and over again. "Looks that way."

"And he didn't give you a reason for all this hurry?" Finn pressed. He really *hated* things that didn't make any sense.

"I already told you," she said, bone-weary, "he's the boss. He doesn't have to explain himself or give reasons. He just gives orders."

Connie kept looking at him, silently begging Finn to tell her not to go. To come up with some lame excuse why she just couldn't pick up and leave right now. *Any* excuse.

But there was only silence in the trailer.

"The men aren't going to be happy," Finn finally said, speaking up.

"They need the money," she reminded him. That was what he'd told her at the outset of the job, that most of the people being hired were taking this on as an extra job. "They'll adjust."

Finn snorted. "Not readily."

"But eventually," Connie countered sadly.

She knew she was right. Within a few months, nobody would even remember that she had been here, Connie thought sadly. She felt as if someone had dropped an anvil on her chest. The upshot was that she was having trouble catching her breath as well as organizing her thoughts into a coherent whole.

Most of all, she was trying to deal with the realization that Finn seemed to be all right with the thought of her leaving. He hadn't said a word of protest, just asked her a few questions about the situation, that's all.

Well, what did you expect? That he'd fall down on one knee and beg you to stay? That he'd ask you to marry him because he just couldn't live a day without you? Get real, Con. This was a nice little interlude as far as he's concerned, but now it's over and it's time for him to move on. You move on, too. Move on, or become a laughingstock.

Connie raised her head and glanced in his direction. "If you don't mind, I've got a lot of things to do before I can leave, and I can do it faster if I'm by myself."

"Sure," he told her. "I'll get out of your hair" were his parting words as he left.

Connie nodded numbly in response.

But how do I get you out of my soul? she asked him silently, staring at the closed door.

With no need for restraint any longer, she allowed her tears to fall.

"Hey, what the hell happened to you?" Brett asked when Finn walked into the saloon a few minutes later.

Murphy's didn't officially open for another few hours although the doors weren't locked and even if they were, all three of the brothers had keys to the establishment since it belonged to all of them.

"You look like you just lost your best friend," Brett said, concerned when Finn didn't answer him.

Finn shrugged his shoulders, leaving his brother's question unanswered. Instead, he went behind the bar, took out a shot glass and then grabbed the first bottle of hard liquor within reach.

When he went to pour, Brett pushed the shot glass away. The alcohol wound up spilling onto the bar.

"I can always pour another shot," Finn said.

"And it'll land on the bar, same as the first shot," Brett informed him, "so unless you plan to lick yourself into a drunken stupor, put down the bottle and tell me what's going on with you."

"Always the big brother," Finn said sarcastically.

"Yeah, I am, so deal with it. Now what the hell's going on with you? You're not going anywhere until you tell me," Brett declared with finality.

Finn's throat felt incredibly dry as he said, "She's leaving."

"When the hotel is finished," Brett said, reviewing the facts as he knew them.

Finn's expression darkened further. "No, now. Today," he snapped. The hotel had a ways to go before it was completed. He still felt that Connie's abruptly leaving for a new project didn't make any sense. Though, he could admit he was more invested than he'd thought.

"Why? Did you two have a fight?"

"No, we didn't 'have a fight,'" Finn retorted angrily. "Her father decided he wanted her working on something else."

"What does Connie say about it?" Brett asked him quietly.

Finn blew out a shaky breath, angrier than he could ever remember being. "She isn't saying anything about it. She's going."

Brett continued to study his brother as he responded. "Did you ask her not to?"

"No," Finn bit off. It wasn't up to him to ask. It was up to her to *want* to stay, he thought, totally frustrated.

Brett gave up standing quietly on the sidelines. "Why the hell not?"

"What am I supposed to say?" Finn demanded.

"How about 'Connie, don't go. I love you.' From where I stand, that sounds pretty simple to me," Brett told him.

Didn't Brett understand what was at stake here? "I'd be asking her to give up everything, that big house, the future she's been working toward all these years. Give it all up and stay here in Forever with me." The inequality of that was staggering, Finn thought.

Brett nodded his head. "Sounds about right."

"Damn it, Brett. I haven't got anything to offer her," Finn cried angrily.

Brett looked at him for a long, long moment. And then he shook his head sadly. "If you think that, then you're dumber than I thought you were."

Finn gritted his teeth and ground out, "You're not helping."

"You're not listening," Brett countered. "Connie grew up in pretty much the lap of luxury from what she said—and she didn't seem able to crack a smile when she first got here. After working in Forever—and associating with your sorry ass—she's a completely different person. She looks *happy.* That's what you can do for her. You can make her happy," Brett emphasized. "That's not as common a gift as you might think."

Finn waved a hand at his brother. Brett was giving him platitudes. "You don't know what you're talking about."

"Ask her to stay," Brett urged. "Honestly, what have you got to lose?"

"Face," Finn retorted. "If she turns me down, I can lose face."

Brett raised and lowered his shoulders in a careless, dismissive shrug. "It's not such a great face. No big loss. Might even be an improvement," he told Finn, keeping a straight face. And then he turned serious. "And if you don't ask her to stay, you'll never know if she would have."

Finn shook his head, rejecting the suggestion. "If she wanted to stay, she would."

Brett threaded his arm around his brother's shoulders. "Women operate under a whole different set of guidelines than we do, Finn. You should know that by now." Brett suddenly pushed his brother toward the front door. "Now stop being such a stubborn jerk and go tell her you want her to stay. That you *need* her to stay."

"It's not going to work," Finn insisted.

Brett pretended to consider that outcome. "Then you'll have the satisfaction of proving me wrong for the first time in your life."

Finn opened his mouth to argue that rather unenlightened assessment, then decided he didn't want to stay here, going round and round about a subject he felt neither one of them could successfully resolve.

Instead, he shoved the bottle he'd pulled from the shelf earlier back on the bar and stormed out of the saloon.

"Make me proud!" Brett called after him.

He didn't knock this time. Instead, Finn burst into the trailer, swinging the door open so hard that it hit the opposite side, making a resounding noise.

In the middle of packing, Connie jumped and swung

around. "Finn, you scared the hell out of me," she cried, her hand covering her heart, which was pounding hard for more than one reason. Hope began to infuse itself through her—hope that maybe, just maybe happily-ever-after wasn't completely off the table. A hint of a smile broke through even as she held her breath.

And prayed that he would say something she needed to hear.

"Well, then we're even," he replied. "Because the thought of you leaving Forever is scaring the hell out of me."

She let the shirt she'd been folding drop from her hand as she regarded him. Just what was he up to? "You certainly didn't act like it did." It was an accusation more than an observation.

"No, I didn't," he agreed. The temper he'd been grappling with since he'd left her trailer was only beginning to come under control. "And you used the right word— act. I was *acting* like it didn't bother me because I knew that was what you'd wanted since you got here, to show your father that you could handle a project on your own, to show him that you were damn good for the company and deserved to be treated with respect instead of being treated like a lackey.

"And I knew that once you were finished building the hotel, you'd leave. I figured I was okay with that. But just now I had to *act* as if I was—because I wasn't. I wasn't *okay* with that. I wasn't *okay* with you leaving."

"You weren't?"

"No, I wasn't. And I'm not," he told her, changing his tenses to make her understand that his feelings were still ongoing. "Look, I know I don't have the right to ask you to stay, and I don't have anything that's close to measuring up to what you have waiting for you back in Houston. I don't even—"

Connie cut him off. "Ask me to stay," she said softly.

Finn was desperately searching for the right words to convince her to stay. When she interrupted, his train of thought came to a screeching halt. He *couldn't* have heard her right.

"What?"

"Ask me to stay," Connie repeated. "Say the word."

He stared at her in disbelief for a long moment, stunned into silence.

"Stay," he whispered quietly, certain that she was seeing how far she could get him to go. He honestly didn't know his limits right now.

And then he thought he was dreaming when he saw the smile that blossomed on her lips. It almost blinded him with its brilliance.

Connie stood on her tiptoes as she reached up and wrapped her arms around his neck.

"Okay," she replied, the word all but ringing with immeasurable joy.

"You're serious?" he asked.

Her eyes never left his. "I am if you are," she answered.

He hadn't known that a person could be this excited and happy while struggling with shock, all at the very same time.

"I love you," he told her. "You know that, right?"

He could have sworn that her eyes were laughing. "I do now."

"Don't you have anything you want to say to me?" he prodded. He'd laid himself on the line here, opened up his heart to her—and she hadn't told him how she felt about him. He held his breath, hoping that it wasn't all going to blow up on him.

"Kiss me, stupid," Connie responded, doing her best not to laugh.

He tried again. "Don't you have anything to say to me besides that?"

The smile slid over her lips by degrees, widening a little more every second. "Oh, yeah, right." And then she said in the most serious voice she could summon, "I love you, too."

"*Now* I'm going to kiss you stupid," he vowed. "As well as senseless."

She was ready and willing to have him try. All in all, it sounded like a lovely way to go.

"You have your work cut out for you," Connie warned him.

Finn's arms tightened around her a little more, bringing their bodies even closer together. "I sure hope so," he told her.

And he was prepared to love every second of it.

Epilogue

"And you're sure you're up to this?" Brett asked Liam for what seemed like the umpteenth time since yesterday morning when the wedding was given the green light by all concerned.

Standing beside him, Finn and Liam exchanged looks. In their joint recollection, they couldn't remember *ever* seeing their older brother look anywhere so nervous and unsettled. But then, Brett had never been in this sort of a situation before, either.

Brett and Alisha's wedding ceremony was only moments away from unfolding. Because of the extensive guest list—everyone wanted to attend—the couple was getting married in an outdoor ceremony performed at the ranch Brett had inherited.

Everything, including Liam's band, which was providing the music, had been set up outside. A canopy was put up to protect the food just in case the weather decided to reverse itself and go from the predicted sunny to rainy at the last moment.

Right now, the sun was shining, but Brett scarcely noticed. His attention was otherwise occupied by the thousand and one details that apparently went into planning a wedding. Brett was concerning himself needlessly inasmuch as his brothers, especially Finn, had for the most part taken over making all the arrangements.

But, as the oldest, Brett found he had trouble relinquishing control and just sitting back. He had just too much riding on all this.

"It's the 'Wedding March,'" Liam reminded his older brother. "I think I can handle the 'Wedding March,'" he said.

But Brett had to make sure. Liam was impulsive at times. "You're not going to suddenly decide to jazz it up or put in a beat, right?"

"What the 'Wedding March' needs is to have you calm down, big brother," Liam told him. "Just concentrate on remembering your vows and getting through the ceremony. I'll handle the music, okay?" he asked, flashing a sympathetic smile.

Brett blew out a breath, doing his best to get this unexpected case of nerves under control. "Okay."

"All you have to do is keep it together until the minister pronounces you husband and wife. After that, you're home free," Finn counseled.

"No, Finn. You've got that wrong. He's getting married. He's never going to be free again," Liam deadpanned affectionately.

That was enough to make Brett rally. "You two should be so lucky," he told them.

"Not me. I've got a lot of wild oats to sow yet," Liam informed his brother happily. Glancing at his watch, he announced, "Time to begin. Last chance to do something stupid and run," he said to Brett.

"Not a chance," Brett replied. Squaring his shoulders, he went to stand at his designated spot at the front of the newly constructed altar.

As his best man, Finn stood beside him—and thoughtfully watched the proceedings unfold.

"This has to be the most beautiful ceremony I've ever attended," Connie told Finn as they were dancing at the reception. "And I've been to more than my share," she confided.

At times it seemed like three quarters of her graduating class had all gotten married in recent years. Because of that, she found that it gave her less and less in common with people who used to be her friends. Their priorities slowly changed while hers had remained the same.

Until now.

"It's incredible," she went on to say, "considering that it seemed as if the whole town pitched in." In her book, that should have yielded a hodgepodge. Except that it didn't.

"They pretty much did—which is maybe *why* it turned out so well," Finn speculated. He knew the world she came from involved wedding planners, something that was completely foreign to his way of thinking. "Wedding planners don't have a personal stake in things turning out well, just a professional one. It keeps them removed."

"Bartender, master builder, wedding organizer. I

guess there's just no end to your talents," Connie teased even though she was only half kidding. "A regular Renaissance man, that's you," she told the man who filled her days and her dreams, as well.

"I don't know about that Renaissance part, but I am a regular man," Finn replied.

Not so regular, Connie thought happily. As far as she was concerned, the word for Finn was extraordinary. Each day she felt as if she loved him a little more. Now that she had made the bold move of detaching herself from her father's company—with the stipulation that she be allowed to finish the hotel she'd started—she had half expected Finn to back away from her. After all, she wasn't that rich woman she'd been just a short while ago, just a woman who was still determined to make her mark on the world—but for a whole different reason.

But instead of backing away, Finn had been incredibly supportive, telling her she was doing the right thing, especially when she told him that she wanted to form her own construction company and take on projects that would help improve the community where she chose to do her work.

The first place she intended to start was on the reservation. The buildings there were in desperate need of repair or rebuilding from scratch. She had enough in her trust fund, left to her by her maternal grandfather, to help her with her goals for a very long time to come.

"How do you feel about marrying a regular guy?" he asked her out of the blue, just after twirling her around as the music went from a slow dance to one with a pulsating beat.

It took her a moment to regain her balance. "Depends on who the regular guy is," she said guardedly.

She hung on to her imagination, refusing to allow it to run away with her.

"Me, Connie. Me."

She stopped dancing and stared at Finn, completely stunned. Had she really heard him correctly? "You're asking me to marry you?"

"That's the general gist of this conversation, yes," he acknowledged. "Move your feet, Connie," he coaxed gently. "You're attracting attention."

She did as he asked, hardly aware of moving at all. "Really?"

"Well, you probably always attract attention, looking the way you do, but—"

"No, I'm not asking if I'm attracting attention," she said impatiently. "I'm asking if you're really asking me to marry you. Are you?"

His mouth suddenly felt dry and just like that, he completely understood why Brett had been so nervous earlier. One way or another, this was going to be life-altering for him. If Connie said no, he'd be crushed and if she said yes—well, she *had* to say yes, he told himself. He couldn't live with any other decision.

"With every fiber of my being," he answered her. Then, to further prove he was serious, Finn made it formal. "Constance Carmichael, will you do me the extreme honor of becoming my wife?"

"I don't know about the extreme honor part, but yes, I'll marry you," she told him as her eyes welled up with tears.

As for Finn, his eyes lit up. The next moment, he sealed their agreement with one of the longest kisses that the good citizens of Forever had ever witnessed.

One of Liam's band members, Sam, nudged him in

the ribs and when he looked at Sam, the latter pointed toward the lip-locked couple.

Liam glanced over and then smiled. "Next," he murmured under his breath, because it was clearly indicated that Finn was next when it came to being altar-bound.

Liam knew he would be the last Murphy brother left standing alone.

The thought made him smile even more broadly.

* * * * *

"Sorry," she said. "I just feel so helpless. Talk away. I'll keep my mouth shut."

"I don't want that." Then he caused her to catch her breath by sliding down the couch until he was right beside her. He slipped his arm around her shoulders, and despite her surprise, it seemed the most natural thing in the world to lean into him and finally let her head come to rest on his shoulder.

"Holding you is nice," he said quietly. "You quiet the rat race in my head. Does that sound awful?"

How could it? she wondered, when she'd been amazed at the way he had caused her to melt, as if everything else went away and she was in a warm, soft, safe space. If she could offer him any part of that, she would, gladly.

"If that sounds like I'm using you…"

"Man, don't you ever stop? Do you ever just go with the flow?" Turning and tilting her head a bit, she pressed a quick kiss on his lips.

"What the…" He sounded surprised.

"You're analyzing constantly," she told him. "This isn't a mission. Let it go. Let go. Just relax and hold me, and I hope you're enjoying it as much as I am."

Because she was. That wonderful melting filled her again, leaving her soft and very, very content. Maybe even happy.

"You are?" he murmured.

"I am. More than I've ever enjoyed a hug." God, had she ever been this blunt with a man before? But this guy was so bound up behind his walls and drawbridges, she wondered if she'd need a sledgehammer to get through.

But then she remembered Al and the distance she'd sensed in him during his visits. Not exactly alone, but alone among family. These guys had been deeply changed by their training and experience. Where did they find comfort now? Real comfort?

Her thoughts were slipping away in response to a growing anticipation and anxiety. She was close, so close to him, and his strength drew her like a bee to nectar. He even smelled good, still carrying the scents from the storm outside and his earlier shower, but beneath that the aroma of male.

Everything inside her became focused on one trembling hope, that he'd take this hug further, that he'd draw her closer and begin to explore her with his hands and mouth.

Don't miss
A SOLDIER IN CONARD COUNTY by Rachel Lee,
available February 2018 wherever
Harlequin® Special Edition books and ebooks are sold.

www.Harlequin.com

Looking for more satisfying love stories with community and family at their core?

Check out **Harlequin® Special Edition** and **Harlequin® Western Romance** books!

New books available every month!

CONNECT WITH US AT:

Harlequin.com/Community

 Facebook.com/HarlequinBooks

Twitter.com/HarlequinBooks

Instagram.com/HarlequinBooks

Pinterest.com/HarlequinBooks

ReaderService.com

**ROMANCE WHEN
YOU NEED IT**